D1369678

DATE DUE

12-23-98			
9-17-99			
11-19-99			
1-18-2000			

Gemma's Journey

Gemma's Journey

Beryl Kingston

Thorndike Press • Chivers Press
Thorndike, Maine USA   Bath England

This Large Print edition is published by Thorndike Press, USA and by Chivers Press, England.

Published in 1998 in the U.S. by arrangement with Darley Anderson Literary, TV & Film Agency.

Published in 1999 in the U.K. by arrangement with Random House UK Ltd.

U.S. Hardcover   0-7862-1648-4   (Basic Series Edition)
U.K. Hardcover   0-7540-1227-1   (Windsor Large Print)
U.K. Softcover   0-7540-2165-3   (Paragon Large Print)

The text of this Large Print edition is unabridged.
Other aspects of the book may vary from the original edition.

Set in 16 pt. Plantin.

Printed in the United States on permanent paper.

British Library Cataloguing in Publication Data available

Library of Congress Cataloging in Publication Data

Kingston, Beryl.
    Gemma's journey / Beryl Kingston.
      p. (large print) cm.
    ISBN 0-7862-1648-4 (lg. print : hc : alk. paper)
    1. Large type books. I. Title.
[PR6061.I494G46 1998]
823'.914—dc21   98-40400

To Dr Robin Luff and
the staff at the rehabilitation
centre at Crystal Palace.

Chapter 1

It all happened so quickly. Which shouldn't have been a surprise because everything was happening quickly, the train hurtling along the tracks at such speed that the wheels squealed, the carriages groaned and the passengers were jerked from side to side, their heads lolling like puppets.

Ever since she stepped aboard at East Croydon, Gemma had been sunning herself in her corner seat, watching idly as the London terraces flicked past the window in their long familiar rows. She knew she looked cool and elegant — designer jeans, Italian boots, neat cream body with a suitably low neckline, casual scarf, leather jacket, new gold earrings, old gold medallion — but her thoughts were spinning, caught between two impossibly contradictory needs — to get herself thoroughly psyched up for the audition and yet to appear relaxed and in control. Now, suddenly flung from the pressure of the moment, she looked across to grimace at the woman in the seat opposite.

'Making up for lost time,' the woman

agreed. She put a restraining hand on her son's arm. 'Mind what you're doing with that Coke!' Her warning was too late. The brown liquid was already slopping out of the can and streaming down the sides on to the little boy's trousers. 'Look at the state of you! I shall be glad when you're old enough to go to school.'

Gemma turned her head away, praying that he wouldn't spill any of his wretched Coke on her new clean clothes. The train was racketing under a road bridge and the comparative lack of sunshine gave her a chance to check her reflection in the window. She'd been taking surreptitious glances at herself all through the journey. Not because she was vain — she *was* a bit vain, she had to admit, but no worse than most girls her age — but because her appearance was all-important if she was to make an impression on the casting director. This was her sixth audition since leaving drama school and, after five rejections, she was only too well aware that first impressions were half the battle.

She checked the outline of her face, pale in the distorting glass of the window and as the train swayed, her hair swung across her cheek, thick, dark, straight, newly washed and beautifully cut. She'd spent an arm and a leg on that haircut so it had better be worth it. She still wasn't quite sure about it, although her flatmates had all been very impressed.

Jerry said she looked like the Snow Queen. 'You'll knock 'em dead,' he predicted, adding with well-trained dramatic rapture, 'Pale skin, heart-shaped face, brown eyes, black hair, mouth like Cupid's bow, cute bum, great tits, this girl has everything.'

Except you, she thought, but she was warmed by his admiration just the same. 'You ought to be in PR,' she teased, applying her third coat of mascara. 'You're wasted on McDonald's.' Since she'd told him their relationship was over, she'd teased him rather a lot, and usually by reminding him of his present low status. 'Anyway, it's a musical. Not a fairy story. A raunchy musical.'

He wasn't a bit abashed. But that didn't surprise her. Nothing ever seemed to dent his self-esteem, not even working in that awful burger bar. In the three years she'd known him, he'd always been the same: brash, self-assured and impossibly cheerful, bouncing from job to job and bed to bed without the least sign of concern about either. There were times when she couldn't decide whether his insouciance was admirable or annoying. Which was one of the reasons for ending their affair.

But he certainly had the right touch when it came to big occasions. That morning he'd organised the other two to bring her breakfast in bed, complete with a red rose in a vase, and as she'd walked off down the road towards the station, long legs striding in her tight jeans, leather jacket slung over her shoulder, he'd thrown open the window and called after her to wish her luck. 'Break a leg!'

'I'll do my best,' she called back.

And so she would. Her very best. This time she was going to succeed. She was on her way. She felt it in her bones.

The train threw her against the window again. Such a filthy window. The corners were caked with yellow grime. Why don't they ever clean these carriages? she wondered. It's disgusting making us travel in all this . . . But before she had time to finish the thought, there was a crash like a building falling. She caught a glimpse of her fellow travellers startled and open mouthed, as she knew she was herself, then the carriage tipped and rolled over on its side, throwing her forward out of her seat on to the floor.

Something hard and sharp hit her on the

side of the head as she fell and there was a dreadful smell of burning. For a confused second, as she was buffeted about among carrier bags and other people's arms and legs, she couldn't think where she was and felt guilty, afraid that she must have left the iron on and that her flatmates would be cross. They were always cross when she left the iron on. But then the movement stopped and she came back to the present and put out her hands for something to grip. She touched an attaché case — where had that come from? — brushed against the rough moquette of the tumbled seats, but before she could find her balance and scramble to her feet again, there was a second and longer crash and, in a moment of total horror, another carriage loomed in towards her spreadeagled body in a blur of white, red and blue, huge and heavy and inexorable as a guillotine. It'll cut me in half, she thought, and she struggled to pull her body away from it. But it was right on top of her and she was pinned under the seat and couldn't move anything except her hands. She was so frightened she could hardly breathe.

Shattered glass showered down on her, hitting her face and shoulders and tumbling into her vision like green hail. The grinding

11

and crashing went on. It was so loud it made her ears ache but even through the noise, she could hear people screaming and a child screeching 'Mummy! Mummy!' over and over again. There was a terrible pressure on her legs, a great weight forcing her down, and below that, a new and awful pain burning and throbbing. She knew she was trapped and that she ought to try to get out, but she seemed to have lost all her energy. And understanding grew in her mind at last, like something huge and black and obscene, and she knew that she was in the middle of a rail crash and that she was injured and that she was passing out.

For a while she drifted in and out of consciousness as if she were far out at sea, borne up and down by immense waves, almost beyond caring. Then she became aware that a child was somewhere nearby and that it was crying in terror. And she remembered the little boy with the Coke can and made a great effort to open her eyes and call out to him. She was lying on her side hemmed in with broken spars and bits of seat and luggage rack. The underside of the other carriage had come to rest at a precarious angle, massive and threatening, a mere six inches from her face. Her mouth was so full of dust that her voice was little more than a croak.

'It's all right,' she managed at last. 'I'm here.' But she was looking at the crumpled mass of metal above her and thinking, if it falls it will crush me. I must be sensible, she told herself. There's no point in panicking. And she turned her mind to the child. If I'm frightened, he must be terrified, poor little thing. 'It's all right. I'm here.'

She couldn't be sure he'd heard her but at least he stopped crying. The dust swirled before her eyes and she could hear people groaning but it was all unreal, as if it was happening in a dream, as if she wasn't really there. The only reality was the threat of that crushed carriage. She made another great effort and turned her head so as not to look at it.

There was a very long pause. Then a little voice called, 'I want my mummy!'

He's still alive, she thought, and she tried to moisten her mouth to call out to him again. But she had very little saliva and it took a long time. 'Can you hear me?' she croaked.

And he answered her. 'Yes.'

That was better. Having someone else to look after gave her a focus. 'Are you all right?'

'Yes. Where are you?'

'Not far away,' she said, trying to reassure

him. She was surprised by what an effort it took her to speak. But somewhere in the back of her mind she remembered that you had to keep injured people talking. She couldn't remember why, but she knew it was important. 'What's your name?'

'Jack,' the voice said tearfully. 'I want my mummy. I can't see my mummy.'

'It's all right, Jack. She'll be all right.' It wearied her to talk as if she were pushing a weight off her chest with every word. I'll have to take it slowly, she thought, pace myself, be sure to get enough breath. What a good job I studied voice production. 'I expect — she's been — pushed — a bit further along. — We've been — sort of — thrown about.'

He was weeping again.

She moved her one free hand, in what little space there was, and tried to wipe the dirt out of her eyes and mouth. Her fingers came away red with blood but she was too numb and weary to respond. 'People — will soon — be here,' she said, keeping her voice calm. Please God let them be! It was awful being trapped. Awful thinking you could be crushed to death at any minute. 'They'll — get us — all — out.'

'Will they?'

She had less and less energy and it was

getting more and more difficult to breathe but she made another effort. 'Yes. I promise.'

'When?'

'Soon. — You'll see,' she said, blinking. The air was still full of dust, swirling in front of her eyes. Where was it all coming from? 'There's — lots — of houses. Someone — will dial — 999.'

But then the ache in her left foot suddenly became a searing pain that rose into her leg in terrible, unendurable waves, each one more severe than the last. Christ! Dear sweet Christ, make it stop. But it didn't. It went on and on rising higher and higher until it had reached her chest and she had to struggle to endure it, drenched with the sweat of it. She knew she was making the most dreadful groaning noise, and that she couldn't stop it. It was too urgent and primitive for that, as if agony was pushing the sound from her throat. There was nothing in the world except pain. Make it stop! she prayed. Please, please, make it stop!

Then she was unconscious again.

Chapter 2

'I must say I do like the autumn,' Dr Quennell said. 'It's such a peaceful season. Restful.' He was standing by the window of the men's surgical ward in St Thomas's Hospital, his hands clasped behind his back, looking out over the Thames at the familiar sunlit façade of the Houses of Parliament and the long line of yellowing plane trees facing the river.

'You can have it,' his patient said rather sourly, shifting in his chair. 'Give me the summer any day.' He was uncomfortable to be slummocking about in his dressing gown at eleven o'clock in the morning and shame was making him tetchy.

'Late September,' Dr Quennell went on happily. 'Leaves changing. Pace of life slowing. Everything peaceful. Even here, right in the city. Sun still warm. Can't beat it.'

'You're showing your age,' his patient mocked. He had known Dr Quennell for more than twenty years and teasing was their principal means of communication. He rubbed the grey stubble on his chin and felt ashamed of that too. You degenerate a bit too quickly once you're in hospital. 'Getting old, that's what's happening to you. Same as me.'

'True,' the doctor agreed cheerfully. But he didn't really believe it. He was only just sixty, for God's sake, and although he might be in the process of taking early retirement, there was too much strength in him to consider himself old — strong hands, strong heart, strong features, strong opinions, good strong head of hair. Middle-aged, maybe, but certainly no more.

'Where's that nice son of yours, then?' his patient asked. 'They're late this morning.'

'No. They're here. They're in with Sister. They'll be doing the rounds presently.'

'You must be proud of him. Following in your footsteps.'

'Yes,' Dr Quennell said, turning from the window. 'We both are.' Proud enough to hang about in the ward on a fine autumn morning just for the chance of a few words. 'He's a good boy. Has his faults, naturally. Don't we all? But a good boy.'

There was a flurry of activity at the other end of the ward. That's not John Barnaby, surely, Dr Quennell thought, charging out of Sister's office like that. But it was. Something must be up.

It was Nick who enlightened him, striding down the ward towards him, white coat flapping, young face full of importance.

They exchanged information in the rapid shorthand of a father and son engaged in the same profession.

'It's an alert.'

'Bomb?'

'Rail crash.'

'Where?'

'Wandsworth Common. Just outside the station. Mr Barnaby said to tell you.'

The message was delivered casually but in fact it was an official call for assistance. Andrew Quennell was one of the many local GPs who were trained for these emergencies. 'Right,' he said.

'Right,' his son echoed. 'See you there, then.'

So much for peace and quiet, Andrew thought, as Nick strode off to join his team. That's what comes of eulogising September. But then his mind jumped into top gear and began to work at speed because he knew how important it was to get to the scene of the crash as soon as he could. Treatment given in the first hour after an accident — the time they called the golden hour — could make the difference between life and death. He said goodbye to his patient — quickly — and called his wife on the mobile as he walked to his car.

'I was just going to phone you,' she said. 'Your call's just come through. I gather it's pretty bad. There was a newsflash on the radio.'

He eased into his car and switched on the ignition. 'I doubt if I'll be back in time for surgery. Tell Grace.'

'Take care, Drew,' she warned.

It was sensible advice for although a combination of height, broad shoulders and strong features made him appear solid and dependable, he was an impetuous man and given to impulsive action.

'You know me,' he joked, as he slipped the car into gear.

She joked back, her voice loving. 'Exactly!'

But this wasn't a time for caution. As soon as he reached the common, he could see from the scale of the response that this was a very serious accident indeed. Some of the emergency services had already arrived, others were approaching, sirens wailing, and the police were in action wherever he looked. They had already removed the sightseers, re-routed the traffic and pulled down the railings near the crash site. Now they were organising the arriving ambulances into a queue all along Nightingale Lane.

He parked where he was directed, put on his emergency jacket, and walked quickly across the common, taking in the details of the crash as he went. Six coaches of a north-bound train were lying on their sides and two others had skewed across the oncoming track and been hit by a second train. Wreckage was piled on either side of the second engine and there were two carriages impacted on one another, the white sides of the broken coaches striped with grease and blood.

Although he knew that what he was seeing was the organised confusion of a major alert, at first shocked sight it looked like a scene from Dante's Inferno. There were people everywhere, with more running in from the common as he was himself, and they all seemed to be brightly coloured: firemen, bold in their yellow helmets and trousers, cutting into the fallen coaches; doctors and nurses and paramedics in fluorescent jackets or waistcoats, lime green, yellow and orange, bending over the first casualties; the injured themselves, sitting between the tracks, stunned, bloodstained, bandaged, grimed with filth and wrapped in scarlet blankets. The men and women from the St

John's Ambulance were already there too, distinctive in their black and white, rapidly bringing in equipment — and there were policemen everywhere, ominous with body bags, their walkie-talkies in urgent use. But it wasn't until he was walking towards the severed coaches that he caught the first scent of the horror that awaited him. The crushed coaches looked appalling but the smell that rose from them was worse. It was the hot, sickly-sweet stink of the abattoir, the alert that had risen into his nose when he reached the lorry on that awful day in Cyprus. But there wasn't time to think about *that*. There was barely time to react.

John Barnaby, Nick's orthopaedic consultant, appeared out of the confusion, as unruffled as though he were simply doing his rounds. 'Ah, Drew, there you are! We've got two major injuries in a very tight space, kiddy about four and a young woman. Both trapped.'

Andrew followed his old friend.

'The Fire Brigade are cutting the kiddy out,' Mr Barnaby went on. 'Todd's with him. The girl's the tricky one. As far as we can see she's pinned by the legs. I'm going through the other side, once the kiddy's out. We might be able to cut in that way.'

Andrew could see their casualty. She was lying right underneath the concertinaed bulk of the second carriage with the wheels and bogey within inches of her face, a small slight girl, pale with shock and covered in filth, her face laced with blood, her dark hair matted, obviously badly injured. Her quietness and patience were enough to tell him that. She's been a pretty girl, he thought as they passed her, and he wondered how on earth they were going to get her out, poor kid.

Gemma had lain in the heat and stink of her metal prison for such a long time that her senses were dulled to it. She'd given up trying to struggle free, accepting that she was too tightly trapped and that the slightest attempt to move brought more pain than she could bear. She knew it was still daylight because she could see glimpses of sky somewhere beyond her, but her awareness of time and place had seeped away along with her energy. Now there was nothing in her world except the terrible looming mass of the coach crushed above her — and pain. While it was just an aching pulse she could endure it and hang on to be rescued, but when it hammered into full, sickening strength, she was mortally afraid and groaned against the agony of it. By the time someone began to wrench away the remains of her coach, she was too exhausted to call out, even though they were within inches of her head. They'd come to rescue her and that was all she needed to know.

Presently she became aware that a young face was looming towards her. She had an impression of strength and determination, caught a glimpse of thick dark hair, very blue eyes, a stubborn mouth. 'Don't worry,' the mouth said. 'You're going to be all right. We're here.'

She tried to swallow so that she could answer him but he was putting a needle into her arm. 'Am I — going — to die?' she asked.

'Good God no,' he said. 'Of course not. I never let any of my patients die. I'll just get this drip set up and then I'll give you something for the pain.'

He was so sure of himself that Gemma was reassured. Perhaps she *was* going to survive after all. She waited until he'd finished with her arm. 'Are you going — to get me out?'

'Of course,' he said. 'But we're going to make you comfortable first. What's your name?'

She told him in what little voice she could

muster and submitted gratefully to the needle that would 'soon take the pain away'. Then she closed her eyes in weariness as he began to examine her.

Now that he was face to face with his first casualty, Nick was in total control and professionally calm, despite the instant rush of adrenalin that had filled him with excitement as soon as he arrived and given him the usual pleasurable sense of importance. He worked automatically, checked her pulse and blood pressure, which were very poor, as he expected, estimated the extent of the injuries he could see. There was a deep gash behind her right ear, but her air passages were clear and there were no other serious injuries to her head, chest and arms apart from superficial cuts and bruises. But she'd lost a great deal of blood and was obviously trapped by the legs, so he knew there would be serious injuries further down her body.

'There's — a little boy — on the other side,' she said, raising her hand vaguely towards the squashed bulk of the carriage above her and opening her eyes again. 'We've been — talking. I haven't — heard him — for ages.'

'Yes,' he said, dismissively. 'We know about him. They're getting him out now.'

'Is he — all right?'

'Of course,' he said, thinking what courage she had. Fancy being concerned about someone else when you're lying underneath a wrecked train. 'I told you. *We're* here now.'

She saw that he was moving away from her. 'You're not going?' she begged.

'No,' he said. And when she looked an anxious question at him, 'I'm going to squeeze in and check over the rest of you. Sally here's going to put a temporary dressing on your head. All right?'

Gemma didn't look to see who Sally was. Now that the pain had receded she was so weary that her eyes were closing of their own accord. She was aware that a pad was being put on her forehead and that the doctor was wriggling in alongside her underneath the bogey. If it falls now, she thought, it will squash us both. But she couldn't imagine it falling on this young man. He was too full of confidence for that.

As he switched on the light on his helmet and inched into the dark and filth under the bogey, Nick knew it would be a hard job to examine his patient. There was so little room between the crushed seats of the first coach and the overhanging bogey of the second. He removed a chunk of bloodstained seating and passed it out to one of the firemen, then a crushed attaché case and various other bits of smashed luggage and torn clothing, shiny with blood, then more seating, but there was still far too little space. He eased his scissors from his jacket and began to cut away the girl's blood-soaked jeans, passing the material out in the same way.

Once he'd hacked off her boot, he could see that the girl's right foot was broken and swollen and the leg above it was badly lacerated. Both looked dreadful but the bleeding wasn't excessive and they were injuries that could be dealt with. It was the other limb that was causing the bleeding and that was a horror. Her left foot and part of her lower leg were crushed under the edge of the bogey. He knew at once that it was much too badly injured to be saved. So much blood had pumped from her wounds that the entire area was sticky with it and he could see that the bones were splintered and that her flesh was dark and torn. For a few appalled seconds he felt such a rush of pity for her that he was dizzied by it and couldn't go on. No wonder she was in pain. To be crushed like this, trapped like this. And lying there so patiently, waiting to be rescued. What courage! Then he gathered his senses and started to deal with the bleeding. She was in a very bad way but he wasn't going to let her die — not if he had anything to do with it.

'Well?' Mr Barnaby asked, when he'd wriggled out into the air again. He and Andrew had finished their inspection on the other side of the carriage and were worried by what they'd found.

Nick gave his report. His clothes were covered in blood and his hands and face smeared with grease, but he was splendidly professional.

Mr Barnaby was thinking. 'That's a pig,' he said. 'But I suppose we had to expect it.' He turned to the fire chief who was standing at his elbow. 'You're sure you can't cut through the bogey from the other side?'

'No,' the fire chief said. 'It's too risky. You can see the angle it's at. It'll have to be lifted, like I told you.'

'So we've either got to wait for that damned crane,' Mr Barnaby said. 'Or we've got to amputate the leg.'

'We radioed in when we got here,' the fire chief told him. 'It's on its way.'

'How long?'

'Another ten minutes, I should say. Shouldn't be long now. Then half an hour. Hour at the outside.'

'Too long,' Mr Barnaby said. 'What do you think, Drew?'

'I don't think we've got a choice,' Andrew answered sombrely. 'We'll *have* to amputate.'

'How much room have we got in there?' Mr Barnaby wanted to know.

'Very little,' Nick told him.

'Ah well. Let's get on with it.'

'Right,' Nick said. 'I'll get things organised.' And he went off to tell the rest of the team.

Gemma was so quiet and peaceful she looked as though she was asleep. 'Yes?' she said, when Andrew began to prepare her for the anaesthetic.

'I'm afraid your leg is very badly injured,' he told her.

She was very calm. 'Yes,' she said. 'I thought it was.'

There was no time to break it to her gradually. 'I'm afraid you're going to lose it.'

She took that calmly too. Her courage was very impressive. 'You're going to cut it off,' she said. It was a statement not a question.

'Yes.'

She sighed and closed her eyes. 'Can't you do anything else?'

'I'm afraid not,' he said gently. 'It's the

only way to get you out.'

'Can't they cut me out?' she begged. But the expression on her face revealed that she understood what a vain hope it was.

He gave her an honest answer, estimating that she was tough enough to take it. 'No. I'm sorry my dear, but it wouldn't make any difference if they could. Your leg is too badly injured to be saved.'

He expected her to weep or argue or rage. But she didn't. She digested what he'd said, her eyes closed. When she opened them, the strain on her face was plain for all her rescuers to see. Sally, the nurse who'd put the dressing on her head wound, was so close to tears that she had to turn her head away. And the firemen were grim-faced. 'Then you'll have to do it, I suppose.'

'Yes. You won't feel anything. I'm going to give you an anaesthetic.'

'You *will* be able to get me out of here?'

'Yes. We will. The sooner we can get you to theatre the better.'

She gave him a wry smile, her eyes full of distress. 'That's where I was going,' she remembered, as he prepared the first injection. 'To a theatre.'

'Were you?' Andrew said, bending towards her as he made professional conversation. 'Why was that then?'

'I was going to an audition. For a part in a play.'

'Ah! You're an actress?'

'Yes.'

'Can you count to ten for me?'

She began to count, patiently obedient. 'One, two, thr . . .'

She was out but he smoothed her hair and praised her as though she could hear him. 'You're a good brave girl,' he said.

It took a long time for Nick and Mr Barnaby to amputate her leg and even longer to inch her unconscious body gradually and carefully from beneath the bogey and on to its waiting stretcher, even though there was a gang of firemen and paramedics to help them do it. As she was carried to the ambulance, wrapped and strapped, with a drip held above her bandaged head and a cradle humped over her severed leg, the rescue teams gave her a cheer.

Mr Barnaby was pale from the stress of the operation but Nick was looking pleased with himself.

'That was a job well done,' he told his father.

You're so young and so conceited, Andrew thought. 'This is just the beginning,' he warned. 'She'll need careful nursing.

There's always the chance of a wound infection in an accident like this.'

Nick smiled the idea aside. 'Not the way we work nowadays,' he said, and teased, 'you're being old-fashioned.'

Andrew didn't argue with him. This was neither the time nor the place. 'Let's hope so,' he said drily and followed Mr Barnaby to their next casualty.

It was well into the evening before the last injured person had been ferried away to hospital and the last mangled body withdrawn from the wreckage and certified dead. By then the rescue teams were so numb with the accumulated horror of what they'd seen that they were beyond speech.

Andrew stayed on the tracks after the last ambulance had gone to give himself a chance to recover a little before he drove home. He took out his handkerchief to wipe the worst of the dirt from his face. To right and left, the sky above the common was the rich blue of twilight, and the roofs and chimneys below it were a lilac outline where the street lights shone like strings of amber beads. It looked peaceful and romantic and impossibly distant against the terrible reality of the crashed coaches and the arc lights that blazed above the debris. Their artificial light was so strong that it cast the landscape immediately behind them into total darkness and lit up the luminescent coats of the departing rescue teams as though they were actors on some surreal film set. To Andrew's exhausted eyes, they made the scene bizarre, diminishing it, as if the pain he'd been witnessing all afternoon had been set up as an entertainment.

And to add to the impression, the TV crews had arrived. He'd been vaguely aware of them while he'd been working, but he'd been too busy to take much notice of them. Now he could see three from where he stood and one was endeavouring to interview John Barnaby who was striding off towards his car with Nick behind him.

'No,' Andrew heard his old friend say. 'I can't. Not now.'

Quite right, Andrew thought, but then he realised that the young man was heading his way, the fluffy sausage of the microphone borne before him like a Roman standard. 'Excuse me, sir. Could you give us a few words? Your reaction.'

Anger rose in Andrew Quennell. Bloody, intrusive monsters, he thought, poking their damned cameras in. Can't they see they're not wanted? Blowflies, the lot of them, rushing in to find the corpses. And anger

brought a flow of language as it always did with him. All right then, he thought. I'll give you a few words and see how you like them. 'It's a total, God-awful waste,' he said. 'It should have been prevented.'

His outspokenness was just what the presenter wanted. The camera was turned in his direction at once.

'Are you saying,' the presenter prodded to open the interview, 'that this accident was avoidable?'

'Oh for God's sake, of course it was avoidable,' Andrew told him angrily. 'Accidents don't just happen. They're caused.'

'Human error?' the presenter suggested.

'That's glib,' Andrew said. 'That's what politicians say. Human error. Can't be helped. These things happen. All very cosy. Lets everybody off the hook. Then we can all go away and forget about it.'

'So you don't think this was human error?'

'I've treated hundreds of accidents in m time,' Andrew said. 'Every single one w caused. By fatigue, poverty, carelessne hyperactivity, you name it. Most could ha been prevented. The ones caused by fatig *certainly* could have been. We know h dangerous fatigue is. We know how caused. A driver works excessive hours,

dangerous. Right? A man under stress is at risk. He puts everyone around him at risk. Right? Accidents are caused. And I'll tell you something else. You don't have to look far to find the root cause of most of today's accidents.'

'Which is?'

'Greed.'

That wasn't what the presenter expected. 'Greed?'

'Take a look at this rolling stock,' Andrew said, gesturing towards it. He looked magnificent in that harsh light, his face passionate, grey eyes gleaming, chin determined, brow and cheekbones strongly defined, thick hair blazing like a silver halo. 'It's twenty years old if it's a day. That's dangerously old. It should have been replaced years ago. But no. It's still in use. It should have been very carefully maintained. The older vehicles are, the more maintenance they need. Any fool knows that. But has it been? Look at it. Greed.'

'Are you saying that this accident was due to poor maintenance?'

Andrew was into his stride and too angry to be cautious. 'I'd lay money it was,' he said. 'It's not vandalism. There's no sign of that. So it's either badly maintained signals, or rotten cables that should have been re-

placed, or dangerously outmoded rolling stock, or a driver working when he should have been resting. We live in penny-pinching times. British Rail is being privatised. So we don't spend taxpayers' money on rolling stock, or safety measures, as we ought to if we had any sense. We use it to bribe the buyers. We use it to ensure a good profit for the shareholders. Profit. That's what this is about. If this accident turns out to be the result of poor maintenance, or the lack of proper investment, I hope no one will forget that the casualties will have paid the price for it.

'We've just had to amputate the lower leg of a young actress who was on her way to an audition, at the very start of her career. She was incredibly brave. *Incredibly* brave. Her bravery ought to put the profit-makers to shame. But I doubt if it will. Their greed ought to be revealed for the selfishness it is. But I doubt if *that* will either. We value money more highly than human life, that's the message of this accident. It's a very sick world.'

'Well thank you, Doctor,' the presenter said, wrapping it up. 'If we can just take your name for the caption.'

'Ye gods!' the cameraman said as they sped off to find another talking head.

'Tell it like it is!' the presenter grinned. 'That'll rattle a few cages. How did it look?'

'Great. He's got a good face. The hair was magic.'

'Thought so. You can't beat a man who knows his mind.'

'If they run it,' the cameraman said.

The presenter had no doubt about it. 'They'll run it,' he said. 'He's a natural. Never seen anyone so sure of himself.'

At that moment, the natural was sitting in his car, feeling peculiarly unsure of himself. The interview had been so quick and so full of fury that now he couldn't remember half of what he'd said. What if he'd gone too far? Said too much. It wouldn't be the first time. He'd lost count of the number of occasions he'd wrecked a situation by saying too much. Especially when he was young.

He picked up his mobile phone and dialled home, persuading himself that he ought to warn Catherine that he was on his way, but actually yearning for the reassurance of her voice. But the line was engaged. Ah well, he thought, switching on lights and ignition, it's too late for anyone to do anything about it now. What's said is said. At least they can't sack me, not when I've just asked for early retirement. As he inched into the oncoming traffic, he comforted himself with the thought that, angry or not, everything he'd said was true. In any case, they might not run it.

Chapter 3

When the phone rang that evening, Catherine Quennell put down the onion she was peeling and answered it at once. She knew it would be Drew because he always called her on his way home from an accident. He said it was his first step back into the normal world and, after a lifetime in nursing and more medical emergencies than she could count, she knew how important *that* was. She was skilled in the art of easing him back from the horrors. Everything was ready, whisky and soda waiting on the sideboard, bath towel heating on the rail, clean clothes laid out on the bed. When the phone interrupted her, she'd been preparing a vegetable soup for their evening meal because that might be all he could eat if the crash had been a bad one.

'Hello darling,' she said, her voice full of sympathy. 'How's it been?'

But it was her daughter Susan who answered. 'Pretty dreadful,' she said, as if she'd been expecting the question. 'It was a major incident, I'm afraid. Twenty-seven fatalities at the last count, and a hundred and eighty-two injured. The news has been coming through here all afternoon.'

Catherine was shocked. 'That's awful.'

'Yes,' Susan agreed. 'It is. There've been some ghastly stories. Apparently one of the injured had to have her leg amputated to get her out. Has it been on the television yet?'

'I don't know. I've been in the clinic all afternoon. I missed the early evening news.'

'So did I,' Susan said. 'It's been a hell of a day. We shall have to watch at ten o'clock.'

'I shall hear about it when your father gets home.'

'Ah,' Susan understood. 'He was on call.'

'Yes. I'm waiting for him now.'

'I thought he'd be there,' Susan said, 'being south London. Give him my love. Tell him there's going to be an inquiry and they've asked me to organise it.'

Catherine caught the pride in her voice. 'Congratulations,' she said. 'That's a feather in your cap.'

'It is rather,' Susan agreed. 'If I do it well.'

'You will. Where will it be?'

'London, I expect. I'd rather it was York but being a London incident, we shall probably have to come down to take evidence.' She'd lived in York ever since she married, which was nearly fifteen years ago, and would have preferred to have been based there but for a job as prestigious as this one she had to be prepared to go anywhere.

'So we shall see you,' Catherine hoped.

'Yes. I'll make sure you do.'

'When?'

'Quite soon I should think. It's a top priority.'

'Will you bring the girls with you?' The thought of seeing her two granddaughters again made her warm with pleasure.

It was short-lived. 'No,' Susan said. 'I don't think so. Not unless it runs into half-term. They'd have to be left on their own all day and they'd hate *that*.'

'I could take a few days off and look after them,' Catherine offered, adding, 'if you'd like them here with you.' Now that she worked part-time it shouldn't be too difficult. She could swap shifts with Marjorie.

The offer was dismissed — brusquely but cheerfully. 'No, no. There's no need for that. They'll manage. They've got their nanny. And Rob. They're used to me being away. Anyway they'll be at school. There's no need to uproot them.'

Catherine sighed. Sometimes she thought there was something a little too ambitious about this daughter of hers. It was understandable that her career was important to her — after all, not many women made it to an executive post with British Rail — but she really ought to consider her children just a little more. She didn't always seem to realise how much you have to compromise when you've got children. 'I wouldn't mind looking after them, you know.'

'It's not a problem,' Susan said. 'They're used to it. They'll cope.' And when her mother was silent, 'Oh come on, Mum, I'm a working woman. Just like you. *You* worked and I coped, didn't I? I can't *remember* a time when you weren't working.'

'That was slightly different,' Catherine pointed out. 'I was a single parent. I had to work. And I was always just round the corner, now wasn't I? I never left you. Not when you were in infant school, anyway.'

'Helen's in the Juniors,' Susan corrected, and now her mother could hear irritation in her voice; 'she's nearly ten, for heaven's sake. I wish you wouldn't exaggerate.'

She's still young, Catherine thought, and Naomi's only seven. It wouldn't hurt you to let them come down here and stay with me for a while. School's not that important. But she decided it would be judicious to change the subject, especially now, when she needed her energy to support Drew. 'How's Rob?'

'Up to his neck in greenery,' Susan said, glad to be able to talk about her husband. 'He's got a huge order for Christmas. Hotel chain. Chrysanthemums . . .'

As she put the phone down after the call, Catherine couldn't prevent another sigh. It would have been so nice to see the girls again. But there wasn't time to brood on it. She picked up her kitchen knife and set to work on the onion again, slicing neatly and rapidly before the juice could make her eyes water. Within seconds she had relaxed into the comfort of cooking, contented in her comfortable kitchen, at ease in her familiar house.

She and Drew had lived in the place for the last twenty-eight years, ever since 1968, when he first decided to set up in general practice. It was a detached, double-fronted Victorian house on the east side of Putney Hill and a very pretty one, built in the Italianate style with a long back garden full of established fruit trees and a short front garden full of flowering shrubs. They'd loved it from the moment they first saw it and Andrew always said that buying it was the best move he'd ever made, even though the mortgage had been more than they could really afford. The repayments were so large in that first year that the thought of them had kept Catherine awake at nights. She'd been easily worried in those days, perhaps because she'd had a lot to worry about. Their marriage was a mere two years old, Christopher had been a babe in arms, and very fretful, particularly at night, and his half-sister, Susan, had been a surly eleven-year-old, self-consciously wearing glasses for the first time, hating her new school, still not quite sure about her new stepfather and struggling not to be jealous of her unwanted brother.

But they'd settled down with surprising speed. By the time Nick was born, two years later, Chris had become an entertaining toddler, Susan was doing well at school and had grown really fond of her new father and they were so much at ease in their rambling home that it was hard to believe they'd ever lived anywhere else.

Now it was almost an extension of their personalities. It contained them, as it contained their memories, of the early days when they ran the surgery in two of the downstairs rooms, of the children growing up, the years when Gran lived with them in her little flat — dear Gran — Susan leaving for York and Chris for Quebec. It was a family house, the place they returned to for rest and recuperation. They knew every creak and quirk of it, every scent and sight, season by season. The very dust was familiar.

The soup was simmering when Catherine heard Drew's key in the lock. She went out into the hall at once to put her arms round his weary neck and comfort him. They stood cheek to cheek until he had relaxed a little.

'Bad?' she sympathised, standing back from him at last.

He covered his mouth with his hand, pretending to rub the dusting of stubble on his chin. 'Hideous.'

The gesture told her more than any words could have done. She kissed him briefly but lovingly. 'Whisky's on the sideboard,' she comforted.

He picked it up on his way through to the kitchen and sat at the table with the glass between his hands, his shoulders hunched, staring into the middle distance. Yes, she thought, reading his body cues, it *has* been hideous. You're done in. But she didn't prompt him to talk about what had happened and she didn't tell him about Susan's phone call either. What he needed now was peace and quiet and the space to recover.

So he had his bath and shaved and put on his clean clothes and they ate their soup together in companionable silence in the kitchen with the radio playing soothing music turned down low. It was the best room in the house for recuperation, a warm, welcoming place, with its range of wooden units and its rich colours — that maroon oven had been an inspiration and so had the red saucepans. They sat in their accustomed places at the farmhouse table with everything they needed easily to hand and the curtains drawn against the night and the world. By the time he set down his spoon, he'd recovered himself enough to smile at her.

'What would I do without you?' he said lovingly, admiring her. Such a good, strong face she had, with those fine blue eyes — air force blue he'd always told her — and that tangle of short curly hair. When they'd first met it had been a sort of pale auburn colour; now it was partly white and partly sandy, like salt and pepper. Not a beauty his Kate, neither of them had ever pretended that — her features were too irregular, her nose too large, her teeth too crooked, her chin too small — but it made him yearn with affection just to look at her.

'Cook your own supper, I expect,' she

said lightly. 'Are we going to watch the news?'

The question brought him up short. Did he really want to be taken back to the accident? Now that he was home and he'd put it behind him, he wanted to avoid it and forget it. But, at the same time, he was proud to think he'd been part of an incident that was going to make the national news and he couldn't help being curious about what they would show. 'It's up to you,' he said, ducking the decision.

She recognised his hesitation, understood it and answered it, as he'd intended she should. 'I think I'd like to see it,' she said and led him into the living room.

The crash was the lead story and it started arrestingly with a close-up of that poor girl being carried away on her stretcher, drowsy and bloodstained, with the cradle mounded over her leg. The shock of seeing her again was more profound than Andrew had expected. It brought back all his irritation and anger but before he could tell Catherine anything about it, they were featuring some asinine bureaucrat in a clean suit who was holding forth in praise of the emergency services.

'So I should think!' Catherine said. She'd recognised his anger and this was a chance for him to give vent to it.

'Nothing about the impact this'll have on normal service in the NHS, you notice,' he grumbled.

Then, suddenly and shockingly, there was his own face blazing at him from the screen. Good God! he thought. Do I really look like that? His face seemed lop-sided, as if it had been twisted out of shape. Very odd. Then he realised that this was not his mirror-image that he was seeing but his face as others saw it. He wasn't sure he liked it.

Catherine was listening to his voice on the television. *'Accidents don't happen. They're caused.'*

'Quite right,' she agreed.

He shrugged. 'But not politic to say so, perhaps.'

'There are always people who don't like hearing the truth,' she conceded, 'but that doesn't mean it shouldn't be told.'

He was speaking on screen again, so they both listened, she impressed by what he was saying and thinking how handsome he looked, he with a mixture of pride and embarrassment. Rabbie Burns was right, he thought. It's chastening to see yourself as others see you. The camera zoomed in on his face, revealing his anger. *'We value money more highly than human life,'* his mouth said. *'That's the message of this accident. It's a very sick world.'*

'I was thinking of what Susan said,' he explained, as the next item of news began. 'You remember. About the state of the rolling stock. The way they've cut back on maintenance. She foresaw this. She *said* there'd be an accident sooner or later and now we've had it.'

That alarmed Catherine. 'You didn't mention her name, did you?'

He brushed that aside. 'No. Of course not. Give me credit for a little tact.'

She retracted her implied criticism by changing direction. 'I wonder what she'll think of it.'

'She might not have seen it.'

'Oh no. She'll have seen it. She was going to watch. She told me so.'

He remembered the engaged phone. 'She called you this evening.'

'There's going to be an inquiry. She's been asked to organise it.'

He was impressed. 'Good for her.' Then he grinned. 'This is turning out to be quite a family affair. Nick was there too. Did I tell you that?'

Her eyes widened with concern. 'At the crash?'

'With John. Yes.'

Now there was anxiety on her face. 'Was he all right?'

'He was fine,' he said, but there was more annoyance in his voice than reassurance. 'Bit too fine to tell you the truth. He's getting too bloody cocky for his own good. Thinks he knows it all. He was trying to teach me my business, saucy young devil.'

So that's what the anger's about, she thought, as he ploughed into an account of Nick's impertinence after the accident.

'You should be glad to think he's so confident,' she said, springing to the defence of her young. 'I'd say that was an asset.'

'Confidence is one thing,' his father growled, 'arrogance is another.'

She smiled at him. 'He's just like you,' she said, 'only you can't see it. You were over-confident when you were his age.'

Now it was his turn to be defensive. 'I was not,' he said, half teasing, half serious. 'I've always had a perfect sense of my own fallibility.'

And that made them both laugh because it was so obviously and manifestly untrue.

'You were over-confident,' she repeated. 'You made me feel you could cope with anything. It was one of the things I liked about you.'

Now they were teasing and easy again. 'Well I'm glad there was something you liked about me,' he joked.

'That among other things,' she joked back.

Chapter 4

Gemma was swimming in a warm sea, on her back with her long hair streaming like silk in the water, moving her arms languidly, kicking her feet so that spray leapt and dazzled before her eyes. The sky above her upturned face was cobalt blue and the beach was a crescent of sun-bright sand edged by the greenest of trees. She was supremely and effortlessly happy, young, tanned, well-fed, relaxed, drop-dead-gorgeous. If only that wasp would stop buzzing.

She put up a hand to brush it away but it was right in front of her face and she couldn't shift it. Right in front of her face and getting bigger and bigger, a huge, dust-covered, metallic horror, with great wheels coming to squash her, slimy with grease and spitting gobbets of impacted dirt as it shrieked towards her. It was enormous, obscene, grinding her down, the weight of it compressing her ribs. She had to struggle to breathe, pushing with all her strength against the horror of it, the heavy, filthy, unspeakable horror, fighting like a mad thing, frantic to escape. She had to get away from it. She had to get away. She had to. But she couldn't move because both her legs were set in concrete. She was pinned to the ground as it screamed and crumpled, in a blur of blue and white and scarlet so that blood gushed in the air in long, red plumes like the red breath of dragons, and she knew that it was going to crush her and kill her and she couldn't do anything about it.

'She's waking up,' Sister said to her junior. 'Gemma. Can you open your eyes for me, dear? That's fine. We're going to take your blood pressure again. Just lift your arm up a bit, there's a good girl.'

Gemma opened her eyes but horror still weighed her down and for a few seconds she couldn't think where she was. Although she had a vague memory of coming round in a very white room and of somebody offering her a sip of water. She lifted her left arm obediently and tried to gather her thoughts, recognised that she was very, very tired and that her arm was surprisingly heavy, gradually took in the blue checked curtains round her bed, the blue uniforms, the distinctive smell of the place. Hospital, she thought. Yes, that's it, I'm in hospital and in a ward. But her mind was too full of nightmare to cope with anything more than that.

The nurse began to take her blood pressure and, turning her head to watch, she saw that the bedclothes were mounded over a support of some kind and then she recalled it all, everything, all at once, with a return of terror that constricted her throat and an overwhelming pain pulsing in her memory. They were going to cut off her leg. That white-haired doctor had been explaining it to her. They were going to cut off her leg and she had to let them do it because it was the only way to get out of the wreckage. Oh God! They were going to cut off her leg. How could she endure it?

But even as panic washed over her, she could feel both her feet quite clearly. One was in plaster and very heavy and the other was irritating, really rather badly. She could feel the irritation right down to her big toe. She would have to put down a hand and scratch it when they'd finished taking her blood pressure. So they couldn't have done it, after all. They must have got her out some other way. What a relief! Thank God! Thank God!

'That's good,' the nurse said, removing the stethoscope from her ears. She was a pretty West Indian with an easy smile and friendly eyes. 'How about a cup of tea?'

The thought of tea brought a lump to Gemma's throat. It was so blessedly normal. But when she tried to sit up to drink it, she discovered that she was attached to a trailing tube and felt a great deal weaker than she'd expected.

'That's just to help you over your operation,' the nurse explained, supporting her as she drank. 'It looks worse than it is. You lost a lot of blood, so we're putting it back.'

Loss of blood sounded ominous. But she didn't dare ask questions in case she was told something she didn't want to hear. 'What time is it?' she compromised.

'Half-past eleven.'

That was a surprise. 'Half-past eleven?' It couldn't be half-past eleven. I caught the twenty-past ten train and I was hours in the wreckage. 'What day is it?'

'Friday. You've been sleeping.'

All that time, Gemma thought and she looked up at the drip and wondered how mobile she could be. 'Can I get out to the loo?' she asked.

'You don't need to worry about that,' the nurse told her. 'You've got a catheter in.'

Oh how vile! How demoralising! 'Do I have to have it? Can't it come out? I could get down to the loo, couldn't I? I know my right foot's in plaster but my left's OK, isn't it? I mean they haven't plastered that. I can feel my toes.'

There was a pause while the nurse looked at her, her pretty face thoughtful. 'I'll get you a chair,' she said. And did, manoeuvring it until it was right against the bed. Then she turned back the bedclothes and removed the support. And Gemma saw the full extent of her injuries. The full, inescapable extent.

Her right leg was striped with stitches and the foot was encased in plaster just as she expected, but the lower part of her left leg was gone, ending below the knee in a bandaged stump. The shock of it was so searing that for a few seconds she just sat where she was and stared at it, feeling sick to the pit of her stomach. How could it be gone when she could feel her toes? It was worse than the nightmare. Perhaps she was still dreaming and it *was* a nightmare. 'But I can feel it,' she protested. 'I can see it's gone but I can feel it.'

'It often happens,' the nurse told her. 'We don't know why. Lots of amputees can feel their limbs. It goes off.'

Amputees, Gemma thought. The word was like a blow. That's what I am now. An amputee. It sounded less than human. This is what I'm like now. This is what I look like and this is how I'm going to look from now on. Incomplete, deformed, hideous. She wanted to run away, to hide in a corner and cry and cry. But where could she hide in a hospital ward? And what would be the point of it if she did? All the crying in the world wouldn't bring her leg back.

The nurse was removing the catheter and being brisk and practical about it. 'Now then,' she said, when it was done, 'let's see if we can get you into this chair. Take your time. It's a bit tricky the first time you try it.'

It wasn't just tricky. It was painful. As soon as Gemma bent her knees, the stump began to throb.

'It always does that,' the nurse explained, as Gemma winced. 'It's the force of gravity. It'll go off.'

I wish she wouldn't keep saying things'll go off, Gemma thought. 'So I should hope,' she said grimly.

'It adjusts after a day or so,' the nurse re-assured. 'The first few days after any op are always the worst. Tell me when you're ready.'

The pulse was dying away as she spoke. 'Another minute,' Gemma decided.

'Now we get to the comedy bit,' the nurse told her, picking up the drip. 'It's like carry-ing a coat-hanger around. Hold on and I'll bring all this stuff round the other side.' She was doing her best to distract her patient by making a joke of it.

But it horrified Gemma to be wheeled away, drip and all, with her stump propped before her on a special board. And the contortions she had to go through once she was in the toilet upset her terribly. By the time she got back to her bed again she was miserable and exhausted.

The nurse was still determined to be cheerful. 'Now then,' she said, arranging the bedclothes over the cradle, 'you've got some visitors, if you're up to it.'

It depended who they were.

'One of them says he's your boyfriend. Jerry, is it? And two girls from your flat.'

Yes, Gemma thought. It might be nice to see *them*. They were such fun and so full of life. They might be just what she needed.

They trooped into the ward, bearing flowers and magazines and a huge box of her favourite chocolates, tied with a red ribbon. Trudi had come straight from the office in her serviceable black and white and Tracey had dressed up for the occasion in a flowing Laura Ashley skirt and a shawl and full make-up.

'Your poor old thing,' the two girls said, as they kissed her. 'What a thing to happen!

Are you all right? You look awful!'

Their good health and crashing lack of tact made her unexpectedly angry. 'Well of course I look awful,' she said. 'What d'you expect? I've just had my leg cut off, for Christ's sake.'

That embarrassed them, but only temporarily. 'I brought you the latest Trollope,' Trudi said, putting the paperback on the bedspread.

'I don't like Trollope.'

'Don't you?' Tracey said, raising her eyebrows with surprise. 'I thought everybody did. Oh well I'll have it then.'

'Do you mind?' Trudi remonstrated, resting her weight on the bed to lean forward and grab the book. '*I* bought it. If she doesn't want it, *I'll* have it.'

They're not going to quarrel over it, surely, Gemma thought. Not when I'm in this state. 'Mind my legs!' she warned.

Jerry was carrying a bundle of newspapers. 'You were on the telly last night,' he said. 'Star of the show. Don't suppose you saw it though, did you.'

Gemma made a grimace. 'I was otherwise engaged.'

'Right,' he said, easily. 'Right. Anyway you're in all the papers this morning so you haven't missed anything. Old Ma Edmunds brought hers up first thing to show us, fairly frothing. I was still in bed. She said I was a layabout. Probably right. Anyway I nipped out later on and bought the lot. Thought you'd like to see them.' He dropped the wedge of papers on to the bed. 'Great, eh?'

Gemma couldn't see anything great about it, but she was certainly front-page news.

'FEISTY HEROINE OF WANDSWORTH COMMON DISASTER,' she read. The *Chronicle* had even got her name. 'TWO-HOUR ORDEAL FOR PLUCKY GEMMA.' And so had the *Mirror*. 'GEMMA SMILES AS SHE IS PULLED FROM THE CRASH,' their headline said, and they had a picture of her being carried off to the ambulance with an oxygen mask over her face, her head bandaged, her cheeks streaked with blood, the shredded arm of her leather jacket swinging below the blanket. It looked dreadful and yet she couldn't help a feeling of pride. It was fame, of a sort, and God knows she'd earned it. She *had* been brave. She was being brave now. There had to be some consolation for all this.

'Great, eh?' Jerry repeated. 'D'you want some choccies?' He was busily opening the box. 'What's your rave?'

'No thanks,' Gemma said. 'Actually I feel a bit sick.'

'Yes,' he said, 'I suppose you would. That'll be the anaesthetic.' Did he have to be quite so matter-of-fact about it? 'How about you, Trace?'

Tracey chose an orange cream, Trudi a caramel. Soon all three of them were sitting by the bedside gobbling their way through the box, while they told Gemma how easy it had been to wangle time off to see her and regaled her with tales of all the 'gross' things that had happened to them the previous day. It was what they always did of an evening while they were eating their communal meal and they saw no incongruity in continuing the tradition that morning. But Gemma did. It was inappropriate and thoughtless. How shallow they are, she thought, listening to their prattle. How they mock people and how little they care. She was surprised she hadn't noticed it before.

Finally they pulled their attention back to her.

'How long are they going to keep you in?' Tracey wanted to know.

Gemma hadn't even thought about it. 'I've no idea. Depends how quickly I recover, I suppose.'

'They won't let you back to the flat though, will they?' Tracey said amiably. 'Because of the stairs. I mean, you'll never be able to manage the stairs, will you?'

Gemma was shocked by such a question. It sounded callous — and felt contrived, as if it was being asked for a purpose. But she answered it as honestly as she could. 'I don't know what I'll be able to manage yet.'

'Not two flights,' Trudi said, tucking her hair behind her ear. 'Not with only one leg.' The hair escaped from the temporary restriction of her earlobe and swung across her cheek again, as it always did. 'I mean, think about it.'

I'd rather not, Gemma thought. It made her feel that life without her leg was going to be altogether too complicated and difficult.

'The thing is,' Tracey went on, adjusting her shawl, 'we've been thinking, haven't we, Jerry? And what we've been thinking is — well — as you're not going to be able to come back — because of the stairs and everything — maybe we ought to find someone else to take your room. Sort of temporary or something like that. Course, we don't want you to think we're turning you out or anything. We wouldn't do that, would we Jez. I mean, if you could manage it, we'd be . . . It's just it's the stairs — and the rent. Isn't that right, Trudi?'

'Shared between three,' Trudi explained, attending to her hair again. 'I mean it's a lot of money shared between three, when you've been used to it being four.'

'You need the rent,' Gemma understood.

'There's no rush,' Trudi said. 'Only Jerry's got this friend, haven't you Jez?'

They don't care about me at all, Gemma realised. They're fair-weather friends and that's all they've ever been. I just haven't seen it until now. 'When does he want to move in?' she asked.

'It's a her, actually,' Jerry admitted, rather shamefacedly. And hastened to justify himself. 'She's a laugh. You'd love her. We thought she'd be just the one.'

I've been replaced, Gemma thought. That's how much I meant to him. That's how much I meant to all of them. If she'd been on her feet — if she'd *had* feet — she would have walked away from them. 'You'll have to go now,' she said. 'I'm tired.'

Trudi persisted. 'What about the flat?'

'Do what you like with it,' Gemma said, turning on her side. 'It's nothing to do with me, is it? Not now. You've made your decision.' And she slithered down the bed, pulled the covers over her ears and closed her eyes. She wanted to weep and shout at them. How could they be so unkind?

'That's settled then is it?' Trudi's voice said from behind her. 'See you later, then.'

Gemma didn't bother to answer. She heard them make their exit, the tone of their voices light, cheerful, teasing, unchanged by what they'd just done to her, unmoved by what she'd just said, unaware of how much they'd just hurt her. *We don't want you to think we're turning you out,* she thought. But that's exactly what they were doing. How could I have liked them? Any of them. Even for a minute. They're shallow, selfish monsters. Not like Pippa. If *she'd* come to see me she'd have been quite different. Pippa had been the best friend she'd ever had and she missed her terribly. Oh Pippa! she mourned, as the tears pricked behind her eyelids, why did you have to go round the world? I need you here. Now. But what's the good of even thinking about it? She's not here. I've lost her. I've lost my leg and my job and my flat. Everything. Nothing will ever be the same again.

There was a rustle beside her bed. Somebody was behind her, bending towards her. Had one of them come back? Surely not. Hadn't they done enough damage?

But it wasn't either of the girls. Ringed fingers touched her hair, stroked it and withdrew. 'Darling!' a familiar voice said lovingly. 'Are you awake?'

It was her mother, leaning across the bed

to kiss her cheek, so that her beads swung and clinked across the straight stylish jacket of her best Chanel-style suit. She was wearing high heels and her blonde hair was immaculate, so she'd obviously come straight from the boutique. And her brown eyes were swimming with tears.

'I got your message,' she said, as Gemma struggled to sit up. 'They rang from the hospital. It must have been just after you got here. Oh my darling, this is so awful!' And she stretched out a hand to try and help.

Gemma shook it away. 'I can manage,' she said, hauling herself into a better position. She knew she was being ungracious but she couldn't help it. She *had* to be independent.

'I've been trying to see you for ages,' her mother told her. 'I came as soon as I got the phone call but you weren't down from the operating theatre then. They let me have a peep at you yesterday evening but you were sound asleep. Dead to the world. Like a little baby. So I thought I'd pop in early this morning and I saw Sister that time, and she said to try during my lunch break. So here I am. Oh my poor dear darling. What can I say?'

'I'm all right,' Gemma said, making a bleak attempt to smile and failing. 'Don't fuss.' It always took such an effort to cope with her mother, and she didn't have the energy for it. Not now. Not after Trudi and Tracey. Just keep off the modelling career, she willed her dominating parent, and don't run my life for me. I've got enough to cope with this morning without that.

Billie Goodeve put her shopping bag on the bed and began to unpack it. 'I brought you some things. I didn't know what you'd like so I thought grapes. Well they're generally acceptable, aren't they, and I don't suppose the food is up to much. It never is in these places.'

'I haven't had any yet,' Gemma said.

'No, poor darling,' Billie sympathised. 'I don't suppose you have. Now I've put some washing things in this little dolly-bag. Just necessities, soap and flannel, that sort of thing. Little box of tissues. I'll put that on the cabinet shall I? And your hairbrush. The one you had when you were a little girl, d'you remember? You used to brush the cat with it, poor thing. I used to say leave it be, but would you? No you wouldn't. You used to dress it up in your doll's clothes — bonnet on its poor little head and everything. You said it was your baby. You used to take it for walks in the pram. D'you remember? Never knew a cat so long-suffering. And a nightie, look. I was going to pop round to your flat and get one for you there, then I remembered this one and I thought, it's just the thing.' She pulled a hideous piece of middle-aged silk from the shopping bag, like a magician producing a rabbit from a hat.

I wouldn't be seen dead in it, Gemma thought, even if I very nearly was. And she wondered what had happened to her expensive clothes. Torn to shreds, probably. Didn't they cut off her jeans? The memory of what happened at the accident was curiously jumbled. It was only the faces she could remember in any detail, the nice reassuring one with the white hair and the handsome one who said, *'I don't let my patients die.'*

Her mother had finished unpacking and was arranging fruit in an old bowl on Gemma's bedside table. 'Now then, my darling,' she said, 'what else do you need?'

My leg, Gemma thought, but she tried to answer in the way her mother expected. 'I can't think of anything for the moment, thanks.'

'Well if you do, get one of these nice nurses to give me a ring and I'll see to it. I'm sure they won't mind. You're not to worry about a thing.'

The banality of the conversation was so irritating that Gemma had to turn her head away from it. I've lost my leg, she thought, and she tells me not to worry about a thing. But she held on to her control and didn't complain.

'Well that's that then,' her mother said, settling herself into the armchair beside the bed. 'Now we must think about the future.'

That was too much, 'Not now, Mother,' Gemma begged. 'Not yet. Leave it.'

'We can't leave it,' her mother said. 'I mean, there are things to be decided. You'll have to tell them where you're going when you leave here, for a start. They'll want to know. And you can't go back to the flat, can you? Tracey was telling me last night. Because of the stairs. So, I've thought it all out. You can come home with me. You can have your old room. I know we're on the second floor but I'm sure we can manage the lift between us. Will they provide you with a wheelchair or will you have to buy your own? Not that it matters, because you've got insurance haven't you?'

Gemma was beginning to feel dizzy. 'What?'

'Insurance. You told me. Remember? For being an actress. In case you got injured on stage. Little did they know!'

'Look!' Gemma said. 'I don't want to talk about this. Not now. I can't take it. It'll have to wait.'

'Of course,' her mother agreed affably. 'I can understand that. Oh, it's so unfair for this to happen to you. My poor baby!'

Gemma didn't want this cloying sympathy either. 'I'm twenty-one, Mother,' she said. 'Going on twenty-two.'

'I know, I know,' Billie crooned. 'And now this. It's iniquitous. But don't you worry about a thing, darling. I'll look after you.'

She was irritating Gemma so much that she simply had to speak up. 'I don't want to be looked after,' she said. 'I can stand on my own two feet. Even if I've only got one.' The irony of the joke pleased her.

But it was lost on her mother. 'Of course,' she agreed again, with happy insincerity. 'Don't you worry about a thing.'

Gemma rolled her eyes in exasperation. 'It's no good talking to you,' she complained. 'You don't listen to a word I'm saying. Read my lips. *I don't want to be looked after.*'

'You might not want it,' Billie said, 'but everything's changed now, hasn't it?' It was breaking her heart to see her beautiful daughter reduced to such a state but they both had to accept it.

'It hasn't! I won't let it!'

'Oh come on, Gemma. Face facts. You'll have to face them sooner or later. You're ... a ... well you're a cripple, darling, aren't you really?'

'I'm not! I won't be! You're not to say such a thing.'

Battle had been joined between them, as it so often was and although neither of them had intended it. 'I have to, darling,' Billie said, 'it's the truth. I mean, they'll never take you on as a model now, not with one leg. And when I think what you were like when you were Miss Pears! Oh it's so unfair!'

'I knew we'd get round to this,' Gemma said. 'You can't leave it alone, can you? I don't want to be a model. I never have. I never will. I've told you over and over again.'

'You were a model when you were four and you were Miss Pears,' Billie insisted. 'You couldn't have had a better start than that. And then there was all the work you did for the catalogues. You were a wonderful little model. They all loved you. But what's the good of talking about it now you're crippled?'

That word again. It was like a sting. 'I'm

not crippled. How many more times? I've been in a rail crash, that's what's the matter with me. I've been in a rail crash and I've lost my leg because they had to cut me out of the wreckage. I'm lucky to be alive. I damn nearly wasn't. They had to cut me out of the wreckage, don't you understand?'

Her mother pulled her jacket straight. 'Yes darling. Yes I know,' she murmured. 'But it'll be all right.'

'What are you talking about?'

'I'm talking about your future,' Billie told her. 'It's no good talking about the past. We've got to think about the future. You must come home with me and let me look after you. That's all there is to it.' And as Gemma was glaring at her, she tried to persuade. 'It'll all be for the best, darling, you'll see. After all, I know your ways, don't I? And there's no one to beat your mother when you're not well.'

Gemma was as close to beating her mother as she'd ever been. 'You're not listening to me,' she said angrily. 'I don't want to come home with you. I don't want to be looked after. Not by you. Not by anyone. I want to stand on my own feet.'

Anger triggered annoyance. 'You don't face facts, Gemma. That's always been your trouble,' Billie said. 'You never have.

You're too self-willed. You always have to know best. Well it'll have to stop now. You'll *have* to be looked after whether you like it or not.'

'No,' Gemma insisted. 'I won't. I'm going to get better and I'm going to look after myself. And while we're on the subject, I'm not going to be a model. Not. N O T. I'm going to be an actress.'

Billie's face was wrinkled with distress. 'Oh my poor darling,' she said. 'You'll never get an acting job now. Not with your face in this state. And all your lovely hair gone.'

Until that moment, Gemma hadn't thought about any other part of her body except her missing leg. 'What?' she said, putting up her hand to touch her hair. Lumps. Spikes. Nasty tacky . . .

'They haven't shown you.' Billie understood. 'You haven't seen.' She was fishing in her handbag for her powder compact, flicking it open, dusting the powder from the surface of the mirror. 'They should have let you see. I mean to say, it's not fair to keep it from you.'

Gemma didn't want to look but it was already too late. The mirror gleamed before her and the image in it was unavoidable. There was her forehead scored with red

71

scars and pitted with black spots as if she'd been peppered with shot, her eyes, not brown and shining as she knew them but small and bloodshot, the left one half closed by swollen flesh and purple bruises. But above her face — and far, far worse — were the roughly cropped remains of her hair, spiky with blood and grease, standing on end, grotesque as a clown's wig, and running through it from the left side of her forehead and round behind her ear, a long hideous wound. It was sutured together with great black stitches like a strip of barbed wire and all the hair on either side of it had been shaved away. The shock of such a terrible change of image was so shattering it ripped away the last of her control. She hurled the mirror from her mother's hand and began to scream.

'It isn't me! It isn't! It isn't! I don't look like that. I won't!' Then she burst into passionate weeping, unable to bear it a second longer, because she *did* look like that, she was changed for ever, wrecked, ruined, finished. 'What did you have to go and do that for?'

Billie was shattered. She hadn't meant to upset her poor daughter. Not like this. She hadn't thought . . . If only she'd . . . Faced with such a terrible reaction, she didn't know what to do or say. She dithered, patted Gemma's arm and was thrown off violently, took two paces into the ward, called for the nurse, returned to the bedside, her face taut with concern, tried to defend herself. 'You had to see sooner or later, darling. I mean to say . . . They couldn't keep it from you for ever.'

Gemma went on weeping, hiding her face in her hands, her shoulders shaking. 'Oh, don't cry, darling,' Billie pleaded. 'Please don't cry. You'll make yourself ill. Please, please don't cry. It's not as bad as all that. I mean, scars fade, don't they, in time. And your hair'll grow back. You think how quickly it grows. There's always a bright side. Every cloud has a silver lining. You'll get *enormous* damages.'

That made matters worse. 'Go away!' Gemma shouted. 'I can't stand this. Go away! Do you hear?' The entire ward could hear but she was too far gone to care. 'I can't bear to see you. I can't bear to see . . .'

A nurse had arrived at the foot of the bed. 'Oh, nurse,' Billie tried to explain. 'She's had a bit of an upset.'

'Yes,' the nurse said. 'I can see.' And she drew the curtains round her patient. 'If you wouldn't mind leaving us for a moment, Mrs Goodeve,' she suggested. 'It's time for

Gemma's medication. She was in theatre a very long time.'

Now that her tears had begun, Gemma lay back on her pillows and wept with abandon, crying out Thursday's terror and pain, her friends' rejection, her stupid, stupid weakness, her utter revulsion at what she had become. She took the proffered pills still weeping, heard the nurse's commiserations still weeping, closed her eyes still weeping. It was a very long time before she slipped into the relief of sleep.

She woke to a changed world. Even before she opened her eyes she could feel the change. It was so peaceful — quiet and soothing and contained. It made her feel secure, as though she were tucked in a cradle. And it smelt heavenly. She opened her good eye, saw that the curtains were opened too and peeped sideways at the ward. It was empty of everything except beds and patients and so quiet that she could hear the slip-slop of footsteps slummocking away along the corridor and the clatter of cutlery from the central table where the rest of the patients were eating their supper, talking to one another in gentle easy voices. The blue daylight of the morning had softened, deepening the colour of the curtains and veiling the walls with lilac shadow, and the square of sky in the window opposite was peach pink and suffused with soft light. It was afternoon.

Then she noticed the flowers.

They were heaped on every surface all round her bed, two glass vases full of roses and gypsophila on the cabinet and vases and baskets and pots of every kind filling the table at the foot of the bed. She'd never seen such a display except in a florist's. She sat up carefully and smiled at the women sitting round the table.

'Better?' one of them called.

She agreed that she was. 'I'm sorry I made such a fuss.'

'You go ahead, duck,' the woman said. She was a comfortable woman in a pink dressing gown and a large neck brace. 'Make as much fuss as you like. If *you* can't, I don't know who can.'

'Why have they put all those flowers on my table?' Gemma asked.

One of the other women got up and strolled across the ward to Gemma's bed. 'They're yours,' she said. 'Been coming in all afternoon.'

'Good heavens! Who from?'

'Well-wishers,' the woman said. 'Sister Foster was telling us. You been in the papers. You're a heroine. We been reading about you.'

Gemma leant across the bed and picked up the card attached to the nearest vase of roses. *Get well soon,* it said, *dear brave girl, from Mrs Elliott and the girls at Ivymount Engineering.*

Surprise gave way to pleasure. The sense of being cared for brought an unexpected feeling of well-being. All these flowers, she thought. All these people I've never met taking the time and trouble to send me flowers. She picked up the second card. That said much the same thing as the first: *We hope you soon get better, from Rainbow class.* 'How kind!'

'People are,' the woman told her. 'Given half a chance. You got a lotta cards too. They're in your drawer. I'm Patsy, by the way. I was in the crash an' all. Broken collarbone and concussion. There's five of us from the crash in here.'

Gemma looked round the ward at her fellow sufferers, who nodded and smiled. Seeing them made her feel ashamed of herself for making a fuss like that when she was surrounded by so many other people who'd been hurt in the accident too. 'Are you all right?' she asked Patsy.

'Yes,' Patsy said shortly. 'Well I'm better

now anyway. All right if I take the painkillers. Mustn't grumble. We're the lucky ones. There was twenty-seven killed. We been reading about it in the papers. Would you like to see them?'

Gemma took the papers and read them one after the other. The pictures gave her a shock even though she knew how serious the accident had been but the text was worse. Twenty-seven dead. It was horrific. It should never have happened. And reading about it brought it all back to her.

'There was a little boy,' she remembered, as she opened the third paper in the pile. 'He was in the carriage with me. I wonder what happened to him.'

And there he was, in the first picture on the centre pages, wrapped in a blanket and being carried away by an ambulance woman. *'Miraculous escape,'* she read. *'Little Jack Turner pulled from the wreckage alive after being trapped for nearly an hour, escaped with cuts and bruises, despite fears for his life. Sadly his mother, Maureen, was one of the fatalities.'*

The news crushed Gernma with sadness. 'That's awful,' she said. 'She was telling him off when we crashed.' She remembered it too clearly. 'He was drinking Coke and it was all slopping out of the can. And she told him off. It must have been the last thing she did. Oh poor woman!' It was so awful it made her cry.

'It was a bad business,' Patsy agreed.

I mustn't make any more fuss, Gemma thought, stanching her tears. And trying to be positive, she turned her attention to the flowers. 'We ought to put these all round the ward,' she said. 'They're as much for you as for me. We were all in it together.' It was suddenly important to her to share her good fortune.

'They was sent to *you*,' Patsy pointed out.

'Only because I was in the paper and they knew who I was,' Gemma said. 'If you'd been in the paper they'd have come to you. Let's spread them around. They'd look better spread around.'

So the flowers were borne away to every cabinet, the cards were read and hung on strings above the bed and, having recovered enough to find an appetite, Gemma was given some supper.

'That's better,' the woman in the pink dressing gown said. 'That's put some colour in your cheeks. That'll please our Doctor Quennell.'

Gemma was enjoying the sight of her roses. She wasn't particularly interested in doctors at that moment. But to make conversation she asked who he was.

'He's our doctor,' Patsy said. 'You'd have seen him yesterday if you hadn't been asleep all the time. He was in and out all day. Ever so kind. Couldn't do enough for us. You'll see him tomorrow when he does his rounds. You'll love him. He's gorgeous.'

Chapter 5

When Dr Nicholas Quennell eased himself out of bed on Saturday morning he was far from gorgeous. After two very bad nights, he felt as though he hadn't slept for a fortnight and one wince at the wall mirror revealed that he looked as though he hadn't either. But that was par for the course in this job and there was too much pride in him to complain.

As the much-loved, youngest child in an almost entirely medical family, he'd never had the slightest doubt about the direction his life would take nor the success he would make of it — to Dulwich College, where his father and older brother had been scholars before him, then to King's — College and Hospital — where they had trained, then on to the wards in one of the London hospitals. Medicine was the right profession for him. It was familiar, it suited his idealistic nature, and it gave him the daily opportunity to help and cure. When he told Gemma Goodeve he never allowed his patients to die, he was simply stating what he believed.

Death was his enemy and he fought it with all the high-tech he could command. Nothing was sweeter to him than the knowledge that he had pulled another patient through. His sister Susan teased him for 'playing God' but that was just the sort of thing she *would* say and could be easily ignored. Inside his personality he'd always been secure and certain of himself.

But now, and without warning, the crash had brought him face to face with two brutal, inevitable facts — that all life is limited and that no doctor can work miracles, however talented he might be. Having to certify the death of so many terribly mangled bodies had been an appalling thing for him to do, hence the bad nights.

And it was a miserable morning. As he made his way between the tall buildings of the hospital towards the main entrance and the café where he usually had breakfast with his friends, it was threatening rain and a chill wind was blowing. He lengthened his stride. The sooner he got to the café, the sooner he would cheer up.

He liked the main entrance. It gave him a sense of importance every time he saw it, with its triangular glass roof and the foyer beneath it full of people all cheerfully milling about. Despite the statues that flanked the automatic doors — Florence Nightingale carved in green stone on one side and the boy king, Edward VI, equally verdant and angelic on the other — it looked more like a shopping mall than a hospital. Some people complained about it, saying it was part of the general commercialisation of medicine, but it seemed right to him, like a cosmopolitan bridge between the wards and the outside world, where staff and patients and visitors could mingle on equal terms, buying sweets and papers in Menzies, flowers at the florist's, using the NatWest, eating at the café or the restaurant, taking their clothes to the dry cleaner's. Its cheerfulness marked the start of his morning routine. He couldn't wait to get inside.

But that Saturday there was a gauntlet to run. Since the crash, the hospital had sent out a spokesman night and morning in order to keep the press informed. Now, early though it was, there were already half a dozen reporters lurking on the walkway, blue jeans sagging, cameras and microphones at the ready. As he approached, one of them left the group and began to stride towards him. He was a thickset man with a solid beer-belly and a determined expression, and he plainly meant business. Damn, Nick thought. He's not after me, is he? But he was.

'Excuse me, Doctor!' he called. 'Just a minute! Excuse me!'

Now what shall I do? Nick thought. If I press on he'll follow me into the café and I shall never get rid of him. I'd better backtrack. He turned on his heel and began to stride back the way he'd come, his shoulders hunched with annoyance. If he walked quickly he could get in through one of the side doors and give him the slip.

The reporter was quicker than he was — and insistent. He was alongside in a dozen paces. 'Don't I recognise you?' he said.

Nick walked on, barely glancing at him. 'I shouldn't think so.'

'You were at the crash.'

That had to be admitted, grudgingly.

'You were the guy who cut our Gemma Goodeve out of the wreckage. Can you tell me how she is?'

I'll have to stop and say something, Nick thought. I can't just go on walking away. 'The hospital spokesman will be giving another press statement at ten o'clock this morning,' he said stiffly, giving the official response. 'As you obviously know. That's who you're waiting for isn't it? He will answer all your questions.'

'How was she the last time you saw her?'

'The hospital spokesman . . .'

'Yeah, yeah! We know all that,' the reporter grinned and quoted the clichéd phrases, his voice mocking, *'As well as can be expected. Stable condition. Making good progress.* But how *is* she? That's what our readers want to know. Right? How's she coping, poor kid? It must have been quite a shock.' He was standing right in front of Nick now, blocking the way.

'I'm sorry,' Nick said, looking at him aggressively but keeping his voice massively polite. 'I can't discuss my patients. Doctors don't. It's against our code. You'll have to ask the spokesman.' And he walked on.

'Doctors don't!' the reporter mocked, striding beside him. 'What a load of crap. That old feller on the news told us all sorts.'

Bloody nerve, Nick thought angrily. *That old feller.* That's my father you're talking about. 'Excuse me,' he said, pushing past the man's bulk. 'I've got work to do.' And he squeezed through the nearest side entrance as quickly as he could. So quickly that the edge of his white coat was caught between the two doors as they swung back and he had to stop, red-faced with annoyance and embarrassment, to disentangle himself.

'A quick quote!' the reporter suggested, looming before him.

Fury and mortification got the better of good sense. 'Bugger off!'

The reporter was delighted. 'Naughty, naughty!' he said, waving an admonitory finger.

Bloody hacks, Nick thought as he charged down the corridor. They make monkeys of us. We ought to do something about them. Calling my father *that old feller*. But as his long stride took him further away from trouble and he began to cool down, he had to admit that his father had asked for it. He *had* given the interview. And everybody knew that doctors don't give interviews, especially to television and straight off the cuff. The BMA handle that sort of thing, or an official spokesman, never the doctor on the case.

His two friends Rick and Abdul were half-way through their breakfast. Abdul was sprinkled with crumbs. 'What kept you?' he said, brushing at his coat.

'Hacks.'

'What did they want?'

'Gemma Goodeve, basically.'

'Who?' Rick wanted to know.

'The crash girl.'

'They say she's beautiful,' Abdul observed. 'An actress or something. Is that right?'

Nick had started his breakfast. 'No idea,' he said. 'I was too busy to notice.'

'Aren't you doing old Barnaby's rounds today?' Rick asked, stretching his long legs out beyond the table.

'Yes,' Nick admitted, grimacing. 'For my sins.'

'Then you can ask her.'

Nick didn't think much of that for an idea. Although he was cool in theatre and something of a whiz-kid when it came to diagnosis, he found ward rounds difficult. Patients had a tendency to emotional outbursts once they were back on the ward, and as grief and anger were a little too hard for him to handle, he was careful not to provoke them. 'I shall do no such thing,' he said.

But when he walked into Page Ward later that morning, everybody in the office was talking about his famous patient, and the place was full of flowers. He'd never seen so many in a ward. He was used to the odd vase here and there but not this sort of abundance: roses, lilies, dahlias, chrysanthemums, there was no end to them, their massed colours dazzling after the grey light of the morning, their scent overpowering. He stood for a moment just inside the swing doors, breathing it in.

Sister Foster explained. 'They're because of our Gemma,' she said. 'She's quite a star. They've been coming in since yesterday afternoon. Mr Barnaby was very impressed. Good publicity, he said.'

Nick didn't want to talk about publicity. It wasn't relevant. He pulled his medical dignity about him and began his routine questions. 'Any problems I should know about?'

They brought him up to date. The oldest inhabitant had been a nuisance during the night but the casualties from the crash were all making steady progress. 'Gemma had a bit of a setback after her mother's visit.'

'In what way?' he asked, and listened carefully while they told him what had happened.

'Right,' he said. 'I'll see her first, in that case.' If she was going to be a problem it would be best to get it over at once.

She looked different from the girl he remembered. When they'd been inching her out of the wreckage she'd seemed tall, but now lying in her regulation bed, with her legs under their cradle and her cropped hair spiky against the pillows, she seemed surprisingly small, as if she'd been cut down to size. Under the train she'd been a beauty —

yes, he *had* noticed — calm and stoical despite her bloodstains, enduring everything that happened to her. Now her face was bruised and swollen and she had a black eye and hair like an old Brillo pad. She was staring into space, her expression pained.

'Good morning,' he said in his professional voice as he picked up her notes. 'How are you this morning?'

She turned her head, looked from his name-tag to his face and smiled at him, as well as she could for her injuries. 'It's you,' she said. 'The one who saved my life.'

Her praise pleased him and so did the smile. It was a good start. 'That's my job,' he said, coolly.

He's different here on the ward, she thought, very handsome with all that thick hair and those blue eyes, but different. Formal and haughty as if he's deliberately putting a distance between us. The change in him disappointed her. 'I never thanked you.'

'There's no need to,' he said, studying her notes. 'You seem to be making good progress. How do you feel?'

She looked at him steadily, aware of the discomfort her smile had caused as it stretched her swollen flesh. She'd been awake most of the night buffeted from one strong emotion to another, depressed by her helplessness, guilty to have made such a fuss the previous day, aggravated by her flat-mates, furious at her mother's bossiness, proud and touched to be the centre of so much public attention, burning with fury at what had happened to her. But she couldn't tell him any of that. Not now he was being so formal. 'All right,' she said.

He admired her self-control. Perhaps she wasn't going to be a problem after all. 'Are you in any pain?'

'Not now.'

'Good,' he said. 'I'll just examine you, then.' And he signalled to Sister that the dressings were to be removed.

As the nurse swished the curtains around the bed, Gemma shivered. This was the moment she'd been dreading. 'Look at the stump, you mean?'

'Yes.'

Which meant she would have to look at it too. At the wreck of her leg. At the scar.

'I have to see if it's healing properly,' he explained, as the nurse removed the cradle.

Seeing his stern expression, she controlled herself, the effort visible. 'It's all right,' she said. 'I haven't got used to it yet, that's all.' The dressing was being peeled away, painfully. The stump was revealed, raw, swollen and held together with horrible stitches. She was appalled by it, aching at the sight of such ugliness. Her lovely, long striding leg reduced to this. But she swallowed her tears and didn't say anything. She wasn't going to let him see her cry. That would be demeaning. From this moment on she was going to get better. As quickly as she could.

'That's fine,' Nick said, looking at the stump so as to avoid her eyes until she'd recovered from the first shock. 'Nice and healthy.'

It didn't seem nice or healthy to Gemma. Nothing about her body seemed nice and healthy now. She submitted to the rest of his examination, turning her head, wriggling her remaining toes. Despite his aloofness he was thorough and his hands were gentle. But it was an anguish to face what had happened to her, even so.

'Right,' he finished, signalling to Sister Foster that the stump could be dressed again. 'That's all.'

But Gemma wasn't listening to him. There was a voice complaining, very loudly, just beyond the swing doors and she'd turned her head towards it and was straining to hear it.

'Now look here,' it protested, 'I've been

here twenty minutes. It's not right.'

Nick was alerted by her tension. She's not going to get emotional on me now, he thought. Not when she's done so well. 'What is it?'

She gave an involuntary grimace. 'My mother.'

'Don't worry about her for the moment,' he advised. And he swept out through the closed curtains thinking, I'll deal with *her*.

Billie Goodeve was standing beside the nurses' station, holding forth to the nurse on duty, and she was so enraged it was several seconds before she realised that he'd arrived to speak to her. Then she turned to give him the full force of her displeasure, brown eyes flashing, well-upholstered bosom visibly heaving her jewellery up and down.

'Now look here,' she complained, 'I've been waiting here for twenty minutes and it's not good enough. I haven't got all day. I run a boutique and it can't be left.'

He dealt with her as though she were any other relation of any other patient, asking who she wanted to see and explaining the delay with magisterial politeness. 'I'm sorry we can't let you in for the moment,' he said. 'Your daughter's having her wound dressed. That's why we've drawn the curtains.'

'And how long's that going to take?'

'Quite a while,' he told her. 'It's not a thing we can hurry.'

'Well how long, then? Five minutes? Ten? I'm a busy woman.'

'Another half an hour at least,' he said. 'It's a major injury. We have to attend to it properly.'

Being reminded of Gemma's injuries triggered Billie's concern. 'Is she all right?'

It was the first sign of any interest in his patient's well-being. And about time too, he thought. If you'd been halfway decent you'd have asked me that first. 'She's making good progress,' he told her, adding, 'We shouldn't be more than forty minutes. Would you like to wait in the day room?'

She hesitated, her face baleful. It was aggravating to be kept out like this but her time *was* precious. 'No,' she decided finally. 'It's no good. I'll have to go. I can't wait another forty minutes. I've been here long enough already. Tell her I'll come back tomorrow.'

He decided it was time to end the interview. He'd achieved his object. 'I'm sorry I can't be more helpful,' he said, turning on his heel. 'Now I must go. I've got rather a lot of patients to see.'

The curtains were still drawn round Gemma's bed and the space inside was so rich with the scent of flowers she felt as though she was sitting in a bower. Now that her stump was covered up again and her mother had stopped complaining she felt easier.

'I can't cope with my mother just at the moment,' she explained to Sister Foster. 'She's a bit heavy sometimes. Well very heavy, actually. Normally I can stand it but now I'm like this . . .'

Sister smiled, her hands busy.

'She wants to live my life for me, that's the trouble,' Gemma went on. 'She will keep on about how she wants me to be a model. She's been pressurising me about it since I was four. Well I shan't do it now, shall I?'

Sister Foster took her question seriously. 'I don't see any reason why not.'

'A one-legged model,' Gemma joked. 'I can just see it. Hopping down the catwalk. I'd be a sensation. I mean, whoever heard of a model with one leg?'

'We had one last year.'

'You mean a model who lost her leg?'

Sister Foster's answer astonished her. 'No, I don't. I mean a model with one leg.

She was a model when she had her accident and we fitted her with an artificial leg and she went on modelling.'

'Really?'

'There's no end to the marvels of modern science,' Sister smiled. 'You'll be surprised what we can do once we get started.'

Gemma was so much easier now that it was possible to ask, 'When will you fit me with a new leg?'

That answer was even more surprising. 'In about a fortnight, I should think,' Sister said. 'When your wound's healed.'

The thought of being back on two feet so quickly lifted Gemma's spirits as powerfully as the sight of her injuries had cast them down. 'Good God!'

Sister Foster laughed. 'We don't hang about,' she said. 'You'll be back on the cat-walk in no time.'

'Actually,' Gemma confessed, 'I don't want to be a model. I never did. That was all my mother's idea. *I* want to be an actress.'

'No problem,' Sister said, smiling at her. 'There's a good precedent. Sarah Bernhardt played Hamlet with a wooden leg. And in tights too. How about that?'

'Brilliant!' she approved. 'A woman after my own heart. If she could do it, so can I.' Her bruised face was fierce with determination. 'I'm not giving in to this,' she said. 'I'm not going to let it change my life. If my mother can't do it, half a leg won't either.'

'You're doing well,' Sister told her as the nurse put the cradle back over her stump. 'Go on like this and we'll have you in the West End for Christmas.'

And at that point, just as she was happy again and feeling that she'd be able to cope with her mother now that her stump was back under the bedclothes, Dr Quennell put his head through the curtain, looking pleased with himself.

'Right,' he said to Gemma. 'I've dealt with your mother.' His voice was full of cheerful confidence. 'You don't need to worry.'

Her precarious peace was instantly broken. She was so surprised she hardly knew what to say. What was he talking about, 'dealt with your mother'? 'I beg your pardon.'

'She's gone,' he explained and he paused for her approval, smiling at her. 'You don't have to see her. I've sent her away.'

She didn't approve at all. She was very annoyed. How dare he take it on himself to do such a thing! 'I never asked you to.'

He was surprised to see that he'd made her angry and, thrown off balance, took refuge in formality. 'I made a professional judgement,' he said stiffly. 'It was for your own good. I can't allow visitors to upset you.'

Anger sparked in the air between them. He might be handsome but that didn't give him the right to play God. 'They're *my* visitors,' she told him, 'and *I'll* cope with them. I'm not a child.'

'You're my patient,' he retorted angrily. 'And it's my judgement. I can't allow you to be upset by outsiders.'

'Outsiders!' she said, brown eyes flashing. Her voice was so loud she was very nearly shouting. 'That's my mother you're talking about. How dare you call my mother an outsider?'

'As far as this ward is concerned she *is* an outsider,' he said furiously, thrown even further off balance by the impact of those eyes. And he left her quickly before they could quarrel outright. What was she thinking of to question his judgement? His professional judgement. She really was the most difficult patient he'd ever known. And the least grateful.

He's as bad as my bloody mother, Gemma thought, as she watched him stride away down the ward. He's pushing me around in exactly the same way. I won't have it. How dare he send her away! The nerve of it!

'And he's supposed to be gorgeous,' she complained to the nurse. 'If that's being gorgeous, I can do without it.'

The nurse was as surprised as she was. 'I've never known him go on like that,' she confessed. 'He's usually lovely. Ever so calm. Never a cross word. I don't know what's got into him.'

Chapter 6

When Billie Goodeve stormed into the lift, she was in a bad mood too, furious with the doctor for sending her away and furious with herself for allowing him to do it. By the time she reached the ground floor, she was steaming with resentment. She strode through the shops towards the entrance, clutching her handbag like a weapon.

There was a knot of people standing on the walkway almost in front of her, youngsters most of them, all in blue jeans, and all talking earnestly to a woman in a green anorak. She'd almost passed them before she realised who they were and what they were doing.

'Still in traction of course, poor little man,' the woman was saying, 'but ever so much better.'

'You didn't happen to see Gemma Goodeve, did you?' one young man asked.

The name echoed in Billie's head like a challenge. Right! she thought. There's my chance! I'll be even with you, young feller-me-lad, you see if I won't. And she strode into the crowd. 'If you want to know anything about Gemma Goodeve,' she said, '*I'm* the one you should be asking.'

The effect was electrifying. She'd never had such instant attention. Faces and microphones swung her way at once. Young bodies surrounded her, all eager to hear what she was going to say. It was wonderful. Made her feel ten feet tall.

'And you are?' the young man asked.

'I'm Gemma's mother,' she said, turning towards the cameraman. 'I'm Mrs Billie Goodeve.'

He held his microphone towards her. 'What can you tell us, Mrs Goodeve?' he asked. 'How is she?'

'Ruined,' she said, 'if you really want to know. She's being very brave about it, of course, but her life's over. She was going to be a model, you see. The photographers loved her. They said she was a natural.'

'You haven't got a snap of her, have you?'

'Well actually, as it happens, I have,' Billie said, opening her bag to find it. 'She had a portfolio done. I've got one of the proofs here somewhere.' It was paining her to remember the fuss there'd been over that portfolio. She'd had to literally drag the silly girl to the photographer's, kicking and screaming all the way. And then she hadn't used them. 'There you are. Wasn't she a beauty?'

The reporter took the little portrait and looked at it, plainly impressed. 'Could we borrow it for a day or two, Mrs Goodeve? We'll give it back.'

'Why not?' she said. 'She can't use it now, can she, poor girl. Not with one leg and a great scar all down her face. And God knows what other injuries.'

'Have you seen her this morning?' another reporter asked.

'No I haven't,' Billie told him, anger renewing. 'I wasn't allowed to.'

'Why was that?'

'I couldn't tell you. They said they were attending to her. She had the curtains drawn all round her bed. I couldn't even see her from a distance.'

'So she's worse?'

'I hope not. But how can I tell?' Billie said, delighted by the way the interview was going. 'Poor girl. Still, she'll get massive compensation.'

That interested them all very much. 'Is she going to sue?'

At that point Billie realised with a pang that she might have gone too far. But it was too late now. The words were said. She had to continue. 'Well of course she will,' she said firmly. 'I should just think so with injuries like that! She'll never work again. Not in that state. She'll have to come home with me and be looked after for the rest of her life. It won't be easy. She'll need all the help she can get.'

'Have you any idea how much you'll go for?'

Billie hadn't thought about a sum of money. 'As much as possible,' she supposed. 'It will depend on the inquiry, won't it? Who's to blame and that sort of thing.'

'A quarter of a million?' the reporter suggested. 'Half?'

Billie smiled at that. It would be like winning the lottery. 'Probably. Who knows?'

It was just what they wanted to hear. They thanked her profusely, took her address, checked what time she'd be back the following day, told her she was a star.

'What papers are you from?' she asked as they parted company.

All the Sunday tabloids, apparently. Excellent! Put that in your pipe and smoke it, Dr Whoever-you-are! 'I shall look out for them,' she said.

'Watch the front page!' they told her.

And the front page it was, as she discovered early the next morning when she went down to the newsagent's. They'd made a wonderful spread of it — a big picture from the portfolio, looking really glamorous, and a smaller one of the poor darling on a stretcher all bloodstained, alongside huge headlines: CRASH HEROINE TO SUE. She bought all three papers on display and took them home to enjoy with her breakfast.

That was a lovely photograph. What a good job she'd kept it. But the memory of the making of that portfolio set a suspicion sneaking into her mind. She shouldn't have told those reporters quite so much. Not yet anyway. Not until Gemma had made up her mind. She'd really jumped the gun a bit. But then again it was too good an opportunity to miss and, if she'd left it to Gemma, it would have gone on and on before *she* did anything. She'd always been the same. In any case this was different. An accident is not the same thing as a few photographs. She's going to need that compensation. She'd've gone for it anyway, sooner or later. I've done her a good turn really, if you think about it.

She bundled the papers together and put them on the sideboard out of harm's way. I'll take them in with me this evening and let her see them. They've said some lovely things about her. She'll be thrilled. Poor darling.

Actually newspapers were the last thing on Gemma's mind at that moment because morning rounds had just finished and most of her fellow patients were being allowed home. The girl called Patsy was the first to leave. Lucky thing!

'I'm off then,' she said, breezing across to Gemma's bed when the doctor had gone. 'Told you he'd sign me off, didn't I? He's a sweetie, our Dr Quennell.'

Gemma kept her opinion of the doctor to herself. 'I shall miss you,' she said. 'What about the others?'

'Them an' all,' Patsy said happily. 'We're all signed off.'

'The place'll be quite empty.'

'It'll be full again by evening, I betcher,' Patsy said. 'You look after yourself. There's the Sundays. Thought you'd like to see them. You're on the front page again.'

Gemma frowned. 'I'm not, am I. What for?'

'Says you're going to sue for damages,' Patsy said, spreading out the paper so that she could see it.

'News to me,' Gemma said.

'You go for it, kid,' Patsy advised. 'Screw

'em for every penny you can get. Why not? If they give it to you, they might shell out for us an' all. Here's my old man come for me. I gotta go.' And she bent to give Gemma a kiss.

There was a bustle of leave-taking and then all four of them were gone. The ward was horribly quiet. The oldest inhabitant was fast asleep in her bed at the end, the woman with the heart bypass was concentrating on her knitting and the kid with crossed eyes had taken herself off to the day room to watch television with her one good eye. The two nurses on duty swished in as soon as the last patient had left but they'd come to make up the empty beds ready for their next occupants. So there was no one for Gemma to talk to and nothing to do except read the papers, even though she didn't particularly want to. The headline was enough to put her off for a start with its ghastly pun, DAMAGES FOR DAMAGED GEMMA, and she had a nasty feeling she knew what they were going to say in the article. And there it was, sure enough: 'Mrs Billie Goodeve, speaking at the hospital yesterday . . .'

Oh Mother! she mourned, letting the paper slip out of her hand, why must you always interfere? Why can't you just leave me alone? This is my business, not yours. I haven't had a chance to think about it and you go to the press. You don't let me breathe. The combination of anger and impotence was making her feel really down. And to make matters worse, her stump was hurting.

One of the nurses smiled across the ward at her. 'You all right?' she called.

'Bit down, that's all.'

The nurse walked across to her. 'Do you need some painkillers?'

'What I need,' Gemma told her, 'is a pill to stop my mother living my life for me.'

Susan Pengilly breezed into York station, glanced up at the clock on W. H. Smith's and decided she just had time to pick up a paper before she caught the London train. The headlines caught her eye, the minute she stepped through the door. She wasn't particularly surprised. It had to happen. There is always someone ready to make capital out of any misfortune and this girl had a good case, if the papers were to be believed.

As soon as she was on the train and settled in her reserved seat, with coffee at her elbow, she scanned through all five papers so as to sort fact from speculation, and discovered that the information had come from the kid's mother, which in her opinion made matters worse. Once families were involved things usually got sticky. Then she phoned the chairman of the inquiry to tell him she was on her way and to keep him informed.

He was having a leisurely breakfast and, although he'd heard the news on the radio, he was determined not to be influenced by it. 'Early days,' he said. 'It shouldn't affect the inquiry. We'll keep an eye on it.'

'Maybe compensation should be on the agenda,' Susan suggested. 'Perhaps we should pre-empt them.'

The chairman didn't see the necessity. 'It's outside our remit, I'm glad to say. Let the accountants handle it. That's what we pay 'em for.'

'But it could have a bearing,' Susan pressed. 'We ought to consider it.'

He was courteous. 'There is that, of course.'

'Maybe I'm being over-cautious but I think we need to cover all the angles.' It was his favourite catch-phrase, so he had to hear it.

There was a pause while he digested what she'd said and gazed at his waffles, wishing he could digest *them* instead. 'I'll give it thought,' he temporised.

Susan smiled with satisfaction as she put down the phone. She prided herself on her ability to handle executives and this one was going to be nicely malleable. It made for smooth running if secretary and chairman were in accord, particularly if he were more in accord than she was. Then she made a happy return to her notes.

Although she wouldn't have acknowledged the fact and certainly not to herself, she was only unquestionably happy when she was at work. It was the one environment in which she truly belonged and the only one in which she was in control. As a child she'd always had the uncomfortable feeling that she was on trial, watched for faults, supervised for unacceptable behaviour. She was honest enough to admit that there'd never been any justification for the feeling. She hadn't been beaten or treated harshly. It was just something she'd picked up from her mother's perpetual anxiety. In many ways she was fonder of her stepfather. He was a more open character and easier to understand. Like Rob, who was so laid back she sometimes forgot he was in the house at all.

But, whatever the reason, work was her solace and she carried it with her wherever she went, travelling with a briefcase crammed full of papers and a laptop primed to receive her thoughts. In her neat business suits, large spectacles, discreet jewellery, with her dark hair sensibly bobbed and face and fingernails immaculately painted, she looked like the high-powered executive she was. Even her over-large spectacles were a status symbol. She'd chosen them four years ago in a moment of drunken bravado, declaring that since her eyesight was so poor she might as well make a virtue of necessity. And had then discovered that they suited her to perfection, giving her rather ordinary face a certain panache.

She had her mother's air force blue eyes. It was the one feature that she shared with her brothers, but few people outside the family realised it. For where Catherine's eyes were hooded and slightly protuberant, and the boys' were frank and tender, Susan's were contained behind her glasses, their shape and colour defined by the latest fashion in eye shadow and mascara, their expression guarded. A flash of temper was so rare that her colleagues would remark on it but the warmth of her smile was an equally remarkable reward.

Now she smiled at the guard as he came to inspect her travel pass, greeting him by name — having checked what it was from his name-tag.

'Nice to have you aboard, Mrs Pengilly. Euston, is it?'

'That's right, Bob,' she said, returning her attention to her laptop. 'All the way.' Just time to write up yesterday's report and then she'd have lunch. As a railway executive she had travel down to a fine art.

By the time the train pulled into Euston, the brakes filling her pressurised carriage with the smell of burning rubber, the inquiry team were organised down to the last name-tag. She gathered her belongings, feeling pleased with her morning's work. There would be a hired car waiting for her on the forecourt. And it had better be an improvement on the one they provided last time, or there would be words to say. Slick, neat and ready for action, she stepped out into the capital.

Andrew and Catherine always got up late on Sunday mornings so they didn't read the news until it was nearly midday and they were having brunch.

'I see the girl from the crash is suing the railway,' Catherine observed, pouring herself a second cup of coffee.

'Quite right too,' Andrew said. 'So she should. Good luck to her. Might make them realise you can't play politics with people's safety.' He cut into his fried egg and let the yolk run over the bacon.

'OK?' she asked, as she always did.

'Superb,' he told her. As he always did. 'I like Sunday. Best day of the week.'

'When we retire it'll be Sunday every day,' she told him. 'How about that?'

He grinned with pleasure at the thought. 'We've earned it,' he said. 'We've done our share of rushing about. Now it's time to put our feet up and read the papers.'

Nick Quennell was so hard at work in the surgical wards that day that he didn't get a chance to look at a newspaper, let alone read one, and he certainly didn't put his feet up. Lunch was a sandwich eaten standing up, at four o'clock he got himself a cup of tea but not the time to drink it, and by dinner time he was tired out and ravenously hungry.

'Duodenal, here I come!' he said to Abdul, as the three friends carried their trays to one of the window seats in the hospital restaurant.

'Me too,' Abdul said. 'I could do with a nice long cruise to recuperate.'

'Round the world,' Rick suggested, unloading his tray.

'Anywhere except A and E,' Abdul said. 'It's been mayhem today.'

On the other side of the Thames the Houses of Parliament blazed with yellow light and behind it the evening sky was indigo blue. 'I wonder what they're cooking up for us tonight,' Rick said.

'Read the papers tomorrow and you'll find out,' Abdul said.

'I haven't read today's yet,' Rick told him.

There was a discarded collection heaped on a nearby seat. 'There you are,' Nick said, handing the bundle across to him. 'Read it now. What d'you want? Review, news, colour supp, sport?'

The various sections were distributed and for a few restful minutes they browsed and fed. They'd reached the lemon meringue pie before Abdul discovered the piece about Gemma Goodeve. 'Your crash girl's going to sue for compensation,' he said to Nick. 'What d'you think of that?'

Nick was still feeling sore about Miss Goodeve. 'It's her business, not mine,' he said shortly.

His friends pulled a face at one another. But at that moment his bleeper sounded, so he didn't have to continue the conversation, which was quite a relief because he could see they were going to tease.

It was the staff nurse on Page Ward. Would he come and take a look at Gemma.

'Back in a minute,' he said to the others and strode off to the lift, white coat flapping.

She was lying on her side in exactly the same position as she'd been in under the wreckage and was obviously ill, her cheeks flushed and her eyes swimmy with fever. He knew the wound was infected even before he looked at it. Damn, damn, damn.

'She'll have to go back to theatre,' he said to Staff.

Gemma took the news with the calm he'd come to expect. Whatever else he might think about her, she was certainly brave.

'When?' she asked.

'Tonight,' he told her. 'As soon as I can arrange it.'

She managed a smile, faint and lop-sided but a smile. 'Will you let my mother know?' she said. 'You owe her that at least.'

Was she daring him, or teasing him, or what? There was a lot about this young woman that he simply didn't understand. 'She'll be told,' he said, stiffly. 'Of course. That goes without saying.'

On Monday, the report of Billie's interview with the tabloids reached the quality press in Cape Town.

It was a fine spring morning and Tim Ledgerwood was sitting on his veranda, sipping orange juice and enjoying the sunshine. It gave him quite a shock to see Gemma's name in his newspaper. Well, well, well, he thought. CRASH HEROINE SEEKING DAMAGES OF HALF A MILLION. Imagine that.

He put the paper down on the table, amused to see that it completely covered all the hideous mail he'd received and hadn't answered for the last awful month — the bills and the letters from creditors, the endless, idiotic demands.

'I think,' he told the sunshine, 'the time has come for me to take a trip to England. This could be the answer.'

Chapter 7

Coming round from an anaesthetic for the second time in three days was a miserable experience for Gemma Goodeve. She felt so ill, weak and confused and nauseous, and the stump was paining her dreadfully. There was no doubt about it being a stump this time, nor that she'd undergone major surgery. She couldn't see properly, there was a foul taste in her mouth and the sounds around her were jangled and confused like a badly tuned radio.

Presently a shape loomed out of the muddle and leant towards her. She could see the blue of a uniform and the double outline of a face, which blurred and shifted as she struggled to focus her eyes. Her brain felt as though it was full of cotton wool and it took a long time to form the question she wanted to ask.

'Where am I?'

'You're in recovery,' the shape said. 'It's all over. No problems.'

A nurse, she thought. Of course. I should have known. The voice was vaguely familiar. 'Are you from the ward? Do I know you?'

'I'm Sally,' the nurse said. 'I was with you at the crash.'

The crash, Gemma thought. Yes. I remember. But it was the vaguest of memories and without pain or distress. She knew there were things she wanted to say but the cotton wool was expanding into her mind, smothering her thoughts, and she had to sleep again.

She was still sleeping when Nick arrived to check on her progress. It was an unnecessary visit because he knew the op had been a success and that she'd come through it well but he felt compelled to make it. He stood beside the trolley for a long time, looking down at her, gowned and still among the tubes and apparatus, her mouth and chin marked by the mask, her skin shock-pale from the anaesthetic, her bruises darkly obvious. Seeing her like this, at her lowest, he felt ashamed of the way he'd shouted at her on Saturday and the sight of her poor battered face made him ache with pity for her. He wanted to comfort her, to smooth her forehead or stroke her cheek and he actually stretched out his hand towards her, before he was fully aware of what he was doing. He checked himself at once, of course, and pretended he was adjusting the oxygen mask, but the impulse had been undeniable. It's not fair, he thought, thwarted tenderness turning to anger. She doesn't deserve this. She's young and strong and brave and she ought to be out there, on the stage, enjoying her life, not lying here struck down like this.

The porters arrived to trundle her out of the recovery room and he stood aside to make way for them. He was aware that he was still feeling uncomfortably emotional and that watching her being wheeled away was making him worse. It wasn't like him to get so involved with a patient. He always felt sympathy for them, naturally, but never this protective responsibility, never this need to comfort, never this yearning to stay with them. It must be because I was at the accident, he told himself, shrugging the thoughts away as he went off to check his other patients. One was a complicated fracture. Old Barnaby had done a superb job with it but it would need careful post-op nursing. It had been quite a night.

'What we want now is a nice straightforward recovery,' he said to Sally, as he left.

Which, to everybody's delight and his relief was what they got. By the time he did the ward rounds later that evening, Gemma was awake; by the following morning she was alert and declaring she was on the mend.

'This is excellent,' he said to Gemma, thinking what a pleasure it was to praise her. 'Much better than last time. We shall have you off the drip in no time at all.' Then, feeling he ought to show some sort of interest to make amends for shouting at her, he added, 'Has your mother been in?'

'Yes,' Gemma said, smiling at him and thinking how charming he could be when he liked. 'Thanks. She came yesterday evening. She brought me some more fruit.' She waved a hand at the carefully arranged bowl. 'Look at it all. I haven't eaten the first lot yet.'

'It looks delicious,' he said.

She agreed that it did but added, 'I'd rather she'd brought me some writing paper.'

They'd established a good contact this time so he let the conversation continue, although he was careful to hide behind his professional voice. 'Why is that?'

'I've had a letter from my flatmates,' she explained, 'and it needs answering.' It was lying on her bedside cabinet and the sight of it rekindled her annoyance at what it said. *'Hope you're getting on all right. Cossie is moving in on Monday. We have put your things in*

*the bathroom cupboard. Can you arrange to
have them collected?'*

'I was their tenant on Thursday morning,'
she told him, 'and now I'm out on my ear.
Apparently my replacement's already
moved in. How's that for friendship?'

This time, her anger pleased him. It was
directed at someone else, so he could see it
as a sign of her recovery. She looked like a
warrior scarred by battle but ready to fight
again. 'Not very nice,' he said and was embarrassed because the words sounded feeble.

But she was still cross about her letter and
didn't seem to notice. 'I shall write and give
them a piece of my mind,' she said. 'They're
treating me as though I don't exist. Can't
wait to get rid of me. It's bloody insulting. I
may have lost a leg but I've still got my mar-
bles.'

He laughed at that. 'So I gather you're not
going back *there* when we've finished with
you?'

'No, I am not.'

He asked the next question casually because it was important. Her lack of accommodation might be a problem and, if it was,
the hospital authority would have to solve it.
'Have you any idea where you will go?'

'No,' she said, and she spoke lightly. 'Not

118

really. Not back to the flat anyway. And not to my mother's either. I've been independent too long to want to "live with mummy". I'll work something out.'

Nick didn't doubt her intentions but, unlike her, he was aware that it would be hard to put them into practice. She would be wheelchair bound for at least five weeks because they wouldn't fit the prosthesis until her remaining leg was out of plaster and fully functional. So she'd need somewhere pro tem, fairly sheltered, ground floor, no steps, maybe with a warden. I'll get Social Services to visit her, he decided. See what they can come up with. And he gave her a smile to indicate that they'd finished their conversation and moved on to his next patient.

Gemma's letter was written, furiously, later that morning. It was short, sharp and to the point, listing the clothes, shoes and make-up that they were to sort out and bring in to her ASAP, together with a personal folder she kept in her dressing table, and ending with the stern instruction that the rest of her things were to be kept clean and safe until she knew where she would be living when she left hospital. *As soon as I have an address I will send it to you,* she wrote, *and then one of you can deliver everything else straight to me, as I am in no fit state to drive, as you well know.'*

After that, as she was in letter-writing mood and anger had recharged her determination, she set to and wrote four more — to the theatre to explain why she hadn't turned up for her audition, to the agency to tell them that she wouldn't be available for stage work, *'until I've recovered'*, to her insurance company to ask for a claim form and to the DSS to discover what benefits she would be entitled to. Both her operations were over, the next phase of her life had begun, there wasn't a second to waste.

By Wednesday morning she'd recovered enough to be taken off the drip, on Wednesday afternoon she persuaded a porter to take her down in the lift and wheel her round the shops, by Wednesday evening she was crowing because someone from the flat had delivered a parcel to the ward, and it contained almost everything she'd asked for.

'I shall get up properly tomorrow,' she said to Sally, 'and have a bath, if that's possible, and get dressed. I want to go to the bank.'

'If you wait till after ward rounds,' Sally said, 'you can have your hair done too. We're going to take your stitches out as soon as we get the OK.'

'Even better,' she said. Her tatty mixture of long and short hair was an irritation and impossible to brush. 'I shall have it all cut short. Make a new start.'

She spoke carelessly as though it was the most natural thing in the world. But, in fact, she was setting herself a formidable challenge, as she explained to the hairdresser the next morning.

'I've had long hair since I was fourteen,' she said ruefully. 'Now look at it. I can't bear to see myself.'

The hairdresser, having dealt with hospital patients for a considerable time, was sensible and sympathetic, 'A new image takes a bit of getting used to,' she said. 'Even when you've planned it, it feels like the end of the world.'

'This *is* the end of the world,' Gemma said, scowling at her reflection.

The hairdresser agreed with her. 'They *have* hacked it about,' she admitted. 'They have to work so quickly, that's the trouble. I think you'd be better to go for a really short cut to even it up. I'll leave enough to cover the scar.'

Gemma took a breath and steadied herself for the next question. 'Will it grow back?'

'Not on the scar tissue,' the hairdresser told her frankly. 'Everywhere else in time but not there.'

Gemma sighed, accepting it because it had to be accepted. I'm going to spend the rest of my life with this then, she thought; with this great train-track running across my head.

'Wait till you see what a good cut can do,' the hairdresser sympathised. And she picked up her scissors.

It gave Gemma a wrench to watch the rest of her lovely long hair being snipped away. All those years growing it to perfection and now there it was being dropped on to the floor like a pile of old rags. The waste of it made her stomach clench with misery. And although the end result was neat and clean and covered the worst of the scar, she didn't like it a bit. It had changed the shape of her face. Before the accident, and framed by her curving curtain of dark hair, it had been a photogenic face, almost heart-shaped with high cheekbones, neat teeth, a shapely mouth, and dominated by her eyes. Now it was all jaw and bruises and hardly any eyes at all. A horrible, lumpy, scarred, unattractive face.

'I shall never make juvenile lead now,' she said. 'I shall have to take up clowning.' And as soon as the word came into her mouth she knew it had to be done at once. That very moment. 'You haven't got one of those red noses anywhere about, have you?'

The hairdresser encouraged her. There were no red noses in her kiosk but she had a wonderful set of false eyelashes 'better than Barbara Cartland's!'

Their effect was devastating even if they *were* painful to apply.

'Big blue tears, I think,' Gemma said, hooking her make-up kit out of her shoulder bag and thinking what a good thing it was that she'd insisted on having it brought to the hospital. She must have known she was going to need it. She began to paint the first teardrop on her swollen cheek, enjoying the sense of power and creativity that make-up always brought. 'Black nose,' she decided. 'Huge red lips. Groucho eyebrows. You won't know me when I've finished! I'll have to tie your haircut in bunches.'

'Not to worry. It'll brush back.'

The finished mask was stunning. It cheered her up just to look at it and caused a stir as her chair was being wheeled back to the ward.

'Cabaret,' she explained to the people who stopped and stared. 'For Page Ward.'

It was like being back on stage, the centre of a buzz of attention, adrenalin running, happy and excited — and nervous. For now that she'd announced a cabaret, she knew she was going to provide one.

She arrived at the ward, was pushed towards her bed.

'Ta-ra!' she called, spreading out her arms. 'What do you think!'

Her fellow patients turned towards her, the bedridden sitting up or craning to see what was going on, the walking wounded gathered around her.

'Whatcher done ter yerself, gel?' the oldest inhabitant grinned.

'I'll tell you,' she said, looking round at them all, and plunged into one of her remembered routines, singing in a rough harsh voice to match her appearance, *'Be a clown, be a clown, all the world loves a clown.'* It was such a bravura performance that her audience burst into spontaneous applause when she'd finished.

'More!' they called. 'Encore!'

She was suddenly very tired: her stump was sore, all she wanted to do was to get back into bed and close her eyes. But her audience was waiting. 'Right!' she said and began another song — to a burst of such noisy applause that the social worker, who'd just come into Sister's office to check that it was a convenient time for her interview, was quite startled and looked through the window to see what was going on.

'That's your patient,' Sister said.

The social worker was troubled. 'She's not going to be another oldest inhabitant, is she?'

'Not for another fifty years or so,' Sister said. 'But she's a feisty girl. Treat with caution.'

By the time the social worker finally reached her bedside, Gemma had been hoisted out of the chair and was sitting up in bed, cotton wool and cleansing lotion in her lap, mirror in hand, carefully removing her make-up. She looked so outlandish with half a clown's face and the other half shiny with grease that the poor girl was rather put out. But she introduced herself valiantly.

'I'm your social worker,' she said. 'Edina.'

'Oh yes?' Gemma said, giving her a brief sideways glance but still hard at work with the cotton wool. And she made a joke. 'I wasn't aware I needed a social worker.'

'Well, no . . .' Edina said. 'Not in the accepted sense, I suppose . . . The thing is, our

Dr Quennell asked me to drop in and see you.'

'Oh yes?' Gemma said again in the same noncommittal tone, her eyes narrowed as she removed her blue tears. 'Why was that, then?'

'He thought I might be able to help you to find some suitable accommodation for when you leave here.'

'Oh did he?' Gemma said, and her voice was decidedly sharper. 'What makes him think I won't be able to find it for myself?'

'You've been having some problems in that direction, I believe.'

The placid assumption that her affairs were common knowledge made Gemma cross. I told him that in confidence, she thought, not to have it blabbed all over the hospital. 'The flat I used to live in isn't suitable,' she agreed. 'But that's my affair.'

'We thought you might like a little help,' Edina insisted. 'I mean, you'll need somewhere . . . well . . . rather specialized.'

Gemma rubbed away the last blue tear. Now it was only her Groucho Marx eyebrows that needed attention. 'So?' she said, turning them fiercely towards her visitor.

'We've got a very nice disabled room,' Edina offered, trying not to be abashed. 'In a sort of, well a housing complex, I suppose you'd say. It's very nice and there's a warden to look after you and everything.'

The mere idea of it filled Gemma with abhorrence. One room, she thought, in a house full of people with problems, hidden away so that 'normal' people needn't see us, with a warden to guard us and see we don't make a nuisance of ourselves. I'd rather live on the streets. 'Now look,' she said. 'I know you mean well and I know Dr Quennell put you up to it but you're barking up the wrong tree. I don't want a disabled room. And I don't want to be looked after. You go back and tell the great Doctor, thanks but no thanks. I can look after myself. And I can find my own flat. Right?'

'He was only trying to be helpful,' Edina said, protecting him. But Gemma's expression was so fierce she decided discretion would be the better part of valour in this instance and beat a hasty retreat.

The oldest inhabitant homed in on the end of the conversation at once, her face avid. 'What was all that about then, gel?'

Gemma explained, crossly. 'They want me to move into a hostel. They've found me a "disabled room", if you ever heard of anything so repulsive.'

'They're buggers at that sorta thing,' the old lady said, settling herself in the bedside chair. 'They reckon they're gonna put me in a home. Bleedin' sauce. Don't you stand for it, gel. Tell 'em they got another think coming.'

'I have.'

'Well good fer you! You paid in fer it, aintcher? Paid yer contributions? Well then. Be like me. Tell 'em you ain't goin'. That's what I done. I like it here. I paid in fer it all me life so why shouldn't I stay here? Worked forty-seven years in that shop, I did, one way an' another. Never took a day off neither. So they can think again. I ain't goin' in no 'ome. You don't get no sorta life at all in a home. I seen 'em, sittin' round in their smelly old chairs, dribblin'.'

'Can't you go back to your own place?' Gemma asked. She was lively enough so they ought to allow it.

The old lady looked shifty. 'Can't,' she admitted, needlessly rearranging the tie of her dressing gown. 'It's gone, see. Been sold. My son-in-law sold it. Had to. Their kids need separate rooms see. There used to be room fer all of us. That's why I dipped in, see. It was all right in them days.' She sighed. 'Anyway, they got a nice little place now, ever so convenient, onny they ain't got room fer me. I'd 'ave ter sleep on the floor if I was to go there an' I don't fancy that. Not at my age.'

'No,' Gemma said. 'I can see that.' And she was thinking, I'll bet she put her savings in that house and they've sold it over her head. Poor old thing. The story put her to shame. Here I am getting cross because I've been offered a room I don't want and she's got nowhere to go at all.

'They're clearin' everyone out,' the old lady confided. 'Mrs What's-it with the hernia's got to go. Gawd knows how she'll make out with that son of hers. They don't care. It's all league tables nowadays. They get you in, chop you up and off 'ome you go. Like a bleedin' conveyor belt. And then you get took bad at 'ome, stands to reason, and they have ter get you in again. They don't care about that neither. They can count you twice, you see. You're another patient by then. It ups the league tables. They think we can't work it out. Must reckon we're all daft. Well they needn't think they can get rid of me.'

Gemma didn't know what to say in answer to all that, partly because it was such a diatribe and partly because the old lady seemed to be blaming the doctors for sending people home too soon. And she was sure it wasn't *their* fault. 'Our Doctor Quennell' might blab your private affairs to soppy social workers but he wouldn't turn you out on your ear. There was too much compassion in him for that. And then, for no apparent reason, she suddenly had a vivid memory of the way he'd treated her at the crash and how gentle and reassuring he'd been.

Chapter 8

Dr Nick Quennell spent the next two days keeping out of Gemma Goodeve's way. She was annoying him so much he was afraid they'd have words again if he had to spend any time with her. And one slanging match had been quite enough. The trouble was, although he kept out of her sight he couldn't stop thinking about her. Fancy refusing Edina's offer like that. Poor old Edina. She couldn't help looking gormless and she was only doing her job. Independence is all very well, he thought crossly, but not when you're recovering from your second operation in three days and not when people are trying to help you. It made him scowl to think of it. The whole thing was ludicrous.

Luckily he knew how to cope. All he had to do was to keep himself busy on the men's surgical wards, which was easy enough, and put in the briefest of appearances on Page Ward, which was difficult but possible. Then, starting on Monday, he had three days' leave, which would solve the problem, at least for the time being. He'd arranged to go and stay with Abdul and his family, right away from the hassle. They were going to take Sacha and the kids to the pictures on Monday afternoon and after that he and Ab planned to spend the next two days out in the wilds somewhere, fishing. It was what they usually did when life got tricky. He'd spent an entire week by the riverside when Deirdre walked out on him in the summer and by the end of it his irritation had been virtually soothed away and he'd come round to the idea that finishing their rela-tionship was actually a good thing. He'd have preferred to end it in a civilised way in-stead of having to endure all that screaming and shouting but ending it was logical and inevitable. They'd been growing apart for months and she'd been much too sharp and much too critical. Was it any wonder he treated women with caution?

There was only one snag in the plans he'd made and that was the fact that he'd agreed to have dinner with the aged Ps and his sis-ter Susan on Sunday evening. Normally that was something he would have enjoyed very much because the food was always su-perb at home and he had a healthy appetite, but this time it was going to be tricky. His father had been in the hospital that morning and someone would have been bound to tell him about Gemma's second op, so now he'd crow. *That* was as predictable as day-break.

Nothing he could do about it, of course. It just had to be endured. Perhaps Susan being there would make it easier. She was very good at turning conversations, especially if she was in one of her powerful executive moods.

Which she was that evening. For despite her meticulous preparation, the inquiry had got off to an inconclusive start, so she was tense with lack of success. Witnesses had been called and given what information they could, but none of it had helped; the signalling system had been examined on site and they'd taken evidence from the railway inspectors but there was no fault there; the track had been put under equally close scrutiny and that had passed muster too, more or less. They'd gone on until late the previous evening and they were still no nearer to discovering what had actually caused the crash. And to cap everything, her fellow investigators were all anxious about the possibility of a court case, just as she'd known they would be.

Now, standing in the hall of her parents' house, she was putting a brave face on things as she and her mother greeted one another with a kiss. When Nick pulled in at the drive and parked his old Peugeot alongside her brand new Rover, she swept out at once to kiss him too and tease him. 'How's my baby brother?'

'Not so much of the baby, *if* you don't mind,' he joked back, walking into the house. 'Where's Dad?'

'Slaving over a hot stove,' Andrew's voice called from the kitchen. 'Where else?'

'And quite right too!' Susan said, leading them all along the corridor to join him. 'Why should women do all the cooking?'

'In this house?' he laughed. He was standing by the oven, stirring a sauce. The chopping board beside him was heaped with debris and the table in the corner was set with roast chicken and assorted vegetables steaming succulently. 'There you are Kate, my lovely. Ready to serve.'

'So how's the hero of the hour?' Susan said, reaching up to brush her cheek against his. 'I saw you on the box. Very dashing.' Then she realised that Nick was looking miffed and paused, wondering why.

'I hope you're hungry, you two,' Catherine said, motioning them towards the table.

'Ravenous,' Nick told her, as he sat down. 'Aren't I always?'

Andrew began to carve the chicken,

breathing in the smell of it as the steam rose towards his face. Maybe he won't say anything now, Nick hoped. Not when we're just about to eat. But his father was grinning at him through the steam.

'Was I right?' he asked. 'Or was I right? Your famous patient *did* get a wound infection, so I hear.'

Nick mumbled agreement, looking at his plate, as Susan sat down beside him, spread her napkin over her lap and wondered what it was all about.

Andrew's grin was so broad it was a wonder it didn't split his face. 'So I might just have known what I was talking about, after all. Not quite such a fuddy-duddy as you thought.'

'OK. OK,' Nick admitted, scowling at him. 'You've made your point. Do I get any of that chicken or have I got to sit in a corner and eat humble pie all night?'

'Who are you talking about?' Susan wanted to know.

'The crash girl,' her father told her. 'Gemma Goodeve. We amputated her leg.'

'Really!' Susan said, with great interest. The girl in the news! What luck! Now if she could get baby brother to tell her whether she was going to sue or not . . . 'I didn't realise she was a patient of *yours*. I've read about her, of course, but the papers don't always tell you the truth, the whole truth and so on. It must be quite an experience to have a famous patient. Especially when she could be a rich, famous patient.'

'Patients are patients,' Andrew told her. 'Wealth and fame really don't come into it.'

'Ah but they do in this case, surely,' Susan tried. 'Or they will if the rumours are true. They say she's going to sue the railway for half a million.'

Nobody answered that so she had to descend to a direct question. 'Is she going to sue, Nick?'

'How should I know?' Nick said, busy with the salt. 'That's her affair.'

'Quite right,' Andrew approved. 'It's called keeping a professional distance, Susan.'

'Poor girl,' Catherine said. 'I don't suppose she's had a chance to think about it in the last few days. She must have had a really awful time.'

Susan tried another tack. 'What's she like?' she asked her brother.

'Bloody hard work,' Nick frowned.

'Not the heroine we've been led to believe?'

'Actually, she's one of the bravest young women I've ever met,' Andrew said. 'Amazingly brave. You should have seen her at the crash.'

'Oh she's brave enough,' Nick agreed. 'I'll give you that. She's a fighter. She doesn't give in. She's got a lot of style.' And he told them how she'd painted herself up like a clown and entertained the ward. 'Caused quite a stir. But . . .'

'But?' Susan prompted.

'She's difficult.'

'With reason,' Andrew said and teased: 'Maybe you're not handling her the right way.'

'Nobody could handle her the right way,' Nick said with feeling. 'She's a law to herself.'

'Good bedside manner, that's all you need.'

'It would bounce off.'

'So what's the problem?' Susan asked.

'She's too independent,' Nick said. 'Won't be helped. Well, take this for an example. She's lost her flat — right? — so she hasn't got anywhere to live when she's discharged and she can't live with her mother because they don't get on. So she needs help — right? So I set everything up for a social worker to come in and find her a room in a hostel. And what does she do? She turns it down. Won't so much as consider it. She's going to find somewhere for herself, she says, if you ever heard of anything so ridiculous.'

Susan was laughing at him. 'Diddums!' she teased. 'Wouldn't she let him play God, then?'

He was needled. 'It's got nothing to do with playing God. It's her behaviour that's at fault, not mine. I'm doing my best, she's just plain pig-headed.'

'Hardly plain,' Andrew said, still teasing. 'I thought she was rather a beauty.'

'She's got one leg in plaster and the other amputated below the knee. She won't be fitted for her prosthesis for another five weeks, never mind learning to walk, and she thinks she can go house-hunting. She's impossible. She won't let anyone help her. It's like . . . It's like trying to cuddle a hedgehog.' Without warning he had a sudden, vivid memory of her anaesthetised face and his own ridiculous urge to hold her and comfort her. And he had to duck his head again, this time to hide his confusion.

Susan sent a rapid eye message to her mother: *Smitten or what?*

But Catherine had decided to rescue her son by changing the subject. 'How's the inquiry going?' she asked.

'According to plan,' Susan said brightly.

'Slow but sure. We're off to Derby tomorrow to look at the coaches.'

'Derby?' Catherine asked.

'That's where they're taken after a crash. Suits me fine. I can go back to York afterwards.'

'And how's Rob?' her father wanted to know.

The conversation slid away into domestic trivia, as wine was poured and appetites were slaked.

'We had a call from Chris on Friday, so Rob says,' Susan told them. 'They can't come to our party after all. His conference date's been moved, apparently.'

'What a shame!' Catherine sighed. 'I thought we were all going to be together again.'

'It was always on the cards,' Andrew said. 'If you're the principal speaker at a major conference like that, you can hardly call off at the last moment. You'll see them at Easter.'

Catherine made a face. 'That's months away.'

'I hope *you'll* all be there,' Susan said and joked, 'I mean you haven't got any major conferences or anything, have you? TV appearances or famous patients to attend?'

'We'll all be there,' Catherine promised.

'Don't worry. We've warned the media. Are we ready to clear?' The first course of their family meal had been Drew's responsibility but the sweet was hers and it was a *pièce de résistance* — a home-made raspberry pavlova, no less. She couldn't wait to bring it to the table.

The phone rang as she was cutting out the first slice. 'Wouldn't you know it!' she said. 'I'll bet it's for you, Drew.'

And of course it was. 'Mrs Courtney,' he explained. 'Fractured femur by the sound of it. Sorry about that, kids.'

'Who'd be a doctor's wife?' Catherine said as they ate the pavlova without him.

They took their coffee into the living room as usual but Andrew's absence filled the room. The evening had grown sombre as if he'd taken the fun out of it. 'Will he be long?' Susan asked.

'Hours,' Nick told her. 'If it's Mrs Courtney.' The old lady was renowned for her spectacular falls. 'If you're going to wait for him, it'll be a long wait. I shall have to go in a minute. I promised Abdul I'd be with him about ten and it's half-past now.'

'In that case I shall make tracks too,' Susan said. 'I've got an early start tomorrow.' It wouldn't have hurt little brother to have told her what she wanted to know but he plainly wasn't going to. 'I'll phone you when I get back from Derby, Mum.'

Catherine watched them drive away into their own lives, Susan waving red-tipped fingers, Nick sounding his horn in his customary farewell. They'd given her a lot to think about and she was still deep in thought when Drew finally came home. It was well past midnight and they were both tired but they finished their day as they always did, discussing the main events as if they were folding it away.

'Nice to see the kids again,' he said, pouring his necessary whisky. 'Sue was on form.'

'Do you think Nick's fallen for that girl?'

'What makes you ask?'

'Sue thinks so and he talked about her rather a lot.'

Andrew considered it. 'It's possible,' he said easily. 'All interns get a crush on their patients at some time or another. Especially if they're pretty. It's fairly normal. Get carried away with sympathy; fall in love; mope around for a week or two; girl goes home; get over it and forget it.'

'Ah!' she teased. 'So that's what you did.'

'Not me,' he told her, teasing back. 'Never got the chance. Not once I'd met you. Hooked I was, as you very well know.'

'Do you think she really is as difficult as he says?'

'No. He can't handle her. That's all. I got on with her rather well. She's a good kid. Sensible. She was quite right to turn the hostel down. She deserves better than that.'

'You'd send her to the Savoy, I suppose.'

'I'd put her in with a family. See she got a bit of TLC. That's what she needs. Somewhere like our granny flat.'

Catherine raised her eyebrows. 'You're not suggesting she comes to live with us?'

He wasn't. But her question made him consider it. 'Why not?' he said. 'She's a good kid and it would only be for a week or two. Yes. Why not? It might be just the thing.'

'Who for?' she asked. He was looking rather too devilish for her comfort.

'Well, Gemma principally. But us too, in a way. It would be nice to have a young face in the house.' He grinned at her. 'And it would show Nick what can be achieved with a good approach.'

'You're impossible,' she laughed at him. 'You can't do this.'

'No, probably not,' he agreed. 'She might turn *us* down too. But we could offer it and see what she says?'

'And who's going to do all this offering?'

He made his familiar grimace. 'In other words I am, is that it?'

'You could go and see her,' he said, suddenly serious. 'Test the water.'

'It won't work,' she warned. But, as he was so insistent, she agreed to visit on her next afternoon off. If Nick really was falling for this girl it would be sensible to meet her. And Drew was right. She might not accept the offer when it came to it. She probably wouldn't.

Having settled things to his satisfaction, Andrew put down his empty glass. 'Time for bed,' he said. 'We're due in the surgery in eight and a half hours.'

In nine and a half hours Susan was carrying her impatience to the railway technical centre at Derby. It didn't take her more than ten seconds after her arrival to discover that it was quite the wrong place for it. After her ineffectual week and her brother's irritating lack of co-operation, she needed speed and success, and this was the slowest place she'd ever been in, a dragons' graveyard, full of rust-stained ruins, crushed and defeated and never to move again. Even the echoes were subdued here and the inspection teams moved among the corpses like boiler-suited undertakers, quiet and sober and speaking in soft voices. As she and her team were led towards the wreckage of their particular crash, she felt completely out of place striding along in her brisk business suit, and that made her even more impatient.

The chief investigator was waiting for them, ready to introduce himself, smiles were exchanged, the chairman established his credentials as a 'former director of safety and quality at British Rail's research division'. Susan was given both her titles, secretary to the inquiry, senior executive with British Rail, York, and the other members of the inquiry were introduced one after the other. It was all very quiet and laid-back and hideously slow. Oh come *on!* she thought, watching the interminable handshakes, or we shall be here for ever.

But as it turned out, the chief investigator was a man who came straight to the point.

'If you will follow me, ladies and gentlemen,' he suggested, leading them to the first battered carriage, 'I think I can show you the cause of your accident.'

It was a fractured axle. 'Collapsed, you see,' he explained, pointing to the break with one broad finger.

'Before or after impact?' the chairman wanted to know.

'Before,' the inspector told them. 'There's no crushing, do you see, which we would have expected if it had been damaged by the crash. No. That's your villain. Fracture, collapse, and over she goes.'

'You're sure about this?' the chairman asked.

'It looks pretty conclusive to me,' the inspector said. 'I've written a full report but I thought you'd like to see the evidence first.'

We've spent a week looking in all the wrong directions, Susan thought, and the answer's been waiting for us here all the time. It seemed appalling that one small piece of metal could have killed twenty-seven people, to say nothing of all the others it had injured.

'What caused it to fracture?' she asked.

The reply was crisp. 'Age and lack of maintenance. That chap on the telly was right. When a public service is required to make a profit for shareholders, safety standards go out of the window.'

'Who owned the stock?' one of the inquiry team wanted to know.

'That I couldn't say for sure,' the inspector told them. 'Changes come in so quickly these days, I can't keep up with them. It's all we can do to cope with accidents and investigations.'

The chairman knew the answer but he didn't tell his team until they were back in their hotel and had gathered in the board-room.

'Railways South,' he told them. 'Ms Pengilly will arrange for them to give evidence.'

'Are we putting out a statement to the press?' Susan asked.

'Not until the inquiry is complete,' the chairman said. 'We must consider all the angles. No need to jump the gun. I suggest we study the report at our leisure and see what the rest of the week will bring.'

It brought two more revelations, although getting them admitted took skill. The suspect carriage had been sold off to an American operator, as part of a job lot after a privatisation deal, and he had then sold them on 'possibly without a maintenance check' to a second company, who faxed that they were sure there had been maintenance work carried out but 'were not, at this point in time, in a position to provide details'. The lack of details hadn't prevented them from selling half the carriages they'd bought to the new private company who were currently running them and who couldn't find any maintenance records for them either, although they assured the inquiry that they were sure they were 'filed away somewhere'.

There was little doubt in Susan's mind that the carriage in question had not been properly maintained for several years, and what was more, that there were four thousand others that could well be in a similar state of disrepair. But proving it in a court of law would be extremely difficult. If that girl of Nick's is really going to sue, she thought, she'll have a job on her hands.

However it was Railtrack's evidence that caused the most concern. They were questioned about the lack of rail-mounted recovery cranes and admitted that six months before the accident the company had reduced the number of such cranes from eleven to five and that there were none at all based in Scotland. Their spokesman claimed that the reduction had no real significance, on the grounds that these were 'train-mounted breakdown cranes we are talking about. They're not like the emergency services. The cranes and the people who work them have no life-saving role.'

But the chairman was quick to point out that fewer cranes of this type meant that Railtrack now had much larger areas to cover and that this was bound to affect their response times to the scene of a derailment. Which had to be admitted.

It was damning evidence, as the chairman

admitted privately to Susan after the other members of the team had gone home.

'We must be very careful how we handle this,' he warned. 'It would be relatively easy to imply negligence — hideously difficult to prove of course with so many companies involved — but relatively easy to imply. It might well lead to litigation. Is there any more news on that front?'

'Only what we can glean from the tabloids,' Susan told him, her annoyance with Nick renewing.

'Um,' the chairman said. 'It occurs to me that it might be politic to send a private note to Railways South to suggest that some sort of compensation should be offered. To the worst injuries perhaps, if nothing else. A pre-emptive strike, as you might say. If this business does come to court, it could be a long hearing with so many interests involved. The expenses could be enormous. What do you think?'

Like the good civil servant she was, Susan forbore to point out that it had been her idea originally. 'Very wise,' she approved. 'Are we issuing a press statement now?'

'I suppose we'll have to give them some sort of preliminary report,' the chairman said. 'Discreet, of course. Oil on troubled waters. That sort of thing.'

But although Susan wrote in the most diplomatic terms she could contrive, even quoting the company excuses verbatim as though they could be believed, the press were quick to pick up the implications.

On Thursday the London *Evening Chronicle* made it front page news in their early edition, with a headline in letters six black inches high: POOR MAINTENANCE CAUSES CRASH. And at lunchtime, the press pack returned to St Thomas's hospital.

Chapter 9

Gemma didn't tell her mother anything about the social worker's ridiculous offer. It would only have upset her and it had all been dealt with so there was no need for her to know. On the other hand, she was disappointed when Dr Quennell didn't appear on ward rounds because she was looking forward to giving him a piece of her mind. Still, she'd been in hospital long enough now to know that doctors work very odd hours, and very long ones, so she knew she would see him sooner or later. And on mature consideration later might be preferable because it would give her time to think of something really stinging to say. In the meantime there were plenty of other things to occupy her.

As the days passed, and one glance at a time, she was gradually coming to terms with her changed appearance, especially now that her lesser scars were fading and her bruises had dimmed from black, blue and mauve to a general greeny-yellow. Her nights were still broken by nightmares but by day she was busy learning how to cope —

discovering how to slide her injured leg out of the bed and into her chair, how to heave herself on to the toilet seat, how to dress herself sitting down, how to arrange her short hair to cover the worst of that scar, even how to take half a shower and leave her encumbered limbs unwatered. And she'd worked out how many weeks she would have to wait until her plaster was removed. It seemed a painfully long time but every day brought her nearer the moment.

On Saturday morning, she persuaded a porter to take her down to the shopping area, and having withdrawn some of her remaining cash from the hospital bank, she asked to be wheeled into the restaurant so that she could treat herself to lunch. She enjoyed it so much that she decided to make a daily habit of it — while the money lasted. It gave her a break from the endless activity of the ward, a time when she could think without being interrupted, and it comforted her to look out at the speed of the city, to be reminded that there was still bustle and purpose beyond the hospital gates and, more importantly, that she would soon be back there and part of it. Her energy was steadily returning and, despite her altered appearance, so was her optimism.

But on Thursday, when she went down to

the ground floor for lunch, she was wheeled out of the lift to find herself confronted by the press. There were so many of them they seemed like a solid wall of faces and cameras, reporters side by side, microphones in hand, photographers ranged beside the lift doors one above the other as if they were ready for royalty. She barely had time to understand what was happening before the flashlights began to pop and the reporters surged forward all talking at once.

'Gemma!' 'What's the latest?' 'Are you still going to be a model?' 'Are you very upset?' 'Are you going to sue?' 'How much?' 'Are you . . . ? Look this way . . . This way . . . Turn your head for us Gemma.' 'Gemma! Gemma! Just a few words . . . Are you going to sue?'

She felt as though she was under attack. They were so fierce and insistent, like birds of prey with their mouths perpetually open, crowding in upon her, wings and lenses flexed and aggressive, following her chair so closely she could feel the heat of their bodies and smell the food and drink on their breath. She tried to wave them away from her face but they pushed in closer. She tried to speak but the clamour was too great for them to hear her. 'Are you going to

sue?' they insisted. 'How much are you asking for?'

'Peace,' she tried joking to the nearest
face, 'that's what I'm asking for. Peace and
the chance to buy some lunch without being
crushed.' But the clamour went on.

'Look this way!' the photographers
begged. 'This way, Gemma.' They were
blocking the corridor completely. People
were having a struggle to get out of the lift,
others were pushing their way through the
scrimmage to get into it. Surely, Gemma
thought, someone must come and deal with
them. They're causing an obstruction. She
felt responsible and ashamed, as if it were all
her fault.

She had to make a decision. And quickly.
She turned her head to speak to the porter,
but there was so much noise he had to lower
his own head until they were mouth to ear.
'Wheel me out,' she said.

'Where to?'

'Out of the hospital,' she told him firmly.
'I can't stay here. We're holding people
up.'

He widened his eyes ready to protest but
she gave him her forceful face. So he did as
he was told and pushed her past the shops,
through the foyer and out into the pale October sunshine beyond the glass entrance.

And the pack followed her, shouting all the way.

It was better out in the open air. Now she could speak to them with some hope of being heard. 'Look,' she said. 'I've come out here so that you can take your pictures without getting in everybody's way. But I shall expect you to do something for me in return.'

'Name it, sweetheart,' a bearded photographer called.

'Go away afterwards and let me have lunch in peace.'

'One interview,' a reporter said.

'Three questions,' Gemma told her. She felt more in command now and better able to argue.

'Six.'

'Three.'

So they agreed to her bargain and the photography session began in earnest. They arranged her chair, her skirt, her hands, her hair and then took so many pictures that her jaw ached with the effort of giving them a smile. But, true to her promise, she answered the first three questions they fired at her. No, she didn't know whether she was going to sue or not. No, she didn't know when she would be leaving hospital. Yes, she was making good progress. 'I shall be walking in no time.'

'Is it true you were going to be a model?'

'No,' she said, refusing the question. 'That's it. That's the last. I'm sorry.'

'Brilliant!' the photographers said, and the bearded one called out by way of farewell. 'See you!'

Gemma had recovered enough to grin at him. 'Not if I see you first,' she said. 'Now I'm going to have my lunch. Right?' And she looked at the porter to show him she was ready to be wheeled back into the hospital.

The press pack began to disperse, some on the run, others, like the reporter and photographer from the *Sunday* and *Evening Chronicles*, rather more slowly.

'OK Nicky,' the photographer said. Now what?'

'We try the parents,' the reporter said.

'Do we know where they are?'

'We know where Mummy is. She'll do for starters. Unless . . .' She stood still for a moment, thinking. 'No. You go on, Jake. I've got an idea. Isn't there a florist's in that shopping mall?'

'Florist's, sweet shop, newsagent's,' he told her. 'You name it.'

Nicky made up her mind. 'Right!' she said.

★ ★ ★

Back in the relative peace of the restaurant, Gemma was feeling rather pleased with herself. She sat in her wheelchair at one of the tables by the window, eating her meal and enjoying the view and congratulating herself on how well she'd handled the mob. It had been a nasty moment but she'd come through it well.

There was cheerful movement everywhere she looked, the sky full of scudding clouds, the pavements thronged with people, all in a rush, the Thames busy with boats. They swished past the Houses of Parliament, hurling white water from their bows and bouncing on the choppy water, as though they hadn't a minute to spare. And on Westminster Bridge cars and buses scurried nose to tail, their metallic colours bold above the grey stone of the bridge.

They're all going somewhere, she thought, getting things done, changing things. Like me. Yet there was a reassuring continuity about the scene too, the Thames following the same old route, the bridge splendidly solid and dependable and dominating the scene, the long elaborate frontage of the Parliament buildings burnished by sunshine and looking as if it had been there for ever, a visible reminder that democracy endures, no matter how many changes it has to weather. As I shall endure, she thought.

She was just finishing her apple pie when a girl arrived and stood beside her table, smiling in the half-hopeful, half-apologetic way of a stranger who wants to open a conversation.

She was an attractive-looking girl, a leggy blonde in a chocolate-coloured trouser suit — long straight jacket, slightly flared trousers, an abundance of gold jewellery — and she was obviously a visitor, as she was carrying a bunch of freesias and a large box of Terry's chocolates.

'Hel-*lo!*' she said, as though she and Gemma were long-time friends. And before Gemma could return her greeting she began to speak again in a gush of half-formed sentences.

'I hope you don't mind me coming here like this . . . Nicky Stretton, by the way . . . I felt I just *had* to see you, you being *so* brave . . . Stuck in that awful train, it must have been . . . We all admired you *so much*. Well we still do. Who wouldn't when you've been *so* brave? You're our heroine. Absolutely. Anyway, these are with our warmest love.' She thrust the flowers into Gemma's lap, put the chocolates on the table and smiled a winsome smile, all bright eyes and thick lipstick.

More flowers, Gemma thought, remembering the overflowing vases in the ward. And how kind to deliver them in person. I wonder how far she's come. 'Who's we?' she asked.

'Sorry?'

'We. You said "we" all admire you.'

'Oh! Oh yes! Me and my colleagues. We're your fan club.'

Gemma was touched. Flowers, get-well messages and now a fan club. 'Well thank you,' she said.

Nicky seemed to be having difficulties with something inside the pocket of her jacket. 'Can I talk to you for a moment?' she asked.

'Why not?' Gemma said, feeling she ought to make her welcome at the very least. 'Take a seat.'

'Let me buy you a coffee.'

So two coffees were bought and the flowers and chocolates were put on the spare seat and the two young women settled to talk.

'Are you better?' Nicky began.

'Much,' Gemma told her. 'As you see.'

Nicky looked down at the bandaged stump propped up on its board and the thickness of plaster around this poor victim's remaining leg. The words of her article were already forming themselves in her head: *Gemma Goodeve, pathetic victim of the Wandsworth rail crash, sits alone in her wheelchair, gazing out over the streets of London, dreaming of what might have been.* 'It must be awful,' she sympathised. 'I couldn't even bear to think about it if it was me . . . to have your life smashed to ruins like this. To be sitting there so helpless and everything . . . A cripple.'

Oh no, Gemma thought, I can't have you saying things like that so let's put paid to it here and now. 'I'm not helpless,' she corrected. 'And I'm not a cripple. That's not a word I answer to. It's a dreadful word. It ought to be wiped out of the language. And my life isn't in ruins. I've had an accident, that's all, and now I'm recovering. I shall be measured for my false leg soon and then I shall get rid of this plaster and after that you won't know me. I shall be leaping about all over the place.'

Nicky adjusted her tone. 'I'll bet you will,' she agreed and drank some coffee, smiling at Gemma across the rim of the cup. 'Is it true you were going to be a model?'

'I did a bit of modelling when I was a child,' Gemma admitted. 'Catalogues and things like that. Miss Pears. My mother's been bragging about it to the papers. That's what you're referring to, isn't it? Right. But there was never any question of me being a model once I grew up. I've been trained as an actress. In fact I was on my way to a theatre when the crash happened. So the minute I get my new leg I'm going to . . . take up again where I left off.' She'd nearly said 'apply for auditions again' but caught herself in time. Taking up again where she left off sounded much better.

'Your parents must have been *so* upset when you got hurt,' Nicky sympathised.

Gemma drank her coffee thinking how friendly this girl was and how easy it was to talk to her. It was like gossiping with Pippa. 'My mother certainly was. Still is.'

'And your father?' Nicky fished. 'What did he think about it?'

'I've never really had a father,' Gemma said, surprised to realise that she wanted to talk about him. 'Except in the biological sense. He left when I was a baby.'

'How sad! Do you miss him?'

'Not really. You can't miss a person you've never known, can you?'

'No, I suppose not. But didn't you ever wonder what he was like? I know I would have done.'

160

'Oh I knew what he was like,' Gemma said. 'My mother's got photographs of him all over the living room.'

'What *was* he like?'

'Handsome, in an Errol Flynn sort of way. Tall and dark with a little moustache. My mother used to call him her dreamboat. It was all dreams when I was little. She used to tell me how wonderful he was and I used to dream about meeting him again. I made up fantasies about it in my head, the way you do. What he'd say. How he'd promise to make things up to me. Bring me presents and tell me he'd always loved me. Come charging in like a knight in armour and right all wrongs. That sort of thing. Silly, isn't it.'

'I don't think so,' Nicky said, thinking, *Deserted, fatherless, crippled, yet she still fights on.* 'I think it's sweet. I'd have loved a knight in shining armour myself.'

'Things like that don't happen in real life.'

'No, I suppose not. We all have to look after ourselves, don't we? Are you going to sue the railway company?'

That's none of your business, Gemma thought, but she gave an honest answer. 'I've no idea. It's much too early to think about it.'

'But you will eventually,' Nicky persisted. 'Given all the things you're going to need.

161

And it *was* sheer negligence.'

'Was it?' Gemma said. 'How do you know?'

'Haven't you seen the *Evening Chronicle*?' Nicky said and produced a folded copy from her shoulder bag. 'Look. There it is. Front page.'

Gemma read the headlines without much surprise. She'd always known that the accident must have had a mechanical cause, unless the driver had gone through a red light, and that had been ruled out right at the start. But as she read on and realised that it was due to something as simple as a broken axle, fury swelled in her chest and filled her throat. I've lost my leg and my looks and all those people were killed because this fucking awful company were too mean to mend their fucking rolling stock. She knew it was useless to feel so angry because no amount of anger or recrimination would bring back her leg, but she couldn't help it. A broken bloody axle!

' "Poor maintenance," ' Nicky was quoting. 'See? Negligence. It could have been avoided. So you will sue, won't you.'

The persistence of the question pulled Gemma's mind away from her anger and into an unexpected clarity. 'Does it matter?'

The answer was instant and honest. 'Of

course it matters. If you go about it the right way you could be a millionaire.'

'And that's important?'

'Well naturally. If I were you, *I'd* go for it. Everyone wants you to. Absolutely every-one. The railway companies can afford it. They're coining it in. All the privatised in-dustries are. Everyone knows that. Look at the salaries the directors are paying them-selves. And think of the sweeteners they were given to get them to buy in the first place. Taxpayers' money that was, every penny of it. If you think of it that way, you'd just be taking back some of your own money, wouldn't you?'

'I've been a student,' Gemma said rea-sonably. 'I haven't paid taxes. At least, not many. I haven't earned enough.'

Rags to riches, Nicky thought. 'Well there you are then. All the more reason. You go for it.'

'You make it sound like some sort of re-venge.'

'It is in a way, when you think what they've done to you. They ought to pay for it. Don't you think so?'

It's tempting, Gemma thought. There's no doubt about that.

But then Nicky said something that made her feel suddenly suspicious. 'We could help you,' she offered. 'Advise you. Put you in touch with a good lawyer. That could make all the difference, a good lawyer.'

'*We* again and *we* with enough resources to hire a lawyer. 'We?' Gemma asked. 'Who's we?' And with a lurch of her heart, she suddenly understood. 'You're a reporter, aren't you?'

The admission was cool. Pretence wasn't necessary now. 'That's right. I'm with the *Chronicle.*'

Gemma gave her an equally cool look. 'And you'd get me a lawyer, would you?'

'Absolutely,' Nicky beamed. 'You're a star. Of course we'd need to know we can depend on your story. That goes without saying. You'd have to give us exclusive rights. But it would be well worth it.'

And that's what this is about, Gemma thought. Selling papers for you. It's got nothing to do with sympathy or friendship. I've been conned. 'At the moment,' she said, speaking carefully, 'I'm just a patient in this hospital receiving treatment. If you look you'll see there's a sister over there who's probably coming to take me back to the ward.' There really was a sister walking towards them. It wasn't anyone she knew but the threat of her arrival might be enough to remove this girl from the restaurant.

Sure enough, the reporter glanced round. 'I'd better go then,' she said, standing up. 'Mustn't hold up the good work. Florence Nightingale and all that sort of thing.' She'd got the information she wanted *and* her headline: *Gemma to sue. With her life in ruins, feisty heroine, Gemma Goodeve, takes on the establishment.* 'Good luck. I'll leave the paper for you. There's the address and the phone number if you want it and I've written my name alongside.' She was fiddling in her pocket again and now, knowing she was a reporter, Gemma realised what she was doing.

'You've been recording this,' she said, her voice spiked with disbelief. 'You've got a microphone in that pocket. And I thought you were a friend.'

'It's only for accuracy,' Nicky said, cheerfully. 'You wouldn't want me to make mistakes, would you? Actually I could have put it on the table only I find it puts people off. You don't mind do you?'

Gemma was so annoyed that for a few seconds she was bereft of words. Then her anger returned, enhanced and terrible — at the incompetence of the railway company, at the insensitivity of this ghastly girl, at her own hideous injuries, her childish gullibility, her dangerous indiscretion. It filled her throat, made her sweat, enlarged every sensation. Feet seemed to be trampling down upon her, the clatter of cutlery from the next table was like the racket of an engine, the busy scene beyond the windows a manic, uncontrollable blur. 'Yes,' she said, 'I do mind. I mind very much. I wouldn't have said a word to you if I'd known you were from the papers. You got this interview under false presences.' Her face was white with fury, the scar across her temple livid against the sudden pallor of her skin.

Which was how Catherine Quennell first saw and heard her.

Catherine had driven to the hospital that morning in a state of suspended indecision, none too sure about what she was doing and suspecting that she was probably making a mistake. In fact, when she reached the ward and was told that Gemma wasn't there, it was almost a relief. But now, one look at that tempestuous face was enough to dispel all her anxieties in a second. She liked this girl at once, instinctively. A fighter, she thought, quickening her pace, a survivor. Like I was when I was left on my own with Susan. She won't be put down. Not with that sort of strength.

'Gemma Goodeve?' she asked, smiling at her.

Gemma turned, took a breath to bring her anger under control and nodded to her as though she'd been expected. 'Yes,' she acknowledged. 'I've got to go back to the ward, is that it?'

Catherine had spent too much time on hospital wards not to recognise a plea for help when she heard one. She picked up the hint at once and smoothly. 'When you're ready,' she said, looking at the other young woman.

'This is — I'm sorry, I've forgotten your name — a reporter,' Gemma explained, adding firmly, 'She's just going.'

At which, still smiling sweetly, she did.

Gemma's anger exploded as soon as she was out of earshot. 'Bloody reporters!' she raged. 'I've had it up to here with them. They pull you to pieces. Peck, peck, peck! They don't care what they do. They're like vultures. If that creature had stayed here a minute longer I'd have hit her.'

'So I gathered,' Catherine smiled.

'She came here with flowers and chocolates,' Gemma said, 'pretending to be a friend and all she really wanted was for me to tell her I was going to sue the railway. She conned me and I let her do it.'

'That's the trouble with a place like this,' Catherine said. 'You can keep them out of the wards but you can't stop them walking into the shopping area.'

'It was all a trick,' Gemma went on. 'I can't believe I fell for it. That's what's so awful. I'm not a fool. I should have seen through it and I didn't. I fell for it.' Then she stopped, feeling suddenly ashamed to be unburdening herself to yet another stranger. And this woman *was* a stranger. She could see that now. Her dark blue uniform wasn't the regulation dress of the hospital, after all, and she had a blue coat over her arm, so she was probably a visitor. 'I'm sorry. I shouldn't be going on like this. I'm keeping you.'

'Actually,' Catherine said, 'you're not. It's you I've come to see.'

Gemma's anger had receded sufficiently for sense — and memory — to return. 'Which is how you knew my name,' she said. And she moved the flowers out of the way so that the sister could sit beside her. The air was suddenly rich with the sharp sweet smell of freesias. 'Is it about my new leg?'

'No,' Catherine said, smiling at her. How easy this was after all! 'It's about your new flat.'

Gemma made a grimace. 'Not the hostel again,' she said.

'No, no,' Catherine reassured her. 'Nothing like that. This is a self-contained flat in a family home.'

'You're not a social worker are you?'

'No. I work in a health centre. In Putney. And before you ask, it's my flat. Mine and my husband's. You met him at the crash. He was the anaesthetist who put you out.'

He was remembered with delight and gratitude. 'He was wonderful,' Gemma said. 'The kindest man. I shall remember *him* for ever. Fancy him being your husband. Will you thank him for me? I never got the chance that morning.'

'Come and take a look at the flat,' Catherine suggested, 'and you can thank him yourself.'

'Well . . .' Gemma hesitated. Thanking him was one thing, taking a flat in his house quite another.

'We thought you might like it,' Catherine said, 'as a sort of halfway house. You wouldn't be there long, naturally, just for the next few weeks until you're happy with your prosthesis and you've learned to walk again. After that you'll want to find somewhere more permanent.' Gemma was nodding agreement, so she went on. 'It might suit you. You can be as independent as you like but we'll be around to keep an eye on you, just in case.' And as Gemma was obviously still thinking about it, she told her a bit more about the flat, explaining how it had come to be built and where it was in relation to the house and how long it had been empty. 'It's not very big, just a bedroom and a shower and a living room and a kitchen, but it's private and it would give you your independence. So there you are, you're welcome to it if you'd like it.'

It was too good to be true. 'Wouldn't someone else in your family want it? I mean, if it was built for your mother-in-law and nobody else has ever lived in it, I might be a bit of an intruder.'

'I've got a son in Canada who uses it when he brings his family over on a long visit, but it'll be empty for the next month or so. Nobody's likely to need it until the spring. I don't think you'd be an intruder.'

'I'd pay rent, wouldn't I?'

'Yes, you would,' Catherine agreed, understanding that this was an important part of this girl's independence. 'So you'll come and see it, will you? I'll give you my card. That's where I work and my address is on the other side.'

'Wellfield Health Centre,' Gemma read. Then she saw the name and her eyes widened. 'Oh!' she said. 'My doctor here's called Quennell. You're not related by any chance?'

'He's my son,' Catherine said, wondering how she would respond.

Gemma frowned. Now this was going to complicate things. 'Does he know you're offering me this flat? Doesn't he want it himself?'

'Oh no. He lives in the hospital. Don't worry. We'll tell him if you take it. It isn't a problem.'

Gemma was thinking hard. 'I ought to warn you,' she said at last. 'I can be . . . a bit tricky.' It was hard to admit it but she had to be honest. 'I won't take charity. I won't let anyone feel sorry for me. I won't be pathetic, or a victim, or a cripple. That's not my style.' And she made her joke again, half laughing, half defiant. 'I shall stand on my own feet, even if I've only got one.'

'Quite right,' Catherine approved. 'So when will you come and see it? How about Tuesday? I could drive over and pick you up.'

He'll be so annoyed, Gemma thought. But it serves him right for offering me a 'disabled' room. I wonder how often he visits them. She would have liked to ask but she couldn't do it yet. It would certainly be interesting to meet him on his home ground, on equal terms. 'Yes,' she said. 'Tuesday would be lovely. Thank you.'

Andrew was on the phone when Catherine got back to Amersham Road. He waved at her but went on speaking into the receiver. 'When would that be?'

The phone buzzed an answer. 'Yes,' he said. 'I think I could manage that. Fax me the details. Yes. The number is . . .'

'What was all that about?' she asked when he finally put the receiver down. His grin was positively devilish.

'I've just been asked to appear on *A Question of Morals*. How about that?'

It was one of the new prestigious programmes, fast making a name for itself as outspoken and hard-hitting. 'I thought you didn't approve of chat shows,' she teased.

'I don't. Most of them are trashy. But this isn't a chat show. It's current affairs. Far more responsible.' And when she grimaced at him: 'Anyway, I've agreed to do it. Apparently they're impressed by the way I predicted the outcome of the inquiry. They want someone who's prepared to speak out. Thought I'd be ideal. It's rather a compliment. Did you see our crash girl?'

'Yes. And she's interested. She's coming

here on Tuesday. I've invited her to dinner.'

'Ah!' he said.

'Is that a problem?'

'The show's on Tuesday,' he said. 'I shan't be here, at least not till it's over. Pity!'

'In that case, we'll watch you,' she promised. 'And if you play your cards right we'll wait dinner for you. How will that be?'

'Sounds a good wheeze!' he said, grinning at her again. 'Did you see Nick?'

'No I didn't,' she told him. 'And you're a wicked old devil.'

Chapter 10

Billie Goodeve lived on her own in a block of flats called 'The High' on the Streatham High Road. It was only a short walk away from the boutique she ran at Streatham Hill and it had once been quite a prestigious address, which is why she'd moved there in the first place. But now she had to admit it had rather come down in the world. Her flat was on the second floor, and had what the estate agents called 'the benefit of a view', which sounded rather grand but actually meant that her living room window overlooked the main road which, in its turn, meant that she had to keep it shut most of the time to avoid the noise and fumes of the traffic.

Nevertheless it was a pleasant flat and she kept it spotless, hoovering and polishing every day even though it made her back ache. It was a point of honour with her to be presentable — just in case anyone came to call. Not that many did, apart from Mrs Cohen from the first floor, and that was usually because she wanted to borrow something. Social life in the High wasn't exactly what you'd call scintillating. So it was rather a surprise when her doorbell rang on that Thursday evening.

Now who's that? she thought, and she walked through the flat to answer it, tucking the hoover into the broom cupboard as she went. Whoever it was, they weren't exactly patient. They'd rung again before she'd reached the door. It'll be Jehovah's Witnesses, she thought. That's just what I need.

But she only had to take one look at the couple standing in the porch to realise that they'd come from the papers. The girl was wearing a smart trouser suit and had a long camel coat slung over her shoulders like a model, and the man was carrying a camera.

'Yes?' she said, patting her hair and wishing she'd stopped to comb it. 'How can I help you? Is it about my Gemma?'

'Got it in one,' the girl said, beaming at her. 'Spot on! I'm doing an article on your Gemma for the *Sunday Chronicle*. Isn't she *fabulous!* We're all such fans. Anyway, I said to Jake here — this is Jake, by the way. I'm Nicky Stretton — I said, I'll bet her mother will be just the one to tell us about her. Could we come in and talk to you?'

Billie wasn't sure. She'd already said rather too much to the newspapers and maybe she ought to draw back a bit. 'Well,' she said. 'To tell the truth, I'm rather busy at the moment.'

'We wouldn't disturb you,' Nicky promised. 'We could come back in half an hour if you'd prefer. It's just that your Gemma is such a *star* and we *do* so want to talk to someone who *really* knows her. I've just been talking to her myself and I *do* so admire her. We just need a little background. And who better to provide it than her mother?'

The persistent flattery had its effect. 'Just for a minute then,' Billie decided, standing aside to let them in. If Gemma'd spoken to them it must be all right. She led them through into the living room, indicated the armchairs they were to sit in and took up a position on the sofa, facing them. This time she would be careful.

Nicky Stretton looked at the pictures on the sideboard, noting how many were of Gemma when young, and thinking: That one must be the father. He does look a bit like Errol Flynn.

'What *lovely* photographs!' she said admiringly. 'Have you got any more — an album or something? I'd love to see it if you have.'

That was easy. And there was no harm in

it. Three bulging albums were produced at once.

'Brilliant!' Nicky applauded, flicking through the pages of the first one. 'These are *wonderful*, Mrs Goodeve. I suppose we couldn't take copies of some of them, could we? We'll send them straight back to you.'

Yes, of course they could.

'We want to write a piece on her childhood,' Nicky explained. 'What she was like as a little girl.' And she began to prompt. 'I'll bet she was a really good kid.'

'Yes,' Billie agreed, plunging straight into her favourite fantasy. 'She *was* good. A dear little girl. I never had any trouble with her. She used to spend hours playing with her dolls, dear little thing. All by herself but she never complained. My neighbours used to say she was the best child they'd ever seen. And she was, although I say it myself. No trouble at all. And pretty! You'd never believe how pretty she was. Well you can see it, can't you, from the snaps.'

'It must have been a shock when she was injured.'

'Oh it was. And of course, she's had to have another operation since then. Did you know that? The wound turned septic. They rang me up in the middle of the night to tell me. She could have died, poor darling. And now it turns out they could have saved her leg if there'd been a crane.'

'I suppose when she leaves hospital she'll be coming home to you?'

The answer was a touch too bold. 'Of course. Where else would she go?'

'But I'll expect you'll move once she gets her money.'

That put Billie on her mettle. 'I couldn't say,' she told them guardedly. 'It depends on her, doesn't it? If she wants to buy a better place, then naturally I wouldn't stand in her way. I want the best for my little girl. We all want that, don't we? The best for our children. But I wouldn't press her. I've never pressed her about anything. It's something I wouldn't do.'

'Could you tell us about her father?' Nicky suggested. 'He left her when she was young, I believe.'

'He was a lovely man,' Billie recalled. 'Terribly good-looking. There's a snap of him, there. So you can see how good-looking he was. He doted on Gemma. She was his little princess.'

Nicky waited.

'She was broken-hearted when he left. Poor little thing. But there you are. It had to be. Life's like that. It was work, you see. We all have to earn a living, don't we?'

'And you've earned your living and Gemma's ever since?'

'Yes, I have,' Billie said, relieved that the conversation had moved away from Gemma's father. If they'd followed that tack for any distance it could have been difficult. 'We were all in all to one another. Like sisters. We still are. I think it comes of having a good home. There's nothing to beat a good home, is there? Somewhere to come back to when you're down — a bit of love and understanding — home comforts — that sort of thing. There's nobody to beat your mother, when all's said and done.'

They taped her every happy self-enhancing word, took so many pictures of her that it made her head spin, borrowed pictures of Gemma and her father, and left her in a trance of euphoria, still relishing the full satisfying flavour of the role she'd been playing. She hadn't enjoyed an evening so much in years.

And when it came out the article was lovely. All about what a good little girl she'd been '. . . *never a moment's trouble . . . We were like sisters . . .*' and how brave she was being: '. . . *deserted, fatherless, crippled, yet she still fights on, taking on the might of the establishment . . .*' and how much she missed her father. The photos they'd taken in the flat were excellent too. *'Mrs Goodeve in her south London home . . . I am looking forward to the day when Gemma can come home and I can look after her . . . we shall be so happy.'*

But she couldn't sit around all Sunday reading the newspapers, pleasant though it was. She had the bedroom to hoover and the ironing to do. She'd only just finished her last white blouse when the doorbell rang. Well aren't you the popular one these days, she said to herself and this time she hurried to answer it.

There was a lone man standing in the hallway, looking away from her down the hall as he waited. But he wasn't a reporter. She could see that at once because he was far too well dressed. It was rather a disappointment. And he wasn't one of the residents either, which was another. She *had* hoped some of them would have seen the article and come up to talk to her about it. She was still wondering about him, when he turned towards her. And then, in a moment of shock and delight and disbelief, she knew who he was.

'Oh my good God!' she said. 'Tim! It can't be.' Tim Ledgerwood, in the flesh, standing on her doorstep as if he'd never been away. 'Oh Tim! What *are* you doing here?'

'Aren't you going to ask me in?' he said, smiling his old charming smile.

'I'm sorry,' she said. 'I'm forgetting my manners.' But surprise was making it difficult to breathe. It couldn't be him. Not after all these years. But it was, and just the same as she remembered him, every bit as handsome, a little shorter maybe, a touch of grey at the temples, a few wrinkles, but he still had the same jaunty air, the same smile, and that lovely thick hair and that little moustache. 'It's just such a shock to see you again. You haven't changed a bit.'

He smoothed the grey hair on his temples and smiled at her as he stepped into the flat. 'Neither have you. You're as beautiful as ever.'

She led the way into the living room, her cheeks flushed with pleasure, her thoughts spinning and fractured. Had he come back to her after all these years? You heard about men returning to their first loves in the end. She'd read a story just like that only last week in the hairdresser's. What if he's going to ask me to take him back? Why has he come here? Why . . . ? What if . . . ? It was all a little unreal.

He was smooth and assured, just as he'd always been. 'I see nothing's changed,' he said, looking around. 'It's all exactly as I remembered it. The display cabinet. Those vases. The clock. I remember that. It used to keep us awake at night. Do you remember, Billie? And you used to turn it off.'

She remembered. Oh how well she remembered!

He asked her permission to smoke and she gave it and provided him with an ashtray. 'You have a lovely home,' he said.

'I try to keep it nice,' she agreed, drinking in the sight of him. It was still hard to believe he was there. They sat in her chintz-covered chairs, facing one another, as he drew the smoke into his lungs in the old familiar way, holding the cigarette elegantly between his fingers, smiling at her.

'I used to dream about this place,' he said, leaning towards her earnestly. 'This place and you. You've no idea how I missed you. Many and many's the time I've lain awake at night wishing I could come back.'

This was the stuff of her dreams, the words she'd always hoped she'd hear him say. 'Oh Tim,' she said, 'why didn't you?'

'I didn't dare. I thought you'd turn me away.'

'I wouldn't have done.'

'I can see that now. But you'd have had every right. Anyway I didn't dare. I was a fool, wasn't I?'

'Never mind,' she said. 'You're here now. Oh it *is* good to see you.'

'I had to come this time, didn't I,' he said. And he picked up her copy of the *Chronicle* and spread it out on the coffee table, flicking it open so that they could see his photograph on the centre page. 'The minute I heard about our poor Gemma, I caught the first flight out.'

'First flight from where?'

'Cape Town,' he told her.

'Is that where you're living now?'

'That's where.'

'So what have you been doing with yourself?'

'This and that,' he said vaguely.

'And did you make your fortune?'

The answer was even more vague, as if it was hardly worth giving. 'Oh yes.' He leant forward towards her, grey eyes full of concern. 'Tell me about Gemma. Poor kid. Is she very badly hurt?'

She told him everything she knew, in the most graphic detail, and was pleased when he winced and even more pleased when tears welled up in his eyes.

'That's horrendous!' he said, stubbing out his cigarette. 'What a good job she's got you to look after her. It says here she's coming back to live with you. Is that right?'

'Well I hope so. We haven't made any firm plans yet.'

'And she's going to sue the railway.'

'Well, possibly. It's early days.'

'Very wise,' he said and he stood up. For a moment she thought he was going to take her in his arms. But he walked across to the window instead and looked down at the street. 'Would you like to come out for a meal?' he asked. 'A little celebration. It's been far too long since we had a meal together. And yes, I know what you're going to say. It was all my fault.'

The invitation and the start of such a charming apology made her heart leap as if she was still a girl. 'When?'

'No time like the present. I ought to start making amends.'

So they went to one of the local restaurants. 'They'll wonder who you are,' she said, as they made an entrance.

'Let them wonder,' he said masterfully. 'We've got other things to think about.'

But oddly, what they talked about was money and how it could be invested. Afterwards she wasn't quite sure how they'd got around to the subject but he was certainly knowledgeable about it.

'There are all sorts of ways to beat the taxman,' he explained. 'Trust funds. PEPs.

And you have to be careful where money's concerned. You ought to look into it. For Gemma's sake. She'll need someone to advise her.'

She supposed so.

'I could get you a few leaflets if you'd like,' he offered. 'You need to be prepared.'

She wasn't sure about that. 'I wouldn't want her to think I was putting her under any pressure.'

'The trouble is,' he told her, 'where money's concerned this world is full of sharks. Absolute sharks, believe me. If we don't look after her, they'll get at her and before she knows where she is the money will be gone.'

'That sounds awful.'

He reached across the table and took her hand. 'Not to worry,' he said. 'I'll help you.'

She held his hand tightly, thrilled by its pressure. 'If you ask me, it's a good job you've come back.'

'I'm glad you think so,' he said and his voice was full of emotion. 'Now the next thing is for me to visit our Gemma. When are you going to see her next? Maybe I could come with you.'

'No,' she said. 'I don't think that's a good idea.' And she explained quickly in case she'd upset him. 'It gave me enough of a shock to see you again and I'm fit and healthy. Let me warn her. Sort of prepare her for it.'

He agreed at once, smiling at her in his most charming way. 'Of course. Very sensible. So when's your next visit?'

'Tuesday,' she said.

'Not tomorrow?'

'I've got the accounts to do tomorrow.'

'Always the worker,' he said, admiring her. 'You're a wonderful woman, there's no doubt about that. One in a million. You see her and give her my love and see what she says.'

'Leave it to me,' Billie said, basking in his admiration.

But when she reached the ward on Tuesday, Gemma wasn't there — not in bed, not in the day room, not in the corridors. She even looked in the disabled toilet but there wasn't a sign of her. After a while she began to get upset. What if she's been taken ill again? she thought, drifting back to the ward. I shall have to find a nurse and ask what's going on.

But there didn't seem to be any nurses around, and there weren't many patients either except for two who were asleep and the oldest inhabitant, who was sitting beside her bed doing her knitting.

The old lady looked up and beckoned to her.

'You looking for Gemma?' she asked. 'Thought you was. She's gone out.'

Billie was relieved. And then cross. 'Gone out? She can't have.'

'For the evening.'

Billie looked down at the wrinkled face below her and decided the old lady didn't know what she was talking about. 'You don't go out for the evening when you're in hospital.'

'You do nowadays,' the old lady said. 'It's all changed now.'

They must have taken her off for some treatment, Billie thought, sighing with annoyance. 'Do you know when she'll be back?'

'Late, I should think. I reckon she's gone out to dinner. Never 'ad no supper and then some woman came to collect her. I seen her bein' wheeled out.'

How very, very annoying, Billie thought. And how typical. Her father comes back to us and she goes out to dinner. 'Well, will you tell her I came to see her,' she asked the old lady, 'and say I'll be back tomorrow. I've got a surprise for her.'

Chapter 11

Despite his outward calm, Andrew Quennell was excited by being in a television studio. His first glimpse of the studio building had been rather a disappointment. It looked too ordinary, single-storeyed, not particularly well lit, right alongside the road, more like a factory than a centre of entertainment and damned difficult to find in the dark. But the studio itself was everything he expected and more. It made him feel important simply to step through the door, there was such an air of purpose and authority there, such a blaze of light, so many cameras. He could even see two being pushed into position on the gallery, right above the raked seats where the audience would sit. There was no doubt about the value of this programme. It was meant to be taken seriously.

A friendly young man with a ponytail explained that Andrew would be one of the principal speakers and escorted him to his seat in the front row, warning him to watch out for the cables. An equally friendly young

woman with a crew cut clipped a microphone to his tie and hid the leads under his
shirt. The studio manager led in the audience, who all looked suitably serious and
well-dressed. There was a gratifying and exciting sense that something important was
about to happen.

'Robert Carpenter will be with us in three
minutes,' the studio manager warned, 'and
he'll have one or two things to tell you before we start. So if you'll all make yourselves
comfortable . . .'

Robert Carpenter, the star of the show,
was taller than Andrew had imagined. He
wore an understated suit and very little
makeup, was effortlessly handsome and entirely without side. He explained that the
programme would begin with a short film
about the Wandsworth crash and 'one or
two comments on the report'.

'There are monitors all round the studio
so that you can watch the film too,' he said.
'But once the discussion begins, don't look
at them. Not unless you want to look a
prat. This is a live show and we can't edit
you out. Don't look at the cameras. Similar
reason. Look at the person who's speaking.
Or at me. If you have something to say,
catch my eye. I shall be walking round all
the time and I don't miss much. You will

feel nervous for thirty seconds, but that's all. I promise.' He smiled at them, the smile as charming and familiar as it was on screen. 'Right. All set?'

Very smooth, Andrew thought with admiration, as he settled to enjoy the film. He was pleased to realise that he didn't feel nervous at all, not even when his own face spoke to him out of the screen. I suppose I've got used to the sight of it now, he thought, and remembered how anxious he'd been after that first interview, afraid that he'd gone too far or said the wrong thing. Well at least there was no fear of that now. He'd been well briefed. He knew what questions he was likely to be asked and, more importantly, he'd planned exactly what he was going to say. Now all he needed to do was to concentrate on the programme. He sat back in his chair, listening intently.

A voice-over was asking, 'Are you saying that this accident was due to poor maintenance?' And there was his own voice speaking. 'I'd lay money it was . . . We live in penny-pinching times. British Rail is being privatised. So we don't spend taxpayers' money on rolling stock, or safety measures, as we ought to if we had any sense. We use it to bribe the buyers. We use it to ensure a good profit for the shareholders. Profit.

That's what this is about. If this accident turns out to be the result of poor maintenance, or the lack of proper investment, I hope no one will forget that the casualties will have paid the price for it.'

'Dr Quennell,' Robert Carpenter said, walking towards him. 'You were very sure of your facts that night.'

'Actually,' Andrew admitted, 'I wasn't sure at all. I thought it likely. I was so angry at the waste of life, I spoke as I felt.'

'And you were proved right. We know from the report that the casualties you tended that night *did* pay the price for inadequate maintenance.'

'Sadly, yes.'

'You stand by what you said?'

'Absolutely. That was an accident waiting to happen.'

'It would appear,' Robert Carpenter said, moving on to his next speaker, 'that no fewer than three companies owned these coaches after privatization. As far as we can ascertain, none of them ran any safety checks before selling them on. We invited all three to send a representative to this debate but all three declined. However we do have with us Mr Graham Vaughan, a regional safety officer who used to work for British Rail. Mr Vaughan, can you tell us

191

what checks you would consider necessary, given the age of the carriages?'

The talk was led from safety standards to the ethics of privatization. Andrew admired the professionalism of it. What I've got to say can wait, he thought. Let the others sound off first and then I'll step in.

The revelation that the accident had been caused by lack of maintenance had touched a public nerve. There were several impassioned speeches from the floor, deploring the lack of care and the general fall in standards. Robert Carpenter moved quietly about, keeping an eye on the studio manager, watching out for new contributors, edging the debate in the direction he wanted. Soon the audience began to take sides, some speaking out for privatization and competition, others castigating the profit motive and corporate greed. It was a lively debate, as Andrew was pleased to see, but it wasn't leading to the opening he was looking for and time was passing. He was just thinking he'd lost his opportunity and should have spoken up right at the beginning, when a woman in the back row began to praise 'the wonderful job' the medical teams had done on the day of the crash.

'If it hadn't been for them,' she said, 'it could all have been much worse. I think we should thank God we've still got a National Health Service.'

This is it, Andrew thought, looking straight at Robert Carpenter. He realised that he suddenly felt very nervous indeed, his heart pounding and his palms wet with sweat. But he was given his invitation to speak. 'Dr Quennell.'

'If you'll take my advice,' he said, looking at the woman, 'you'll make the most of our NHS while you've still got it. I quite agree with you. It's a wonderful institution but it's in its death throes. I'm not supposed to say that, but it's the truth and we all know it. There's a desperate shortage of beds, especially in intensive care units. We could easily have lost patients that night for lack of beds. It was only by the grace of God that we managed to get them all into London hospitals. The problem we've been talking about here is the same problem we're facing in the NHS. Ever since their inception, British Rail and the NHS have been offering a public service. Now we're being required to run a business, which is an entirely different matter.'

'But don't you think competition makes for a better service?' a man's voice asked.

'No,' Andrew said, trenchantly, 'I don't and this programme has been evidence of it.

We've been talking about how railway companies compete. They close lines and sack staff and cut back on essential services like safety checks. Hospital Trusts are in the same position. They have to save money too, so they close wards and sack staff and cut back on beds. Hardly a week goes by without news of a death that should have been avoided, or a helicopter chase for an intensive care bed. When the next rail crash comes we might not be able to deal with it.'

'That's alarmist,' his opponent said.

'That's the truth. We're running two health services now — one for people who can pay and one for the rest. In a good many hospitals, patients arriving at Accident and Emergency are asked whether they have private health insurance almost as soon as they get through the door. If they have, they can expect rapid, specialist treatment. If they haven't, they wait. Imagine that system operating at a major accident.'

There was a murmur of agreement and the hiss of breath drawn in outrage.

The programme was into its last two minutes. 'Are we likely to have another major accident?' Robert Carpenter asked the health and safety expert.

'I'm afraid we are,' Mr Vaughan told him, 'unless the new companies are prepared to spend more on maintenance and keeping up proper safety standards.'

'Which is what you would like to see done?'

'Of course. It's a simple choice. We either spend more on passenger safety or we allow the new managing directors to earn bigger profits.'

'And if we can have a last word from Dr Quennell,' Robert Carpenter said. 'What would you like to see done?'

'I agree with Mr Vaughan,' Andrew said. 'But I would like a proper Health Service too, adequately funded and ready to cope with any emergency. It would cost money because it would mean reopening wards we've been forced to close, employing more doctors and nurses, enlarging our intensive care provision. But I think most people would vote for it.'

'Well that's it for tonight,' Robert Carpenter said, speaking to camera. 'Don't forget to join us next week when we will be examining another moral issue of the day.'

The credits were rolling, the programme's theme tune being played. It was over.

'That was great!' the studio manager told Andrew as the microphone was being unhooked from his tie.

'Good,' Andrew said with satisfaction. 'I hoped it would be.' There was no false modesty with this man.

Back in Putney, Catherine and Gemma had watched the programme with mixed emotions, Catherine proud of the stand he was taking but feeling protective in case the media exploited him, Gemma full of unqualified admiration. It didn't occur to her that the doctor might be making difficulties for himself. She was still angry at the findings of the report and thought it was splendid that he was standing up for the victims and the medical teams who cared for them. Fancy having a man like that for a father.

'Strictly speaking,' Catherine explained, 'doctors aren't supposed to talk to the media.'

'I don't see why they shouldn't,' Gemma said. 'It's *their* Health Service. I think it's great the way he's speaking up for it.' Seeing him like this had made her feel that this flat was a distinct possibility.

'He's furious about what they're doing to the NHS,' Catherine told her. 'His father was in it from the beginning, you see, so he was brought up to it. He can't bear to see it being run down.'

'No. That's obvious.'

'Time to look at the flat,' Catherine said as the programme was faded out. 'There's nothing else we want to watch, is there?'

So the flat it was. They left the living room, Catherine pushing the wheelchair, opened a door to their right and entered the chill of an unused room. It was a bedroom and the biggest and most peculiar Gemma had ever seen. She didn't like it at all.

'Originally it used to be the dining room,' Catherine explained. 'Then it was Drew's surgery. Then Gran had it as a bedroom. It's been all sorts, this room.'

Which is what it looked like. The remains of its original grandeur were still there, china finger plates above and below the brass handles on the door, an elaborate moulded ceiling, a fireplace still complete with Victorian tiles and a marble mantelpiece supporting a Victorian looking-glass in its original gilded surround. There had been similar fittings in the room she'd just left, but there, as she now realised, they'd been matched by the furniture: the doctor's bureau and leather chair, the comfortable armchairs and sofas, the general relaxed affluence of it all. Here, where the only items of furniture were two plain single beds shrinking against the far wall, a small modern chest of drawers and a diminutive wardrobe, they were totally out of place. And to make matters worse, there was a stainless steel sink in the alcove to one side of the fireplace. *Drew used it as his surgery.* She looked at the room rather bleakly, not at all sure that she wanted to live in it. But Catherine was already pushing her towards an archway on the other side of the fireplace, switching on more lights as she went.

They were in a dark inner hall dominated by doors, three white ones giving out to right and left and a Victorian side entrance, stained glass and all, immediately facing her.

'This is the bathroom!' Catherine demonstrated, throwing open the first door to her left. 'We had it specially built when Gran got arthritis, so it's got a shower stool and a handrail and that sort of thing. And this is the kitchen.'

It wasn't a great deal bigger than the bathroom, but there was everything to hand, even a washing machine, which Gemma hadn't expected, and although it was a tight fit, the wheelchair went in and out of the door and could just about be turned round inside the room. There would be problems here, she thought, but I could handle them.

'*Pièce de résistance* now,' Catherine said and manoeuvred her through the last door into the living room.

This time she didn't switch on the lights until they were both through the door and for a split second, as the room bloomed before her, grass green and corn gold, sage, pine, mustard and ginger, Gemma had the impression that she'd been pushed into the garden. It was such a pretty room it could have been designed for her. There wasn't a straight line or a discordant colour anywhere she looked. Flowers curled about each other on cushions and curtains, a wing chair held out curved green arms, the occasional table was circular, the two chests of drawers elegantly bow-fronted; there were two spherical vases, an oval mirror, a clock like a golden orb. Even the three-seater settee was curvaceous, its cushions plumply buttoned. And down by the television set was a little round footstool, not much bigger than a dessert plate, but intricately carved and upholstered in soft brown velvet. It lifted her spirits simply to look at it all.

'Well?' Catherine asked. 'What d'you think?'

'It's gorgeous,' Gemma said.

'The furniture was Gran's,' Catherine explained, 'but we left it as it was. We thought it was too good to change.'

Gemma was suddenly aware that atmosphere in the room was heavy with unspoken emotion. Nothing was said, but to her trained eyes, Catherine's body cues were clear and touching: the anxious expression — eyebrows slightly raised, blue eyes strained — the stoop of her spine and the slight, defensive hunching of her shoulders. She values this room, Gemma thought. She doesn't want it altered.

'If I come here, I won't change a thing,' she promised.

'Haven't you got some furniture you want to bring?' Catherine asked.

'Only odds and ends,' Gemma said. 'Books and clothes and things like that. I've been a student for the last three years. I don't have many possessions.'

There was a rush of cold air in the inner hall and Dr Quennell appeared in the doorway. His arrival changed the atmosphere immediately, as though he'd switched on another, brighter light. His face was glowing with success, his hair bushing above his temples, his grey eyes bright.

'There you are!' he said, taking command. 'Did you see it? What did you think of it? Hello Gemma. Making a good recovery, I see.'

They answered him together. And were then confused by the clamour they'd made.

'First things first,' he laughed and turned to Gemma. 'Are you taking the flat?'

Direct question, direct answer. 'If you'll have me.'

'Oh I think we can put up with you for a week or two,' he said, accepting her as a tenant and prescribing her tenancy in the same breath. 'Until your prosthesis is fitted and you're comfortable with it. That's what you need, isn't it? Halfway house.'

'And an electric wheelchair,' she said, her mind very sharp now that she'd made her decision. 'I shall need to be independently mobile.'

'You'll have to buy one,' he warned. 'They're not cheap.'

'I've got money coming from my insurance.'

'It'll be about a thousand.'

'I can manage that.'

'I'll see to it,' he promised. 'Right. That's settled then.'

And so quickly, Gemma thought, but there wasn't time to say anything else because he was leading them out of the flat, declaring that TV was thirsty work and he needed a drink.

And once they were all back in the living room, he hardly gave either of them a chance to say a word. He dispensed drinks, analysed the programme, told them stories about the way the studio was run, made them laugh and was still entertaining them when the phone rang, its double bell shrill in hall and kitchen.

'I'll get it,' he said and was gone in two strides, leaving them still laughing at his last joke.

Even when the laughter eased, he still focused their attention. They could hear his voice, booming in the hall. 'Speaking.' . . . 'Yes. I am.' . . . 'That's very short notice.' . . . 'What time would you want me to be there?' . . . 'I see.'

'That'll be a call,' Catherine said. 'What a nuisance.' But it was neither, as she could see from the grin on his face when he breezed back into the room.

'That was Capital FM,' he announced, looking round at them both. 'Will I give them an interview about the state of the NHS? How about that? I seem to have started something.'

'When?' Catherine wanted to know.

'Tomorrow evening. I shall have to sneak an hour away from surgery.'

'So you've agreed to do it?' Catherine said.

'Yes, I have. Don't look so worried. It's all right. I'm in a good position. Damn nearly retired. They can't touch my pension. I can say what I like. It'll give me something to do in my retirement.'

'I thought you were going to tackle the garden,' Catherine said, smiling at him.

'There's too much backache in gardening.'

'There's too much heartache in television,' she said. 'You ask Gemma. They trample all over you, don't they, Gemma?'

Gemma wouldn't admit *that*. 'Only if you let them,' she said. 'You have to fight back.'

'You had to handle them in a public place,' Andrew pointed out. 'I shall be in a studio. It's a bit more civilised there.'

'And you'll be the centre of attention,' Catherine said.

'Yes,' he agreed honestly. 'You're right. Undivided attention flatters the ego. And there's nothing so totally undivided as a camera. Makes you feel important. Powerful, even. As if you might have some influence. I could develop a taste for it.'

'Dr Quennell, media star!' she teased.

He made a self-deprecating face. 'I don't know about that,' he said, heading for the drinks cabinet, to refill glasses and change the subject. 'So when are you moving in, Gemma?'

'I don't know,' Gemma said. 'That'll depend on Mr Barnaby, won't it?'

And whether he needs the bed, Andrew thought. But he kept his thoughts to himself.

As Catherine was doing. Now that the decision had been made she was wondering how they were going to break the news to Nick and what he would say when they did. It was all very well offering this girl a helping hand but she didn't want him to be upset by it.

He rang her later that evening and, rather as she'd feared, he wasn't pleased. There was a long pause while he digested what she'd said and when he spoke his voice was full of controlled anger. 'You've done *what?* You're joking!'

'Your father thought it would be a good idea.'

'This is a family house we're talking about, not a convalescent home. Who's going to look after her?'

'She'll look after herself. She's independent. As you very well know.'

He had to admit that but he wasn't mollified. 'And what about Sue's anniversary?' he asked. 'We're all supposed to be going up to York in a fortnight. How's she going to cope *then*, all on her own? I don't suppose you've thought of that. Or are you going to stay at home and look after her?'

'I shall ask Polly to come in on Saturday instead of Friday,' Catherine said. Polly Okino cleaned the house while she and Andrew were at work and over the years had become more of a friend than a housekeeper. 'I'm sure she wouldn't mind.'

'And how will she manage at night? You can't ask Polly to live in. Gernma's had twenty-four-hour care with us.'

Catherine was beginning to feel cross. There was no need for him to be quite so negative. It was out of character. 'She'll be fine,' she said firmly. 'You'll see.'

But he was determined to disapprove. 'It's ridiculous,' he told her and she could hear the scowl in his voice. 'It'll never work out.'

Chapter 12

After such an eventful evening, Gemma found it difficult to settle back into the sedate pace of the ward and almost impossible to get to sleep. The bed was too hard, the night too long, the problem she was facing too pressing. Exciting though it was to think that she would soon be out of hospital and living in her own flat, she couldn't help feeling that *her* Dr Quennell wouldn't approve. She thought about it off and on all through the night, wondering what he would say to her about it and preparing answers, as though she was learning a part, thinking up one-liners and possible put-downs, even jokes about having a patient as a lodger. By breakfast time, she felt she'd covered all the angles and when he finally came striding into the ward for the morning round, she was ready for anything.

It was all a total waste of time because Mr Barnaby was in one of his decision-making moods and took the rounds at such speed that the team had to run to keep up with him. Gemma was examined, congratulated on her progress and told that she could be measured for her prosthesis that morning. Then before she had a chance to answer, and before she could even look at Dr Quennell, they were all whisked down the ward to see what could be done to get the oldest inhabitant into a nursing home. 'High time we sorted that out.'

At which point, it started to rain. As the team charged out of the ward, Gemma could see flurries patterning the window opposite with sharp white dots. She reached for the headphones, took up a magazine, and tried to block out the ward and the weather by listening and reading. But the print sloped away from her understanding and the music was simply a throb. How could they behave like that? It was so impersonal. Crash, bang, interview over, on to the next. It left her feeling flattened and, what was worse, none the wiser about Dr Quennell's reaction.

Despite her strong character, she'd always been careful not to do anything to upset other people. Her mother had dinned that into her from a very early age. She could hear her voice now, chanting their mantra: *We'll make our own way, my darling, and look after ourselves, and we won't be a burden to anyone.* And now she'd probably annoyed this prickly young man and she hadn't had a chance to explain or answer back or anything. It was very irritating. He'd stood there at the foot of her bed, with ink all over the pocket of his white coat, looking horribly handsome and horribly disapproving, and he hadn't had a chance to say a word. Even if he'd wanted to. Had he wanted to?

She was still frowning over it when the physiotherapist arrived to put her through her paces and after that there was no more time for brooding. She'd just about got her breath back from her exercises when Staff appeared with a porter and the wheelchair to tell her that the prosthetist was ready to see her.

'Never a dull moment!' she said to the porter as he wheeled her along the corridor.

'We aim to please,' he smiled, trundling round the corner.

She wondered whether she could ask him what the prosthetist was likely to do but decided against it, because he probably wouldn't know. Were they just going to measure her stump? Or would they bring a new leg and fit it on? Or a selection of legs? If she hadn't been so preoccupied thinking up snappy answers to Dr Quennell she could have asked someone. But she was already outside a door marked 'Fitting Room' and being pushed inside, her heart pounding.

The prosthetist was a cheerful man with very curly hair and a wide smile. He sat in the centre of a room with a nurse beside him and what appeared to be half a bed behind him. There was no sign of a leg of any variety anywhere at all.

'Gemma Goodeve?' he said. 'Let's have a look at you. Can you get up on the table?'

She struggled on to the half-bed and waited while the nurse removed her dressing and displayed her stump. It looked smaller than it had been the last time she saw it, shrunk and pathetic and exposed, and it occurred to her, looking at it with a sinking of the heart, that whatever *was* going to happen to her now would probably hurt.

The prosthetist adjusted the bed to the height he required, sat himself at the end of it, and switched on a spotlight.

'Did you do a lot of walking?' he asked, peering at the stump.

'I did, before all this.'

'And will again,' he said, touching the stump delicately. 'What sort of job did you do?'

She told him the straight truth, that she'd

trained as an actress but hadn't landed any parts — yet — that she'd worked in any job that offered, stacking shelves in Sainsbury's, serving in a greengrocer's, typing letters in an estate agent's, delivering free newspapers door to door.

'Sport?' he said, lifting the stump and examining the scar.

Relieved that he wasn't hurting her too much, she told him that too. Swimming, tennis, athletics at school.

'This is very clean,' he said approvingly. 'You heal well.' Then he asked her a question she didn't expect. 'What do you think of it?'

She gave him an honest answer. 'I think it looks awful.'

'In what way awful?'

'Shrunk. Pathetic. I feel quite sorry for it. If that's not a silly thing to say.'

'Not silly at all. It shows you're learning to love it. That's important.'

'Is it?'

'Oh yes. Very important. We're going to make it do a job it wasn't designed for, you see, so you'll have to look after it like a baby, keep it clean and dry, powder it, give it clean socks every day, really pamper it. Do you massage it?'

'No. Should I? I haven't liked to touch it.'

'It helps. Do it in the shower or the bath. Not a rough massage. Just gently.' He was soothing the stump as he spoke, holding it in both hands. 'Like this. You'll get a lot of benefit from it.'

She could tell that, for really the sensation he was producing wasn't painful at all. In fact, it was almost pleasurable.

'Now,' he said, still massaging the stump, 'what we're going to do today is to take a cast. That's the start of the whole process. Once that's done we'll be able to make an interface that will fit you like a glove. Better than a glove, actually, because it will be a perfect fit. Once we've got a really good interface, we can fit your new leg. Are you ready?'

She was ready for anything, and followed the whole process with great interest.

'First,' he said, working as he spoke, 'I'm going to cover the stump with a layer of cling film so that we can get the cast off afterwards without hurting you. Right? Like that. Now we give you a nice layer of stockinet. Like that. Now we come to the sloppy bit. I enjoy this. Whacking on the plaster. Reminds me of my nursery school, playing with clay.'

He took a very long time over the cast, watching it most carefully as it began to set and marking it with a pen. 'You don't want any pressure,' he told her. 'I know this takes a long time but you want the most comfortable fit I can get for you. It'll be worth it in the end.'

'I don't mind how long you take,' she joked. 'I'm not going anywhere.'

'Are you not?' he asked. 'I understood you were going home tomorrow morning. You've got a flat with Dr Quennell, isn't that right? Can you just turn your leg slightly this way?'

Tomorrow morning, she thought, her heart leaping. Hooray!

But there was still a lot more to be done that day: forms to fill in, instructions to gather, a final check on her plastered leg to ensure that it was still healing as it should, even another fleeting visit from Mr Barnaby 'more to wish you luck than anything' — although no sign of Dr Quennell. Packing had to wait until after tea, by which time she was so excited she couldn't even manage a biscuit. One more evening, she thought, as she folded her clothes, one more night, and then I can start living my life again. Roll on tomorrow.

She was sitting on the edge of the bed with her stump on a pillow, folding up the last of her clothes and tucking them into plastic bags, when her mother arrived, out of breath, flushed and obviously excited.

She didn't stop to ask Gemma how she was but plunged straight into her news. 'You'll never guess what's happened,' she said. 'I came to tell you yesterday only you'd gone out. Where were you? Never mind. You can tell me later. Oh Gemma, darling, you'll never guess. Your father's come back.'

Gemma was so astonished she didn't know what to say. 'What?'

'Your father,' Billie repeated happily. 'Just turned up out of the blue on Sunday afternoon. I was hoovering the bedrooms and there was a knock at the door and there he was.'

'Good God!' Gemma said. She was almost too stunned to take it in. 'After all this time!' I've spent an entire childhood wondering where he was and what he was like and why he'd gone and whether he'd love me if we ever met up again. And now he just turns up. It's like something out of Mills and Boon. But then she was curious. 'What's he like?'

'Well older, naturally, but still a dreamboat.'

'And he just turned up?'

'Yes,' Billie said, her face softening at the

thought of it. 'Out of the blue. All the way from South Africa. He read about the crash — it was in one of their papers — and the minute he knew it was you he caught the first flight here to find out how you are. Isn't that wonderful!'

'But why?' Gemma wanted to know. There had to be a reason. Absent fathers don't just reappear without a reason.

The answer was so exactly what she'd always wanted to hear that it sounded unreal. 'To look after you. What d'you think of that? He's come all this way to look after you.'

She didn't know what to think or say. It was too overwhelming. The old annoyance flickered in her because they were both assuming that she needed looking after but on the other hand it would be wonderful if he really *had* come back because he wanted to care for her. He might have stayed away all these years because he didn't know how to make contact. He could have been too ashamed. And the accident could have given him the chance to show his feelings. What if . . . ?

Her mother was still talking. 'He saw your picture first. That's what did it. It must have been a shock to see you after all these years. His own flesh and blood in a rail crash. He says it brought him up short and I'm sure it did.' Her brown eyes were shining between the butterfly blue of her eye-shadow and the thick fringe of her mascaraed lashes.

She still loves him, Gemma understood. After being left on her own all this time, she still loves him. The knowledge touched her. Poor old Mother.

'He wants to see you,' Billie said, earnestly. 'He'd have come tonight only he thought you ought to have a bit of warning. I mean, he didn't want to give you a shock or anything like that. So I said I'd come here and tell you and then we'd fix a time between us. Isn't it wonderful. I knew he'd come back sooner or later. Didn't I always say so? He says he's always loved us and I've always felt that, haven't I? It was just having to get a good job made him go. That's all it was. A man's got to get on in the world, hasn't he, when all's said and done. You can understand it. Anyway, that's all water under the bridge. He's back now. So what do you think? Shall I bring him tomorrow?'

Gemma's head was still spinning. No, she thought. I can't see him yet. Not in this state. I couldn't face it. Not till I've got my false leg and I can walk about again. She wanted to see him very much, to know what he was like and what he thought of her and if he really *had* loved her all this time. But not yet. Not now.

'Well?' Billie asked, her face bright with entreaty.

'There's not much point coming here,' Gemma said at last, parrying her mother's pressure. 'I've been discharged.'

'Darling!' Billie yelled, seizing her in her arms. 'How lovely! You're coming home.'

Gemma waited until the embrace was over and then leant across the bed and stuffed the plastic bags into her locker. It was a necessary pause. 'No,' she said, as kindly and firmly as she could. 'I'm not. I'm going to a flat.'

Billie's jaw dropped visibly. 'What for?'

Now there'll be a row, Gemma thought. And she prepared herself to fight. 'To live there.'

'But you can't,' Billie cried. 'I've got everything ready for you at home. Everything. I've told your father you're coming home.'

Is he living there? Gemma thought. Whatever else she didn't want to play gooseberry in that little flat. And especially one-legged gooseberry. 'I'm sorry, Mum. I'm not.'

Billie's eyes filled with tears. 'You really are the cruellest girl sometimes,' she said. 'Here's your father come back specially to look after you and you go on like this. I've got everything ready, sheets on the bed and everything.'

'It's no good, Mother,' Gemma said, putting her hand on her mother's arm. 'I've made my mind up. I'm not going to live with you. I've found a flat and that's where I'm going.'

'And when are you going to this precious flat? If I'm allowed to ask.'

'Tomorrow morning.'

Billie's mouth was a round O, pillarbox red. 'Oh!' she cried. 'You can't *do* this, Gemma, you really can't. You'll never manage on your own. You need looking after. You know you do.'

'No,' Gemma said firmly, 'I don't. And that reminds me. What's all this nonsense you've been telling the press?'

Billie's expression was instantly defensive. 'But they'd been talking to you,' she protested. 'They told me so. I had to let them in after that, didn't I?'

It's the girl in the café, Gemma realised, heart sinking. And that made her even angrier. 'You didn't have to tell them fairy stories about how happy we were. *Never a cross word!* How could you possibly say that?'

'They twist things.'

'And all that stuff about how I was coming home to live with you. They didn't twist that, did they?'

'I thought you *were* coming home,' Billie said. 'You ought to be coming home. You'd be better at home. Anyone can see that. I could look after you.'

'I can look after myself,' Gemma insisted. It wearied her to be going over the same old ground again. 'You don't listen to me.'

'Look,' Billie said, opening her bag. 'I'd better write down where you're going. He can come and see you there, can't he?'

No, Gemma thought, stiffening her spine and her resolve, if I do see him it's going to be when *I* want to. And where. I don't want either of them turning up in Putney. 'I'll send you a postcard when I've settled in,' she promised. The trolley was being rattled into the ward and, after the exertions of the day and the lack of tea, she was suddenly hungry. 'They're bringing in the supper now, so you'll have to go. Don't worry. I'll be fine.'

'Oh dear!' Billie said, kissing her automatically. She couldn't understand how this visit had suddenly gone so wrong. It ought to have been wonderful. 'You will write, won't you?' The trolley was halfway down the ward and that nurse looked fierce. She began to quail, as she always did under the pressure of authority and that made her dither. 'I suppose I *had* better go. Oh dear. I don't know what to do for the best. I can't just go off and not know where you are. I mean, where you're going to go. I know I shouldn't have told that reporter woman all those things but they push you so. I mean, I wouldn't have if I'd known . . . I mean . . . You will write, won't you? And you will see your father?'

Her confusion made Gemma feel rather ashamed of herself. She leant across the bed and kissed her mother lovingly. 'I'll write. I promise. And I'll see him as soon as I can.'

'Yes. Well,' Billie said, her face creased with indecision as the nurse bore down upon them. She'd have to go or they'd call that awful doctor and he'd have her frog-marched out of the ward. 'Look after yourself.'

She was so bewildered and upset that the full realization of what a terrible failure this visit had been didn't sink in until she was in the lift on her way to the ground floor. How shall I tell Tim? she thought. Poor man. He's come halfway round the world to see her and now I've got to say . . . But what on earth *was* she going to say?

He'd left three messages on her answer-phone while she'd been out, so she phoned him back at once, before she'd taken her coat off and before her courage could fail her.

'Well?' his voice said eagerly.

'Well it's lovely news,' she said. 'She's getting on ever so well.'

'That's good. So she'll be coming home soon.'

'Well not just yet,' she said, flailing to find the right thing to say. 'She's — um — being moved.'

'Oh!' he said, trying not to let his disappointment show too much. 'Where to?'

'I don't know.'

Now there was a trace of exasperation in his voice. 'What do you mean you don't know? You must know. They don't just move people without telling them where they're going, now do they.'

Inspiration suddenly dropped light into the muddle of her mind. 'She's going convalescent. They haven't told her exactly where.'

'I'm surprised they still do that these days,' he said. 'I thought they'd closed down all the homes.'

'There are some still open,' she floundered. 'For special cases.'

'But you don't know where this one is?'

'She's going to write and tell me,' Billie said, thinking, I knew he'd be cross. I've done this so badly.

There was a long pause and then he spoke again, his voice changed. 'You're upset,' he said.

She had to admit it. 'Well yes, I am a bit. It was a disappointment. Her not coming home, I mean.'

'Shall I come over?'

The offer reduced her to tears. 'Oh,' she said. 'If you would.'

'I'll be with you in half an hour,' he said. And was.

It was so good to see him again and looking so handsome in that classy suit. Tears welled into her eyes for the second time. 'Sorry to fuss,' she said, ducking her head.

'Fuss all you like, my poppet,' he said, using his old pet name for her. 'You've every right.' And he gathered her into his arms.

It was a bitter-sweet moment. To be here, in the flat they'd shared all those years ago, back in his arms, as if they were still lovers. It was too good to be true.

'God, how I've missed you,' he said, his mouth in her hair. 'There's never been anyone half as lovely as you. Not ever. You always *were* the best. What a fool I was to walk out on you. I should have had my head examined. Let me look at you, Poppet.'

She leant back against his encircling arms

and gazed into his eyes. She was too full of emotion to say a word. It was several seconds before she realised that he was talking to her about Gemma.

'How long is she going to be in this home?' he asked. 'Do you know?'

'A couple of weeks?' she wondered. 'Not long anyway.'

'Then we've got a few days on our own,' he said, looking at her amorously. If he'd got to wait another fortnight for this wayward child of his, he might as well make the most of it. 'While the cat's away, what say the mice play a little?'

'What?' Billie asked, feeling dizzy.

'Bed?' he hoped, unbuttoning her blouse.

'What, now?'

'Why not?' he said and his voice was masterful. 'We've waited for it long enough.'

So they went to bed and although his love-making was as rough and quick as she privately remembered, she pretended to be thrilled, the way she'd done in the early days when it hadn't worked. He'd come back to her. That was what mattered. She lay beside him, her nose full of the foreign scent of his skin, and knew that she was happier than she'd been in years. They could get the sex right gradually.

He sat up, took a cigarette from a rather

grand silver case and lit up. 'Tell you what,' he said, removing a shred of tobacco from his lower lip. 'Why don't I move in here for a few days? While we're waiting.'

She was dazzled. Wasn't this what she'd always dreamed about, always hoped for? 'Do you want to?'

Given the state of his finances, the answer was obvious. 'Oh yes, my poppet,' he said. 'Very much.'

Chapter 13

Gemma arrived on the doorstep in Amersham Road at the same time as the postman, she slow in her hospital wheelchair with an ambulance man to push her and her plastic bags mounded on her lap, he brisk and striding with a fistful of letters and a bulky parcel.

'Good heavens!' Catherine said, looking at him as she opened the door. 'What's all this?'

'Somebody's birthday?' he suggested. And when she shook her head, he dropped the mail on to the heap in Gemma's lap and went whistling off to the next house.

Gemma was aware that somebody was carrying a wooden ramp into the hall, a small skinny woman wearing a shabby T-shirt and a pair of ragged jeans. 'This is Polly,' Catherine said. 'She's my right hand. She comes in every morning and looks after the house while I'm at work.'

Not at work this morning, Gemma registered, and wondered why not.

'I swapped shifts,' Catherine told her, answering her unspoken query. 'I thought you'd like a welcome committee.'

'That's very kind.'

'She is,' Polly said cheerfully. 'Hello Gemma! Hang on a tick while we get this fixed.'

'I'll give you a hand,' the ambulance man offered. But even so, it took some time to wedge the ramp safely into position and it seemed longer because it had started to spit with rain and they were all getting wet. Gemma was torn between guilt at being a nuisance and annoyance at her own uselessness.

'Now then,' Catherine said, when the ramp was finally ready, 'we've got something for you. Stay there and we'll bring it out.'

It was an electric wheelchair and obviously very heavy because it took both women to roll it down the ramp.

'That's fantastic!' Gemma said, all smiles at the sight of it. 'How did you get it so quickly?'

'It was advertised at the clinic,' Catherine told her as the ambulance man lifted her out of her hospital chair and lowered her into the new one. 'They brought it round this morning. There! What d'you think?'

It was a high-tech wonder with brakes and

a joystick to turn to the right and the left and to move forwards at a nice brisk speed. And it climbed the ramp with no trouble at all.

'It's wonderful,' Gemma beamed. 'I don't know how to thank you.'

'It'll take a bit of getting used to,' Catherine said. 'It could be quite a job getting it through the doors, especially in your little hall. Let's have the mail. You don't want to take all that in with you. We've got some coffee on the go. Come through when you're ready. Would you like Polly to give you a hand?'

'No, no,' Gemma said quickly. This was her chance to begin as she meant to go on. Whatever else she did in this house, she was determined not to be a burden. 'I can manage.' She spoke lightly, because that would show them there was no doubt in her mind. But, in fact, once she was on her own in the bedroom, managing was difficult, as she'd known it would be.

First she had to master the art of driving her new chair, turning it sideways to open doors and then inching her way through. Then she had to learn how to turn it round in a small space — and the inner hall was a very small space. Then she had to unpack. She soon discovered that there were rather too many drawers and cupboards that were beyond her reach and that the sink in the bedroom was impossibly high. But she did what she could, accepting that clothes that she used to hang in a wardrobe would now have to be folded in a drawer. Then she struggled into the bathroom and managed to heave herself out of the chair to use the loo, without falling on the floor, and to wash her hands, without spilling too much water on her clothes. Finally, delighted to be independently mobile again, she drove out into the hall and through into Catherine's kitchen without bumping into the furniture. It was a small triumph.

Catherine was sitting at the kitchen table drinking coffee and sorting through the mail. 'Look at it!' she said. 'It's all for Andrew. The parcel's from *A Question of Morals* and I'll bet that's full of letters too. It must be the broadcast.'

Gemma thought it very likely. 'What a postbag!' she said.

'Rather him than me,' Polly grinned, as she poured out Gemma's coffee. 'Fancy having to wade through all that lot. Makes me feel weak at the knees just to look at 'em. I never was one for readin', me. Nor writin', to be honest.'

But when Andrew came home for his coffee and saw them, he was cock-a-hoop, especially as the first five letters he opened were from doctors he knew, praising him for the stand he'd taken. He opened the parcel, which was indeed full of letters, with a covering note from the producer to say he'd 'started something'.

'There you are, Kate!' he said. 'Didn't I say it would be worth doing?'

'Will you answer them all?' she wanted to know.

'Probably. It'll take time, though.'

Gemma looked from the letters to the doctor's face and in a moment of delighted revelation knew she'd found a way to justify her existence in his house. 'If you don't mind me saying so,' she ventured, 'what you need are some format letters that you can top and tail to suit the person you're writing to. I could put them on the computer for you, if you'd like.' And when he looked doubtful. 'It's all right. I'm used to word processors. I used to do the mail when I worked in an estate agent's.'

'Right,' he said, grinning at her. 'You're on!'

'He'll work your fingers to the bone,' Catherine warned.

'I don't mind,' Gemma said. 'It'll give me something to do. Anyway, I'd like to help.'

'We'll start after dinner tonight,' Andrew

decided. 'You're having dinner with us, aren't you?'

Put like that, how could she refuse? Providing she could help with the cooking. 'I can't offer to do the washing up,' she said, 'because I can't reach the sink, but I can do the vegetables and things like that.'

It was a happy meal. Gemma felt she'd made a good start in her new home, Catherine was pleased by the success of the electric wheelchair and Andrew was so full of himself that he seemed to be twice his normal size. And when they'd stacked the dishwasher and retreated into the living room for coffee and chocolates, the letters from the parcel provided non-stop and excited conversation for the rest of the evening.

One was from a politician who berated Andrew for 'letting down the country with your unpatriotic carping and unnecessary horror stories'. Another was from a woman who signed herself Mrs Godfrey Gordonson and said he ought to be ashamed of himself. But the majority were from doctors and patients who agreed with everything he'd said and had their own horror stories to tell.

A junior casualty doctor in Kent wrote that he'd spent three hours calling fifteen neurosurgery centres to try to find a bed for an accident victim and that the nearest he'd been offered had been in Yorkshire, two hundred miles away — which he thought was a scandal. They'd flown the man there but he had died the next day. Another wrote of a little boy who'd been ferried from Manchester to Leeds, fifty-five miles across the Pennines in a blizzard, because the scanner at his district hospital only operated during office hours. A transplant surgeon wrote that he'd had to turn down twenty-nine livers in just over a year because of a shortage of intensive care beds. 'In that time we have had eleven patients die on our waiting lists.'

One of the worst stories was about a baby in Birmingham who, as the doctor wrote angrily, 'died as a direct result of health cuts. His operation had been postponed five times because there wasn't a bed for him. That's the sort of scandalous situation we are in.'

But the best letter of all came from an old colleague Andrew had worked with in St Thomas's.

'This is not a sudden crisis,' he wrote. 'We've been warning about it ever since Mr Clarke bulldozed the internal market into being. Hospitals are Trusts now and run like businesses with expensive management teams and decisions taken simply to save money. St Thomas's was the flagship and they closed a hundred and thirty-seven beds in the year the Trust was set up, as you will remember. That's what happens when you turn a service into a market. When tragedies occur, this government tends to portray them as "one-offs" rather than symptoms of a fundamental malaise. You and I and the patients know better. Please go on telling it like it is, Drew. You are doing us all a great service.'

'Now that's justification,' Andrew said, passing the letter to Catherine.

'As if you needed it,' Catherine teased. 'You'd speak out anyway.'

'All I need's the chance,' Andrew told her.

It was soon coming. Later that evening, while they were sorting the letters into piles ready to be answered, he had three phone calls, two from journalists wanting to interview him, the third from ITV, asking him to appear on a programme specifically about the collapse of the NHS. The *Question of Morals* team were right. He really *had* started something.

Gemma was so caught up in the excitement of what was happening that it put all thoughts of her father's extraordinary return right out of her mind. It was still stirring at a lower level of consciousness, but it wasn't until she was in bed that she had a chance to think about it. Then she turned it over in her mind, quietly as though it was an academic problem. She was inquisitive about this unknown father of hers. But did she want to see him? She knew that refusing to make a decision about it had upset her mother but that was what always happened when she started to pile on the pressure. It was almost like a reflex action. I'll write to her tomorrow, she decided. Send her a card or something. I should have written today but she'll understand how busy I've been. I won't give her my address or she'll come rushing round here to see me. And I don't want that. Not till I've settled in and had my new leg fitted. Things'll be different then.

And at that point, lying there in the unfamiliar darkness, she realised that the person she really wanted to see and talk to was *her* Dr Quennell. There was too much unfinished business between them and now she would only see him on rare occasions when he came to visit his parents and wouldn't have time to talk to her anyway. Even if he wanted to. Which he probably wouldn't. She was surprised to realise that she was sighing at the thought, as if she missed him.

How stupid! As if she hadn't got anything else to do.

Sure enough, the next morning she was woken by Polly with a mug of tea and the news that the doctor had left her a lot of letters to write.

'They've both gone to work this morning,' she announced, putting the mug on the bedside table. 'She said to bring you tea and see what you wanted for breakfast and to tell you she'll be back for lunch and he's left the computer switched on for you.'

It took most of the morning to type in the format letters he'd suggested and that afternoon he brought home his dictaphone, asking, 'You *can* work this thing can't you?' and looking happy when she said she could. By that time, there was another parcel of letters waiting for him on his desk.

Gemma had a sandwich for lunch sitting in her green and yellow living room, as the trees shushed and swayed in the green garden beyond the window. And that afternoon, while her hosts were busy tidying the herbaceous borders, she drove her wheelchair all the way down Putney Hill, feeling very pleased with herself, and went shopping in the High Street. She returned with a selection of cards for her mother — one of which she wrote and posted there and then

— flowers for Catherine, whisky for the doctor, groceries to stock her own cupboard and a gâteau for tea, which turned their second meal together into an occasion.

By Sunday she felt so at home that she decided it was time to write to her old flatmates to tell them to bring her possessions over.

'I shouldn't be using your sheets and towels,' she said to Catherine. 'And I'm running out of suitable clothes. Not being able to wear jeans puts a great strain on your wardrobe.'

'I can imagine,' Catherine said. 'I think it's a good idea. You'll feel more settled with your own things round you.'

So the letter was written that night and addressed to Jerry, telling him she would like her belongings to be sent to her as soon as possible. As a helpful afterthought, she drew him a sketch map of the side roads and marked the house with a large red cross, thinking how very appropriate the symbol was.

Unfortunately he arrived on Tuesday evening, just as she and Catherine were setting the kitchen table for dinner which was their routine, the Quennells having established that she would dine with them twice a week.

'I am sorry,' she apologised, wheeling out

of the room to attend to him. 'I'll just see them in and I'll be straight back.'

'Not to worry,' Catherine said. 'We've got plenty of time. It won't take long, will it?'

There was such a lot of luggage, that it took half an hour just to get it out of Jerry's car and bundled into her bedroom. She couldn't think where it had all come from. There were two tennis rackets that she'd forgotten all about, a dead potted plant, trailing cobwebs and clots of earth, three battered suitcases, stuffed to bursting point, and so many cardboard boxes that Jerry ended up stacking them on top of one another. She was quite relieved when he finally threw three broken umbrellas on top of the pile and told her that was the lot, 'except for some letters'.

'Most of the stuff that came for you was junk mail,' he explained, 'so we chucked it. There's one or two things we weren't sure about, so I've brought them, and this one came yesterday. Looks pretty official to me. I thought you'd like to see it.'

Gemma hadn't got time for letters, official or otherwise, not when Dr Quennell would be arriving for dinner at any minute. She stuck the little bundle between the umbrellas. 'I'll look at them later,' she said.

Jerry didn't seem to be in any hurry to leave. 'Nice place,' he said, looking round. 'You've fallen on your feet here — if you'll pardon the pun.'

She agreed that it was and she had. But now that her stuff had been safely delivered she realised that all she wanted to do now was to get rid of him. Poor Jerry, she thought. And you were my part-time lover for three years. I've grown hard-hearted since I saw you last. He looked seedier than she remembered. His shirt was frayed at the collar and his jeans were filthy. And he needed a shave. But she couldn't feel any affection for him at all. She wheeled towards the front door, as a hint that he should follow, and reached up to open it. Then she took momentary pity on him. 'How are things?' she asked. 'Did — what's her name? — Cossie settle in all right?'

He stepped out on to the doorstep, wincing as he went. 'Don't talk to me about Cossie,' he said. 'She's been nothing but trouble. Bickering and fighting. Argue, argue, argue. It's doing my head in.'

She was delighted to hear it. 'Oh dear!' she said, struggling not to smile. Didn't I know she'd be trouble? Well it just serves you right, all of you.

There was a car pulling into the drive. She

watched as the headlights turned the hedges emerald green and listened as the wheels crunched to a halt and the driver pulled on his handbrake.

'You'll have to move,' she said, looking at Jerry's old banger. 'You're in the way. Thanks for bringing the things.' Then she saw that it wasn't the doctor's Rover that was waiting in the drive to park but a dark green Peugeot and that *her* Dr Quennell was sitting at the wheel. Oh shit, she thought. Why didn't they tell me he was coming?

There was an awkward pause as they looked at one another in the darkness of the little front garden while Jerry crunched across the gravel to his old wreck, crashed it into gear and drove off in a cloud of acrid smoke. Nick parked his car, got out, hesitated, and walked to the door. Gemma put her chair into reverse to make way for him, thrown by the sight of those long legs striding towards her. Then they were face to face and neither of them knew what to say.

He's cross, Gemma thought, looking at the stern line of his mouth. I *have* annoyed him. If they'd told me he was coming, I'd have made an excuse not to join them. But she was caught now and she would have to endure his company, whether he wanted it or not and no matter what he was thinking.

In fact she would have been very surprised if she could have read his mind at that moment, because he was actually thinking how gorgeous she was, noticing her dark hair and those great brown eyes and those neat little teeth and her gorgeous figure, almost as if he was seeing her for the first time. And admiring her so much that it was turning him on.

He stepped into the hall, muttered 'Hello' and brushed past her chair, annoyed to see how clumsily he was moving. He was rescued by his mother who came out of the kitchen oven-cloth in hand to see how Gemma was getting on.

'Heavens!' she said looking at the pile on the bedroom floor. 'That'll take a bit of sorting out. What a lot there is! Never mind. You can leave it there for the minute, can't you. There's no rush. I'll give you a hand if you like.'

Gemma was hideously embarrassed. The one thing she *didn't* want was for him to see her tatty belongings. And he was looking straight at them. She turned her chair, awkwardly, and shut the door on the mess as quickly as she could. But he went on looking at the closed door and the expression on his face was one of total disdain. It didn't soften much when his mother kissed him.

'Hello Nick,' she said. 'I thought you were your father.'

'No,' Andrew laughed, stepping in through the front door. 'I'm his father. I'd have thought you'd have got that worked out by now.'

His coming broke the tension and the joke made them all smile — even Nick. He hung up his coat, beaming at all three of them. 'So what's new?' he asked his son.

'Have you seen today's *Herald*?' Nick said.

'Not yet.'

'I've brought my copy. I'll show it to you.'

'Pass it round as we eat,' Catherine urged, shepherding them towards the kitchen. 'I'm ready to dish up. Come on, Gemma.'

There was another short uncomfortable moment as Nick realised that Gemma was joining them and looked at her so sternly that it made her bristle with annoyance. Why shouldn't I be part of this meal? she thought angrily, glaring back at him. I helped to cook it. But the moment was brushed aside by his father, who ushered them all to the table and insisted on sitting next to Gemma and opposite Nick — much to the relief of both of them.

The meal began with the usual business of meat-carving and plate-filling and there

239

were too many tasty things to choose and eat for any irritation to last for long. While his father was still carving, Nick produced his copy of the *Herald*, opened it, and passed it round.

They'd run a half-page article on 'Dr Drew' and very interesting it was, particularly to Gemma, for most of it was about his early career and revealed that he had been awarded a Military Medal for bravery during the troubles in Cyprus in 1956. He'd been in the army at the time, according to the reporter, doing his National Service, and had been behind an army truck when it was blown up by EOKA terrorists. There was a picture of the wrecked truck and another of an injured soldier with a very young Dr Quennell kneeling beside him in the dust. It seemed natural to Gemma that he'd been the one who'd tried to rescue the four men who were injured, *'working under sniper fire and in constant danger'*. And it made her admire him even more than ever.

Nick said it had surprised him. 'I never knew you'd been given a medal,' he said. 'You never told me.'

'I don't tell you everything,' Andrew teased him. 'Actually I hadn't thought about it for years. Almost forgotten it, in fact. And then damn me, if I didn't remember it on the day of the crash. Being there brought it all back. Funny how the mind works. Let's have a look then, Nick.' Holding out his hand for the paper: 'I haven't seen it either, don't forget.'

'Did the reporter get it right?' Gemma asked as he took the paper and began to read. 'Was this really what happened?'

'More or less,' he told her. 'He recorded the interview, so it should be OK. Seemed the sort of young man who would be accurate. I didn't expect them to dig up the pictures though. That's a shock.' And not a pleasant one, for it brought back another and more difficult memory. Sticky heat, dust spurting up like a series of yellow fountains under the impact of that God-awful machine-gun, his tongue stuck to his palate with fear and anger, having to spit before he could roar his order. Christ! I'd really forgotten *that*.

Catherine was looking at him with concern. 'It was all a long time ago,' she said, soothing with her voice.

'Does it upset you to see it again now?' Gemma wanted to know. He'd gone quiet and that made her wonder how she would respond if she were to see pictures of the crash when she wasn't expecting it.

He pulled himself together. Kate was

right. It was all a long time ago. Well in the past. 'No,' he said. 'Not really. Memory softens things. It's part of the body's natural defence system. It puts a distance between you and the horrors. Looking at it now, I feel as if it had happened to someone else. As if it was nothing to do with me. Although, in actual fact, it was a turning point in my life.' And as she waited, watching his face curiously, he gave her as much of an explanation as he thought she needed and knew he could contend with. The full truth certainly wasn't possible. 'I'd always had a vague feeling I would end up as a doctor, you see, like my father. I'd got a place at college waiting for me, the right grades, all that sort of thing, but I wasn't committed. That day made up my mind for me.'

'I know how you felt,' Gemma told him. 'The crash was a turning point in *my* life.'

Andrew looked at her and smiled. 'Yes,' he said seriously, 'so it was. But not all to the bad, I hope. At least, not now.'

'Quite a lot to the good,' she answered, grinning at him, 'except for occasional writer's cramp.'

He suddenly saw a way to turn the conversation. 'There's something really rather good coming up next weekend,' he said. 'Family party. In Yorkshire. Wedding anniversary. How would you like to join us?'

The question had such impact it was as if he'd dropped a bomb. Catherine was so surprised her eyebrows disappeared into her hair, Nick was more annoyed than any of them had ever seen him, while as to Gemma herself, she stopped breathing for at least a second while she took in the implications. She wasn't at all sure about it. In fact, if it hadn't annoyed *her* Dr Quennell so much she wouldn't have considered it. Being here in Amersham Road with them was one thing; being at a party with hordes of other people to look at her would be a very different matter, sitting in a wheelchair, with a face like a gargoyle, as the only stranger.

'Well it's very kind of you,' she said at last, 'but a wedding anniversary's a family affair. Wouldn't I be butting in?'

Andrew laughed that excuse aside at once. 'No, you wouldn't. There'll be lots of people there. You'll be one of many. And they'd love to have you.'

'But they'll all be relations. I mean, I'm . . .'

'The family lodger,' Andrew smiled. 'You'll be a novelty. Just say yes. You'll have a great time. Wouldn't she, Nick?'

Nick was looking impassive and avoiding Gemma's eyes. 'Don't ask me,' he said.

'Don't bully her,' Catherine said. 'Let her make up her own mind. It's a long journey.'

And that was another thing. 'How will you get there?' Gemma said, wondering whether she could face a train again so soon.

'By car,' Andrew reassured her. 'Don't worry. I'll drive you. But it's your decision. If you'd like to come with us, come, if you'd rather not, don't.'

I've got to meet people sooner or later, Gemma thought, looking across the table at him. It's cowardly to hide away. I ought to go. Then she looked at Nick and his disapproval swung the balance. 'If that's the case,' she said, 'I'd love to come.'

'Good!' Andrew said. 'That's settled, then.'

Gemma was pleased to see that once the decision was made it restored Catherine to her usual good humour. But *her* Dr Quennell was still sternly distant, and when his parents got out the photograph albums after the meal to show her snaps of Susan and her husband and their two little girls, he sat apart as though it was nothing to do with him, and didn't become animated again until he and Andrew started talking shop.

How odd he is, Gemma thought, as they all went out into the hall to see him off at the end of the evening. His body cues were so contradictory they were very hard to interpret. One minute so kind he's almost tender — look how wonderful he'd been at the crash — and the next all stiff spine and formality and giving me the full glare treatment. Well he won't put me off no matter what he says and does, and he needn't think it. If his father wants to take me to the party he'll just have to put up with it. She wondered how he would react to her once they were there. It was going to be very interesting. Meantime there were clean clothes to sort out for the morning and she really ought to make a start on that awful heap.

But when she wheeled herself into her bedroom, she was too tired to do more than edge her wheelchair into the pile of boxes to retrieve her letters.

Two were junk as Jerry had predicted, one was a postcard from Pippa with no forwarding address, and the most recent was an official letter which took her breath away for the second time that evening. It was from Railways South, offering her a one-off payment of £10,000 as compensation for her injuries and enclosing an official envelope 'for the courtesy of an early reply'.

Chapter 14

Andrew's second appearance on TV was an even bigger success than his first, which wasn't a surprise to anyone who knew him, especially after the article in the *Herald* and particularly when this programme was entirely concerned with the troubles in the NHS. The presenter gave him his head right from the opening question.

'Many people say that the NHS is becoming a two-tier system. Dr Quennell, would you agree?'

He felt no nervousness this time His answer was instant and trenchant. 'It's a two-tier system already. Has been for years.'

'Could you elaborate?'

He could and did. 'We keep being told that the Health Service operates within finite resources. Very well then, if you allow one set of people to buy swifter service, better care, private rooms, the right to jump waiting lists, there will be consequences. Another set of people — the ones without extra insurance or the money to pay up front

— will have to wait, and put up with over-crowded wards and tardy treatment and ex-hausted doctors. Two tiers. It's the inevitable result of encouraging the rich to buy privileges.'

The debate that followed was hot and furious. And by Friday morning, Andrew's criticism was in all the papers. The *Mirror* dubbed him 'Doctor Truth Teller', the *Sun* declared 'War hero speaks out' and reported his words verbatim, the *Chronicle* ran a banner headline over a very flattering photograph: NHS DYING SAYS DR DREW.

'There'll be mail by the sackload now,' Catherine predicted, as they drove to the surgery.

Andrew wasn't fazed by any of it. 'It won't start coming till Monday,' he said, negotiating the junction. 'And I'm not go-ing to let it get in the way of the party. For-get it.'

That's easier said than done, Catherine thought, even though it *is* sensible advice. But there was no chance to say anything else, because they'd arrived and Grace, their senior receptionist, was waving to them through the window. She couldn't wait to tell them how wonderful she thought the broadcast had been.

'You're speaking for all of us,' she said. 'High time too. It makes me boil the way the politicians will keep saying everything's perfect. They should sit in my seat for a day or two. They'd soon change their tune then.'

'Have Mrs Amraliwahla's results come in yet?' Andrew asked, shifting them both into working mode.

'We're waiting for the post,' she told him, still beaming.

'You and me both,' he grinned.

In St Thomas's hospital the broadcast was the main topic of conversation at every pause in the day and Nick came in for a lot of stick from his friends.

'You never told us your old man was a war hero,' Abdul teased, as the three of them snatched a sandwich and a cup of coffee at what should have been their lunch break.

'I don't tell you everything,' Nick said airily.

'You didn't tell us about the broadcast either,' Rick rebuked. 'I only caught it by accident.'

'I didn't have to tell you,' Nick grinned at him. 'I knew you'd be watching. It followed the football.'

'When are you going to see him next?'

'Saturday. We're driving up to York together.'

'Well, tell him from me it was a great broadcast.'

But when Nick turned in at the drive that Saturday afternoon there was no telling his father anything. He was too full of furious energy, glowering at his car.

'Just look at all this rubbish,' he said. The back seat of the Rover was piled with ungainly luggage, cardboard boxes, a guitar, even Sue's old rocking horse, wrapped in sacking and wedged across the seat at an undignified angle.

Gemma was waiting in her chair, under the porch and out of the rain and Catherine was packing the boot with the hand luggage. She was wearing her anxious expression but she was fighting back. 'It's all necessary,' she said to Andrew. 'I promised I'd bring it. I can't go back on my word.'

'Oh for Christ's sake!' he growled at her. 'Won't it wait till next time?'

'No. It won't. I promised.'

'Bloody ridiculous!'

'We've got two cars,' she said, closing the boot. 'Nick won't mind taking his too, will you, Nick?'

It wasn't possible to refuse her. Not when

249

she was so anxious. 'What do you want me to take?'

'Gemma's chair,' she said at once, 'if you can get it in your boot.'

And Gemma too, he thought, looking across the path at her. Well thanks very much, Mother dear.

His furious expression made Gemma feel uncomfortable. 'Are you sure it's all right?' she asked.

'Course it's all right,' Andrew said, brusquely. 'Get in the car or you'll be drowned.' The rain was increasing by the second and so was his bad temper.

She wheeled to the side of Nick's car as quickly as she could — as there was nothing else she could do — waited for him to open the door and then hauled herself from the chair to the passenger seat, feeling uncomfortable and rather aggrieved. By the time he'd folded the chair into the boot and was back in the driver's seat, the windscreen was smeared with raindrops. He switched on the windscreen wipers, scowling. 'It's going to be one hell of a drive,' he promised.

'Obviously,' she said, as he drove off at speed.

The miles stretched before them like a trial.

'Look,' she said, as he drove down Putney

Hill towards the High Street. 'I'm sorry about this. It wasn't my idea. I thought I was going in your father's car.'

'There's no need to apologise,' he said stiffly, watching the road. 'I said I'd take you, so I'm taking you.' Then he vented his fury on a motorist who was dithering at the junction. 'Well come on then, you stupid woman, make your mind up. We can't sit here all day.'

He really is the most infuriating man I've ever met, Gemma thought, looking at his averted profile. Well if that's the way he wants to go on, let him. I shall watch the world go by. After weeks being cooped up in hospital and days when the furthest journey she could manage was down to the shops, it was a treat to be out on the road and actually going somewhere, even with him. In any case, once she'd decided to attend this party, she'd made up her mind to enjoy everything about it, no matter what the company. Or the weather. Although she couldn't have foreseen how gruesome they would be.

As they reached the High Street, it was so overcast that it was more like evening than early afternoon and the wind was blowing the rain horizontally across the road. All the cars had turned on their headlights and most of the shop lights were lit too, alternately glowing and blurred by sideswept torrents of water. The Saturday shoppers looked wet and miserable, bent against the onslaught, or struggling to control their wind-battered umbrellas.

Nick inched past the church, which sat in its hollow beside the river, brooding as darkly as he was. Then he joined the traffic growling across the bridge. The Thames was a disagreeable putty colour and pock-marked by rain. And they were driving through such a downpour that he had to switch his windscreen wipers to double speed. They clicked and squeaked and shot spurts of water to right and left.

'Damn things!' he complained. 'They don't like rain.'

'It is a bit much,' she agreed, making another effort.

But it was wasted. He didn't answer. The spurt of rain died down, the wipers reverted to their normal swishing action, and they continued in silence.

Gemma looked out at the crowded streets, busy with her thoughts. She was alarmed to find that she was acutely aware of him and it wasn't simply the silent profile that was making her aware. It was the smell of his skin, the sight of those long, gentle, competent hands on the steering wheel, that thick hair falling over his forehead, those dark blue eyes . . . And what eyelashes! Thick and sweeping, like a girl's. She'd call them tender if he'd been a female. He really is the oddest mixture, she thought, deliberately moving her mind away from the fact that he was turning her on, the oddest mixture, even to his clothes, the only man I know who would wear a classy watch with an old jersey. It wouldn't hurt him to be polite. That's all I want.

But he drove on in silence and eventually they left the entertainment of the London streets and took to the M1 where there was nothing to look at except cars spewing water from their wheels, the stained backsides of innumerable, trundling lorries and rain bouncing off the tarmac. Although he switched on the radio, he still didn't speak. The road went monotonously on. It felt as though they'd been driving for days.

They passed Luton in silence, drove through Bedfordshire without a word, passed signs directing them to Coventry, Leicester, Nottingham. She'd never kept quiet for such a long time in the whole of her life. If this goes on much longer, she told herself, I shall forget *how* to speak.

Finally, when they'd reached a stretch of

open road where the driving was easy she decided to tackle him straight out.

'Look,' she said. 'We can't drive all the way to York without speaking. I know you didn't want me to take the flat but it's done now. Can't we just accept it and get on with it?'

He was monosyllabic with annoyance. 'It's nothing to do with me.'

'Then why won't you talk to me?'

His face was sterner than she'd ever seen it. 'There's nothing to talk about.'

'Yes, there is. There's always something to talk about. What you're saying is, there's something you *don't* want to talk about.'

He was angered to be subjected to such criticism. Damn you, he thought, and turned his head to look at her. It disconcerted him that she looked so sure of herself, skin glowing, brown eyes gleaming, and her head held up with such confidence it really annoyed him. There was nothing for it. She would have to be crushed. 'I didn't know actresses had to be trained in psychology these days.'

She laughed. Infuriating woman! 'I don't need psychology to see what's going on. That's just common observation. Which we *are* trained in. You're not talking to me because you're cross about me taking the flat.'

And she looked at him boldly, urging him to admit it.

'All right then,' he said, angrily. 'I don't approve, if you really want to know. It isn't suitable.'

'That's your opinion. I don't share it. And neither do your parents.'

'I went out of my way to provide you with proper accommodation, if you remember. That *would* have been suitable and you . . .'

'Dared to question your judgement,' she mocked. 'That's what all this is about, isn't it. I didn't do as I was told.'

'No,' he said glaring at her. 'That's not what it's about. It's . . .' He was so cross that it took him a second to think what it was. 'It's a matter of my professional judgement.'

'Oh I see,' she mocked. 'If it's your *professional judgement* nobody can question it, is that it?'

It was exactly what he meant but the tone of her voice made him feel he was in the wrong. The little space inside the car was bristling with bad temper, as if they were shooting darts at one another. 'There's no point in making professional judgements,' he told her stiffly, 'if they're just going to be ignored.'

He was driving alarmingly fast and his

speed increased her anger. 'You might be a good doctor,' she said, 'all right, you *are* a good doctor, a very good doctor, but you can't read people's minds. Doesn't it ever occur to you that sometimes — just sometimes — your patients might know what's best for them?'

'No,' he said. 'It doesn't.'

She erupted into fury at that. 'That's so bloody arrogant.'

He was hot with anger too. 'You're the one who's arrogant,' he said, shooting a furious glance at her. 'You think you know better than anyone: doctors, nurses, social workers, you name it. I shouldn't think you've ever done as you were told, not once in the whole of your life.'

That was a bit too near the knuckle. 'What I've done in the rest of my life is my affair, not yours.'

'You can dish it out, you see,' he said, with great satisfaction, 'but you can't take it.'

'It's not a matter of taking it. This is irrelevant.'

'If you really *had* studied psychology, you'd know that the irrelevant is invariably the most significant.'

It was hideously true. And what was worse it had made her lose the thread of her argument. She glowered at him, struggling to reorganise her thoughts.

Victory! he thought and couldn't resist clinching it. 'Now,' he said, with infuriating calm, 'I suggest we stop all this nonsense and get on with the drive.'

'Right!' she said, pink-cheeked. 'That's it! Stop the car! I want to get out.'

He increased his speed. 'We're in the middle of a motorway, you stupid woman.'

'Don't you call me a stupid woman. I know we're on a motorway.' Actually she hadn't even thought about it. 'Turn off at the next junction. I want to get out.'

'And then what?' he said, giving her a sardonic grin. 'What are you going to do then? Drive back to London in your wheelchair?'

That was below the belt. She didn't know what she wanted to do. Only that she couldn't sit in this car with him. 'I'll find a way, don't you worry. Turn off at the next junction,' she said.

'The next junction is twenty miles on.'

It wasn't. It couldn't be.

'There's a road map in the glove compartment. See for yourself.'

She was so full of anger she wanted to scream. She turned her body away from him and glared out of the window. 'Don't talk to me!' she said.

He was triumphant. 'My point exactly!' he said.

The rain bounced on the road ahead, sharp as needles. Anger was making her skin prickle and her heart jump in her chest as if it was struggling to get out. And there was nothing she could do. Bloody motorway! Bloody rain! Bloody doctors!

They drove on. And on and on. They listened to the four o'clock news in heavy silence, left the motorway at six, still not speaking. Finally, after a lifetime of brooding bad temper and private self-justification, they passed a road sign directing them to Poppleton. Nearly there, thank God.

And suddenly he turned his head and spoke to her. 'There's Rob's garden centre,' he said.

They were passing a field fenced by flag poles, a long low bungalow building marked by a green neon sign, PENGILLY'S OF POPPLETON, a phalanx of garden sheds standing in ranks like well-drilled troops, and rows and rows of evergreen trees and shrubs, neat as toys and silhouetted black against the royal blue of a high clear sky. She realised that the rain must have stopped at some point while they were driving and was surprised that she hadn't noticed. But as he'd condescended to speak at last she decided she would answer.

'Who's Rob?'

'Sue's husband.'

'Does he work there?'

His answer was infuriatingly superior. 'Actually he owns it.'

They're rich, Gemma thought, and despite her determination not to be put down, her heart sank a little. He's bloody superior and they're bloody rich. What a good job I brought my silk blouse.

They drove over a level crossing, past a station like a Victorian doll's house, down a long straight well-lit road, where all the houses were neat and affluent, and reached a village green. This was obviously a very well-heeled place.

The road they were following curved and twisted and here the houses stood apart from one another, hidden behind the tangled branches of bare trees and thick hedges. They passed a library and a school. The road curved again and he drove through open gates toward a mansion. Oh it would be, wouldn't it. A wide paved drive lay before a white house, late Victorian and extremely elegant, all windows blazing light. There were cars parked all over the drive, pop music throbbed a welcome from the open door, coloured lanterns glowed among the trees. What a place! she thought. I shall need all my skill to cope with this.

After that things happened very quickly and in some confusion. Before Nick could lift the wheelchair from the boot and let her out of the car, two small girls tumbled out of the front door squealing that Uncle Nick had come and hurled themselves towards him. They had the same fair hair cut in identical bobs, and wore identical black velvet trousers, white cropped tops and huge chunky boots. And they were both very excited. As soon as he saw them Nick stopped looking stern, grinned at them broadly and swept them up, one after the other, to swing them round and round. Then he and the car were surrounded by people who were all introducing themselves to Gemma. There were too many to take in all at once, but she managed to register that Sue was tall and elegant and welcoming, wore a long straight dress made of cream silk and a superb pair of diamond earrings and was clearly in command.

'Where are the ageds?' she said to Nick. 'I thought you were all coming together.' And without waiting for him to answer, 'You've got a wheelchair, haven't you, Gemma? Someone bring it round this side. That's it. I've put you in the den. It's the best place on the ground floor and there's the downstairs loo alongside. I'll show you. Did you bring a bag?'

The den was a huge room at the back of the house, with a pool table in one corner, a console television in another and a bar in a third. There was concealed lighting at every vantage point, faintly pink to match the décor, original watercolours on the walls, and a variety of easy chairs and sofas scattered luxuriously about the room. One had been converted into a bed in the fourth corner.

'There,' Sue said. 'Will this do?'

Gemma felt as though she'd been ushered into a five-star hotel. 'It's gorgeous,' she said.

'I'll give you a few minutes to settle in,' Sue told her. 'We're in the drawing room. Follow the racket. The do's in the Fox. We'll be leaving in about half an hour. OK?'

Then I shall have to work quickly, Gemma thought, and set about her transformation at once, washing as well as she could, changing into her silk, working on her hair until the worst of the scar was covered, making up her face as though she was going on stage. Which, in a way, she was. Whatever happens, she told the image in her hand mirror, whatever anyone says — and especially Nick — you're going to be on top of it.

Finally, with a last glance at her image, she went to join the party.

Racket was the right word for it. The noise was deafening. The long drawing room was full of people, drinking and talking, and children of various sizes, all blondes and all running about as if they were playing tag. Down at the far end was a grand piano — it would be grand! — where a group of men were listening to Andrew and Catherine, who'd just arrived. She couldn't see Nick among so many bodies, but then, as she was beginning to realise, it is hard to distinguish one person from another when your viewpoint is the middle of their chests.

Ah well, she thought, plucking up her courage. It's no good sitting here. And she drove towards the nearest group of legs.

'I'm Gemma,' she said. 'The lodger.'

One of the men put his hand on the arm of her chair and leant towards her. 'I'm Tom,' he said. 'One of Rob's brothers.'

'One?' she said, shaking his hand and smiling. 'You make it sound as though there are lots.'

'There are,' he told her. 'There's seven of us. We were quite a brood. Four brothers, three sisters. Let me introduce you. These are the girls, Anne, Maureen, Gill. You'll remember Gill. She's the little one with the loud voice.'

'I love you too,' Gill said to him as she shook hands.

All three women were as blonde as their children and very friendly. They smiled and teased and laughed a lot, and none of them made any mention of the wheelchair or her injuries because they were too busy looking at Sue. 'They're a lovely couple,' Anne told her. 'We're ever so fond of them.'

Presently Andrew arrived with a glass of wine and a rug. 'See you got here safely,' he said. 'Try that.' He handed her the glass.

She accepted the wine happily but bridled at the sight of the rug. There was no need to treat her like an invalid. 'I've got a coat,' she said. 'I shan't need that.'

He laughed at her. 'It's to keep your toes warm while we walk to the pub,' he said, 'and you're not to argue about it. We're all going across on foot, so that we can drink, and it's a fair old way. You can take it off the minute we get there.' And when she grimaced: 'Trust me. I'm a doctor!'

Somebody was calling over the din. 'All set?' The blonde girls were putting on their jackets. They all seemed to be wearing the same — short, black and padded with black fur collars — as if they were in uniform. Then people began to drift into the hall, depositing glasses on chairs and tables as they went, and Gemma looked at her wine and finished it quickly.

'Come along everybody,' Sue said, appearing at her side. 'More drinks when you get there.'

But just as they were all moving through the hall, the phone rang.

Sue answered it on her way past, holding her free hand over her ear so that she could hear. 'Yes? . . . What?' Then her face bloomed into a delighted smile and she turned to quieten her guests, flicking her fingers at them. 'It's Chris! Shush! Shush! It's my brother from Canada . . . Chris. Yes. Lovely to hear you. No not yet. We're on our way out now . . . Yes, it has. Wonderful . . . He's here. Do you want to speak to him?'

Then there was a long pause while her guests stood around in the hall, waiting patiently and trying to pretend they weren't eavesdropping.

'Yes,' she said eventually. 'That's what we all think. You know Dad. We're quite proud of him actually. I never reckoned he'd make much of a gardener, anyway. Did you? . . . No . . . Hasn't got the patience . . . Yes, yes. I will. Love to Lorraine. And the kids. Yes . . . Thanks for ringing.'

'He was phoning from the conference centre,' she explained as she put the receiver down. 'They've just broken for lunch so he thought he'd phone and wish us many happy returns. Wasn't that nice. Sent his love to you, Dad. He's heard about the broadcast.'

Nick strolled out of the drawing room. 'Didn't want to speak to his little brother, I see,' he pretended to complain.

Sue pulled a face at him. 'You haven't been married fifteen years,' she said. 'What d'you expect? Come on everybody or we shall be late.'

So the party set off along the winding road, Gemma in her wheelchair, Nick walking ahead talking to his father and the kids singing and dancing as they went. It was clear to Gemma that this was going to be a great party, even if Nick didn't approve of her being there. And equally clear that Chris's phone call had set the seal on it. They're all so fond of each other, she thought, tucking her hands under the rug, and the thought made her warm.

The Fox turned out to be a large pub, set well back from the road so as to allow the maximum space for parking cars. They trooped through the ranks of Fords and Vauxhalls and into the building, still singing. Gemma had a vague impression of a bar and a narrow corridor full of legs and backsides, and then they were in a long beamed dining room, hung about with fairy lights and crammed with people who were milling about among the chairs and tables set ready for dinner. To make the crush worse, there were four brick columns rising in the midst of the tables, cheerfully abounce with balloons. They took up a lot of space and would make it difficult for her to manoeuvre the chair. She had a glimpse of a group of black-clad waiters and waitresses standing behind a serving bar to her right and, peering through the crush, saw that there were two large curved windows on the far wall, cosily curtained, and between them a disco going full, light-pulsing blast.

Catherine reappeared and led her to the head of one of the side tables where a space had been left for her chair. She noticed that Nick had taken himself off to another table on the far side of the room and was nodding in conversation with two men on either side of him. But then a man in a red shirt stood on a chair and yelled 'Happy Anniversary!' and the guests cheered and the party began and there wasn't time to think about him or anything else.

Food, wine, muzak thrumming and throbbing, a confusion of voices, speaking party platitudes. 'I'm a neighbour. That's my little boy, Kevin, down the end.' 'Have you come far?' 'Oh that's a long way!' 'How did you get here?' And speeches — from a man with a beard, saying what a fine couple the Pengillys were — from Dr Quennell, saying fifteen years hardly seemed any time at all to him, although he knew Naomi and Helen wouldn't agree with that — the two little blonde girls calling out 'No, we wouldn't, Grandpa' and getting a round of applause — and finally from another bearded man in a checked shirt who thanked everyone for coming and told them the bar would be open while the floor was being cleared.

There were several minutes of such utter confusion as tables were cleared and pushed to the sides of the room and chairs were carried about and rearranged, that Gemma thought it politic to get out of the way and drove herself off to the disabled toilet.

It was already occupied and there was a queue of children gathered beside the door and jigging to the music.

'What have you done with your leg?' one

267

of the boys asked. It was such a sudden and unexpected question it made her catch her breath.

'I broke it,' she said, looking down at the plaster sticking out from under her skirt.

'No,' he insisted. 'The other one. The one that's missing.'

She'd known this was the sort of question that would come sooner or later, and tried to steel herself to face it, but it gave her a shock even so. 'I lost it in a rail crash,' she said.

They were all very interested, gathering round her chair, and staring at the bandaged stump.

'What happened to it?' a little girl asked.

'It was crushed.'

'Where?'

'Under the train,' Gemma said, adding before they could ask her, 'They had to cut it off to get me out.' Now maybe they'll have had enough.

But there is no end to the natural curiosity of the young.

'What do they do with people's legs when they chop them off?' the first boy asked. 'Do they bury them?'

'I don't know,' Gemma admitted. It was the first time she'd thought about it. 'I don't suppose there was much of it left by the time they came to clear the tracks.'

'Ugh!' the boy said, delighted. 'Was it squashed to bits? Did they have to pick all the bits out? Ugh!'

For a sudden and terrible second, Gemma had a vision of her legs as they'd been when she last saw them, long and elegant in her new jeans, lovely, strong, elegant, striding legs. And she would never see them again. Never be long-legged and striding again. Then she realised that she was on the edge of tears, that if she stayed with these awful prying children another moment she would be howling. She looked around wildly for a way to get clear of them.

The loo door was opening. Rescue was at hand. 'Excuse me,' she said, propelling the chair past her innocent tormentors. 'My need is greater than yours.' She got into the cubicle just in time.

Tears streamed down her cheeks in a terrible outpouring of grief and mourning. She couldn't stop them and she didn't try to. Her leg was gone. She was stuck in a chair. Nothing would ever be the same again. And there was nothing she could do but cry. Nothing, nothing, nothing.

Presently she became aware of women's voices outside the cubicle.

'Hop it, you lot. You're not disabled.'

'Neither are you,' a boy's voice said cheekily.

'We're old. We got privileges. Hop it.'

'Who's going first?'

'It's engaged.'

'Oh bugger. I thought we could jump the queue. Who's in there, do you know?'

'Could be the kid in the wheelchair.'

'Yeah. 'Spose so. Poor little devil.' The voices were receding as they walked away. 'What happened to her? Does anyone know?'

'She's the one in the Wandsworth rail crash. The one that was in all the papers. *You* remember.'

'Well I never. I thought her face was familiar. Well good luck to her, poor kid.'

Their sympathy stanched Gemma's tears. Right, she said to herself. You've had your cry. You knew this would happen, and it has, and you've coped with it. Now you can stop feeling sorry for yourself. You're not going to let *anyone* feel sorry for you. You're going to get back in there and show them.

She used the loo — pleased that the handrails were in the right place for her — washed her hands and her face, and repaired her make-up, very carefully. A brave face, she thought, examining it critically.

That's what you need and that's what you're going to put on.

But the party had another blow for her. While she'd been away, the floor had been cleared of tables, the chairs pushed back against the wall, and all the lights dimmed. The disco was playing pop and in the middle of the floral carpet there was a neat square of parquet where all the little girls were solemnly dancing, rocking and swaying on their thin legs, their huge boots clumsy as weights.

She felt such a yearning to dance that it made her chest ache. No, she thought, I can't just sit here and watch. It's too much. I'll have to do it eventually. I know that. But not yet. Not just yet. I'll go outside for a little while. Have a few minutes' peace and quiet. Cool my face and clear my head. I wouldn't like anyone to see I've been crying.

She turned the chair and headed off towards the corridor and the entrance, smiling at the people she passed. There'd been a ramp over the step when she came in and with luck it would still be there. Yes. It was. And so out, out, into the cold and reasonable air of a clear night.

Chapter 15

The garden was full of little boys. Gangs of them were swinging from the branches of a tree, two were belting after one another among the parked cars, and down on the sloping lawn of the garden an excited mob was playing an impromptu game of football, their shouts as sharp as barks above the pounding beat of the disco.

So much for peace and quiet, Gemma thought. But she couldn't go back in again. Not while she was feeling so vulnerable. Then she saw one of the bearded men, the one in the checked shirt who'd given the welcoming speech. He was leaning against the trunk of a tree, smoking a cigarette, the red tip glowing as he inhaled. As she hesitated, he looked across at her. 'You escaping too?' he said.

He sounded so much at ease and was smiling at her in such a friendly way, that she went to join him. If he was her host, it was only polite. 'Not for a smoke,' she said. 'It's the dance I'm running away from. I used to love dancing and now . . .'

'Ah! Is this your first party since the accident?'

'Yes.'

'The next one will be better,' he said, smiling at her again.

'Once I've got my plaster off and they've fitted my new leg,' she said, reassuring them both. 'It's just at the moment it's a bit hard.'

He drew on his cigarette, exhaling the smoke in two long white streams, like a dragon snorting. She noticed he was careful to blow them away from her direction.

'I'm allowed one before the dance,' he explained. 'Then Sue and I have to lead off.'

'I thought that was who you were,' she said. 'I wasn't sure. I expect they introduced us but . . .'

'Among a hundred and fifty others,' he smiled. 'It's a wonder you can remember any of us.'

'Well, thanks for putting me up. It's very kind of you. And congratulations on your anniversary.'

'You're welcome.' His cigarette was almost finished. 'I think I'll have just one more,' he said. 'Then I'll take to the floor. Don't tell Sue.'

There was something in the way he said 'take to the floor' that roused her sympathy. 'You don't like dancing.' She understood.

'Not much. It's ironic, isn't it.'

She looked at him, taking him in and trying to read him. He wasn't the sort of man you would notice in a crowd, although he was tall and rangy in his jeans and that checked shirt. He wasn't the most obvious partner for Sue, either, in her fashionable clothes and her diamond earrings. But he *was* attractive. There was no doubt about that. And all of a piece, his face still and composed, his hair and beard thick but neatly trimmed, the hand that raised the cigarette to his mouth long-fingered and delicate. He's happy in his skin, she thought. That's what it is. That's why he's so easy to talk to. There was a peacefulness about him, a sense of gentleness and repose. It was calming her simply to sit beside him.

'You were an actress, weren't you,' he said after a pause. 'Before.'

'Yes.'

'Sue told me. Will you go back to it?'

'If I can land a part. It's not a secure job at the best of times.'

'Is any job?' he asked, wryly.

She thought about it. 'Probably not. Now.'

'If you'll take my advice,' he said, 'you'll find yourself a second one. To be on the safe side. I tell the kids that. It's no good thinking you can hold down one job for a life-time. You have to be prepared to change, or you get left behind.'

She was impressed by the sense of it. 'Actually,' she said, 'the college I went to trained us to teach drama as well as act. If everything else fails, I suppose I *could* do that.'

'Would you like to?'

'Not much,' she said honestly. 'But it would be better than nothing.'

'We're all in the same boat now,' he went on. 'No job's really safe. Bank managers used to be, executives, people like that. Not any more. It's the age of insecurity.'

She wondered whether his garden centre was at risk but didn't feel she could ask. Probably not. He didn't seem to be insecure about anything. But then she hardly knew him and he could be the sort of man who kept his problems hidden.

'We must go in,' he said, stubbing out his second cigarette. 'Or you'll take cold and I'll take a scolding.'

Gemma couldn't imagine anyone scold-ing him. He seemed too gentle. She de-cided to watch and see how he would be received when they got back into the dining room.

The Quennell family were sitting at the

bar, drinks in hand and head to head in conversation.

'So that's what I reckon,' Sue said. 'I'm being head-hunted. Three lunches in a fortnight. It has to be that.' She was a little the worse for drink or she wouldn't have been confiding in them so freely. Not at this early stage anyway. But now that she'd begun, she was glad she'd spoken because her mother looked so proud.

'Is it a much better job?' she asked.

'Oh yes. Much better. Tougher, natch. But the pay's astronomical.'

'It would be,' Nick laughed at her.

'You'll be able to look after us in our old age then,' Andrew teased.

'From what I hear you'll be able to look after yourselves,' Sue teased back. 'Aren't you the guru of the Health Service?'

He preened but tried to answer modestly. 'So they say.'

'What with you and Gemma,' Sue said, 'there's hardly room for anything else in the papers these days.'

'They're leaving her alone at the moment,' Catherine said. 'Which is just as well. They really hounded her when she was in St Thomas's.'

'But wasn't that because of the compensation?' Sue asked.

'That was a fairy tale,' Catherine told her.

That was news good enough to sober her daughter. 'Was it?'

'So she says. Her mother told the press, apparently. It was all wishful thinking.'

'Then she isn't going to sue?'

'Not for half a million, anyway,' Andrew said. 'She's not that kind of girl.' And when Sue made a doubting face. 'Oh come on, Sue. Look at her. She's not greedy.'

'I can vouch for that,' Catherine put in. 'She's a giver, not a taker.'

Nick made a wry face. You should have seen the way she was going on in the car, he thought. But his parents were concentrating on Susan and didn't notice.

Susan sipped her Martini. 'I wish you'd told me this at the beginning,' she said. 'It would have made my life a lot easier. We spent a lot of time at the inquiry wondering what she was going to do.'

'I didn't know myself until yesterday,' Andrew said. 'She told us at dinner, didn't she Kate?' He was glancing round the room, looking for Gemma. She'd been gone for rather a long time. 'Where's she got to? She ought to be back by now.'

And then suddenly there she was, motoring into the room with Rob beside her, smiling and talking. 'I thought you'd been kidnapped,' he said, as she joined the group.

'Only by me,' Rob told them.

Sue smiled at him lop-sidedly. 'Ready?' she asked. When he nodded, she linked her arm in his and led him to the dance floor. Her elegant head was so close to his shoulder that she was almost resting on it.

That's a love match, Gemma thought, watching them. And she was even more sure of it when they began to dance, for Sue moved into his arms as if that were the most natural place for her to be, and although he danced awkwardly, shuffling his feet, he held her with an obvious tenderness.

Their appearance on the dance floor changed the mood of the occasion. The band began to play 'The Anniversary Waltz', all the other couples stood aside, the children were called off the floor to make way for them and their guests applauded as they danced alone in the centre of the room — and of everyone's attention. And as if *that* were the most natural thing in the world too, Rob bent his dark head and kissed her.

'Aren't they lovely,' Gemma said.

'Well we think so,' Catherine said. 'But then, we're biased.'

'Enjoying yourself?' Andrew asked.

The answer was entirely accurate. Now. 'Very much.'

'Come and join us,' he suggested as the dance ended. 'We've got a table over there. I think we could squeeze you in. You too, Nick.'

She was quite surprised when Nick agreed. Affection for his sister must have made him more affable.

So they were both seated at the table and given another drink and Nick spent the next few minutes talking to his father about 'a difficult case' while the floor gradually re-filled with dancers. Now Gemma didn't worry about sitting it out. She was in good company and that was pleasure enough.

After a while, Nick wandered off to dance with his sister while Rob partnered his daughters, one after the other, and Andrew 'took a turn' with Catherine. The dances went noisily on, growing steadily faster and less and less inhibited. Soon, Rob's three sisters were prancing in line like chorus girls and Sue was hanging round Rob's neck, cheerfully squiffy. Rob's brother Tom flung his jersey to the ground and danced on his own, to raucous applause, shirt-sleeves flapping. Even the little girls shed their solemnity and began to sing and smile. The dance floor was visibly heaving under the weight of so many stomping feet and the bar was doing continual trade.

Then the DJ turned the volume down to announce that the next dance was by special request. As soon as the song began there was a roar of recognition and the dancers scrambled to sit on the floor, legs astride and one behind the other. It was 'The Rowing Boat Song'.

'*Oops upside yer head,*' they sang. '*I said, Oops upside yer head.*'

Andrew appeared beside the table, grinning broadly. 'This one is for you,' he said to Gemma. 'And don't say you can't do it. Come on!'

The announcement startled her. The thought of being down on the floor with the tenderness of her stump exposed to all those trampling feet made her tense with alarm. What if it gets kicked? she thought. What if I can't move it out of the way in time? Yet the thought of being part of a dance again was terribly tempting.

'I'll carry you there,' Andrew said and he bent towards her to lift her out of the chair.

'Oh for God's sake,' Nick's voice rebuked him from somewhere behind him. 'You'll give yourself a hernia. Let me.'

And before Gemma could protest, he was standing in front of her, lifting her bodily out of the chair, carrying her to the dance floor.

The impact of being so close to him took

her breath away and spun her thoughts into an impossible turmoil. He can't be doing this, she thought. But he *was*. I shouldn't be feeling like this. But she *was*.

'Put your arm round my neck,' he said, and even his voice was different.

She did as she was told, overwhelmed by sensation. However this had happened, she wanted it to go on for ever.

But in ten strides they were at the end of the line of seated dancers and he was lowering her to the floor behind Gill, 'the little sister with the loud voice'.

'Hold on,' he said, sitting behind her. It surprised them both but her obvious vulnerability had roused his protective instincts and he was obeying them almost without thought. He leant forward, guarding her injured leg with his arm as more dancers rushed to sit behind him. 'Don't worry,' he reassured her. 'I won't let anyone hurt you.'

'I don't know how to do this dance,' she admitted. Now that he was being so gentle it was possible to let him know how exposed she felt.

'There's nothing to it,' he told her, his cheek against hers. 'Just follow Gill. She's an expert.'

So she followed the movements of the dance and nobody trod on her and after a while she relaxed and began to enjoy her-self. Soon she was singing along with the rest and dancing with abandon. It was the best fun she'd had in a very long time. So much so that when the record came to an end, hers was the loudest voice demanding a repeat performance. '*I don't believe you wanna get up and dance,*' they sang. And she sang with them, thinking how very apposite the words were. If she could dance on the floor, she *didn't* want to get up and dance. By the end of the second playing she was stupid with laughter. This time, when Nick picked her up to carry her back to her chair, she put her arm round his neck, without be-ing told. And this time he looked straight into her eyes and they were both caught up in the sudden magic of desire. He wanted to kiss her and she knew it. She wanted to stay in his arms for hours and he knew that.

But then Rob came lolloping over to tell them they were going to have another floor dance later, and the moment was lost.

The rest of the evening was a happy blur. There was a lot of singing and two more floor dances, as Rob had promised. And on each occasion Nick carried her to the floor, as slowly as he could, and bore her back again taut with desire. The smallest chil-dren fell asleep, some in their mothers' laps, some across two chairs; the bar staff struggled to collect empty glasses; a young man fell on the floor and couldn't get up again, so they left him where he was and walked round him; and most of the couples, including Rob and Sue, were dancing in a dream with their arms about each other. It seemed for ever and no time at all and it was midnight and time for the last waltz.

Rob and his guests walked home along the empty lane, carrying children and happily exhausted. Gemma was so tired she hadn't even got the energy to clean her teeth or to drink the coffee that Sue had left beside her bed, 'as a nightcap'. She'd forgotten about her mother, the compensation offer, the return of her father, even her injuries. All she could think about was the extraordinary events of the day, their long silent journey and their quarrel in the car, the amazement of being in his arms. There was no sense in any of it and yet it had all happened. She would have to think it all out. She tossed her clothes on the floor, fell back into her luxurious bed and was asleep before she could pull the duvet over her plastered leg.

Chapter 16

The spare bedroom where Nick was supposed to be sleeping was directly above the den. It was the room he was usually given when he came to visit his sister and until that night he'd occupied it without giving its position a thought. Now, muddled by drink and the conflict of unexpected emotions, he'd been wakeful most of the night. Wakeful and horny, because there were sounds of love-making emanating from all the bedrooms around him, smothered giggles, throaty murmurs, amorous creaking. Sitting up, plagued and open-eyed, it occurred to him that there was hardly a room in the house that wasn't occupied by a loving couple, except his and Gemma's, and she was so close that he could visualise the space she was occupying in the room below him, fancied he could hear her breathing, even imagined he could feel sparks flying up towards him through the carpet. How could he be expected to settle with all that going on?

Eventually he must have slept, because he

woke with a start to the sound of frantic weeping and the crash of breaking china. He knew it was Gemma, even before he was capable of thought, and was out of the bed at once and straight down the stairs, alarmed and alert, pulling on his bathrobe as he went.

Down in the den, Gemma had woken weeping in terror as she so often did these days. She couldn't remember where she was and as she turned and twisted, her arms flailing, her hand hit the edge of a table. From the corner of her eye, she saw a cup spinning in the air, throwing up a curve of brown liquid as it fell, heard the smash as it hit the wall, and looked down to see the broken halves of it lying on the pink carpet among a scattering of small white chips, and an ominous dark stain where the liquid was seeping into the pile.

She was furious at herself for being so clumsy. Oh Christ! she scolded, as she hauled herself into a sitting position. What a thing to do in her beautiful room! How could you be so stupid? She knew she had to clean it up quickly before the stain spread any further and looked around desperately for something to use as a mop. But there was nothing. Her discarded clothes were too far away. I'll have to get up, she thought, and see if I can find a cloth in the loo or somewhere.

There was someone outside the door, calling her name. 'Gemma! Are you all right?'

'Yes,' she called back, feeling caught out. 'It's nothing.'

The voice insisted. 'Gemma?' And this time she recognised it.

'It's all right,' she said, trying to sound dismissive.

But he came in anyway, in a blue bathrobe, with his feet bare, his chin dark with overnight stubble and a large expanse of hairy leg visible below the robe. Two legs, for God's sake! He should be so lucky! She didn't know whether she was cross or relieved to see him.

'I heard a smash,' he said, tactfully ignoring the cries. '*Are* you all right?' She was sitting on the edge of the bed, getting ready to heave herself into her chair, and his flesh rose just to look at her, those round arms rosy with sleep, her breasts under that T-shirt, her lovely thick hair bushy and tousled, that chin jutting with determination — her breasts under that T-shirt.

'Did I wake you up?' she asked. Now the others would be down. And the stain was growing by the second.

'No,' he reassured her. 'I was awake. Do you want a hand?'

No, she didn't and said so crossly. 'I've broken a cup,' she explained, as she manoeuvred into the chair, 'and there's coffee on the carpet.'

The doctor in him took over. She was his patient, she needed care and she wasn't in any fit state to clean carpets. 'Leave it to me,' he said, walking round to the side of the bed to examine the stain. 'Don't worry. It'll wash out if we're quick. This is washable carpet. It's her speciality. I'll get a cloth.'

'Tell me where it is . . .' she was beginning.

The door opened and Andrew appeared, massive in the door frame, wearing a paisley dressing gown and an inquisitive expression. 'Trouble?' he asked.

They answered him with one voice, neither of them pleased to see him. 'No. We can manage.'

'Nightmare, was it?' he said to Gemma.

His assumption was so certain she had to admit it. 'But it's all right,' she told him. 'I'm over it now. I broke a cup. That's the only problem.'

'And I'm going to clear it up,' Nick said, heading for the door. 'If you'll excuse me.'

'Post traumatic stress,' Andrew diagnosed. 'It's very common after what you've been through. I should have thought of it before. You probably need counselling. I'll get on to John Barnaby and arrange it for you.'

'No,' Gemma said at once, alarmed to be put under pressure. The one thing she didn't want was counselling. The idea of telling her deepest fears to a stranger was abhorrent. 'I can cope. It's been much worse. I'm getting over it.'

'What she needs is a cup of tea and some breakfast,' Nick told his father firmly. 'Which we're going to get as soon as I've cleared up the carpet. If I were you, Dad, I'd go back to bed and finish off your beauty sleep and just let us get on with it.'

It was a direct challenge and all three of them knew it, Andrew weighing up the situation, thinking hard, Nick emboldened by his own daring but alarmed by it too, Gemma watching them with some trepidation in case they had a row. The moment held for a very long time, as the two men stood eye to eye. Then suddenly and rather to Gemma's surprise Andrew backed down.

'OK,' he said, grinning at his son. 'I'll leave it in your hands, then.' He gave Gemma a smile and went.

She could see the tension leaving Nick's shoulders. 'Right,' he said. 'Let's get this cleared up and then we'll put the kettle on.'

I'll bet that's the first time he's ever stood up to his father like that, she thought. He was holding his head in such a cocky way, as if he'd taken on the world. But she didn't comment. Matters between them were too delicate for that. She wheeled out to the washroom to get dressed and left him to clean the carpet and pick up the chips of china. If there was anything to say, they could say it over breakfast.

After the drama of her waking, the house was quiet and very peaceful. As they ate their cornflakes, they could hear trains in the distance, but they were too faint and far away to be alarming and there were no other sounds at all: no traffic, no feet on the stairs and no voices. Outside in the garden, pale sunshine striped the lawn and patterned the trunks of the trees with streaks of palest green. The bare branches were richly brown against an autumnal sky. It's going to be a lovely day, Gemma thought. If only I hadn't begun it so badly.

She hasn't got over that nightmare, Nick thought, reading her expression. She probably doesn't know it, but she does need to talk. And that gave him an idea. 'I tell you what,' he said, as he put their dirty cups and bowls in the dishwasher, 'why don't we go for a walk? The others won't be up for ages and this weather's too good to waste.'

It was an excellent suggestion but she didn't want to annoy her hosts. 'Won't they miss us?'

'We'll leave them a note.'

That solved the problem and the note was written — with a PS.

Dear Sue, I'm sorry about the damp patch on the carpet. I knocked over a cup of coffee. I hope it won't stain. Nick has cleaned it.

Gemma

Then Nick got dressed, they found their coats in the hall and, whispering like conspirators, off they went.

It was a crisp Sunday morning, and they had it entirely to themselves. Frost tipped the long grass with white feathers, the lane was dew-damp and edged with squashy mud, cattle blew steam from their nostrils, placidly observing the world from behind the denuded hedges. The sky was the colour of a thrush's egg. A lovely, lovely day.

'I've been having nightmares too,' he confessed, hoping that would make her feel easier.

'I'm not surprised. It *was* pretty hairy.'

'Worse for you than me.'

'You're not going to suggest counselling, are you?' The question was half warning, half hope of a sensible reply.

'Not everyone needs it,' he told her. 'Depends if you get depressed.' And he gave her a grin. 'I'd say there's too much anger in you for that.'

They were both remembering their journey. 'You can say that again,' she admitted. Nightmare still lurked in the lower reaches of her mind and she needed something else to talk about — but not the journey and not their ridiculous row. In the clear light of this gentle morning it shamed her to remember it.

But at that moment, they turned a bend in the road and there was the inn. Just the thing. 'Good Lord!' she said. 'Is that the Fox?'

'That's the Fox.'

'I wouldn't have recognised it,' she said. 'It looks different.' And ordinary, now that there were no lights and no music and no excited party-goers. The concrete expanse of the empty car park looked vast in the daylight and totally out of place beside the neat grass verges that fronted the Georgian houses further up the road. 'Quite different.'

'Come and see the garden,' he said. 'That's pretty. They've got a little gazebo.' A quiet private place where they could be on their own and she could talk if she needed to. It might even have a seat so that she could get out of that damned chair. He was beginning to realise that one of the difficulties in talking to a girl in a wheelchair was that you couldn't get near her.

She looked puzzled. 'A what?'

'A gazebo. Come and see.'

It was a circular summerhouse, made of stone with a curved wall on the landward side and four slender pillars to face the river and hold up a round flat roof. It was circled by a pathway romantic with lichen but too broken to allow the passage of a chair. Worse, as he realised the moment he stepped inside the little building, it was much too dank and cold inside to encourage conversation.

'What's down there?' she asked, looking down the slope of the garden.

'The river.'

She could just see a gleam of pale blue water between the dark mesh of the branches.

'Could I get down?'

'You could try.'

They walked and wheeled until they came to a series of steps leading to a small jetty. But the steps were a disappointment too. Although they were gently spaced, there were far too many of them to be tackled in a wheelchair. Nick was beginning to get irritated. Wasn't there anywhere around here where they could sit and talk?

At that point he heard a motor boat approaching the jetty and the noise of American voices, talking excitedly.

A pleasure boat from York was pulling in, full of elderly tourists ready for their pub lunch. Plump and cheerful, they stomped up the path, the women in brightly coloured shell-suits, the men in anoraks and baseball caps, all of them hung about with cameras and all talking at once.

'Hi!' they said as they passed. 'Swell place you got here.'

'Are you staying long?' Nick asked.

'Just for lunch,' they told him. 'Then we got a coach drive to a place called Knaresborough. Gonna see Mother Shipton's Cave. Neat, eh?'

'I've got an idea,' Nickn said to Gemma. 'That boat's got to go back to York. Right? And it's empty. Right? So it can take us.

We'll have a day in York.'

It was a preposterous, wonderful, impossible idea. A day in York. Instead of spending her time in Sue's Ideal Home, feeling ashamed of herself for ruining the carpet, and out of place in her wheelchair, a day on the town. But practical as ever, she asked, 'Won't they wonder where we've gone?'

'We'll phone them when we get to York.'

There was another worry too. 'How am I going to get down all these steps?'

Steps didn't deter him in the slightest now. 'I'll carry you. Wait there!' He was already on his way down to the boat, leaping past the Americans and calling to the boatman: 'Two for the return journey.'

Gemma leant forward in her chair and watched him, admiring his long legs and envying his ability to run. She was downcast by her incapacity. If only she could have jumped out of this awful chair and run down the steps with him, instead of sitting in a bloody chair.

He was leaping back up the steps, splendidly tousled and slightly out of breath. 'Come on!' he ordered and picked her up in his arms.

This time the pleasure of it was so intense it took her breath away. She put one arm round his neck and settled her head against the warmth of his chest, the woollen cloth of his jacket soft and multicoloured under her cheek, the rhythm of his heart insistent under her ear, the scent of his skin now both familiar and exciting. She was glad that he had a distance to carry her — all the way down the steps and into the boat — and very loath to be put down again, especially on a wooden seat that struck decidedly cold.

'Won't be a minute,' he promised, blue eyes earnest. And he wasn't, hurtling down the steps with the chair and bounding back to sit beside her. The boatman cast off, the engine churned the river into a froth, and their day out began.

It was cold on the upper deck but neither of them cared because it was so wonderfully private. They sat on the back seat very close together, as the boat chugged them towards the city and ducks squawked away from their passing in a rush of white water and frantic wings. They were on their own, in a magical, blue and green world, enclosed by overhanging branches and green banks, with wide empty fields on either side and not a sign or sound of any other human being to disturb them — apart from the boatman, of course, and he had his back to them and was tactfully occupied at the wheel. They passed empty footpaths and mud banks where coots paddled among the weeds and unseen birds called and twittered in the branches. The pale sky arched above their heads and the wash of pale blue water spread into a gentle fan behind them. And at last, as the bells of the Minster rang out over the winter fields, Gemma began to talk out her pain.

'Have you had a lot of nightmares?' she asked, her face strained. 'If you don't mind me asking.'

'Yes,' he admitted, thinking, I was right. She does need to talk. 'I have. Especially in the first few days. I kept going back to it all the time. I couldn't get it out of my head.'

'I relive it,' she confessed. 'I have the same dream over and over again. Reliving it. It doesn't matter what I've been doing during the day.'

He waited, wondering whether he should say something to prompt her. But after a while she went on. 'Always the same,' she said, 'that awful carriage coming in on top of me and thinking, I shall be crushed. It's going to cut me in half.' And then she began to cry. 'Oh! I'm sorry.'

He put an arm round her and held her as she wept. 'It's all right,' he said. 'Cry all you like. There's no one to see you. You're safe with me.'

'I can't get away from it,' she wept. And out it all came in a torrent of stumbling phrases and shuddering memory. 'I could hear that little boy . . . and when I put up my hand it was covered in blood . . . And then the pain began . . . I shall never forget it. I thought I was going to die . . .'

'But you didn't. You came through.'

She found a tissue in her pocket and tried to dry her eyes. 'Oh God!' she said. 'I'm sorry to make such a fuss. I'm such a coward.'

'It's not a fuss,' he said. 'It's part of the healing process. Just go with it. And you're not a coward. You're the bravest girl I've ever met.'

'It didn't feel like brave to me,' she admitted, trying to force herself back to normal. 'It just felt inevitable. I can remember thinking, I'm going to die. I think I was accepting it. Well I *was* accepting it, until you came along.'

But she couldn't keep her voice steady and her tears flowed no matter how hard she tried to hold them back. Now that she'd unlocked them, memories surged into her mind, too strong to be denied, and everything she saw triggered another one. The sound of children squealing at play reminded her of the screams she'd heard, a sudden flight of finches was green as falling glass, even something as peaceful as a riverside path bordered by trees recalled her last glimpse of Wandsworth Common as the train rolled over.

They passed a derelict building, labelled YORKSHIRE HERALD but long out of use. The brickwork was fusty with grime and all the windows were smashed and splintered, gaping like a mouth full of broken teeth. And that brought a torrent of images, of broken debris, the filth and grease of that dreadful bogey, the terror in the darkness.

Even when they passed a huge modern building, a pseudo-castle of turrets and gables, expensively grand in cream stone and with bold black windows like empty eyes, she still cried, remembering the hospital and coming round in that white recovery room and having to face the loss of her leg.

'We're nearly there,' he warned, as she dried her eyes for the fifth time. 'This is Lendal Bridge. We stop here at the boatyard.'

She made such a valiant effort to control herself that it tore him to see it. 'It's all right,' she said. 'I *am* all right. Really.'

He was concerned because her eyes were red and her face blotchy with weeping. But they were manoeuvring into position at the boatyard and there was nothing he could do to hide her from inquisitive eyes now that they were in the city. Perhaps this hadn't been such a good idea after all. He took his time getting the chair ashore and carried her off the boat most gently, glad that it wasn't a thing that could be done in a hurry. Luckily it was a struggle to get out of the yard, and that took time too. The ground was rough, and the incline too steep for the chair's limited engine. But they finally managed it by a combination of her electricity and his muscle power, and found themselves in the isolated darkness of the tunnel under the river.

'We'll stop here for a minute or two,' he said, adding tactfully, 'I need to get my breath back.'

'Do I look a sight?' she asked.

'Not to me,' he said. 'Your eyes are a bit red, that's all.'

'I'll bet,' she said, making a self-deprecating face. But she was recovering. The horrors were receding. 'You won't tell anyone about this, will you?' she asked.

'Of course not,' he reassured her. 'Trust me. I'm a doctor.'

'That's what your father said last night,' she recalled.

'It's a family joke. Chris says it too. Fact, I think he started it.'

There was an oddly yearning expression on his face. 'You miss him.' She understood.

'I do rather. Well we all do, to be honest. But it's only for four years.' He grinned. 'Then he'll be back and driving us crazy and we'll be telling him to go away again.'

'I envy you,' she said, 'having a brother and a sister. I was an only.'

Which is why your mother's so heavy, he thought, but it wasn't something he wanted to talk about. Not yet anyway. 'OK to move on?' he asked.

She touched the skin under her eyes with her fingertips. 'Has it gone down a bit? I don't want people to stare. I'm sorry to sound so vain but you feel exposed when you're in a wheelchair.'

'They won't stare,' he promised. 'Come on.'

They emerged, blinking, into the bright daylight of the town. The streets were full of tourists, most of them Japanese. They walked in long trailing columns, meekly following the upheld umbrellas of their leaders and they were much too busy looking at the buildings to notice a girl in a wheelchair.

'This is Museum Street,' Nick told her, and waved at the park they were passing. 'The museum's in there but you don't want to see that, do you?'

'Are you taking me on a tour?' she wondered.

'If you like,' he said. 'Now we're here. It's a great place. We could go to a pub and have something to eat first, if you like. Then I'll take you round. What do you think?'

So they had a pub meal, rang Sue and explained where they were and then set off to see the sights, from Bootham Bar with its black portcullis at one end of the town to the little round keep of Clifford's Tower, aloof on its high green mound at the other. And Gemma gradually recovered her spirits. They went to the Minster, naturally, and along the Petergates, High and Low, to admire the Elizabethan shop front of Mulberry Hall and walk under the banner advertising the Star Inn and dodge in and out of another straggling column of Japanese tourists. They stopped in King's Square, which delighted Gemma because it was triangular, and listened to a flautist who was entertaining the crowds, with a coin-spotted cap at his feet. And then they reached the Shambles, where butchers' hooks were still visible above the shop windows and the upper storeys sagged into the lesser storeys below them like a row of fat ladies sitting on tiny stools.

Halfway down the street, Nick remembered the house where Saint Margaret had been crushed to death for her faith. That was far too near the knuckle for Gemma to see in her present tender state. He would have to try and smuggle her past before she asked questions. Fortunately the cobbles gave him the opportunity.

'They're not made for wheelchairs,' she said, as the chair rocked on the uneven stones.

'I shall have to push you,' he said and manoeuvred the chair rapidly along the rest of the street, off the cobbles and out of harm's way. 'Parliament Street next. Then we'll take a look at the Yorvik Centre. I've never been there, so it'll be new to me too.'

She was impressed by his knowledge of the place.

'We used to come here for half-term holidays,' he told her, 'when Sue and Rob were first living together. They had a flat in Blossom Street, over a shop.'

'You and Chris?'

'Yep. I was still in primary school then. It was great. Rob was a jobbing gardener in those days. He used to take us round to all these wild gardens and give us rides in wheelbarrows and squirt us with hoses.'

Gemma found it hard to imagine the elegant Sue putting up with that sort of behaviour. 'And what was Sue doing while all this went on?'

'She was at the university here. We used to meet up for lunch and then she'd cut lectures and he'd pack up work and we'd go to the pictures and after that we'd . . . Which reminds me. It's getting on for teatime. Let's go to Betty's and have tea and cakes.'

'I've done nothing but eat all day,' she protested. 'What about my figure?'

He dared a compliment. 'Your figure's perfect.'

'Oh this *has* been a lovely day!' she said, turning in her chair to look at him. 'I didn't think it was going to be when it started but it has.'

'We'll do it again,' he said.

'Yes. I'd like that.'

'The next time I get a day off,' he promised. And as she smiled at him, he thought how very different their return journey was going to be.

It was. But not in the way he imagined.

They took a taxi back to Poppleton and arrived as Andrew was packing his car and the drive was full of departing guests.

'Just in the nick of time,' Andrew said. 'If you'll just get your things, Gemma, we can be on our way. Told you they'd make it, Kate.'

He was in such an overpowering rush — and Nick didn't oppose him or offer to give her a lift home — and there were so many people all running in and out of the house and saying goodbye, that for once Gemma simply did as she was told. She collected her bag, said her goodbyes to Susan and Rob, and 'hopped in' to the back seat of the Rover, as she was instructed. There was no sign of Nick but as the Rover turned out of the drive, he came out of the house carrying his bag and stood on the doorstep to watch them go. She waved to him, but he didn't wave back, and she wasn't sure he'd seen her. It was a miserable anticlimax after their day together. 'And that's the way the world ends,' she thought. 'Not with a bang but a whimper.'

'What a weekend!' Andrew beamed, as they headed out of the village.

'Now you'll have to tackle your fan mail,' Catherine warned him.

'If any comes.'

'It will,' she said. 'Don't you think so, Gemma?'

Sure enough, two parcels were delivered the very next morning. And with them was a letter for Gemma. It was from the rehabilitation centre, offering her an appointment on 9 November.

Chapter 17

The rehabilitation centre at Crystal Palace is a new, brick and glass, bungalow complex built below the parade on the site of the old railway station that used to serve the Crystal Palace in the glory days before it was burnt down. Few of the thousands who drive along the parade today have any idea it is there. Why should they? They drive with two feet and both hands. But to amputees it is a special place, staffed by people who are there to help them, and purpose built to suit their needs, with wide windows to admit as much light as possible and wide doorways to admit their wheelchairs. The tiled floors reflect light like long wide mirrors, there are louvred blinds at the windows for privacy, and the furnishings are subdued and subtle, chairs and curtains a quiet gray-blue, carpet an unobtrusive buff.

Had she not been a patient, Gemma would have liked it a lot. As it was, she approached it with caution and considerable apprehension. And, most important of all, entirely on her own.

Catherine had offered to come with her as soon as she heard about the appointment. 'I could swap shifts with Marjorie,' she offered. 'It wouldn't be a problem.'

'*I'm* the problem,' Gemma told her. 'I don't mean to sound ungrateful but I've got to do this on my own.' If she was going to be hurt, or make a fuss, or burst into tears, or, worse still, fail at her first attempt to walk on her new leg, she didn't want anyone she knew to be around to see it.

Catherine took her refusal sympathetically. 'That's all right,' she said. 'The offer's open if you want it.'

'Thanks,' Gemma said, thinking how kind she was, 'but, if you don't mind, no thanks.'

As she was lowered out of the ambulance and wheeled herself into the reception area, she knew she'd been right to face this on her own. There were already several patients waiting there, either sitting in their wheelchairs or in a group of armchairs ranged in front of a shoulder-height TV set — an old lady, a girl in her teens, three old men and two young ones who had to be soldiers if their haircuts were anything to go by — and they all had limbs missing. Amputees, she thought, wincing at the word. That's what we all are. And the day ahead loomed in upon her like the ordeal she feared it would be.

But everybody was kind. The receptionist smiled at her warmly, the other patients chatted to her as she waited to be called, the nurse who finally came to escort her to the consulting room was cheerful and pretty.

As they progressed along the corridor, a young man in a pale green shirt and squeaky shoes strode past them carrying four artificial legs as though they were shopping baskets. He grinned at Gemma as he passed and she wondered whose legs they were and whether one of them was for her. But he strode on, legs and all, and squeaked in through a door marked 'Socks'.

'Here we are,' the nurse said. 'This is it.'

Gemma moistened her lips and propelled herself into the room, where two men and a young woman were waiting beside a handsome man in his fifties who was obviously the consultant — the expensive suit would have revealed that without the earnest attention of his team. Gemma's senses were working at full stretch now, taking everything in, a white examination table like a bed with no covers, a full-length mirror — have I got to look at myself ? — a zimmer frame — I'm not going to need *that*, surely — a desk facing the wall. The desk pleased her. It showed that this man put patients before paperwork.

Sure enough, his greeting was warm. 'Gemma,' he said. 'Nice to see you. I'm Mr Pearce. Could you bring your chair up to the desk? Fine. There are quite a few people for you to meet today, but you'll see who we all are as we go along. Peter's worked with you already, hasn't he?'

Peter was the prosthetist and among so many new faces he looked like an old friend.

'Are you going to fit my new leg?' she asked hopefully.

Apparently not. First she had to submit to yet another examination and then her plaster had to be removed. It was the oddest sensation, even though the saw looked more alarming than it felt, and it took a long time. But eventually, there was her leg at last, very white, wrinkled like an old lady's and shrunk to a matchstick. She was horrified by the state of it.

'Muscles disappear very quickly if they're not used,' Mr Pearce comforted her. 'Once you're walking about it'll build up again in no time. Now let's see how well you can stand up.'

She put on the sock and trainer they'd advised her to bring, but standing up was another matter on such a fragile limb. For a start it was extremely difficult to find her balance on one leg, even with two crutches and a physiotherapist to help her. It was also painful.

'All right?' they asked, as she gasped and staggered, the crutches hard in her armpits.

'Yes,' she lied. 'Fine.' And gritted her teeth, determined not to be beaten.

'There's a mirror at the end of the room,' the physiotherapist said. 'Take a look at it from time to time. It will help you to work out where to aim your foot.'

Gemma had been concentrating so hard that she hadn't looked at anything beyond her trainer but now she glanced up and there she was, right in the middle of the mirror, centre stage, standing, looking like herself again — only one-legged. Despite her discomfort, it was a lovely moment. 'Watch out Sarah Bernhardt,' she joked. 'I'm on my way.'

'Let's see if you can get a good swing this time,' the physiotherapist advised.

'By Christmas,' Gemma told her, 'I'm going to walk out of here with two legs and perfect balance.'

'That's our aim too,' Mr Pearce said. 'Now we're going to teach you some exercises to strengthen your muscles.'

They worked for an hour, took a rest,

worked for another hour, asked her to walk again. By the end of the morning, her calf ached and her arms were heavy with fatigue.

'That's it for now,' Mr Pearce said. 'Time for the ambulance to take you home.'

She was disappointed. 'What about my new leg?'

'Take a week to get used to this one,' he advised. 'Do your exercises every hour on the hour, then we'll put you on two.'

By this time she felt secure enough to joke. 'Promises, promises,' she complained.

But it was wonderful to wheel her chair into the hall at Amersham Road with her plaster gone and crutches balanced across her knees and even better to know that she could get up and walk whenever she felt up to it. Especially as Catherine and Nick came out of the kitchen the moment she stood up.

She was surprised to see Nick, although she shouldn't have been because it *was* his home. After their day in York, and that emotional river trip, and the abrupt way they'd parted, she *had* hoped he would phone her to ask how she was. As the days passed and there'd been no call she'd been rather cast down. But what did that matter now? She was too high to worry about something as trivial as a phone call that hadn't been made.

'Impressed or what?' she asked, leaning on her crutches and beaming at them.

'Very,' Catherine said. 'Come and have lunch. It's all ready for you.'

Gemma began her slow hobble towards the kitchen. 'How did you know I'd be back in time?'

'Nick rang the centre.'

It was petty to be annoyed about it but she was annoyed, because his action felt more like interference than concern. But he didn't seem to notice that she was frowning. He was too busy urging them both into the kitchen.

'I've only got an hour,' he said, 'and then I'm due back on the wards. So tell me, who did you see and what did they say?'

He's more interested in my symptoms than he is in me, Gemma thought. There are times when I don't feel my legs are my own. But she told him what he wanted to know, adding 'I've got a week to get my act together with one leg and then they're going to give me the other one.'

'So Dad'll have to answer his own mail,' Nick said.

She assured him she could do her exercises *and* answer letters at the same time. 'No problem.' And he said he could well imagine it and helped himself to more salad.

Despite her initial annoyance with him, the hour and the meal passed pleasantly and were over too soon.

'I must go,' Catherine said, 'or I shall be late for my clinic. Have you got time to fill the dishwasher, Nick?'

He had but only just. 'If I'm quick,' he said, glancing at his watch. And he was quick. But he didn't speak again until his mother had gone and the table was almost clear.

How tense he is, Gemma thought as she handed him the last dirty plate. And right back to being formal and distant again. But then he suddenly smiled at her and said, 'I suppose the next time I shall see you is at the ageds' retirement party.'

That was news to her. 'I didn't know they were retiring,' she said. 'They don't seem old enough.'

'Oh they're retiring!' he confirmed. 'In just over four weeks. There's a party organised. Invitations going out tomorrow. You're invited.'

'Am I?'

'Of course,' he said and he relaxed enough to laugh. 'I'm the organiser. I/c balloons and streamers. That sort of thing.'

The thought of another party warmed her. 'Have you ordered a cake?'

'No,' he said, switching on the dishwasher. 'I never thought of a cake. Do we need one?'

'You can't have a party without a cake,' she told him. 'I'll make one for you if you like.'

They were conspirators again, grinning at one another. 'You're on,' he said. Now we shall talk, Gemma thought. But he was halfway out the door. 'See you!' he said. And was gone.

Left on her own in the empty kitchen, Gemma felt deflated. They'd been together for nearly ten minutes and he hadn't said a word about their day out. But never one to brood for long, she shrugged her thoughts away. Why should there be any sort of intimacy between them? He was a doctor and she was a patient. And that was all there was to it. Then she hobbled into her flat to write a list of the ingredients she would need for the cake.

The next few days were disjointed by exercises and fraught with impatience: at her slow progress, at the aches and pains the exercises produced, at the intolerable wait before she could get back to the rehab centre. Her invitation arrived as he'd promised but there was no letter with it, not even so much as a little note. Fortunately letters arrived for Andrew in every post and that kept her occupied.

So the long week passed and at last she was back in Crystal Palace, with the medical team around her and the consultant finally agreeing that she'd made sufficient progress to be introduced to her new leg.

It was a hideous thing, like an enormous light socket with a carbon fibre peg emerging from the middle of it, where the calf should have been, and a clumsy-looking plastic foot attached to the end of the peg. There was a grey leather strap to fit over her knee and hold the socket in position and, laid out ready for her, a selection of socks to pad the stump so that the liner didn't rub. The one the prosthetist recommended was called an Ottobock sock and was made of cotton but there were woollen socks and fluffy socks too and the choice would depend on what felt most comfortable to her.

The sight of it upset her so much that she had to joke about it to recover her balance. 'Peg-leg the pirate,' she said.

'It is a bit,' Mr Pearce agreed. 'But this isn't what you'll finish up with, of course. This is just your primary limb.'

'How many am I going to have?'

'Three, probably,' the prosthetist said. 'Maybe more.'

This is going to take months, she realised, and her heart sank. But he was talking about socks. '. . . lots of socks.'

She pulled her mind back to the moment. 'Lots of socks?'

'They've got to act like shock absorbers,' he explained. 'The one thing you *must* avoid is any chafing and we've got to get a perfect fit. We'll see how many pairs you need to be comfortable, which will vary according to how much shrinkage there is in your stump. Shouldn't be too many in your case because you've had to wait for such a long time to be fitted and most of the swelling should have gone down. Let's see, shall we?'

It was two, one woollen and one fluffy cotton. Then at last, at last, the prosthesis was eased over her stump — and it did fit, exactly as they'd promised, like the prover-bial glove — and she managed to stand on two legs, admiring her new wonderful im-age in the long mirror. Two legs, two feet, too good to be true.

'Now,' Mr Pearce said, bringing her back to the earth she would tread on, 'let's see what you can do. Two steps forward, if you will.'

Although she was walking between the two long handrails, they were the most diffi-cult steps she'd ever taken. Her remaining leg was still weak and the stump didn't move her new leg in the direction she wanted, so she straddled and staggered like an overgrown toddler. The effort it took was out of all proportion to the distance she was able to move. She was glad it was only two steps he'd asked for.

'Now we'll take a look at your pelvis,' he ordered.

This was the physiotherapist's job and it was done very thoroughly.

'We've got to be sure the new limb isn't going to tilt your hip bones,' she explained, 'because that would change the alignment of your spine and then you could be in trouble. No. It's all in order. You can walk again when you're ready.'

The next two steps were simply comic. It was like being on stilts. 'I'll get the hang of it in a minute,' she promised, as much to herself as her audience. But they were all too busy to answer, watching her closely and taking notes.

The prosthetist produced a set of tools and followed her on his hands and knees, adjusting the leg after every step, gradually working his way round the various adjustment screws all over the alignment device. At one point he stuck a slice of wood underneath her new foot to get the level right. It looked ugly and untidy but was obviously necessary, as the next step she took was a slight improvement. She staggered on, one uncoordinated pace after another, up and down between the rails, hanging on for balance and dear life. The observation and the adjustments continued.

'And I always said I didn't do patience,' she observed to Mr Pearce as she passed him for the second time.

'This takes time,' he told her. 'It's not a thing we can hurry.'

'It's all necessary,' the prosthetist added from the floor. 'You'll thank us for it when you get your perfect leg. And it will be perfect, I promise you.'

'Break for lunch,' Mr Pearce decided, checking his watch. 'Back here at 2.15.'

Gemma was glad to sit in her chair and wheel off for something to eat. This was much, much worse than walking on her real leg had been. Her entire body was aching: calf, hips, back, neck, shoulders. Even her hands. It was as if she'd been gardening non-stop for a week. Thank God for a snack and the chance to sit down.

A pretty woman was limping towards her table, carrying a tray. Late thirties, neat figure, fluffy fair hair, snub nose, blue eyes, warm smile. 'You're new aren't you?' she asked. 'Mind if I join you?'

'Please do,' Gemma said. 'I shall be glad of the company.'

'Bad morning?'

'Exhausting.'

The woman understood at once. 'Was it your first fitting?' she asked and nodded sagely when Gemma said it was.

They introduced themselves — 'Janey Medlicott' 'Gemma Goodeve' — and told one another what limbs they'd lost and how, as calmly as though they were discussing a visit to a hairdresser. Janey had lost an arm and a leg in a road accident.

'I'm over the worst of it now,' she said. 'Getting back to work helps a lot. And driving again. You've no idea how much better that makes you feel.'

That made Gemma stare. 'Isn't it a bit difficult, driving?'

'Not these days,' Janey said. 'Providing you've got one foot for the accelerator and the brake. You can do everything else on the steering column, even with a false hand — change gear, switch on the lights, sound your horn, change channels on the radio, put on your make-up. It's great. I recommend it.'

'How long did it take you?' Gemma asked.

'Five months almost exactly,' Janey told her, 'from the day of the accident to the day I was behind the wheel again. Fords do special rates for disabled drivers. I could give you their address, if you're interested. I think I've got a telephone number too, somewhere.'

'Yes please,' Gemma said. 'I'd like both. If I can drive again . . .'

'You will,' Janey encouraged her. 'Just make your mind up to it and it's as good as done.'

'People are very positive here,' Gemma remarked, returning to her sandwiches.

'No point in being anything else,' Janey said. 'When you've been brought down as far as we have, the only way on is up. The thing to remember is you're not alone. There are lots of people here to help you. That's the good thing about a limb centre. There are people in chairs and people with hooks and people with pea-stick limbs wherever you look. We're all in it together and we all help each other.'

'You said you worked,' Gemma asked. 'What do you do? If you don't mind me asking.'

'I *was* a telephonist,' Janey told her. 'With the Post Office. Still am, actually, only I'm part-time now. There aren't so many full-time jobs available these days. Not for anyone. But in a way it doesn't matter. I've got my disability pension so I don't need a full-time job as much as I did. The extra money would be nice because we've got a mortgage, but he's still in work so I'm not desperate for it. And having a bit of time to spare gives me a chance to do something useful.'

Gemma looked a question at her.

'I'm part-time telephonist, part-time disabled helper,' she explained. 'I work in my local hospital with the disabled kids. It helps them to have someone around who knows what they're going through, someone they can ask questions and talk to. Takes one to know one, sort of idea.'

It sounded an excellent arrangement. 'They don't need any more, do they?' Gemma asked.

'I don't think so. Not at the moment anyway. But they're always looking out for people to help in the schools. You could try there.'

'I might just do that,' Gemma said. Maybe being trained to teach drama was going to stand her in good stead after all. She hadn't been near a school since her last teaching practice, but there was no harm in offering. 'I am glad I met you,' she said.

'You've given me a lot to think about.'

'Good to hear it,' Janey said, finishing her tea. 'Now it's back to the catwalk, I suppose.'

The word rang bells in Gemma's mind. 'The what?'

'The catwalk. That's what we call the bars. You know, the ones you hang on to while you're walking up and down and they're all looking at you.'

Gemma was enjoying the joke. 'My mother always reckoned I'd end up as a model,' she said. 'Little did she know!'

'Well good luck!' Janey said. 'I'll see you around.'

'Parking in the next bay,' Gemma promised. It was extraordinary how much she'd cheered up. She was on her way. Anything was possible now.

That night, she wrote a postcard to her mother. She hadn't written to her for days, so it was high time. I shall have to go and see her soon, she thought, as she picked up her pen. And there was still the business of meeting her father. She really did want to see him. She knew that now. But not in this state. Not until she was walking properly and had found herself a job and her scars had faded a bit more. They were too obvious at the moment. There was no rush.

What were a few more weeks after the years she'd spent without him?

Thought I'd better let you know how I'm getting on. I have had the plaster removed from my right leg and have been fitted with my prosthesis. I can now walk again using crutches. It will make a lot of difference in the flat. Being in a chair all the time was awkward. I will write again after my next appointment and when I can walk well enough I will come and see you. Luv, Gemma.

Chapter 18

When Billie got home from work the next afternoon, Tim was in the bedroom sitting at her dressing table trimming his moustache with her nail scissors.

'You've had another postcard,' he said, flashing his charming smile through the mirror and out to where she stood in the hall. 'It's on the hall table. Came second post. She's not in the convalescent home any more, apparently. She's got a flat.'

'Was there any address?' Billie asked but she could see from his disappointed face that there wasn't. She picked up the card and read it quickly. 'Oh dear! She *is* being naughty.'

'We must make allowances,' Tim said gallantly, as he returned to his trimming. 'She's been to hell and back, poor kid.'

Billie walked into the kitchen to make a pot of tea. 'It wouldn't hurt her to put her address even so,' she grumbled. 'If she's got a place of her own she ought to tell us where it is. I mean, time's going on. It's six weeks since the crash. She ought to consider our feelings a bit. Yours certainly, when you've come all this way to see her. It's not nice to spurn you.'

He followed her into the kitchen and, standing behind her, put his arms round her waist and kissed her neck. 'You're such a tender heart,' he said. 'I'm not being spurned. How can you say such a thing when I'm here with you? Nothing could be further from the truth.'

She leant back into his embrace, charmed by the compliment.

'That's a smart blouse,' he murmured into her hair. 'Is it new?'

'I bought it this afternoon. Out of stock.' She'd worn it home specially to please him. 'Do you like it?'

'It's charming,' he said, kissing her to prove it. 'That pink always suited you. It's your colour. English rose.'

She turned in his arms so that she could face him. 'Oh Tim,' she said. 'I do love you.'

But he was sighing. 'I *would* like to see her, naturally,' he said. 'You're right about that. Still, she'll come round in her own time. I must be patient.'

My poor Tim, she thought, pitying the sigh. 'I wish there was something I could do,' she told him, sighing too. 'I mean, if I could think of something, I'd do it like a shot. You know that, don't you?'

'Of course you would,' he soothed. Then he seemed to be thinking. 'What if we were to try the hospital again?'

'*They* won't tell us anything,' she said, reaching for the teapot. 'You know they won't. It's against their policy. They said so.' She'd gone back to ask them for an address after Gemma's first postcard was delivered and they'd made her feel so unwelcome she certainly didn't want to repeat the performance. 'I've had enough of hospitals and their blessed rules all the time. No, my darling, I'm afraid we'll just have to wait till she writes a proper letter to us. Or comes to see us. Maybe she'll come over Christmas. I mean, families always get together for Christmas, don't they?'

'That's over six weeks away,' he said, sitting at the kitchen table. 'And like you said, time's getting on. She ought to be putting in her claim soon or she'll miss the boat.'

Billie had almost forgotten about the claim. 'Oh that!' she said. 'Maybe she's done it already and not told us.'

He shook his head. 'If she'd done it, it would have been in the papers. Half a million's a lot of money. And that's news.'

True. 'I don't suppose she's been well

enough to think about it,' Billie said, watching the kettle. 'They make you rest all the time when you're convalescent, don't they.'

'I couldn't say. I've never been convalescent.'

'No,' she said, turning to admire him. 'I don't suppose you have.'

He preened under her admiration. 'Luck of the draw,' he said, modestly.

'You were always fit,' she said. 'Strong and healthy I always used to say.'

Her praise was enhancing his ego most rewardingly but there were other matters to get settled. 'I tell you what I think we ought to do, my poppet,' he said. 'We ought to set the wheels in motion.'

She put their two cups on the table beside the milk jug and the sugar bowl and her little rose-covered biscuit barrel. 'What do you mean, set the wheels in motion?'

'Go and see a solicitor,' he said. And when she looked doubtful: 'If she hasn't made up her mind — and I'm not saying she should, not while she's feeling poorly, and I dare say you're right, she *is* resting — but if she hasn't, then we ought to do it for her. There could be a time limit on compensation claims and we wouldn't want her to miss out, now would we?'

She hadn't thought of time limits. 'Is there?'

'Of course. There's bound to be. I think we ought to go and see a solicitor and get things started on her behalf. I haven't been much of a father to her. I know that. But I'm going to make up for it now, to think of her welfare. This is one way to do it. It's not fair to her for me to sit around doing nothing. There are some dreadful sharks out there when it comes to money, and for all I know they could be after her already, getting her to sign things and putting pressure on her. I should be protecting her. That's what parents are for.'

She could see that. Look at all those nature programmes on the television.

'You're such a good man,' she said. 'The only thing is, won't it cost a lot of money?'

'Don't you worry your pretty little head about money,' he said, wearing his masterful expression. 'She's *my* girl. Leave it to me. It's no problem.'

'Well . . .' she dithered.

'I'll make an appointment, shall I? We'll both go along and see. There'd be no harm in that. Let's say Monday morning when you haven't got much trade. You could wear this blouse and we'll go out for lunch afterwards.'

She wasn't entirely convinced but she was

persuaded. So the appointment was made.

It was a nasty cold morning but she dressed herself up in her new blouse and her best suit, regardless of the weather. It was a silly thing to do really because the suit was a thin wool and didn't give her any warmth at all. But you have to make sacrifices when it's your children, and she did look nice in it.

But she wasn't a bit impressed with the solicitors. Their offices had a fine brass plate, *Gresham, Gresham, Philpott and Mainwaring, Family Solicitors* but they were up four flights of stairs and jolly steep at that. She was out of breath by the time she got to the top. And the office they were ushered into was small and hot and crammed with enormous furniture — a desk like a dining-room table and two great leather armchairs you could have put together and turned into a double bed. They would have been lovely in her living room but in a titchy little room like that they were just a waste of space.

The solicitor was a disappointment too. She'd expected an upstanding sort of man with white hair and a theatrical voice but this one was small and seedy with a long narrow face that looked as if someone had squashed it between two bookends.

But he assured them both that he was at

their service, that damages of half a million pounds were well within the bounds of possibility and that he would be happy to do anything within his power to help their 'poor dear daughter'.

The words triggered a recollection in Billie's mind of Gemma at her fiercest, which she found rather disquieting. But Tim liked them and repeated them with approval.

'Our poor dear daughter,' he said. 'That's exactly it, Mr Gresham. Spot on. We've got to help her, poor girl. It's the least we can do, as I told you on the phone. This is too big a burden for her, after all she's been through.'

'She will have to come in and sign the papers,' Mr Gresham pointed out. 'Eventually. You understand that, don't you? Good, good. In the meantime we will do the donkey work, as the saying goes. It might be helpful if I were to take you through the legal process at this point. Yes?'

It was a droning explanation and Billie lost interest in it after the first thirty seconds. What a bore solicitors are, she thought. Still, I suppose it's all for the best. Those roses are pretty. I wonder how much they cost. I bet it's a lot, being out of season. Different in the summer of course. And she remembered the great bunch that Gemma had given her on her last birthday, roses and great white daisies, larkspur, antirrhinums. They were gorgeous.

Mr Gresham had come to a halt in his peroration. He took out a large stained handkerchief and wiped various parts of his face, lingeringly, as if polishing buffed up his thought processes: forehead, nose, chin, the back of his neck. He avoided the top of his head because he didn't want to disturb his hair. He hadn't got very much of it, and it took him a lot of time and care to arrange what little there was so as to cover his balding scalp. 'Now,' he said, 'if you will permit me to take down a few details. She was very badly injured, I believe you said?'

Both men looked at Billie for information. 'Oh dreadful!' she told them, pulling herself back to the moment. 'She lost her leg, poor girl, and she was terribly scarred. Terribly. All across her poor little face. They had to cut off all her hair too — imagine that — and she was going to be a model. I've got a photograph of her here if you'd like to see it. As she was, I mean.'

'A lovely girl,' Mr Gresham said, when he'd glanced at it. 'Which, sad though it is, will make our job all the easier.'

'Of course her life's ruined,' Billie said,

brown eyes filling with tears. 'She'll never be a model now. Not in this state. Not now she's a cripple. She can't do anything, really. Not a thing. She'll need looking after for the rest of her life.'

'Then we must see to it that she has the wherewithal to make that life as meaningful as possible,' Mr Gresham oiled. 'Now as to my fee. An unpleasant business, talking about money, but it's sensible to get these things in order from the outset.'

What if she doesn't agree to all this? Billie quailed as an astronomical fee was mentioned. Oh, if only she'd write and tell me where she is, we could go and see her and ask her what she thinks. We shouldn't go ahead without telling her, just in case.

The two men shook hands, well pleased with their morning's work, while Billie looked at the roses. That was a lovely birthday, she thought. All those flowers and a party and that lovely birthday cake. She was ever so good to me, my little Gemma. She did that flat up in my honour — balloons in the corners of the room and everything — and it couldn't have been easy with all the others in and out all the time and that funny boy lying on the sofa. And suddenly she knew how she could find out where her daughter was. She'd go to her old flat and ask her friends. They'd be bound to know. Now why hadn't she thought of it before? For a moment, staring at the scarlet blooms, she wondered whether to tell Tim. Then she decided against it. I'll go there first, she thought, and see how I get on. It might not work and I wouldn't like to tell him about it and get him excited and then have to tell him I'd failed. It'll have to wait a week because I can't take any more time off this week or I shan't break even. Next Monday maybe. In the afternoon.

The old flat was ever so easy to find on that Monday afternoon and just the same as she remembered it. Bit more paint flaked off the windowsills and half a motorbike in the garden but other than that it had hardly changed at all. The funny boy put his head out of the window when she knocked and called out 'Who is it?' but he came down to let her in. Quite friendly, really.

Once upstairs she was a bit embarrassed because there wasn't anyone else there and he was lounging about in his underpants and not much else apart from a pair of terrible holey socks and a jersey that had seen better days. But he didn't seem to mind so she decided she wouldn't either. When in Rome, sort of thing.

He looked for Gemma's address as soon as she asked. 'Yes,' he said. 'I do know where she is, as it happens. She sent me a letter. Hang on a tick and I'll see if I can find it.'

It took him quite a while because he had to grub about in a very untidy drawer, but when he finally pulled it from the debris there was a map to go with it.

'There you are,' he said. 'Good job I never throw anything away, right?'

It was a nice clear map with all the roads neatly named and the house marked with a big red cross. Amersham Road, Putney, Billie read. Well now I know. 'Do you see her much?' she asked, tucking the two precious bits of paper into the inner pocket of her handbag. He was a kind boy, even if he *was* half-dressed.

'No,' he said. 'I delivered her things, that's all. She's got her own life now. Gone up in the world.'

Billie liked the sound of that. And quite right too. She ought to go up in the world, especially if she's going to sue the railway for half a million.

'Well thank you,' she said. 'I'm obliged.'

'I'd offer you tea,' he said, flinging himself backwards on to the sofa, 'only all the cups are dirty and I'm knackered.'

She assured him it was all right and that she'd better be getting along, and at that he closed his eyes and asked if she could see herself out. Which she did, thinking that he must have been working really hard, poor boy, to be as tired as that.

All the way back on the bus she kept patting her handbag with satisfaction. I know where she is, she thought. The fact that she could have found out right at the start, if she'd used her wits, didn't trouble her. It was done now. That's what counted. It was done now. Won't Tim be pleased.

He was delighted, especially as he'd had a letter from Mr Gresham that morning, mentioning the half-million in splendidly official black and white. 'That's my gel!' he said, taking her into his arms. 'Now we're on our way!'

'We shall have to go out and celebrate,' she suggested happily. 'Somewhere special this Saturday, what d'you say?'

But to her disappointment, he said not. 'I've got to go up north for a day or two. See a man about a dog.'

Ah, she understood, business. That was why he was wearing his important face. 'When you get back, then,' she agreed.

I'll go and see Gemma while he's away, she decided. Prepare the ground sort of thing. Then we can have a grand celebration when he comes back, all three of us together. It'll be a little treat for her. She must get bored sitting around all day with nothing to do. I can just see her, poor darling, sitting sadly in that awful ugly chair drooping with boredom. Poor Gemma! If I knew where she was I could take her out for a little ride. Give her a breath of fresh air. It would be like the old days when she was a little girl. And a vision of the old days bloomed in her mind like one of those nostalgia ads on television — herself when young taking the infant Gemma, all dimples and chuckles and babbled nursery rhymes, sitting in her pram and wearing a spotless white dress, over Streatham Common, or some other expanse of bright green grass, under a canopy of summertime foliage with the sun so bright it shimmered haloes round their heads. Lovely!

In his sleep-frowsy room in St Thomas's, Nick was planning an outing for Gemma too.

Ever since his return from York, he'd been trying to think of a way to ask her out again without being too obvious about it or too pushy. Their day in York had been so extraordinary that it ought to have been easy to follow up. But not to him. Any successful excursion, with any girl since Deirdre — and quite a few before her, if he was honest — led to the possibility of failure on a subsequent occasion. York could have been a one-off. Probably was. It would have been easier if they hadn't parted so abruptly. It still hurt him to remember how she'd driven off with his parents without even stopping to say goodbye. It was a very bad sign, particularly after that boat trip. But, even so, he knew he wanted to spend more time with her and now one of his elderly patients had given him the opportunity.

That morning, when he'd gone down to the ward to sign him off, the old feller had pressed an envelope into his hand, mumbling that it was 'to say thank you for all you've done for me'. Inside were two tickets for *Cats*.

'You're not on duty that night,' the old man beamed. 'I asked Nurse to find out for me. You go an' have a good night out, Doctor. You've earned it.'

It was heaven-sent. He'd arranged to go to Amersham Road on Friday afternoon, to collect the cake for the ageds' party and smuggle it into the surgery while they were occupied elsewhere. He'd take the tickets with him and offer them to her in the car on the way there, sort of casually.

It didn't work out that way. When he arrived, there was such an atmosphere in the kitchen that he couldn't have missed it even if Polly hadn't been pulling a face and signalling.

'What's up?' he asked them.

'You can see what's up,' Gemma told him, her face dark with fury. 'Bloody thing! Look at it.'

The fruit cake was on a silver plinth in the centre of the table, not round and cake-shaped but lop-sided and sunk in the middle, like the aftermath of an underground explosion.

'It was all right yesterday when I took it out of the oven,' she stormed. 'And now look at it! Wouldn't you *know* it would sink.'

He'd laughed before he realised it was the wrong thing to do. Oops!

She glared at him and then at the cake. 'What am I going to do with it?'

'Bung something over the top,' he suggested. 'That's what you do with this sort of cake anyway, isn't it?'

That earned him another glare.

'Nothing turns out the way you expect,' Polly commiserated. 'You could try butter icing. That covers a multitude a' sins, butter icing. I swear by it.'

Gemma had been working in the kitchen all afternoon and now she was hot and tired and felt more like swearing *at* it. She'd got the marzipan all rolled out and the royal icing made and what was the good of it now? 'I was going to write "Happy Retirement" on it,' she said. 'I've got the icing pen and everything. I can't do that on butter icing.'

'Then there's only one thing,' Nick told her. 'You'll have to opt for radical surgery. Cut out the middle and turn it into a polo cake and write round the edges. I'll do it if you like.' And he picked up the bread knife.

'You will not!'

'Trust me,' he joked. 'I'm a surgeon.'

Sparks were leaping between them again. 'I'm the cook,' she said angrily. 'If anyone's going to do it, it'll be me.'

'Well hurry up then,' he said. 'We've got twenty minutes.'

It took two minutes to reshape the thing, but it was thirty before it was iced to her satisfaction.

'It looks very presentable,' Polly said encouragingly.

'Until they cut it,' Gemma grimaced, 'and see the state of the inside.'

'No one'll notice the inside,' Nick told her. 'Not in the sort of crush there'll be.

They'll all be too busy eating it. Now come on, for heaven's sake or it'll be over before we get there.'

It was such a scramble to get into the car and he had to drive to the surgery at such speed that he forgot all about the tickets until they were inside the building. And then, of course, it was too late because the party *had* begun and they were instantly engulfed in the excitement of it.

Crush was the right description. For although the reception was held in the waiting room, which was the largest space in the surgery, so many people had turned up to say goodbye to the Quennells that there was barely room to turn round. The four present doctors were there with their husbands and wives, together with Andrew's original two partners and all the nurses and midwives, physiotherapists and receptionists who'd ever worked in the practice. They milled around, champagne glasses in hand, greeting old friends, swapping gossip, enjoying the nibbles, applauding as the cake was cut — and it *did* look good once it was placed in the centre of the table — and waiting for the speeches, which came when Grace was sure that everyone who'd promised to be there had arrived and had been 'fed and watered' and just at the moment when Nick had decided to push through the mob and talk to Gemma about the tickets. Damn, damn, damn, he thought. Now I'll have to wait till *this* is over.

'We drew lots for this job,' Grace said, blushing slightly. 'And I got the short straw. But seriously, what I want to say to you, Dr Quennell, Catherine, is this. We're going to miss you dreadfully, both of you. This practice would never have existed if it hadn't been for you. You've been an inspiration to us all. I know I speak for everyone when I say that. Anyway, we hope you'll have a long and happy retirement together and we've got two little gifts to wish you well. This is for you, Catherine. A little token of our appreciation.'

It was a silver locket 'with four spaces for your four grandchildren', which was instantly hung round Catherine's neck, to happy applause.

Then Grace turned to her boss.

'Now to you, Dr Quennell,' she went on. 'I hope you realise you've put us in an impossible position. We *were* going to buy you a set of garden tools to mark this retirement of yours. But now you're running about all over the country being a television personality, we've had to rethink.' She pulled a second parcel from under the table and handed it across to him. 'We hope this will do instead.'

The accompanying card was signed by every member of the partnership, past and present, all with their own personal messages. The package contained a rather splendid silver hip flask, inscribed with Andrew's name and that day's date.

'I'm touched,' he told them in his response. 'It's going to be very useful in my new career.'

'Dashing about the country?' his senior partner called.

'Spilling the beans on TV?' their junior hoped.

'Well actually,' Andrew grinned, savouring the moment that was to come, 'when I'm burning the midnight oil, trying to write a newspaper column. It seems I'm going to be a journalist. Been offered a weekly column in the *Indie*. Life in the NHS. Health provision in the 1990s. That sort of thing. Spilling the beans on paper. I'm going there on Monday afternoon to discuss terms.'

His audience were as impressed as he'd hoped they would be. But, as Nick saw only too clearly, there was no possibility of edging across the room yet.

'You are a dark horse,' Catherine rebuked

him, when the buzz died down. 'You never told me that.'

'Only came this morning,' he said. 'I thought it would make a good conclusion to the ceremony.' Then he turned to his guests. 'I give you a toast,' he said. 'As so many of us seem to be setting out on new careers —' looking at his senior partner — 'or in a new life —' looking at Gemma — 'or in a new variation of the old one —' smiling at everyone there: 'Here's to new directions!'

'New directions!' Gemma echoed. She could certainly drink to that. It was time to take a new direction of her own.

The party was over. People were already saying goodbye and drifting away. If I'm not quick, Nick thought, she'll up and go too. She's a bit too good at that. He shouldered his way through the mob.

She was standing by the table looking at the remains of her cake.

'Great cake,' he said.

'Well, they ate it,' she admitted, 'and nobody's dropped dead.'

'Great party.'

'Yes.'

'Look,' he said, 'I know this isn't the time for it, but how would you like to go to the theatre?'

'What to see?'

He took the tickets out of his pocket and showed them to her.

'Next Friday,' she said. 'That's a week to-day.'

He agreed that it was, adding carelessly, 'You've probably seen it.'

She had, but she decided not to tell him. 'They say it's a very good show.'

'Then you'll come?'

'Yes,' she said, 'thanks.'

But the words were barely out of her mouth before Andrew loomed in upon them, booming that it had been a great party and demanding that Nick come and talk to old Campbell before he goes. 'He's been doing some fascinating work with duodenals.'

It wasn't the moment for another toe-to-toe so Nick allowed himself to be led away. 'Six o'clock?' he said to Gemma as he turned into the throng, smiled as she nodded, and was lost to her sight.

Is it a date? she wondered. Or what? It had been offered so casually it was hard to tell. She started to clear the table, glad to have something to occupy her. Before the accident she would have teased him and found out what his feelings were; now she didn't feel capable of that sort of teasing and wouldn't have dared it anyway just in case he was asking her for the wrong reasons. It would have been different if she hadn't been his patient, different if she hadn't confessed so much to him out in the boat, different if she still had both her legs. I must get a job, she decided. Keep myself busy. All this sitting about being introspective isn't good for me.

Chapter 19

Not being one to waste time once she'd made a decision, Gemma took the first step in her new direction the very next morning. The Quennells were sleeping late now that they'd retired, the house was quiet, and, as the flow of letters had more or less dried up, there was no work she felt compelled to do. With a copy of the telephone directory to provide addresses, and the gas fire lit to provide a pleasant heat, she sat on the sofa in her green and gold living room and wrote to the four nearest primary schools to offer her services as a disabled helper 'should you have any pupils who might need me', stressing that she'd been trained as a teacher as well as an actress, and adding: 'besides losing my left lower leg which has given me the experience of knowing what newly disabled people need'. Then, feeling she'd made as good a case for herself as she could, she took a walk to the postbox.

It was a clear, cold, breezy morning and there were only two other people in the street — a man exercising his dog and one of her neighbours returning home with the Saturday newspaper tucked under his arm. He waved and smiled as he passed. 'Off for the papers?' he asked.

Until that moment Gemma hadn't thought of papers — the Quennells had theirs delivered — but the question gave her an idea. She would walk round the corner and see if the newsagent had a copy of *Stage and Television* or *Plays and Players*. It wasn't far and if she took it gently she ought to be able to manage it.

It was actually further than she thought and, by the time she'd struggled there and back, her stump was decidedly uncomfortable, but she'd found a copy of both magazines and bought them at once. It was a good move. Simply looking at their familiar covers made her feel she was back in charge of her life again. She would take off her prosthesis as soon as she got home, check that the stump hadn't chafed and attend to it if it had. Then she would see what was on offer in the London theatre world.

It wasn't very much. One show was asking for singers and dancers, so that was out. A small firm needed extras for an ad, and that would be too active for her too. Another required an ASM for a Christmas pantomime on the south coast and she wasn't sure she was up to facing digs just yet. She put the magazines down, feeling rather demoralised. Just as well I've got two irons in the fire, she thought. Rob Pengilly had been right.

Andrew was demoralised that Saturday too, because his first foray into journalism proved to be more of a challenge than any of them had expected. Even with a computer to count them, he couldn't get the words right. First there were too many, then there were too few. The stories he told were either hideously stilted or rambled like weeds. Sustained by black coffee and Classic FM, he hacked and padded all through the day, thought and sweated, rewrote and rewrote and rewrote, but the harder he tried, the more abysmal the prose he produced.

'If you'd told me before I started, I'd never have believed it could be so difficult,' he complained to Catherine. 'It's only a thousand words, for Christ's sake!'

By Monday evening he was in such a black mood that Catherine served him dinner in his study on a tray and left him to cope with frustration and indigestion on his own.

'I'm not cut out for this,' he admitted at dinner the next day.

Gemma was mashing potatoes and gave

him a sympathetic grin but Catherine, lifting the hot-pot from the oven, said there was no reason why he should be and advised him not to worry about it.

It was wasted advice. 'I shall miss the deadline,' he told her, scowling with agitation. 'My first deadline.'

She was aggravatingly calm. 'Then phone them and tell them you can't do it.'

'Admit defeat?' He was horrified at the very idea. 'Good God, woman, I can't do that. This is the chance of a lifetime. Look at the timing of it. Election coming, people *thinking*. And they give me the chance to speak out just when I've retired and I can say what I like. I'm one of the few people around who can actually afford to tell the truth and shame the devil. I can't walk away from *that*.'

It's a campaign, Catherine thought, looking across the table at his tempestuous face. He'll write this article no matter what it costs him. Or us. 'Well if that's the case,' she smiled at him, as she spooned hot-pot on to his plate, 'I suppose we shall have to put up with you until you've finished it. I'm going to York on Friday, don't forget.'

'Finished!' he sighed. 'I can't get the bloody thing started, never mind finished. It's ridiculous. I was all right on television, so why not on paper?'

It was Gemma who gave him the answer as he was helping himself to potatoes. 'Maybe you should use the dictaphone,' she suggested. 'Speak what you think instead of writing it.'

'What a very good idea,' he said, smiling at last. 'What made you think of that?'

'I've been swatting up my lesson notes,' she explained, taking her plate from Catherine. 'The ones I made at college. Doing a bit of revision. That's one of the tricks to get reluctant pupils to put pen to paper. I read about it last night.'

'It might well work. Can't think why I didn't think of it myself. You could type it up for me, couldn't you?'

'I could do the first article,' she said. 'After that, I'm not so sure. I might be at work.' What a wonderful thing to be able to say. And she'd done it with style, casually, as though it wasn't important. 'I'll show you how to use the dictaphone, if you like, and then you can do it yourself. It's not hard.'

That seemed sensible, especially if he was going to make a career of this writing business. He couldn't depend on her help for ever. Nor should he. She had a life of her own. 'Are you thinking of leaving us, then?'

he asked, starting his meal. 'Have you got a job?'

'Not yet,' she said, 'and I'm not thinking of leaving yet either. Not if you can put up with me a bit longer. But I'm looking.' And as she began her own meal, she told them about her four applications.

'Excellent!' Andrew applauded. 'They'll jump at you, if they've got any sense.'

Which, the next day, and to her delight, one of them did.

The letter was from the headmistress of Fairmead School who said she would be interested to meet Gemma and suggested that she might like to come in at ten o'clock on Friday morning. 'We have three disabled children in the school,' she wrote, 'and all of them need help.'

'I can see Friday's going to be quite a day,' Andrew said when she told him at coffee time. 'Kate's off to York for two days with the girls and I'm going to Cardiff for an interview on the radio. Ben Clifford's arranged it,' he explained to Catherine. 'Did I tell you that? No? I thought I had. You remember Ben, don't you? Used to be in St Thomas's. We thought it would be an idea to go on for a meal afterwards so I'll probably stay over till Sunday morning. Good job we've got you to look after the house, Gemma.'

'Actually I shall be at the theatre on Friday,' she told him, as casually as she could, 'so it'll have to look after itself for one evening. Nick's got tickets for *Cats*.' Then she waited to see how they would take it.

There was an almost imperceptible pause, while husband and wife exchanged glances — his amused, hers saying 'what did I tell you?' — then they began to tease.

'So we're *all* going to be gadabouts,' Catherine smiled. 'There must be something in the stars!'

'Let's hope they're on our side, if that's the case,' Andrew said. 'Success to all our endeavours, that's what I say.' And he smiled at Gemma too.

It was a pleasant moment and a positive one. So far so good, Gemma thought, smiling back at them. If it *is* a date at least they approve of it. 'Amen to that!' she said.

Catherine was the first to leave the house that Friday morning, in a rush and scowlingly worried because she was afraid she was going to miss her train. Andrew was late too. Not that it worried him. Radio interviews were a doddle these days and he fully expected to enjoy his weekend.

Ten minutes after he'd gone, Polly arrived, out of breath and only just on time, explaining that the cat had been sick on her daughter's bed and she'd had to clear it up before she could come out. 'Couldn't very well leave it, could I?'

Gemma agreed that of course she couldn't, but with her interview so close, her mind was preoccupied, checking off half-remembered lists of teaching aids and 'aims and objectives', and trying to prepare herself for anything else that the headmistress might question her about. It was worse than revising for an exam.

And all totally unnecessary. For Mrs Muldoony, the headmistress of Fairmead School, didn't look a bit like a headmistress and wasn't out to test her at all. She was small and skinny, with grey eyes and greying hair, and scruffily dressed in denim and Doc Martens. All she wanted to do 'at this stage', as she explained at once, was to meet Gemma 'to see if she'd suit'.

'I think the best way to do that is for you to meet the children,' she said. 'There are three of them. I think I told you that, didn't I? Kevin has cerebral palsy so he has a full-time helper because of his speech difficulties. The two I'd like you to meet are Francine and Matthew. They're both in wheelchairs at the moment. Francine lost the use of her legs after a virus and Matt had his right leg amputated after a road accident. He's got a prosthesis but he won't use it. Quite a problem, our Matthew.' They'd reached a classroom leading out of the hall. 'Here we are.'

Matthew was a small scowling boy with black hair and enormous dark brown eyes. He was sitting in his wheelchair in a corner of the room, picking holes in a strip of coloured paper, all on his own. He looked trapped and resentful as if he were sitting in a cage. He made Gemma think of a beleaguered bush-baby she'd seen in a zoo when she was a child.

'Hello,' she said, limping to his side. 'I'm Gemma.'

But he didn't answer. He didn't even look up.

'What's that you're making?' she tried.

The answer was little more than a grunt. 'Nothing.'

'Well what are you supposed to be making?'

He went on picking holes. 'Nothing.'

'That's not much fun,' she said. 'What would you like to do instead?'

'Nothing.'

'Come and meet Francine,' Mrs Muldoony suggested to Gemma. 'Maybe Matt will feel more like talking to us later on.

You're not too happy at the moment, are you Matt?' And she swept Gemma off to another classroom.

Francine was a different sort of child altogether, a plump West Indian with a bubbly personality. She befriended Gemma at once, showing her the project she was working on and telling her about her mum and her two brothers and how they were going to Jamaica for their Christmas holiday.

'A lovely family,' Mrs Muldoony said, as she and Gemma walked back to her study. 'Yes, Svetta, that's very good. I'll be back in a minute to see it, tell Mr Rainer . . . Shouldn't you be in your classroom, Paul?'

The more she saw of Mrs Muldoony, the more Gemma liked her. For such a small woman she had amazing presence. Nothing fazed her and she seemed to be able to give her attention to at least four things at once.

'So what do you think of them?' she asked when they were back in her study again.

'Francine's a lovely kid,' Gemma said, starting with the child she could praise. 'She'd be pretty easy to help. At least, I think she would. She'd take help when she needed it. She wouldn't feel put down by needing it — if that makes sense. Of course, I could be wrong. It's hard to judge in such a short time. She must get upset now and then. That's only natural. But she looks like the sort of kid who would come out of it easily.'

'And Matt?'

'He's mourning, isn't he?'

The dark eyebrows raised slightly over eyes grown shrewd. 'Go on.'

'They told me at the rehab centre that we all have to mourn what we've lost,' Gemma explained. 'I cried a lot. Usually in the bathroom. We all mourn in different ways. Some of us get angry. I think that's where he is. Hurt and angry.'

'And what's the answer?'

'Time. Finding others in the same boat. Accepting that life goes on. That it might even get better in some ways. Finding a bit of hope. All sorts of things.'

Mrs Muldoony was looking at her thoughtfully, grey eyes narrowed. I've said too much, Gemma thought. I've gone on too long. I should have waited for her to ask me.

But the headmistress was smiling. 'Bang to rights,' she said. And when Gemma smiled in response, she added, 'You'll do.'

'You mean I've got the job?' Gemma said. It was almost too good to be true.

'As good as,' Mrs Muldoony said. 'If I could offer it to you here and now, I would, but life isn't quite so simple these days. The governors have to agree to rustle up the funding before I can make an appointment. I should warn you, though. It's not full time — just one full day a week and four half-days — and the pay's not good. It'll probably work out at about £4.75 an hour.'

'That's all right,' Gemma said. 'I've got a mobility allowance.'

'In that case, I'll set the wheels in motion. Incidentally, you're supposed to come to me through an agency. Don't worry. It shouldn't be a problem. I tell them I want you and you apply to them for work half an hour later. I'll give you the address. I've got it here somewhere. Yes. Here it is. Can you get there?' And when Gemma nodded: 'Right. I should be able to let you know officially in a day or two. Certainly by the end of next week.'

'Thanks!'

'Welcome aboard,' Mrs Muldoony said and held out a skinny hand for Gemma to shake.

The agency was easy to find but difficult to enter, being up a flight of stairs and along a corridor. Going up the stairs was tricky, coming down was painful. But it was worth the effort. She'd made her application, filled in forms, and seemed to have been accepted. By the time she got back to the empty house in Amersham Road she was weary but triumphant.

'Guess what?' she said to Nick as she opened the front door to him that evening. She couldn't wait to tell him her news.

'The place looks empty,' he said. 'Are they away?'

She explained where his parents were and then tumbled back into her story, telling him about the school and Mrs Muldoony and Matt and Francine and how she managed to get up and down stairs for the first time. 'I feel on top of the world,' she said. 'A job. And straight away. Imagine it. Almost the first time of asking. I know I haven't actually got it yet and I ought not to count chickens but it's as good as mine. I can't believe my luck. Aren't you going to congratulate me?'

'Yes,' he said. 'Of course. Are we taking the chair?'

She ought to have said yes but she'd done so well that day she couldn't face being reduced to a wheelchair for the evening. It would be losing face, chickening out, and she was made of sterner stuff.

'No,' she said airily. 'We don't want to cart that about all over London. We'll leave it in the bedroom. I'm a big girl now. I can manage without it. You just watch me.'

It was a mistake. Her stump was already uncomfortable from the pounding it had taken at the agency, so the walk from the car park to the theatre was more than she should have undertaken and she knew it after the first three steps.

But once they were in their seats, *Cats* took her mind off her discomfort and being in a theatre again was such a pleasure that a little soreness was an easy price to pay for it. And in the interval there was so much to talk about — his day on the wards and hers in school, musicals in general and this one in particular — that she quickly forgot all about it, especially when they began to discover how many tastes and opinions they shared. If this isn't a date, she thought, it's the next-best thing.

Back in Amersham Road, Billie Goodeve was standing in the porch, waiting for someone to answer the bell. She'd been there for over five minutes and she'd rung every thirty seconds or so but there was no sign of life in the house at all, no movement, no sound, no lights, except for the courtesy light over the front door, and you couldn't count that. Now she was getting cold and beginning to shiver. Where *was* the girl? She couldn't be out. Not at this time of night and not in the state she was in. And it was much too early for her to be in bed. Oh come on, do!

Presently she became aware that there was a light in the kitchen of the house next door. She could see a young woman busy at the cooker and a young man drifting about with a bottle in his hand. Maybe she'd just knock and see if they knew what was going on.

They were polite and friendly and didn't know very much.

'They must be away,' the young woman said, vaguely. 'Can't have gone for long or they'd have said. Who did you want to see?'

'Gemma Goodeve,' Billie said, suppressing a shiver. 'The girl in the wheelchair. She does live there, doesn't she?'

'Nice kid,' the young woman said. 'Yes, she lives there. She's got the granny flat.'

'Then why doesn't she answer the door?' Billie asked. 'She's not ill or anything, is she?'

'Not as far as I know. She looked bonny the last time I saw her. She must be out. Did she know you were coming?'

This time the shiver couldn't be controlled. I'm catching cold, standing around here, Billie thought. And all to no point, that's the nuisance of it. It's too bad. It really is. She's got no business being out at this time of night. What's the good of knowing where she is, if she's not there? She thanked the young couple politely and set off for home.

And after all that, she had to wait half an hour at one bus stop and nearly an hour at the other and consequently didn't get back to Streatham until very late. By which time there was no doubt she'd caught a cold. Miserable with disappointment and with an increasing temperature, she made herself a hot milk, added a liberal dose of whisky, and grumbled to bed.

Chapter 20

Nick and Gemma emerged from the blaze and boom of *Cats* into the evening chill of a mundane Drury Lane, arm in happy arm.

'I'm starving,' Nick said. 'Let's go and get something to eat. I don't have to be back on the wards till two o'clock. Do you like Chinese? There's a really good one in Leicester Square and they're very quick. It's only down Long Acre. We could get a cab if you like.'

So they took a cab to Irving Street and walked from there into the familiar, pedestrianised bustle of the square. She looked up at the neon lights of the cinemas and told him that the Odeon used to be the old Alhambra Music Hall and he looked across at a drunk staggering about in the central garden and told her that the police were always picking up junkies and winos and bringing them into Casualty.

'What do you do with them?' she asked.

'Not a lot, really,' he admitted. 'Patch them up and send them out again. Most of them need psychiatric care and full-time nursing but they're "in the community" now so they don't get it.'

'So your father's right,' she said as they walked to the restaurant.

'Absolutely right,' he agreed. 'The government thought they'd be saving money when they closed down the psychiatric hospitals but all they've actually done is to shift the problems on to someone else.'

'Like the police.'

'And A and E, especially over the weekends.'

'You must be proud of him,' she said. 'The stand he's taking.'

She expected to see some sign of pride or pleasure on his face but he was suddenly wearing his distant expression. 'You don't approve,' she said.

'It's not that exactly,' he told her, trying to be fair. 'He's honest and he's got the courage of his convictions but you need more than that if you're going to speak out the way he does.'

'Why?'

'It could be dangerous.'

That sounded over the top. 'Dangerous?'

They'd reached the restaurant so he didn't answer for the moment but stood aside to usher her in. Then he moderated his words. 'Well, harmful then. He's a whistle-blower, and whistle-blowers get hurt. I know he says they can't touch him because he's retired but I'm not so sure. I think he's being over-confident. If he's not careful he'll end up paying a price for it.'

Gemma thought that was cynical but they were being escorted to a table and the menu was being placed before them, so there was no more time to talk politics.

The food was as good as Nick had promised and they both enjoyed it very much. Then well fed, happily entertained, still talking and feeling decidedly pleased with themselves, they took another taxi to the car park and drove back to Amersham Road.

It was dark and private in the front garden and very quiet when he'd switched off the ignition. There was enough pale light from the courtesy lamp for them to be able to look into one another's eyes and no necessity for them to bring their evening to an end. Hadn't he said he wasn't due back on the ward until two o'clock? They sat so close together they were almost touching. And the magic began again, just as it had when he carried her down to the river, holding them still and enraptured and hopeful.

He put his arm round her shoulders and kissed her. At last. It was a tentative kiss and very gentle but it roused them both.

'Beauty!' he said, gazing at her tender-eyed. And kissed her again, this time with more passion. This time she kissed him back, her eyes closing of their own volition with the pleasure of it.

The empty house waited obligingly in the darkness. 'Are you going to ask me in for coffee?' he asked hopefully.

She teased him. 'I've only got Nescafé.'

Nescafé would be fine. What did it matter what it was? It was only an excuse and with luck they wouldn't get to drink it. Good old ageds, he thought, as he got out of the car. Their timing's perfect. But then he noticed that Gemma was wincing as she stood up. 'Are you all right?'

She tried to make light of it. 'I've done too much walking, that's all. It's a bit sore.'

They strolled to the side door with their arms around each other but now, besides being acutely aware of her and wanting to kiss her again, the doctor in him was noticing how badly she was limping.

'It's more than a bit sore,' he said, as she took up a careful stance before putting her key in the lock. 'It's hurting you to stand. You'd better let me have a look at it when we get in.'

'There's no need,' she said, opening the

door. 'Really.' His abrupt change from lover to doctor upset her. Surely her leg could wait. Or didn't he want to kiss her again?

But he was insistent. 'You're limping,' he said firmly. 'It needs checking. You don't want another op, do you?'

She could see there was no hope of ignoring it now. 'All right then,' she said quite crossly. 'I'll go to the bathroom and sort it out. Will that satisfy you?'

She thought he would wait in the living room but he followed her into the bathroom determined to see the state of the stump for himself and without the slightest inkling that he might be invading her privacy.

She was miserably embarrassed. In hospital it had been the norm to be seen by any number of young men and women, but never like this. The fact that he'd just been kissing her turned this sudden descent into helpless patient into a mortification.

She sat on the toilet seat and took off her shoes and socks, so that her false foot was exposed. She had to steel herself not to wince at it. Oh if only she'd got a nice normal foot covered in flesh like everybody else. 'I can manage,' she begged, looking up at him.

But he was massively adamant, wearing

his serious face and waiting, as immovable as a tree.

There was nothing for it. She had to take off her jeans and let him see the damage. She set about it gingerly, as he was quick to notice, good leg first, then the prosthesis, easing the tight cloth down towards her false foot as gently as she could.

And of course, the stump *was* chafed. It looked red and sore and was obviously swollen. Damn, damn, damn!

'You'll have to come into St Thomas's,' he decided. 'Have you got a skirt you could put on?'

'There's no need for that,' she protested. 'It'll be all right. I'll put a dressing on it.'

'It needs more than a dressing,' he said, already on his way to the bedroom. 'Where do you keep your skirts?'

'Look,' she called after him. 'I'll go to the rehab centre first thing Monday morning. That's all it needs.'

The offer fell on stony medical ground. 'Much too late,' he said, returning with a red skirt that didn't match anything she was wearing. 'You can't spend the weekend in this state. Put this on.'

'I'll phone them tomorrow and see what they say.'

'Tomorrow's Saturday. They won't be

there. Put this on.'

'Don't boss me about, Nick.'

'It's for your own good. Believe me. You don't want another op do you?'

She had to admit that she didn't. But she still thought he was making a fuss.

'Allow me to be the judge of that,' he said. 'I'd rather have you cross with me now and be sure you're properly looked after than give in to you and have to watch you come round from another op.'

So she had to put on her unsightly skirt and use her crutches to get out to the car — because she certainly wasn't going to allow him to carry her when he was being so officious — and be driven to the hospital. She argued with him all the way but he was impervious to everything she said. It didn't seem possible to her that they'd been kissing one another in this same car less than half an hour ago.

And things got worse when they reached St Thomas's because the A and E department was full of casualties and obviously much too busy to attend to a swollen stump, as she told him at once.

'We'll go through the side door,' he said, undeterred, 'and jump the queue.' And shot off at once to get a wheelchair.

'I don't need this,' she said.

He was calm and implacable. 'I'm going to see if I can find Ab,' he said. 'He'll know who's on. You'll have to sit in with the others for a few minutes but I shouldn't be long.'

The others were all so much worse than she was that she felt uncomfortable to be among them. There were two drunks in mud-coloured overcoats and stained trousers held up with string, clutching cans and stinking the place out, one with blood-stained fists and the other with a blood-smeared face; two young men, pale-faced with shock and with a policeman in attendance; an old lady groaning on a stretcher with a neck brace holding up her chin and tears oozing out of her eyes; a skinhead, with six earrings in each ear and spikes through his nose and his eyebrows, being sick between his boots; ambulance men coming and going, two paramedics waiting by the entrance, nurses looking harassed, a doctor rushing through the swing doors as if the place was on fire.

This is a waste of time, Gemma thought, as the minutes ticked monotonously by. Names were called and casualties led away to be examined, but more arrived by the minute, some very belligerently. They've got enough to attend to here without me. If only Nick had waited with her instead of rushing away like that. It was frustrating just sitting about. And it got more frustrating the longer she sat there. She was trying to work out how she could get home by herself, when Nick emerged from one of the curtained cubicles with a tall Indian doctor, who smiled at her as if they knew one another.

'This is Ab,' Nick said, wheeling her into the cubicle. 'He'll look after you. You're in safe hands. I'm due on the wards in five minutes. Sorry about that. I'll be back. I'll arrange for an ambulance to take you home. Look after her, Ab.' And he was gone before she could catch her breath.

'Not to worry,' Ab said, seeing how confused and annoyed she was. 'Let's have a look at this stump of yours, shall we.'

She submitted to yet another examination and waited again while a consultant was called. There was no sign of Nick but by then she was past caring. It was half an hour before the consultant appeared. Not one she knew, but he was quick and decisive, told her she was wise to come in, prescribed anti-inflammatory drugs, advised her to use her chair until the swelling had gone down and suggested that she should get back to the rehab centre.

'That's arranged,' Ab said. 'Dr Quennell phoned down. He's ordered the ambulance for nine o'clock on Monday morning.'

I might as well not be here, Gemma thought, they're all so busy living my life for me. Then she felt ashamed of herself for being ungrateful. They *were* doing their best. So she smiled and said thank you, and the consultant wrote his notes and departed. But Nick didn't come back.

'Now what?' she said to Ab, as a nurse arrived to wheel her back into the waiting area.

'There's an ambulance on its way to take you home. Shouldn't be long. Nick said to tell you he'd be down to say goodbye.'

But he wasn't, even though it was another three-quarters of an hour before an ambulance man arrived to collect her. By the time she hopped awkwardly into her flat, it was past three o'clock in the morning and all she wanted to do was cry.

How could I have been such a fool? she wept as she lay in the darkness of her ugly bedroom. How could I have sat out in that car and imagined I was going to start a relationship when I've got one leg missing and a stump that lets me down at the crucial moment and I don't even *look* normal, for Christ's sake? It was time to face up to the facts. And the first one was her own changed image.

The lesser scars on her face were fading but the great tramline across her scalp would never go away. It was there and she would have to live with it. And it couldn't be completely hidden by her hair, no matter how cunningly she arranged it and no matter how strongly it was growing back. The scars on her leg would always be there too and so would the deformity of that stump. No matter how well she was managing her life, the bare brute facts would always be the same. She had one more or less normal leg and one that ended in an ugly stump of flesh. How could any man love a woman in a state like that? Even a doctor who knows what I've been through. I thought he might be an exception, a man strong enough to accept me for what I am, but he's not. How could he be? He's a doctor and I'm his patient. That's all there is to it, all there'll ever be to it, and I'm a fool to imagine it could ever be anything else. That's how they think of me in this house — as a patient. That's how they'll go on thinking of me as long as I stay here. They're all in a mind-set. And I can't put up with it. It's too painful. Well there's only one thing to be done. I shall have to move out. I've got a job, or as good as, now I'll find a flat and set up on my own.

Making plans restored her. I'll go tomorrow, she decided, closing her eyes. Well, today really. Later on today. And with that, she slept.

In the Pengillys' stylish living room in Poppleton, Susan and Catherine were still awake. Catherine had spent a cheerful afternoon in York, Christmas shopping with the two girls, who'd had an Inset day off school, and tomorrow they were all going to Leeds for a day's shopping there. But now, although it was well into the small hours, she and Susan were sitting up, enjoying the warmth of the log fire, talking and drinking yet another late-night whisky. Catherine joked that she was too bushed to go to bed. She *was* tired, that was true enough, but there was another and more pressing reason for her delay and that was her need to know what was troubling her daughter. They'd been gossiping off and on since the girls went to bed but she was still none the wiser and now they were on to yet another new topic.

For, as Susan refilled her mother's glass, she'd asked, 'How are our lovebirds?'

'Difficult to say,' Catherine answered. 'I'd hardly call them lovebirds.'

'Are they an item?'

'They went to the theatre tonight,' Catherine said. 'Thanks. Gemma told me. But I'm not sure there's anything in it.'

'What does Nick say about it?'

'He hasn't said anything yet. And I haven't asked. It's not something you ask your son. He'll tell me in his own good time, if there's anything to tell. Like Chris.'

'Is she still living in the flat?'

'Oh yes.'

'And does he phone her?'

'No.'

'Now that's odd,' Susan said. 'Why is he being so slow? I thought they were getting on so well.'

Catherine was puzzled by these questions, just as she'd been by all the others Sue had asked her. Why the interest? she wondered. It's not like her to quiz me about her brothers. Or to be so edgy. She's always been quick and tense but nothing like this. She's like a greyhound in the slips, all bolting eyes and straining at the leash. New lines on her forehead, that trick of flexing her fingers before she tackles the next chore. That's new too. She's doing it now. It reminded her of that awful time when the fifteen-year-old Susan had failed her mocks and locked herself in the bedroom and refused to talk to anybody. Maybe I should ask a direct question and see if I can get her to talk about what's really troubling her. If I do it gently . . .

'Is anything up?'

It was too direct and the answer was aggressive. 'No. Why should there be?'

So there is, Catherine thought and backtracked at once. 'No reason. I just wondered.'

'I think I'm going to accept the job I told you about.'

A clue? Catherine wondered and asked, 'Do I congratulate you or would that be premature?'

'I don't know.'

'Well, let me put it another way. Is it a good thing or a bad thing?'

Susan put down her glass and looked her mother directly in the eye. 'I don't know that either. There's a snag. Matter of fact, I phoned Chris about it yesterday. To see what he'd have to say.'

So this is what she really wants to talk about, Catherine thought, considering how much a call like that would have cost, and it's serious. I shall have to be very careful.

'And what *did* he say?'

'He said go for it. But that's Chris all over.' She sighed. 'I don't know. I suppose it's what you'd call a moral dilemma.'

Catherine waited.

'It's a matter of telling the whole truth,' Susan said, plunging into confession at last. 'Or not quite the whole truth. What it boils down to is this. Do I tell my new bosses I'm Dad's daughter and risk not being offered the job? Or do I keep my mouth shut and risk them finding out later on?'

'Is it a risk?'

'I think so. But that's part of the trouble. I can't be sure. If he hadn't started all this by slagging off the railways it might have been all right. Or if he wasn't in the news all the time slagging off the government. I just don't know what to do for the best.'

Catherine smiled. 'Is that how you see what he's doing? Slagging off the government?'

This time it was Susan's turn to backtrack. It wouldn't do to let her mother think she was criticising her father. 'Well no, not exactly. That was anger talking.' And when Catherine's eyebrows rose at the word, she explained. 'I know he doesn't mean to but he's making my life very difficult at the moment.'

'He's writing a column for the *Independent*,' Catherine felt she ought to warn her.

'Well let's hope they restrict him to talking about medicine,' Susan sighed. 'If he starts on about the railways again, I shall be sunk.'

'But that's all over, isn't it?' Catherine said. 'The report's published. There haven't been any side-effects.'

'If you discount twenty-four claims for damages.'

'But it's history.'

Susan sighed again. 'I only wish it were. The trouble is there's going to be another inquiry. By Railtrack.'

Ah, Catherine thought. So this is politics. 'What for?'

'To inquire into the availability of cranes. Railways South have been pressing for it. They say that if the cranes had been brought in more rapidly there wouldn't have been so many fatalities. They've been pressing for someone else to be involved for weeks — ever since our report was published, in fact. It's what comes of being privatised. When we were BR there was never a problem. It was all done centrally and we could withstand any number of claims. Now the network's been broken down, there are dozens of companies and we're into buck-passing time. Nobody wants to take the blame.'

Catherine could see the problem. 'Have you talked this over with Rob?' she asked.

Susan made a grimace. 'No,' she said. 'He wouldn't understand. They don't go in for office politics in the gardening world. Besides, he's been in Leeds rather a lot recently with this Christmas show. I haven't had much chance to talk to him about anything.' He was there at the moment at a gardeners' conference, which was why Catherine had come to visit and why they were all going to Leeds the next day. 'Not that it would make any difference if I had. He's so laid back he'd just say, "What's the problem?" and forget about it. No, when it comes down to it I've got to work this one out on my own. It's a straight choice. Do I tell the whole truth and risk not being offered the job? Or do I keep my mouth shut and get the job and hope I won't get found out?'

It was a dilemma. And it kept Catherine awake for what little was left of the night. What *could* she advise? What could anyone advise? Maybe I ought to say something to Drew. But what? And how? Why was family life so hideously complicated?

Chapter 21

Saturday was one of those bleak December days, when the sun is so weak that every trace of colour is leached away from earth, sky and human countenance. The winter grass was so pale that it was almost grey and the tatty hedges and denuded trees were reduced to a dull monochrome, their branches grey against the dirty white of the sky.

Billie woke that morning feeling ill and one look at the world beyond her window made her feel worse, but she got up and made herself a cup of tea and tried to get on with her day. While she was sipping the tea, the post arrived but it was only a letter for Tim from Gresham, Gresham, Philpott and Mainwaring and she didn't have the energy to think about *that*. It would have to wait until he got back. She swathed herself in her warmest coat, found a hat and a very thick scarf and set off to work, even though her nose was running like a tap and her throat felt as though she'd been eating barbed wire. Saturday was her busiest day and she couldn't afford to miss the trade.

Nick was hard at work on the wards and too weary to notice what the weather was like. From time to time he wondered how Gemma was and promised himself that he'd ring her as soon as he got the chance, because he really should have tried to find the time to go down and say goodbye to her. But once he was off duty he fell across his bed and slept as though he'd been anaesthetised.

In Poppleton, Helen and Naomi were up at six, loud and ready for their day in Leeds. They were so excited they didn't care what colour the sky was, and wouldn't have noticed if it had fallen on their heads, Chicken-Licken style.

Only Gemma paid any attention to it and that was because she was reduced to travelling in her chair. She knew she ought to take a rug to keep herself warm but decided against it. She was young and strong and, after the humiliation of the previous night, she needed to prove it. There was no necessity to appear more of an invalid than she was. She jammed a red woollen hat on her head, arranged a red paisley scarf round her neck, found her one and only pair of gloves, tucked her crutches beside her and set off for Putney High Street and the letting agencies.

And didn't find anything suitable, which, despite her deliberately cheerful mood, was rather dispiriting. The trouble was that nearly all the flats she visited were impossible for a wheelchair, the first because there were awkward steps, the second because the door was too narrow for her to get through. The third had a better entrance but was poorly lit and hideously ugly inside. The fourth looked so dour she didn't even bother with it.

By this time the estate agent, who was young and conceited, was beginning to get sick of her. 'Well that's it,' he told her, walking away from the fifth flat. 'I haven't got anything else.'

'Just as well you're not the only letting agent in town,' she said, grinning at him to keep up her spirits.

But the other one hadn't got anything suitable either. By lunchtime she'd annoyed him too by turning down every single flat he suggested. Bar one.

'I'll come back after lunch and see that,' she said. 'Is there a restaurant or a McDonald's anywhere that can take a wheelchair?'

He didn't know and plainly didn't care.

'Not to worry,' she said. 'I'll find one.'

But like finding a flat, it was easier said

than done. Why is everything so complicated when you're in a chair? she thought, buzzing past yet another impossible entrance. And then, as if to show her that there were complications she hadn't even thought about, the chair suddenly seized up and stopped.

It didn't take her long to realise what had happened. The wretched batteries had gone flat. She'd noticed how low they were on Friday morning when she went to the school, so she ought to have put them on charge overnight. But she'd been in such a rush to get out to the theatre that she'd forgotten all about them, and later on she'd been too upset. How could she have been so careless? More to the point, what was she going to do now? It was much too far for her to walk back home, even if her stump was up to it, which it certainly wasn't. What was worse, there was no one she could phone to come and rescue her, because Andrew and Catherine weren't due back until tomorrow morning. What was she going to do?

By this time the chair was causing an obstruction and people were giving her odd looks. 'I've broken down,' she explained and tried to cover her embarrassment with a joke. 'I'm waiting for the AA.'

'Would you like a push?' two young men offered.

'I live at the top of the hill,' she told them. 'And it's very heavy.'

The weight of the chair deterred them. 'We'll get it out the way then,' the older one compromised.

So they heaved it to one side and parked it beside the nearest shop front. I shall have to phone for a taxi, Gemma thought. But there was no sign of a phone box anywhere — wouldn't you know it?

Now that she wasn't in the middle of the pavement, the shoppers passed her without giving her much attention, apart from the occasional sympathetic look from those who'd stopped to gaze at the shop window, and an unexpected wave from a dilapidated lady on the other side of the road. She was a funny-looking old thing, not much better than a tramp, in an ancient tweed coat tied round the middle with a man's belt, Wellington boots and a woolly hat that had fallen over one eye, but she was smiling happily and didn't seem a bit abashed when Gemma stared at her. Quite the reverse, in fact. She stepped to the kerb, looked carefully to left and right, crossed, and walked straight towards the chair.

'Hello duck,' she said. 'Didn'tcher get yer

new leg after all, then?'

The sound of her voice revealed who she was — the oldest inhabitant from Page Ward.

'Well hello to you,' Gemma said, smiling at her. 'How are you?'

'Fell on me feet, didn't I,' the old lady said, sucking her teeth.

'You didn't go to a home, then?'

'Not likely. I told you I wouldn't, didn't I. No, I got one a them sheltered flats up the 'ill. Lovely it is. We got a warden an' a club room an' a nice little bus to bring us down here shopping. All sorts. Worth waitin' for. But never mind me, what are *you* doin' here? I thought they was gonna fit you with a new leg.'

Gemma explained, shivering a little in the cold wind.

'Good job I was passin' then,' the old lady said. 'How far can you walk?'

'About a hundred yards, I should think. I don't want to go too far in case of making it worse.'

'That'll do,' the old lady said, nodding and smiling. 'Come on.'

'Where to?'

'Why, the church. Where else? They'll help yer. Ever so nice they are. I go every Sunday. It's just up the road.'

Gemma wasn't hopeful. For a start she

doubted whether there would be anyone there. Most churches were locked up during the week these days, weren't they? And if there *was* someone around, it was even less likely that there'd be a phone. From what she remembered of churches they were dull empty places with rows and rows of dusty pews facing a distant high altar where you had to creep about and whisper. But she struggled to her surviving foot, balanced on her crutches and limped off towards the church.

'How's yer mum?' the oldest inhabitant asked as they struggled down the slope towards the church entrance.

The question provoked a stab of conscience. So much had happened in the last few days, she'd forgotten all about her. She'd even forgotten about her father. 'She's fine.'

'She's ever so fond of you, you know,' the old lady said. 'She used ter come an' talk to me when you wasn't there. I still got all them cuttings. You remember. You as a little gel. I show 'em to the old folks. I say, See that gel. Famous, she is, I was in hospital with her. I tell 'em about your flowers. D'you remember? An' how you dressed up as a clown that time. D'you remember that? Give her my regards next time you see her.'

'I will,' Gemma said, speaking the words automatically but wondering when it would be. I really ought to ring her.

But there wasn't time to feel guilty about it because the old lady was bustling her through a side door. 'Here we are then,' she said. 'This is St Mary's.'

It wasn't a bit what Gemma expected. The side door led into a modern vestibule made of a richly coloured wood. Beech, was it? Or ash? And when she hobbled through into the church itself she found a place transformed. The side aisles were gone and there were no pews, only rows of wide chairs, upholstered in leather and arranged in long curved rows to face north, towards the river. The altar wasn't where she expected it to be either, but in the centre of the north side of the building, below a new stained-glass window designed in long strips of shiny primary colour, like a stage curtain or a collection of bright, furled flags. The impact of the place was extraordinary, uplifting and decidedly friendly.

'Stay there,' the oldest inhabitant ordered. 'An' I'll get John.'

She returned within seconds with a middle-aged man in a fleecy T-shirt and corduroy trousers. He reminded Gemma of someone but for the moment she couldn't think who it was — middle-aged, dark eyes, gentle face, brown beard going grey.

'I gather you need a lift home,' he said. 'You've come at the right moment. I was just going to take my wife shopping. My car's just outside.'

Gemma was touched. 'That's very kind of you.'

'We *are* kind,' he said. 'That's us. If you'll just wait here a minute while I get Sarah . . . We'll pick up your chair *en route*.'

'I shall sit here and admire your church,' she told him. 'I've never seen one like this.'

'Ah!' he said. 'Thereby hangs a tale, which I'll tell you on the way.'

So the oldest inhabitant took herself off, saying she'd have to look sharp or she'd miss her bus, and Sarah was collected from the office and away they went.

'Right,' John said, when the chair had been picked up and they were driving up the High Street, following Gemma's directions. 'About the church. It's quite a story. We had a fire, you see. A really bad one. The whole place was gutted. By the time the Fire Brigade got it under control, there was nothing left but the outer walls. It took us ten years to rebuild it, didn't it, Sarah? We only reopened in 1983. But as you see, it gave us a chance to redesign, to think about the sort of church we wanted, to start anew in the way we wanted. I suppose you could say we made a virtue of necessity.'

'And now you've got a beautiful new church,' Gemma said.

'Well we think so.'

'With a larger congregation,' Sarah smiled. 'I'm happy to say.' She was an old-fashioned foil to his dark gentleness, being slight and pale with her fair hair caught up in a bun at the nape of her neck.

'It must have seemed like the end when it was burnt down,' Gemma sympathised. 'I know how that feels. It seemed like the end to me when I knew my leg had been cut off.'

'It never is the end, though, is it?' John smiled. 'Sometimes it's a beginning.'

'Yes,' she agreed. 'Sometimes it is.' And she suddenly realised who he reminded her of, with that gentle face and that neat greying beard. It was Rob Pengilly.

When they reached Amersham Road, it was an effort for her helpers to struggle with the heavy wheelchair into the flat, which embarrassed Gemma, even though they assured her it was quite all right.

'You've been so kind,' she said to them. 'I don't know how to thank you.'

'It's all part of the service,' John told her, as he got his breath back. 'Incidentally,

Mabel said you were flat-hunting when your chair broke down. Have you found what you wanted?'

She shook her head. 'I wish I had.'

'Have you tried St Mary's Court?'

She hadn't even heard of it.

'Oh well, if that's the case, let me recommend it,' he said. 'It's a new complex down by the river, built by a housing trust. Mostly family flats and houses but they've got a block of sheltered flats too. They might be just the thing. What do you think, Sarah?'

Sarah thought they would be ideal. 'They're really rather nice,' she said. 'I've seen them. They've got lifts and special fitments and all that sort of thing. Would you be interested in one?'

'Yes,' Gemma told her. 'If I could afford the rent. Very interested.'

'I don't know about the rent,' John admitted. 'But it shouldn't be prohibitive. Why don't you go and see?'

It was the third time since her accident that she'd been picked up from a miserable state by the unexpected kindness of strangers — first the flowers, then Catherine with her offer of the granny flat and now this. 'I will,' she told her new friends. 'And thank you very much. For everything. I'm really grateful.'

She went the very next morning, driving her newly charged chair down the long hill towards the High Street in a state of such happy expectation that only success was possible. The sun was shining again, colour had returned to the world, and she sang as she drove, *'Let it be! Let it be!'* past the Edwardian villas and the prestigious flats of Manor Fields, round the crossing and past the curved frontage of Bernard Marcus Estate Agents, along a High Street which was empty of everything except two red buses and a family car, down to the river and the friendly tower of St Mary's Church.

St Mary's Court was on a smaller site than she expected but, once inside, she found herself in a spacious courtyard, neatly paved with flowerbeds, with a fountain in the middle, and blocks of pristine new houses to north, east and west. They were built of sandy London brick richly ornamented with terracotta and in several variations of the Victorian style with gables and bay windows and wrought-iron balconies. She liked them at once and set off to find the site office.

That turned out to be the living room of one of the unoccupied houses and was manned by a woman with pebbledash glasses, thin beige hair and a long beige cardigan who was knitting with furious concentration when Gemma limped in through the door.

'You're just our sort of tenant,' she said, beaming at Gemma. 'The very person we had in mind when we were designing these places.' She got up to show her the site map and to explain where the sheltered flats had been built. 'Number 6 is for wheelchairs,' she said, 'and I believe it's about ready for occupation.' She checked the papers on her desk. 'Yes, after Christmas. Would you like to see it?'

It was on the ground floor — which was good for a start — with a ramp leading up to the door which was wide and handsome under a gabled porch. There was a flowerbed planted with shrubs alongside the ramp and another set neatly underneath the kitchen window. The whole place looked so clean and orderly and white-painted and welcoming she couldn't wait to get inside.

So the key was produced and in they went. The front door was wide enough to accommodate her chair and so was the hall, which was painted magnolia like every other room. And from the hall there were only two other doors to negotiate, one leading into the bedroom which had an archway through to an *en suite* bathroom, and the other which led to the kitchen and thence through another archway to a very pretty living room. It had a Victorian fireplace, white skirting boards and coving, magnolia walls and a huge bay window overlooking the River Thames.

Gemma wheeled her chair into the bay to enjoy the view. Beyond the window, the river was glamorous with winter sunlight, its sharp waves tipped with flashes of crystal, its width a rolling pattern of olive green and sky blue. On the opposite bank the terraces were made of the old familiar London brick, dirty yellow, smudged smoke-gray, and the row of windows flashed in the sun as if they'd just been washed, reflecting the blue of the sky like a string of mirrors. Looking at it, she felt as if she'd come home. It made her think of all the other river scenes she'd enjoyed in her life, and especially the ones that had comforted her since her accident — the view of the Houses of Parliament from the restaurant in St Thomas's, the milky blue water that had lapped around her on that river journey to York. There was no doubt in her mind. If she could afford this flat, she would rent it. No, damn it, she would rent it even if she couldn't afford it. It was simply too good to pass up.

Chapter 22

Because the girls were clowning about, Catherine missed her train that Sunday morning, so she got home an hour later than she intended. She was surprised to see the ramp in position because that meant Gemma must be out. As she walked into the living room to check the answerphone, she wondered briefly where she could have got to and hoped she was with Nick. But there wasn't time for speculation. The machine was flashing and there were five calls waiting, one from Grace wondering whether they would like to come to dinner with her on Thursday, one from a man from the *Independent*, who said he'd call back, and three who hadn't left a message. Blanks made her feel anxious, but there wasn't time to worry about *them* either. Not when there was a dinner to cook and she was an hour behind schedule. She hung up her coat and headed for the kitchen.

The lamb was roasting nicely and most of the vegetables were prepared before Gemma limped in, using her crutches and not wearing her prosthesis.

'Oh dear,' Catherine said. 'Trouble?'

Gemma grinned to show that it was nothing. She'd rehearsed what she was going to say and how it was going to be said. 'Bit sore. That's all. I walked too far yesterday.' There was no need to mention going to hospital. Nick could tell them that — if he wanted to. 'Wait till you hear what I've got to tell you. I've got a job. *And* I've found a flat.'

'Well done, you!' Catherine applauded. 'Stay to dinner and tell me all about it.'

They were still talking happily when Andrew breezed into the kitchen, grey eyes beaming, hair bushing about his temples, wearing triumph like a cloak.

'Great broadcast,' he said. 'That smells good! How were the kids?'

His arrival pushed Catherine straight back to the problem that had kept her awake for the past two nights. How can I possibly tell him what to do? she thought. Or what not to do? Even for Susan. It would be like telling the tide not to come in. She gave Gemma a smile to signal that the rest of their conversation would have to wait and turned to give him her full attention. 'What was it about?' she asked.

'Rationing,' he told her briefly, lifting the

lid of the saucepan to examine the contents. 'Got pretty technical. Are we having almonds with these?'

'We are. And the carrots are cooked in cider. All your favourites. So I gather you had plenty to say.'

'Oh, this and that,' he teased. 'Actually that's not the best news.' And he waited happily for them to look at him. Which they both did. 'I've written my next article.' Oh the pride of being able to say that.

Catherine laughed. 'Good heavens! What happened to your writer's block?'

'Solved,' he said, taking a copy of the *Chronicle* out of his bag. 'I've got an enemy. Look at that.'

It was an article by a reporter called Garry McKendrick, headlined QUACK-QUACK QUENNELL and printed alongside a very unflattering photograph obviously taken from a television broadcast: Andrew was in full flow with his mouth wide open.

'Dr Know-it-all, self-opinionated Quennell,' the article said, 'is getting on my nerves. You can't turn on the telly these days without him popping up all over the place, giving everybody stick and rabbiting on about how bad the NHS is. There's a rumour he's got a column in the *Independent* so he can bend our ears in print. We should be so lucky! If it goes on much longer nobody will be able to get a word in edgeways for his endless quack-quack-quack. There's no end to the man. So I've got a message for him. Pin back your lug-holes, Dr Quack-quack. Here it comes.

'We're fed up to the back teeth with your complaining. And it's got to stop. There's a lot right with our Health Service in case you haven't noticed. It's had *millions* spent on it in the last five years. Some of us would prefer to hear about *that* instead of having our ears bent with doom and gloom. So put a sock in it Doctor and give us a break.'

'What a revolting man,' Catherine said, hotly. 'And isn't he *crude!*'

'He's perfect,' Andrew told her, grinning. 'A gift. He sounds off, you see, and all I've got to do is answer him. Do you want to see what I've written? It's really rather good. All about the way those millions have been wasted.'

They read the article over dinner and Gemma promised to type it up for him when she got back from the rehab centre. Then she told him *her* news. They'd reached the coffee stage and she'd just handed him the brochure from St Mary's Court, when the phone rang.

Catherine got up to answer it but Andrew was on his feet before her. 'It'll be for me,' he said splendidly.

It was Nick. 'Ah!' he said. 'You're back.'

'So it would appear,' Andrew agreed. 'Didn't you think we would be?' And he mouthed 'Nick' at Catherine.

'Ask him if he rang earlier,' Catherine said. But he ignored her.

Gemma sat at the table, trying not to look as though she was listening and feeling ill at ease. Would he ask to speak to her and, if he did, what would she say? Did she want to speak to him? She had to admit she did, despite the way he'd behaved. But only to tease him. She sat quite still, gathering her strength and honing her wits, bracing herself as if she was putting on armour, ready for a fight. Or if not a fight, a show of force. Or if not a show of force . . .

Andrew had taken full charge of the call and was off on a happy account of his weekend, urging Nick to get a copy of the *Chronicle* and describing his newly written article. 'Absolute piece of cake! Flowed like water. I should have found myself an enemy right at the start.' To Gemma's troubled eyes he seemed to be growing by the minute, filling the room. If only he wasn't quite so dominant all the time, she thought. Nick can hardly get a word in edgeways.

As Nick himself was miserably aware. This was his lunch break and he only had a couple of minutes left so he couldn't afford to waste them. Work was waiting and his bleeper lay in his pocket like a grenade about to explode. If he'd been talking to his mother, he'd have asked her to hand the phone over to Gemma. As it was, the best he could manage was to ask how she was when his father paused for breath.

'She's all right,' Andrew said. 'Got herself a job.'

'I know,' Nick said. 'She told me.' And he willed his father to put her on.

'And a flat,' Andrew went on easily. 'Did she tell you that? We shall be losing her.'

The news was so sudden it made Nick's heart sink. 'When?' he said, although the question he wanted to ask was 'Why?'

'Don't know. Week or two, I expect. Could be earlier. I shall have to learn to do my own typing.' He smiled at Gemma.

He's not going to speak to me, Gemma thought. Just about me. One doctor to another, discussing their patient. There's no point in sitting here. It's just embarrassing.

And she got up, made a mumbled excuse to Catherine and limped back to her flat.

'Is she there?' Nick asked at last.

'No. Actually she's just gone out of the room.'

She's putting a distance between us, Nick understood. She's not interested. Well if that's the way she wants it, so be it. I can handle it. 'I must go,' he said, stern with disappointment. 'Duty calls.'

'Shall we see you Tuesday?' Andrew asked.

'No,' Nick decided. He couldn't face a visit quite so soon. 'Tell Mother I'll come round on Wednesday week. About teatime.' He hung up.

'They've had a tiff,' Catherine said as Andrew rejoined her at the table.

He laughed at her. 'Now how could you possibly know that?'

'They were going out. Remember? To the theatre. Neither of them have said a word about it. He didn't, did he? And he's rung here four times.'

'Well if that's the case,' Andrew said easily, 'I suggest we keep well out of it. Let them sort it out for themselves. Much the best thing. Is there any more coffee? This lot's cold.'

Once she was back in her green and gold

living room, Gemma recovered deliberately quickly. She took out the brochure and studied it until she felt calm again. Then, feeling bolder than she'd done for a long time, she wrote an application for the least impossible job in her trade magazine, as an ASM at a theatre she'd never heard of, and folded it into her largest envelope, along with a stamped, addressed envelope for their reply. Then she found a notebook and began to work out what furniture and fittings she would need for her new life in her new flat and how much they would cost. The minute I know I've got this job, she decided, I'll put down a deposit. Then I can get on with it. I might even hear tomorrow.

But she didn't, so it was a long week, even though there was plenty in it to keep her occupied. On Monday she went to the rehab centre, where she was prescribed special dressings and a week's rest because the stump was still sore.

'Use the chair,' the consultant advised, 'and give yourself a chance to heal again.'

On Tuesday, she typed up Andrew's article for him and showed him how to operate the dictaphone. It was a way to avoid facing the fact that Nick hadn't visited.

But by Thursday, when the letter still hadn't come and Nick still hadn't phoned or written, her limited patience deserted her and she spent the entire day fretting from one domestic catastrophe to another. Pens ran out of ink, the kettle boiled dry, the duvet wouldn't stay on the bed. She made cakes and burnt them brown, did her ironing sitting down and scorched her best blouse, tried to dust her living room and ended up spraying so much polish on the clock face that she couldn't see the hands.

'I hope to God they write and tell me tomorrow,' she said to Catherine that evening. 'I'm a walking disaster area.'

But at last the letter arrived, in the second post on Friday morning, and the job was hers. She put on her coat and drove her chair to St Mary's Court at once, as if there wasn't a minute to lose. The sooner she was fully independent the better.

Tim Ledgerwood returned to Streatham that evening in a brand new BMW, a designer suit and an expansive mood. He wore his hat at a jaunty angle and his arms were full of flowers.

Billie had been sitting by the gas fire watching a film on the television and feeling miserable, with a scarf wound round her neck to ease her sore throat and a hot-water bottle in the small of her back to ease her aching bones, but his arrival lifted her spirits at once.

'Oh!' she said, as she received the flowers. 'You shouldn't have. You're spoiling me.'

'Sweets to the sweet!' he said, giving her his well-worn smile. 'Come and see my new car.'

Billie wasn't terribly interested in cars, not being a driver, but she remembered how much he enjoyed being praised so she went to the window and said the right things, commenting that business must have been good.

'So-so,' he said, looking modest. In fact, it had been far less conclusive than he'd hoped, even with the solicitor's letter as collateral, but he certainly wasn't going to tell her that. Now, what with the purchase of the suit and the hire of the car, to say nothing of business lunches and cigars, he was considerably out of pocket. 'Was there any mail?'

'You've had two from Mr Gresham,' she said, taking them out from behind the clock. 'That one came this morning.' Then she went off to the kitchen to put the flowers in water so as to give him time to read them. He was still reading when she got back, and his forehead was quite wrinkled. Better not disturb him, she thought. It'll only make him angry and I don't want to do that. He'll tell me in his own good time. She put the flowers on the sideboard and returned to the fire, where she settled against the heat of the hot-water bottle and blew her nose as discreetly as she could.

'You've got a cold,' he observed mildly, his eyes still on the letters. But he didn't sound particularly concerned.

I'm ill, she thought, and despite the pleasure she'd felt at seeing him again, she was niggled by his lack of sympathy. He'd never been good about illness. In fact, he'd been quite heartless when she was carrying Gemma and being sick all the time. She'd forgotten all about it until now. But even as the thought was in her head, she felt ashamed of it. She was remembering far too many negative things about him and it was no way to treat him, when he'd come back to her, and he still loved her, and he'd brought her all those lovely flowers. Especially when he was looking so worried. He needed support, not criticism.

'Problems?' she asked.

He changed his expression at once and smiled at her. 'Nothing I can't handle,' he said. 'He's drawn up the application. Looks fine to me. For half a million, as we specified. Now he's ready for Gemma to sign it.'

He was also ready to be paid and had sent an invoice to prove it. Damned man! 'I don't suppose we've had any news of her, have we?'

'Well, yes,' Billie smiled, feeling pleased with herself. 'I've found her.'

His response was wonderfully dramatic. 'Brilliant!' he said, looking up at her, eyes gleaming. 'You clever, clever girl! How is she? When's she coming over? Did you tell her I wanted to see her?'

If only she could have told him what he wanted to hear instead of having to confess to a partial failure. 'Actually,' she said, 'what I mean is, I found out where she lives. She wasn't there when I went. Nobody was. They were all out for the weekend. I was hanging about for hours. That's how I caught this cold.'

'But you've been back,' he insisted. 'You've seen her?'

'Well no,' she admitted. 'I've been in bed ill. I was so bad I had to take Monday and Tuesday off work.'

'My poor poppet!' he sympathised. 'How beastly for you. Well it can't be helped. In a way it's quite a good thing. We can go back together. It's a bit late tonight, but first thing tomorrow.'

His enthusiasm made her feel tired. 'I've

got work to do,' she pointed out. 'Saturday's my busiest day. I've missed two days already this week. I can't afford to take any more time off, not if I'm to pay the mortgage.'

'Sunday, then.'

But on Sunday she would be doing her books, which had to be brought up to date because the Christmas stock was coming in on Monday and Tuesday.

He lit a cigarette and inhaled deeply, so as to hang on to his patience. 'I tell you what,' he said. 'Why don't I go on my own? You go to work and leave it all to me. How about that?'

She was horrified by such an idea. 'You can't do that, Tim. I *must* prepare her. She can be very tricky when she likes.' It would be awful if she refused to see him. It would break his poor heart. And you never really knew with Gemma.

'All right then, Poppet,' Tim conceded. 'We'll do it your way. But we must find her soon. I can stall old Gresham until after Christmas but he'll get suspicious if we don't produce her then. What about Wednesday? That's a pretty slack day. You said so yourself.'

So she agreed to Wednesday.

'We'll invite her here for Christmas,' he

said. 'That'll be nice. A real family Christmas. We'll just have time to get everything ready.'

'If she'll come.'

'You *are* down in the dumps,' he said. 'You leave her to me. She'll come. I'll handle her. Now give me a smile and tell me where you'd like me to take you for dinner.'

In Poppleton, Christmas had already begun. The decorations were up and Helen and Naomi were singing at the tops of their voices, beating time on the kitchen table with two wooden spoons:

*'Jingle Bells, Batman smells, Robin's
 flown away.
 The batmobile has lost a wheel, and landed
 in the hay.'*

Mummy hadn't come home yet so Daddy was looking after them and that meant they could sing as many rude songs as they wanted. They'd had chocolate fudge cake, peanut butter and lemon jelly sandwiches, mince pies *and* ice-cream for tea and their school jerseys were well messy, although they *had* licked their fingers clean. If Mummy'd been there they'd have got done.

But Daddy hadn't said *anything*. He'd just sat there drinking tea and smiling.

'Are there any choccy biscuits?' Naomi asked. 'I'm starving!'

'After all you've just put away!' her father grinned, producing the biscuit tin. 'No wonder you keep growing out of your clothes.' He glanced at his watch, for the tenth time since they got home. This interview was going on too long for comfort.

'When's she coming home?' Helen said, catching her father's concern.

'Now,' their mother's voice answered from the hall. And there she was, in her smart blue suit, looking pleased with herself. 'Oh for heaven's sake, you girls!' she rebuked. 'The state of your jerseys! What have you been eating?'

Fortunately Daddy spoke up before either of them could admit to anything. 'Did you get it?' he asked.

'You're looking at the new senior executive of Rail North East,' she told him, striking a pose. 'Da-daaa!'

'Pleased?' he asked. She'd been edgy before she went for this interview so there was some anxiety in the question.

She gave him a sharp look but a measured answer. 'All things considered, yes, I am.

Why shouldn't I be?'

He decided not to pursue it. If there *was* something untoward about the job she'd tell him in her own time. 'Your mother called,' he said. 'I told her you'd ring back when you got in.'

'I'll do it now,' she decided and reached for the phone at once, pausing just long enough to ask if there was any more tea in the pot, to check that the groceries had been delivered, that Mrs Jarvis had collected the dry cleaning and paid the window cleaner, and to suggest that her daughters ought to change their jerseys and get on with their homework.

'Yes,' she said, when her mother answered. 'It's me . . . Yes. I did . . . Yes I am rather . . . Well let's say I decided discretion was the better part of valour . . .'

So she's had to be discreet about something, Rob noted, as he made a fresh pot of tea. I was right. This hasn't been a straightforward promotion.

'Have you still got your lodger?' Susan asked. 'Right. Right. When's moving day?'

She's changing the subject, Rob thought. And that was a bad sign too. She's proud of her success but she doesn't want to go into details.

Catherine had picked up the same message. It was easier to talk about Gemma and her new flat than to worry over what had or had not been said at the interview. 'They're letting her move in gradually,' she said. 'The official moving day isn't until after Christmas, but they don't seem to mind. She's there now as a matter of fact.'

'Where's she going for Christmas?'

'She's staying with us, according to your father.'

'Did he ask her or tell her?' Susan laughed.

'You know your father.'

'And how is he?'

'He's gone to see Dr Thomas at the moment. Very full of himself. He's just finished another column.'

'What about, this time?'

'Coughs and colds at Christmas, which doesn't please him. He'd rather be campaigning but they don't want whistles blown at Christmas, apparently.'

'Well give him my love. Tell him I'm glad he's giving the soapbox a miss for once in a while. See you Christmas Day, if we don't get snowed in.'

'That's not likely, is it?'

'Well let's put it this way. It's not snowing yet, but it's not for want of trying. We've had sleet all afternoon. Hideous.'

'Rather you than us,' Catherine laughed.

'Don't gloat!' her daughter laughed back. 'According to the weather forecast, it's coming your way.'

Chapter 23

Although there was no sleet in Putney, it was a dark, damp afternoon and nose-pinchingly cold. But as Gemma drove her chair along the pavement, with her crutches tucked beside her and her shopping basket on her lap, she was singing to herself with the sheer joy of the season. Her stump had almost recovered, her scars were fading fast, her latest haircut looked stylish, neat and thick and really quite pretty, and now Christmas was erupting all around her, like some vast, effulgent, multicoloured flower bursting into bloom in the midwinter darkness. Lights blazed above her head, the local Lions were parading their decorated float along the High Street with a great deal of noise and excitement, playing carols at full blast on the Tannoy, shop windows rained tinsel, everyone was smiling. It might be her first one-legged Christmas, Nick might have cooled, her theatre application had been turned down, just as she expected, and she still hadn't met her father, but it was going to be a triumph. She was positive about it.

She'd been positive about Nick's visit too — in a negative sort of way. As soon as Catherine told her he was coming for tea that afternoon, she decided to be out of the house until he'd gone. The excuse was easy — she had to be at the flat — and true because she'd made it her business to be there. She'd spent the first part of the afternoon hanging up her clothes in the built-in wardrobes and measuring the windows for curtains, and now she was filling in the last hour buying Christmas presents — a string of blue beads for her mother, with stud earrings to match, and because she was spending Christmas Day with the Quennells, malt whisky for Dr Andrew and a bottle of champagne for Catherine to thank them for their kindness during the year, a scarf for Susan, gloves for Rob and two Christmas stockings full of chocolates for the girls. It was quite a haul for one expedition.

Nick was the only person she hadn't thought about that afternoon and that was because his was the first present she'd bought. Not because he meant anything to her — she was far too sensible to think that — but because it took so much consideration.

When Andrew invited her to spend

Christmas with his family she'd accepted at once and happily, partly because it seemed the obvious place for her to be — at least for part of the time — and partly because he'd asked her with the cheerful assumption that she *would* accept. 'You'll come in with us, of course.'

Catherine had laughed at that and told him not to be such a bully, but that hadn't deterred him.

'I suppose you want the poor girl to sit in her flat for two days on her own,' he'd teased. 'No, no. You spend them with us, Gemma. You'll have a whale of a time.'

At first, the only thing that worried her was the fact that Nick was being distant. But they'd got hordes of people coming so she wouldn't have to spend any time with him if he didn't want her to. But then it occurred to her that she would have to buy the family presents and that meant she would have to buy him a present too because it would look a bit pointed if she left him out. The trouble was, what could she get? It had to be just right, not too personal and not too expensive so that he could accept it in any way he pleased — as a token of friendship or a sign that she liked him as much as the rest of his family, or whatever.

She'd deliberated about it for days. And

in the end she'd been visited with an idea of such brilliant suitability that she couldn't imagine why it hadn't occurred to her before. It came as she was remembering him striding down the ward with his white coat flapping and ink stains all over the pocket. But of course! She would buy him a fountain pen.

It was already wrapped up in its Christmas paper with a splendidly noncommittal card attached which read, 'Christmas greetings from Gemma. I hope this will save your white coat from further spills.'

Now the rest of her shopping was done and in about half an hour it would be safe to head for home. And because it was Christmas time, there was plenty to entertain her while she was waiting. She wheeled across the street towards the float where the Tannoy was still singing in its raucously tinny way, '*And with true love and brotherhood each other now embrace. The holy tide of Christmas all other doth deface. Oh-oh tidings of comfort and joy!*'

The words made her remember her mother. The one discordant note in the cheerful music of the afternoon had been the intermittent growl of her conscience and now it was too loud for comfort. She still hadn't sent her an address nor fixed a time to meet her father and the nearer she got to Christmas the more it troubled her. Poor Mother, she thought, as she stopped to enjoy the procession. There's been precious little comfort and joy in her life and she means well, even if she is dominating. She *does* love me, in her own way. She came to see me when I was in hospital. She didn't exactly cheer me up but she *did* come. It isn't kind to go on sending her scrappy little cards, especially at a time when everybody remembers their parents. I'll phone her and arrange to go and see her over Christmas — and him too, if he's still there. I ought to be able to manage a bus ride by now. Catherine would know which ones to take. And as she searched in her purse for a coin to put in the collecting box, she wondered fondly where her mother was at that moment and what she was doing.

She was wearing her warmest suit and sitting beside Tim Ledgerwood in his new BMW as they purred into Amersham Road.

'That's the place,' she said, pointing to the house.

'Very nice!' Tim approved, admiring the tree-lined pavements and the size of the houses. 'Now you're sure you don't want me to come with you?'

'Yes,' she said. 'Quite sure. I told you. Let

me break the ice first. You wait here. I won't be long.'

He wasn't entirely convinced of the wisdom of letting her go alone but he gave her his charming smile and parked the car where he could watch the house. Then he watched her as she walked towards the front door, blonde hair pale in the fading light, shoulders hunched, high heels squeaking on the damp pavement.

As she reached the porch, Billie knew that there were people in the house this time. There was a lived-in air about the place and she fancied she could hear them talking. But it took ages for them to answer and that made her uncomfortable. The lady who opened the door looked at her in a guarded way as though she had no right to be there. And that made her belligerent.

'I've come to see Gemma Goodeve,' she announced.

'I'm sorry,' the lady said. She had a nice smile. Quite changed her face. 'She's not here.'

Billie could feel her own face falling. 'Oh,' she said, struggling to take it in. She couldn't be out again, not with one leg. You don't go out a lot if you're a cripple, do you? Perhaps she's gone to the doctor's. 'When will she be back?'

There was somebody walking towards them in the hall. A dark-haired young man with long legs, wearing jeans and a Marks and Spencer jumper. 'Who is it, Mother?' he asked.

'Somebody for Gemma,' the lady said, as the young man stepped up to the door.

They recognised one another instantly but before Billie could say a word, he'd taken over.

'I'm afraid Gemma's not here,' he said. 'She doesn't live here any more.' She'd be gone after Christmas so it was more or less the truth. And she was in her wretched flat at the moment, according to his mother, so the next thing he was going to say was certainly true. 'She's got a place of her own.'

'You're that doctor, aren't you?' she accused him. 'I remember you from the hospital.' And she remembered his name-tag too. She could see it clearly in her mind's eye. 'Dr Quennell.'

He was much too cool, looking at her boldly, the way he'd done on the ward. 'That's right.'

'Then you can just tell me where she is, *Dr Quennell*. I've got a right to know.'

'No,' he said, happy to fight her. 'I can't. She's particularly asked me not to. She wants time to settle in.'

'Time!' Billie exploded. 'What's she talking about? She's had *ages*.'

He didn't bother to answer. Arrogant young puppy.

'Now look here,' she said. 'I don't know what she's playing at but it can't go on. I mean it's gone on long enough already. I mean, it's weeks and weeks and weeks. Months. I'm her mother and I need to know where she is. So you just stop all this nonsense and tell me.'

He drew himself up to his full six foot, face stern and eyes dark with determination. It was always pleasant to use his authority but this was doubly satisfying because this woman deserved it and because it gave him an outlet for his annoyance with her daughter. 'You're not listening to what I'm telling you,' he said. 'She doesn't want *anyone* to know where she is. You'll just have to take "no" for an answer, I'm afraid. She'll tell you in her own time.'

To have come so far, to be so near to finding her darling and then to be balked by this horrid young man was more than Billie could bear. 'I see how it is,' she spat at him. 'This is to do with her money, isn't it? You're after the money.'

He smiled at her pityingly. 'No, Mrs Goodeve. It's nothing to do with money.'

His condescension tipped her into fury. 'Oh yes it is,' she said. 'You don't fool me.' He turned to make a grimace at his mother and at that she began to rant. She knew she shouldn't do it, but she was too far gone to control herself. 'Call yourself a doctor! You're a fine one. Just because you wear a white coat that doesn't make you a god. You ought to be ashamed of yourself! After a poor girl for her money. And don't think I don't know what you've been up to. It's as plain as the nose on your face. She'd have written long since if it hadn't been for you. You've enticed her away from us. *I* know. He always said you would. Well you needn't think you can get away with it. I'll get the law on to you. You haven't heard the last of this, and don't you think so.'

But he'd closed the door. He'd actually closed the door in her face. How could he be so foul! She was so upset she burst into tears.

In the sudden peace of the hall, mother and son looked at one another for a long second, she horrified to think that Gemma could have such a dreadful mother, he bristling with well-used aggression.

'What an exhibition!' Catherine said, speaking so low that her voice was little more than a whisper. 'I thought you were being unkind to her at first — but really! I can see why Gemma doesn't want any contact with her.'

Nick was remembering his first meeting with Mrs Goodeve. 'She's a tricky woman,' he said. 'She used to make scenes like that on the ward. I had to head her off *then*.'

The shrill voice seemed to have stopped. 'Has she gone, do you think?' Catherine said. She peered through the stained glass of the front door. The garden was blessedly empty.

Nick had no more time for the woman and didn't even bother to look. 'Let's hope so.'

'What if she comes back?'

'Oh, I don't think she will,' he said airily. 'She knows when she's beaten. But if she does, don't answer the door.' It was the sort of treatment she deserved after shrieking abuse like that. It had shaken him despite his apparent cool. His blood pressure was well up. And now it was time for him to go back to St Thomas's and Gemma still hadn't come home so she was obviously keeping out of his way.

'It's a good job your father wasn't here,' Catherine said, 'or he'd have had her sectioned. Shall we tell Gemma?'

'I wouldn't,' he said, opening the door.

'But it's up to you. I must go or I'll be late. Give Dad my love.'

She kissed him goodbye. 'Mind she isn't waiting round the corner,' she warned and it was only half a joke.

When Billie ran away from the house, she was crying so much she could barely see where she was going. She crossed the road without checking for traffic and fell towards the BMW, her cheeks flushed and streaked with tears. The sight of her was so alarming that Tim got out of the car and rushed towards her.

'Poppet! What is it?' he said, putting his arms round her.

'She's not there,' Billie wept into his chest. 'She's gone and they wouldn't tell me where. They shut the door in my face.'

'Right!' he said, on tiptoe to rush for the house. 'That's it. They need sorting out.'

But she hung on to his arm to restrain him. 'No, don't! Please, Tim. I couldn't bear another scene.'

'They needn't think they can get away with this,' he bristled. 'Upsetting you like this.'

'Please, Tim. Please. Just take me home. Please.'

She was too distraught to face another

row. He could see that. 'Well . . .' he said.

She opened the car door and slid inside. 'Just take me home,' she begged.

'I shall deal with them,' he told her as he followed her into the car.

'Yes, but later.'

'Enticement,' he said, sniffing so that his moustache shifted sideways. 'That's what this is, isn't it?' And when she nodded: 'I told you so, didn't I. Right at the outset. I knew someone was enticing her. Don't you worry, Poppet. You leave it to me. I'll fix them. They can't refuse to tell us where she is.'

Now that she was safely inside the car she began to recover. 'Fancy shutting the door in my face.'

'They'll live to regret it,' he promised, patting her hand. But then his tone changed. 'Hello!' he said. 'Who's this?' A Rover had just passed them and was turning in at the Quennells' drive. He peered through the windscreen at it, his eyes narrowed. 'I know that feller. Well bugger me! That's Quack-quack Quennell, the one in the papers.'

'Yes,' she said. 'That's right. That *is* their name. Quennell. He must be the son. My one, I mean.'

'Perfect!' Tim said, still watching as Andrew got out of the car. 'A man with a public face. Couldn't be better. Now we've got a stick to beat them with. I'll make them wish they'd never been born. Taking our girl away from us. You leave it all to me.'

Curiosity dried the last of her tears. 'What will you do?'

'I shall find out where she is, for a start.'

'But they won't tell us.'

'I shan't ask them,' he said, putting the car into gear. 'I shall stalk them. Softly softly catchee monkey.'

She was very impressed. 'Like a private eye, do you mean?'

He drove out into the main road and turned to smile at her. 'That's about the size of it,' he said. 'You just go back to work, my poppet, and don't you worry your pretty little head about a thing. You can leave it all to me from now on.'

Billie snuggled into her luxurious seat. 'You're so good,' she said.

'Yes,' he agreed. 'I am.' Taking action always gave him a kick and taking action for half a million pounds was the best kick of all.

He started his stalking the very next day, rising early for once and driving to Amersham Road as soon as he'd had his breakfast. He found a parking space where he could see the front door of the Quennells' house. Then he watched.

Within two days, he'd discovered that the Quennells had a charlady who came in every morning and left at noon, that Dr Quennell went in and out a lot and that Mrs Quennell took her car to the supermarket early on Friday morning. I'll bet she does that every week, he thought, as she left the house that Friday calling out to her charlady, 'I'm off then, Polly.' Especially when Polly came to the door to wave her goodbye and promised to have the coffee on when she got back.

Polly, he wrote in his notebook. *Mrs Q Supermarket out 9.35.* Now all he needed was a time when *she* was out shopping and *he* was out wherever he went.

And at that moment, wonderfully on cue, the doctor appeared, wearing a smart suit and carrying a briefcase, and set off along the road, on foot.

This is it! Tim thought. He stretched out his hand to open the car door.

And somebody tapped on the window. The sound was so unexpected, it was all he could do not to jump. Police? he thought. Traffic warden? He put on his most charming smile to face them, whoever they were.

The face peering down at him belonged to

an elderly lady and was wearing a very fierce expression. 'Excuse me, young man,' she said. 'Can you tell me what you're doing here?'

Now he was aware that there was an elderly man hovering behind her, white-haired, tweedy, baffled expression. So she's the boss. And a sharp-faced Dobermann pinscher standing beside her, ready to bite.

'No problem,' he said, easing himself out of the car. His mind was spinning in a frantic effort to think up a plausible excuse, but he held his smile and stayed calm. 'No problem.'

'We're the neighbourhood watch,' the old lady announced importantly. 'We've seen you here two days running, haven't we Oswald? Sitting in your car. You'd better explain yourself.'

'Actually,' he said, pulsing charm at the highest voltage he could manage. 'I'm being a coward. It's my daughter, you see.'

The woman was taking mental note of his clothes, his car and his accent, her face full of suspicion. 'Oh yes?'

'I'd better come clean,' he said, appealing to the old man. 'My daughter used to live in that house over there. Dr Quennell's house. You've probably seen her. In a wheelchair, poor kid. Gemma Goodeve, the girl in the rail crash.' Then he hesitated, wondering what else he could say.

'Ah yes,' Oswald said, brightening. 'We know Gemma. We read all about her in the papers. So brave. An inspiration, you might say.'

His wife was still pecking-fierce. 'According to the papers, Mr Goodeve,' she said, 'Gemma's father walked out on her when she was an infant.'

'All true,' he confessed, looking suitably contrite. 'I was young and silly.'

She snorted.

'I've regretted it ever since,' he went on. 'I came straight back the minute I heard about the accident.'

'If you ask me,' she said, 'it's just as well she's got Dr Quennell to look after her, don't you think so, Oswald?'

'He's a good chap,' Oswald agreed. 'War hero, you know. Won the Military Cross in Cyprus during the troubles. Kept very quiet about it though. Never said a word to anyone. We wouldn't have known to this day if it hadn't been in the *Herald*. Very modest, our Dr Quennell. Odd that, for a man who speaks out the way he does. You'd think he'd want everyone to know about it. I know I would if I'd won a medal. But he never said a word to anyone, did he Christabel?'

Christabel brushed his comments away with a wave of her hand. She had something more interesting to occupy her wits. 'You haven't seen her yet, have you Mr Goodeve?' she accused. 'You've come back but you haven't seen her yet. That's why you've been sitting out here in this car. I'm right, aren't I?'

He admitted it, suitably shamefaced.

'Then I'll give you a bit of advice,' she said grandly. 'If I were you, I'd get back in that car of yours and drive right away. You can't come bouncing back into a girl's life whenever you think fit. That's not fair. You just get back in the car and drive away.'

'You could be right,' he said, thinking fast. He could drive round the block, park somewhere out of their sight and walk back to the house from the opposite direction when they'd gone back indoors.

'You know I am,' she said and nodded with great satisfaction when he climbed into the car and switched on the ignition. She even waved as he drove off. Nosy old bat!

He allowed them ample time to get indoors before he walked back into the road. And he slipped into the Quennells' front garden like a thief, feeling anxiously excited in case the heroic doctor came home while he was still there. It was quite an adventure.

The charlady came to the door with an expression on her face which said, 'No we don't want it, whatever it is.'

'Good morning,' he greeted her, all charm. 'Polly, isn't it?'

She was suspicious and none too pleased. 'How d'you know my name?'

'My little girl told me,' he explained. 'She's always talking about you. And Mrs Quennell, of course. Mustn't forget Mrs Quennell. I don't know what we'd have done without her. She's always saying how good you've been to her. My little girl, I mean. Gemma. Gemma Goodeve. I'm her father.'

'Oh!' Polly said, relaxing. 'I see. She's not here.' She'd gone off in her chair barely two minutes ago.

'I know,' he said, easily. 'She's at her flat. The thing is, I've got a little present for her, and I was going to take it over there, and now I can't find the address. I feel such a fool, losing it. I'm always losing things. It's the story of my life. I don't suppose you know what it is, by any chance?'

She couldn't remember it off hand but if he'd like to wait a minute she'd go and find it for him. Mrs Quennell would have it in her address book. 'Yes. There it is. St Mary's Court. Number 6. Have you got a pen to write it down?'

'I'm much obliged to you, Polly,' he said, writing happily. 'I can see why Gemma thinks so highly of you. You're a star! Thanks very much.'

As he strutted back to his car he felt like a million dollars. Or half a million pounds. He'd got it sussed in two days. Two days! And Billie had been faffing about for months. He should have taken over right from the start. There's no doubt about it, he thought, as he drove off, if you want a thing doing, do it yourself. Now he'd go straight to the flat and beard the silly girl in her den.

But the place was empty, as he could see when he peered through the kitchen windows, having rung twice without reply. She must have gone out shopping or something. It was rather an anticlimax after the speed of his success. And an irritating one.

I'll go and have lunch, he decided, and come back this afternoon. Now that he knew where she lived, there was no urgency. He could visit her whenever he felt like it. Meantime there was the pleasure of knowing how skilful he'd been — and of being admired as he drove his classy car through the south London streets.

So it was odd that he barely noticed the envious glances he was earning. And even odder that it was the voice of that funny old man that filled his thoughts all the way home. *'War hero . . . you'd think he'd want everyone to know . . . a man who speaks out . . . kept very quiet about it . . . never said a word.'*

Billie was cooking lunch when he got in. 'How did you get on?' she called. 'Did you find anything out?'

'Quite a lot,' he said and began to tell her about the old feller from the neighbourhood watch. But she was too involved with what she was doing to give him more than a glancing attention.

'I won't be a tick,' she promised when he sighed. 'You can watch the news while you wait, can't you.'

It wasn't the welcome he wanted or expected. He sighed again as he turned the television on, feeling hard-done-by. And to add insult to injury that wretched Quack-quack's face swam into focus in the huge close-up of a one-to-one interview.

'You won a medal, I believe?' the presenter was prompting. Nice young girl, blonde and eager.

'It was a long time ago,' Dr Quennell said.

'But I dare say you remember it as if it was yesterday,' the presenter hoped. 'Would you care to tell us about it?'

'No,' Dr Quennell said, shifting his head

as if he was trying to avoid something. 'I wouldn't. Not really. There are other more important things . . .'

Now that's peculiar, Tim thought. The old feller was right. He *doesn't* want to talk about it. He's looking downright shifty, as if he's ashamed. And a new and intriguing possibility began to form in his mind.

As they ate their lunch he tested the idea on Billie. 'Now don't you think it's odd,' he finished. 'This man loves publicity. Courts it, you might say. And yet he doesn't tell anyone about that medal and doesn't want to. Now why? That's the question.'

Billie had no idea.

'I tell you what I think. I think he was up to no good while he was out in Cyprus. I think he did something he's ashamed of, something he wants to keep hidden. Right? That's why he never talks about it. So I'm going to find out what it is.'

She was impressed but couldn't see how he would go about it nor how it would help them find Gemma. 'Anyway,' she said, 'the one you want to get at is that young doctor. He's the cruel one. He's the one who won't tell us where she is.'

'We'll get at him through his father,' Tim told her. 'Shoot the father, wound the son.'

But she didn't see how he was going to get

at either of them.

'It's a matter of putting pressure on,' he explained. 'If Quack-quack's got a guilty secret and I know what it is, they're not so likely to go shutting doors in our faces. Right? And Gemma won't think he's so wonderful once she knows what he's really like. She'll listen to *us* then. He won't be such an influence on her. When you're in the public eye, you're vulnerable. He ought to remember that. If we play our cards right, we'll have him over a barrel.' His excitement was growing by the second.

'So what will you do?' she asked.

He knew exactly what he was going to do now. 'I shall go to the *Herald* and check through their files. See what they've got on disc.'

'But it's Christmas. They won't be there, will they?'

'Newspaper men are *always* there,' he told her with feeling. 'But I'll leave it till afterwards if you like. When things are slack. They'll have more time to attend to it then.'

'But what about Gemma?' Billie said. 'Aren't you going to find our Gemma?'

He was tempted to let her into his secret but decided against it. It was better for her to be in the dark. 'Quack-quack first,' he told her. 'Then I'll find Gemma.'

There's no stopping him now, Billie thought. She wasn't at all sure this scheme would work although she could see the sense of putting pressure on that awful Dr Quennell. But what she really wanted was to see Gemma again, to have her home for Christmas and look after her. It was miserable not knowing where she was, especially when there was no news from her. Not even a Christmas card. It wouldn't hurt her to send a Christmas card, she thought sadly. I mean that's not very much to ask, is it? Most daughters visit their mothers at Christmas. I visited mine right up to the very end, even when she was half-daft and cantankerous and didn't know who I was.

Had she known it, Gemma was planning her visit at that very moment, as she and Catherine were cooking their lunch.

'You haven't got a local bus timetable, have you?' she asked, as she peeled the last potato.

'Is there such a thing these days?' Catherine wondered. 'Where do you want to go?'

'To Streatham to see my mother.'

'Ah!' Catherine said and the word carried so much meaning that Gemma stopped work to look at her.

'What is it?'

'I wasn't going to tell you this,' Catherine confessed. 'But if you're going to see her, you'd better know.' And she told Gemma about her mother's visit.

'Oh God!' Gemma said. 'How embarrassing! I'm *so* sorry.'

'It's not your fault,' Catherine said. 'I just thought you ought to know, that's all.'

'She does that sometimes,' Gemma felt she ought to explain. 'I'm not trying to excuse her. It's the way she is. I wish she hadn't done it to you.'

'Not to worry. I didn't take it seriously.'

'I'm glad you told me anyway,' Gemma said. 'I've got a present for her, you see. I was going to deliver it in person. But if she's in one of those moods I'll send it through the post and give her time to cool off.'

'Very wise,' Catherine approved, remembering that awful shrill voice. 'Have Christmas first. You've earned it.'

Chapter 24

Despite her misgivings, that Christmas was one of the best that Gemma had ever known. Christmases with her mother had always been strained, no matter how hard they tried to make them happy, the decorations too elaborate, the food too rich, the presents they felt compelled to buy for one another too lavish and, more often than not, unsuitable. This one was simple and easy, and the dinner was Dickensian, eight happy faces round a loaded table, the turkey steaming as Andrew carved the first slice and so many dishes of vegetables and stuffings and sauces that it took five cheerful minutes before they were all served. The pudding was borne in ablaze with a sprig of holly stuck on top as the kids clapped and cheered. There was even a glass of vintage port to round off the meal. And although Nick sat right down at the other end of the table, as far away from her as he could get, and hadn't said a word to her beyond 'Hello', he looked happy, and very handsome, and it didn't seem to worry him that she was being treated like one of the family.

There were underlying tensions, of course — what family can gather without them? — but few difficult moments. One came when the meal was over and they were gathered round the fire for the exchange of presents — Andrew in his armchair, Catherine in hers, Rob and Susan on one of the two sofas, he with his arm around her shoulders. By this time the two girls had taken Gemma over and insisted that she sit on the second sofa squashed between them. Which left Nick rather apart, sitting on a leather stool, where he looked distinctly uncomfortable, his long legs bent at an inelegant angle.

'You'll get cramp sitting there like that,' Catherine told him. 'Why don't you go and get an armchair from Gemma's flat?'

But he dismissed her concern, telling her not to fuss, and ordered Naomi to pick the first parcel from the pile under the Christmas tree. 'I've got to be back in St Thomas's by six,' he said to her. 'So look sharp.'

Despite her determination to be cool, Gemma was rather cast down to hear how little time he had. She hadn't imagined he would be on duty over Christmas. It was none of her business but it seemed sad somehow. She didn't like to think of him missing out on the fun. Then she became aware that he was looking at her and turned her head to find herself in the full beam of a mocking smile.

'It's a rotten job,' he joked, 'but somebody has to do it.'

The smile confused her, and confusion undermined her ability to answer him. Should she commiserate or make a joke? But before she could say anything, Naomi appeared before them with a small parcel in her hand.

'How about this one?' she asked. 'It's for you, Uncle Nick.'

It was the fountain pen.

He accepted it seriously, opened it and read the gift tag aloud: *'I hope this will save your white coat from further spills.'* Then to Gemma's consternation, he blushed. 'Well thanks,' he said, ducking his head towards the firelight. 'That's very . . . I can't reciprocate I'm afraid. I didn't know you were going to be with us until this morning. I thought you'd be at your new flat.' And the blush deepened.

Oh dear, she thought. I've embarrassed him. 'It's more for your coat than for you,' she said, trying to reassure him. 'An act of compassion.'

'Quite right!' Andrew laughed. 'His

coats are a disgrace!'

'He's the disgrace,' Sue teased, giving her brother a wicked grin. 'He's a true blue meanie. That's what he is. Never mind Gemma, *we* didn't forget you. *We've* got you a present.'

'We couldn't wrap it,' Rob said. 'As you'll see. Hang on a tick and I'll get it.'

It was a four-foot yucca plant, 'to bring some green into your new flat'.

Gemma didn't know what to say. 'However did you get it here?'

'That's why we came down in the van,' Sue explained. 'We'll take it over for you if you like. Saturday's your moving day, isn't it?'

It was. 'I haven't got a lot to move, though.'

'You have now,' Rob laughed, looking at the plant. 'We'll give you a hand.'

'We'll *all* give you a hand,' Andrew said. 'How would that be?'

'All of us?' Helen hoped.

'Well why not?' Susan said. 'If Gemma can withstand us. Many hands make light work.'

Gemma glanced at Nick to see whether he was being included, but apparently he wasn't, for he stood up without looking at her, strolled round the furniture until he reached the tree, stooped, picked up two small parcels and tossed them to his nieces. 'These are for you kids!' he said, changing the subject. 'From me.'

They contained two old-fashioned books with marbled covers and gold lettering, Helen's announcing that it was an *Address Book*, Naomi's simply labelled *Birthdays*. They were an instant success and had to be filled in at once with every known and remembered date and address, even Gemma's, new telephone number and all.

So the awkward moment passed and after that they went on exchanging luxuries: chocolates, silk shirts, expensive slippers, books, toys, CDs, until the day faded and the room grew dark. And then they sat on in the firelight too replete and satisfied to move. And talked. About Susan's promotion, the kids' school play, Andrew's journalism, Gemma's new job.

'Rob's got a new job too,' Susan said. 'Did we tell you?'

'A new assignment,' Rob corrected. 'You make it sound as though I've sold the centre.'

'I can't imagine you ever doing that,' Andrew told him.

'I couldn't imagine *you* writing a newspaper column,' Susan said. 'But you're doing it.'

'True!'

'So what's the assignment?' Nick wanted to know.

'The gardens of the Alhambra Hotel,' Rob said. 'Big place by the station in York. Do you remember it, Nick? Used to be rather grand when you and Chris were little. Four-star stuff. Might even have been five. It's been tatty for ages, really going downhill, and now they're going to refurbish it. We've been asked to resuscitate the gardens. It's quite a challenge. But as Sue's taken a new job I thought I'd better strike out too.'

Naomi yawned like a cat. All this grown-up talk was boring. 'Are we going to play charades?' she asked.

'When the others come,' Susan told her. There was to be a party that evening for friends and neighbours. 'Then I suppose you'll be fighting over who has Gemma on their side.'

'No we won't,' Helen said. And when her mother made a face at her, 'Why would we?'

'Because she's an actress.'

Both girls swivelled round to look at her. 'Really!'

'She's just applied for a part in a play,'

Catherine said. 'In the West End. Haven't you, Gemma?'

'Have you been on television?' Naomi wanted to know.

Gemma grinned at that. 'Only in a non-acting capacity.'

And Helen asked, 'Can you really act? Can you show us?'

'You can see her after supper,' Catherine said, 'when we play charades. How will that be?'

They answered with one voice, both looking at Gemma. 'Wicked! Can I be in your team?'

'You see what I mean,' Susan laughed. But before they could protest against her teasing, the phone rang and they all rushed to answer it knowing it would be Chris on the line to wish them happy Christmas. As it was. 'Chris! Lovely to hear you! Yes. We're all here.'

Gemma stayed where she was on the sofa and watched them. Although none of them had anything particular to say, their affection for this absent member of the family was as clear as daylight. His wife took the phone and was told the same things in varied detail, and after that their two sons came chirruping on to the line, their voices so bright and tinny with excitement that

Gemma could hear them where she sat. She looked across the hearth to Rob, who, like her, was still sitting by the fire, watching the action, half smiling. We're the outsiders here, she realised, but it seemed an odd thing to think because she hadn't been made to feel like an outsider at all that day.

'Family tribe in action,' he observed, nodding towards them.

'They're very fond of him,' she said. 'And his wife.'

'Yes,' he agreed and added rather wryly, 'Whatever else you might say about them, they include you in.'

It seemed a rather odd phrase to use and his body cues were awkward too, his shoulders hunched and his head turned too stiffly towards the group round the phone. But there wasn't time to say anything more, even if she could have thought of something, because Andrew had put the receiver down and they were all on their way back to the fire and Nick was saying he'd got to be off.

A flurry of leave-taking, kisses, last-minute instructions. Then he was gone and the next phase of the day was beginning, with the drawing room fire to attend to and the table to be set for their buffet supper. There wasn't time to miss him but Gemma missed him acutely, tantalised by those few short hours in his company and the dearth of communication between them.

But then the guests began to arrive and soon they were acting charades, where she was in her element, and joining in quiz games that all seemed to be designed to baffle her and talking and joking well into Boxing Day. Which consequently began very late indeed with a yawning brunch and the casually given information that Nick wouldn't be with them again until Saturday evening.

As Helen said, 'Poor old Uncle Nick. He does work hard.'

And on Saturday, Gemma thought, I shall be moving so I shan't see him. I thought we were getting on so well when we were in York that day but I was wrong. I was reading too much into it. No wonder he was embarrassed when I gave him that pen. And despite the pleasure of the day she yearned to be on her own in her flat, leading her independent life.

It was just as well there was plenty to entertain her until the move, with another party that night for old friends from the practice, and a trip to the winter sales and finally a visit to a pantomime, where they hissed Abanazer and screamed advice at

Aladdin and Helen was scathing about the acting ability of the princess, telling Gemma, 'You could do it much better than *her*.'

And then it was Saturday at last and she had to face the mayhem of the move. Many hands may make light work but the countless bags and boxes they carried on this occasion filled the little flat beyond its capacity. To make matters worse, Helen and Naomi decided that the wheelchair would make a splendid trolley and took it in turns to sit in it and ferry the biggest boxes into the flat on their laps. They even tried it with the yucca plant and ended up dropping it and spilling compost all over Gemma's new carpet, to Susan's annoyance.

'I warned you that would happen,' she scolded. 'Now look at the mess. *And* you're getting in everyone's way. We can't turn round in here with you under our feet all the time.'

'I'll get a dust shovel and brush,' Helen offered quickly, but Gemma couldn't remember where she packed them. Now and too late in the day, she realised that she should have labelled the boxes.

'That's the lot,' Rob said, coming into the hall with the last cardboard box. 'Where d'you want this putting?'

'It had better go in the living room with the others,' Gemma said. 'If I open them I shall see what's what.'

But they'd barely opened three before the bell rang and it was the furniture store delivering her new bed and the table and chairs.

'If I live through this day the rest of my life will be a doddle,' Gemma said and she was only half joking.

'We'll get the bed put up and the kitchen more or less straight,' Catherine promised. 'They're the main things. You can sort everything else out at your leisure.'

'I start work on the sixth,' Gemma pointed out, looking at the wreckage in her once-neat rooms. 'Leisure's going to be in short supply.'

Which was true enough for there were far too many things to do in those few short days and, as she soon discovered, far too many physical problems in her new environment. Working in a new kitchen took practice, she fell twice in her new shower and, by New Year's Eve she'd bruised her thigh so many times by misjudging the position of her new furniture that it was quite tender. But she was independent now and if she made mistakes there was no one there to see them. She could get on with her life in peace. New Year, new start.

Billie and Tim saw in the New Year in their local pub, where Tim acquired a circle of instant friends most of whom were reeling before they arrived. Billie would have preferred a twosome at home in the comfort of her flat, but she drank to the New Year gamely and proposed a special and private toast to Tim as the clock struck twelve.

'Success to your endeavours, my darling!'

'Starting tomorrow,' he promised. 'Just you watch me.'

But in fact it took several days and much heavily enforced patience before he found what he wanted. There were so many obstacles in his way that he began to complain that they were 'doing it deliberately'. First the journalist he needed to see was away, then it wasn't convenient for him to use the microfiche, then there was nobody who could date the picture they'd used in their recent article on Dr Quennell. But at last he was given the information he needed and allowed to sit before a relevant screen and trawl his way through the ancient pages on the microfiche.

The history of the Cyprus troubles scrolled past. He read about British paratroopers patrolling the streets of Nicosia and Limassol, and Turks threatening to take *'five Greek lives for every Turk'*.

Vaguely remembered, once-famous names jumped out of the print, Field Marshall Sir John Harding, Archbishop Makarios, Colonel Grivas. But there was no mention of a soldier called Quennell.

Until he reached 25th March 1956 and an article headlined 'Bombs thrown at army patrol'.

'Despite the restrictions,' the article said, 'bombs were thrown yesterday at army patrols in Paphos in Western Cyprus. In one incident a medical orderly, Corporal A.S. Quennell, rescued three members of a four-man patrol hit on the road into the Troödos mountains. Interviewed afterwards, Corporal Quennell said he had acted instinctively. "There wasn't time to think." '

Specious git! Tim thought, as he went on scrolling. Just the sort of thing he would say. Right. Now I know where he was and where he was based. If there *was* something else going on, and it was bad enough for him to want to keep quiet about it, there ought to be some mention of it somewhere.

It took him three more days before he found what he was looking for and then it was such an insignificant item he could have missed it if he hadn't noticed a familiar phrase.

'Killed on the road to the Troödos mountains,' the item said. 'Residents of the village of Herapheton turned out in force yesterday for the funeral of Andreas Papagathangelou (16) who, according to his relatives, was shot and killed by a British medical orderly on the road to the Troödos mountains on Greek Independence Day. Troops were put on stand-by but the event passed off without incident.'

That's it! Tim thought. A medical orderly. On Greek Independence Day. It had to be him. The man's a killer. No wonder he didn't want to talk about it. With his heart pounding in triumph, he copied the item into his notebook, detail by detail, and went whistling back to Streatham.

Billie was setting the table for the evening meal and cast down by the fact that she'd had another postcard from Gemma, still without an address.

'It's all very well for her,' she complained. 'She sounds quite perky. It was all about her flat. I still think she'd be better here with me but what's the good of thinking when I can't tell her.'

'No good at all,' he agreed. 'Not while she's under Quack-quack's influence. And no address, you say?'

'No.'

He was relieved to hear it. This whole thing needed careful stage management; an ill-judged visit could put the mockers on it. 'Not to worry, Poppet,' he said, expansive with the importance of what he was going to tell her. 'I've found his Achilles' heel. Didn't I tell you I would? Look at that.' And when she'd read it: 'Now all I need to do is to go to Cyprus and find a relative and get them to spill the beans. We shan't have any more trouble from Quack-quack Quennell then. You mark my words.'

'But how do you know it's him?' she asked. 'It doesn't say it's him.'

'I *don't* know. I must follow my hunch, that's all. That's why I've got to go there. It's the only way to find out.' And a bit of freedom wouldn't come amiss. Domestic life was getting very wearing. All this fussing about with flowers and tablecloths.

'Now?' Billie asked. 'In this weather?'

'The weather's not important,' he told her grandly. 'This is our daughter's future we're talking about here. I'd go at once, if I could. I could be there and back in a week or two. The trouble is I've got a bit of a cash-flow problem and I might have to wait a few weeks or two for capital.'

His anxious expression roused her sympathy. 'How much do you need?'

'About a grand,' he hazarded. 'Depends how long I have to stay. Seven hundred and fifty, maybe.'

'I've got some savings,' she told him. 'You could borrow them if you like. Just to tide you over. You'd give them back afterwards, wouldn't you?'

'You're a star,' he said, rewarding her with a kiss. 'How soon can you lay your hands on it?'

He was gone four days later. The flat seemed horribly empty without him and the bed miserably cold. But it was necessary, she knew that. If they were going to get Gemma back, it had to be done. She couldn't go on living in that flat all by herself, poor girl.

Chapter 25

The New Year began in a confusion of blizzards and blocked roads. The television screens shone white with romantic visions of glistening snowscapes and delicately falling snow, but in the real world, cars inched and fumed, or stood moodily immobilised under thick white hoods, or slid out of control on ice their drivers couldn't see. Tim's flight was delayed for six hours, Billie's boutique unvisited for as many days. Despite all-night work by gritters, it was hardly the most auspicious time to start a new job.

Phlegmatic as ever, Rob set off to work in his Land Rover as though the roads were clear and it was just another day. But Susan decided to let the train take the strain, saying 'I've earned it if anyone has'. The service from their little station at Poppleton was very good, even in bad weather, and she had no intention of reporting for her first day dishevelled by a difficult drive.

She'd organised the start of the day down to the last meticulous detail. Her new Black Watch tartan trouser suit was laid out in the spare bedroom with all its carefully chosen accessories neatly arranged beside it, her new executive rail pass was in its gold-edged docket in her handbag, her new nanny had been told to arrive half an hour before she was actually needed so as to ensure that she turned up more or less on time, the girls had new toys to play with and a video to keep them entertained and there was enough food in the freezer to feed a regiment. Whatever problems the day might drop on her desk, she was ready.

'Now be good girls,' she said to Helen and Naomi as she put on her last layer of mascara, leaning towards her dressing-table mirror. Eye make-up is irritatingly difficult when you are shortsighted. 'Do what Nanny says.'

Her daughters stood behind her, neat and clean in their designer jeans and their new Christmas sweaters, watching apprehensively.

'Do we *have* to have another nanny?' Helen complained, wiping her nose on her fingers.

'Don't do that,' Susan rebuked. 'Take a tissue. Yes, you do. You can't stay in the house with no one to look after you.'

Helen took a tissue but persisted in her complaint. 'I don't see why not. We're not babies. I'm ten, in case you've forgotten.'

'And don't be rude,' her mother said.

'I hate nannies,' Naomi weighed in, sensing from her mother's irritation that Helen had scored a point. 'They're gross.'

'You'll like this one,' Susan instructed them. 'Her name's Sheryl and she's very nice.'

'You said that about the last one,' Helen reminded her. 'And she broke your crystal vase.'

'Time you cleaned your teeth,' Susan said, putting the mascara in her make-up bag. 'Unless you're waiting for her to do it for you.'

'No fear!'

'Well then,' Susan said. They always made such a fuss over a new nanny and it wasn't necessary, even if the last one had been dire. But there you are, it was the price she had to pay for continuing her career.

There was movement in the garden below her. A dark figure was battling in through the gate, doubled against the wind and clutching a wide-brimmed hat to her head. Not a very prepossessing figure, Susan thought, ginger hair, very long and tatty, glasses — although I suppose I can't fault her for that — red maxi coat flapping behind her, fashionable boots with sharp high heels. Not exactly Norland! And thirty-three minutes late. 'She's here!'

The two girls came down the stairs to be introduced, their faces set and sullen. 'My name's Helen,' that damsel announced. 'And she's Naomi and we don't have nick-names and we don't like cocoa and we always have chocolate biscuits at half-past ten.'

The new nanny was vague and looked as if she'd just woken up. 'Yeah!' she said. 'Right!'

'They'll show you where everything is,' Susan said, putting on her coat. 'Won't you, girls?'

'If we have to,' Helen said.

A bad start, Susan thought, but there wasn't time to do anything about it. Not if she was going to catch her train. 'Be good!' she warned. And left them to it.

It was a difficult first day. For a start, there was as much frost inside the building as on the pavements outside. The central heating system had broken down and although there seemed to be an army of men in boiler suits trying to get it running again, it was so cold that the staff were all still in their coats. Even in her personal office on the fourth floor, which was close carpeted and sumptuously furnished and had enough radiators in it to be comfortably warm, if only they'd been working, the desk was chill to the touch and her breath streamed before her every time she spoke.

'Sorry about this, Ms Pengilly,' her secretary said.

'That's the winter for you,' Susan said, determined not to be discouraged. 'Is there any coffee?'

'You generally have coffee during the board meeting,' the secretary told her.

Susan opened her desk diary. 'When's that?'

'Ten o'clock.'

'Let's spoil ourselves and have our first cup now or we shall be too cold to do any work.'

The secretary made a moue. 'With respect, Ms Pengilly,' she said. 'It would be better not to. They're very hot on conformity here. Place for everything, everything in its place.'

'Even coffee?'

'Particularly coffee. The chairman has a thing about dirty cups.'

He also had things about punctuality and brevity. The board meeting began at ten o'clock precisely and business was brisked through because, as Susan was quick to notice, no one — except the chairman — was allowed to speak for more than thirty seconds. He prided himself, he told them, that Rail North East was a lean machine. 'Work smart,' he said to Susan. 'That's our motto. That's what pays dividends.'

But, as Susan also saw, it had an anxious board, and item six on the agenda that morning 'Railtrack inquiry' revealed one of the causes.

'You'll doubtless have been hearing rumours about this one over the break,' the chairman said, 'so I thought I would put you in the picture. There is likely to be — ah — um — legal action of some kind. Between you and me, Railtrack are dragging their feet over this inquiry of theirs and — ah — um — Railways South want to force them to publish. Their own report, which was largely the responsibility of — ah — um — Ms Pengilly here, was very full and frank and came out in October, if my memory serves me correctly. The findings of the Railtrack report will of course be — ah — um — instrumental in determining liability for compensation claims. This will affect us in three ways. Firstly because it is the first sizeable action of its kind since BR was privatised, so there is bound to be considerable media interest, secondly because we need to be — ah — um — mindful of our own relationship with Railtrack and aware of the impact of adverse publicity, and thirdly because we have been — ah — um — specifically asked to be — ah — um — circumspect in our own dealings with the media.'

So we're under a government gagging order, Susan thought. It didn't surprise her, given public sensitivity about rail privatization, but it left a nasty taste in the mouth, even so.

The chairman was looking at her. 'Of course Ms Pengilly, you had some — ah — um — dealings with the media in your capacity as secretary to the Railways South inquiry, did you not?'

'I published the report,' Susan told him firmly. 'There was never any question of me giving interviews. Nor was I ever asked to. I did the job I was required to do and kept in the background.'

'Quite,' the chairman said. 'Point taken. Given the — ah — um — complexion of the media these days, we all need to be quite clear where we stand. Any questions? No. Then we will adjourn for coffee.'

It was a long, cold, trying day. The bad weather brought non-stop problems, the computer crashed when she was in the middle of a complicated transaction and the damned central heating wasn't switched on again until nearly half past five.

She came home bone tired, filthy with cold and feeling that she'd more than earned her money that day.

'There'd better be an improvement to-morrow,' she said to Rob. 'I've never worked under such pressure.'

But, as she was to discover as the month wore on, pressure was the norm in her new environment and she had to get used to it.

In St Thomas's hospital, Nick was under pressure too, far too hard at work in a ward full of elderly patients suffering from the usual ailments of a spell of bad weather: falls, flu and pneumonia. In a way, he was glad to be busy because it stopped him brooding over his relationship with Gemma. If it had *been* a relationship, which looked less and less likely the more he thought about it.

In the clinical light of a hospital morning, he found it hard to understand why it had all come to such an abrupt end. They'd had a great day together in York and, as far as he could see, their night out at *Cats* had been great too. And then, suddenly, she'd taken that flat, and she didn't have any time for him. True, she'd given him a Christmas present, but she'd done it as if it wasn't important. It might have been better if he'd followed his instincts and bought *her* a present. But he hadn't and there was no point in thinking about it now. It wouldn't have hurt her to talk to him over Christmas instead of sitting on the other side of the room all the time. Then he could have explained. It wasn't his fault that he hadn't gone back to A and E that night to say goodbye to her. That was the way life was in a big hospital and she ought to understand it. If there'd been a problem about it, she should have talked it through with him, not gone rushing off to live on her own. That was a slap in the face. Why did she have to be so bloody independent all the time?

And yet for all his irritation, he couldn't get her out of his mind. He remembered her when he was in the restaurant, when he was on his own at night, when he woke in the morning, even when he was on the ward. Only a rush of work kept his mind away from his preoccupation. As it was about to do at that moment, for there were two more casualties coming up from A and E and nowhere to put them.

'We shall have to move our two geriatrics for the time being,' Sister Taylor said. 'We could do with another ward.'

'And twice the number of nurses and doctors,' he agreed, examining their case notes. 'If only!'

It was a point that was being made in the editorial offices of the tabloids that morning, where the headlines that were being set up read BED CLOSURES SCANDAL and HEALTH SERVICE IN CRISIS. The story that was about to break was one that combined bad weather, bureaucratic muddle and loss of life. A pensioner, who had fallen on ice and broken her hip, had been left on a stretcher in a busy Accident and Emergency ward for 'five long terrible hours' without food or attention, and had died before anyone had time to attend to her. Now her son was threatening legal action against the Hospital Trust. It was good strong stuff and they were beefing it up for all it was worth.

Gemma heard it on Radio 4 as she was putting on her Ottoback socks in the bathroom later that morning. She'd slept until nearly midday and woke feeling oddly sad. Now, showered and half dressed, she paused, one sock on and the next in hand, to listen and sympathise. It seemed dreadful for someone to die like that. Having come close to death herself, she felt she understood how the poor old thing must have felt, lying there in pain, looking at the ceiling, in a strange place, all on her own, as the hours went by and nobody came to help.

She was still listening and still torn with sympathy when the phone rang with a message that cheered her up at once. It was the local Ford dealer to tell her that her disabled car had arrived. When would she like to take delivery?

She hadn't expected to have it delivered for several weeks so she was delighted by the news and didn't stop to consider the bad weather or the state of the roads or how long it would take to have something to eat. 'Now,' she said.

It was with her forty minutes and a rushed breakfast later, a neat metallic blue Fiesta specially adapted, as the dealer explained, 'for one right foot and two hands'. She couldn't wait to try it out.

'Shall I sit in with you till you're used to it?' the dealer offered.

But she told him she could manage. She hadn't driven since she'd sold her original old banger to pay the deposit on her first shared flat and that was nearly eighteen months ago, but, as she told them both with cheerful confidence, 'Driving is something you never forget, isn't it?'

So he asked her to sign the agreement,

gave her the keys and left her to it.

It was a hair-raising morning, as she gradually found out how to handle the controls along roads that were silvered with salt, occasionally slippery and far too full of traffic. Her prosthesis was heavy and useless, pinning her false foot to the floor when all her instincts were urging her to use it to change gear. She bumped the kerb every time she took a left turn, misjudged distances and even managed to stall the engine before she could drive with anything approaching confidence, but by the time a flurry of snow made her stop for lunch and a rest, she was more or less proficient again. As she turned off the ignition, she decided she would drive to school on Thursday and start her new job in style.

It had been an eventful morning for Andrew Quennell too. As Gemma was edging her new car gingerly back into St Mary's Court, he was taking a call from Thames Television.

'It's this story about the pensioner who died in the Casualty department,' a young voice said. 'We're planning a discussion on it this evening and we need our guru. Could you possibly manage it, do you think?'

'I'll be there,' he promised.

'Four days into the New Year and you're off again,' Catherine said.

He grinned at her. 'But think how it'll annoy Garry McKendrick.'

'I'll bet you played with matches when you were a kid.'

'Correct. I was a regular fire-bug.'

She laughed at that. 'Well let's hope we get better weather if you're going to dash about all over the country,' she said.

'I shall take my new hip flask,' he told her.

Gemma could have done with a hip flask on Thursday morning for although it wasn't snowing, it was bitterly cold. But Fairmead School struck warm and the welcome she got when she walked into the staffroom made her feel as if she was coming home. She was introduced to all ten teachers, told that Colin Rainer would be looking after her and given a copy of the school timetable, a peg for her coat and scarf, a locker for 'books and so forth' and a pigeon-hole for letters.

'I've got two folders here you ought to look at before you start,' Mrs Muldoony told her. 'They're the relevant notes on Francine and Matthew. To put you in the picture. And there's a whole lot of teaching information in the green file. I should have sent it to you before but I thought it would get lost in the Christmas post. Right? We always start term with an assembly so you'll have time to look at them before you have to begin and if there's anything more you want to know, pop into my room. Colin's going to be your shepherd for the day. Would you like a cup of tea?'

Gemma accepted the tea gratefully and sat down to drink it, noticing that all the others were either drinking where they stood or carrying their mugs away with them. 'Is it always such a rush?' she asked Colin Rainer.

He considered. 'I'd say this morning is about par for the course,' he said. 'Have you got all you need for the minute? My lot are waiting for me. I'm in Room 6.' And was gone along with everyone else.

So she drank her tea and read up the case notes on her two pupils. Francine turned out to be exactly the sort of child she'd appeared to be — average ability, willing worker, popular with her friends — but there was a sad surprise in Matthew's notes. Before his accident, he'd obviously been one of the leading lights in the school, 'an excellent athlete', 'captain of the school football team and the cricket eleven' and a 'promising scholar'. Poor little boy, she thought, no wonder he's grieving. And she felt even more sorry for him than she'd done when she met him.

But trying to help him that morning was a waste of breath and effort. He was surly and monosyllabic, sitting morosely in his chair and deflecting every suggestion with a shrug or a single word. 'Nothing,' he said, when she asked what he'd done over the holiday. 'Nothing,' when she tried to find out what work he was supposed to be doing.

'You can't do nothing,' she told him. 'That's not the way schools work.'

That at least provoked a sentence. 'It's the way *I* work.'

Colin Rainer came over to provide the answer — in the form of an English worksheet that had to be completed.

'You're a clever boy,' Gemma told the scowling face beside her. 'You could do this with no trouble at all. I'm supposed to help you but I bet you could do it without me. Why not read it?'

'It hurts my head.'

'I'll read it for you,' she told him. 'How will that be? Then you can answer the questions. It won't hurt your head to answer a few questions, will it?'

So the task was done, but mechanically, with no trouble, total accuracy and absolutely no interest at all.

'I'm not sure I was any use to him,' Gemma said to his teacher when the first half of the morning was over and they were back in the staffroom for more tea.

'He did the work,' Colin told her. 'And *that's* progress. Usually he just sits there. You'll get more joy from Francine.'

But Francine was in a weepy mood. She and her family had flown back from Jamaica the previous day and she said she felt cold and was missing her grandmother.

'Tell you what,' Gemma said. 'When you've done your project, I'll get you some coloured paper and you can make her a great big New Year card and put your love on it and send it to her.'

The idea dried the child's tears so they made a start on the project. But it was hard going. And it got harder at the end of the morning when Colin gave her a notebook and reminded her that she had to write up a report of both lessons.

'Yes, I think it's unnecessary too,' he apologised. 'It's all filling in forms and writing reports these days. I sometimes think that's more important than teaching.'

'It's changed a bit since I was at school,' Gemma said.

'You can say that again!'

By the time she got back to the flat that afternoon, Gemma felt so drained that she was thankful to sit by the window and eat a late lunch and watch the river. I hope it gets easier tomorrow, she thought.

But the days that followed were all as difficult as one another. She learned to pace herself better and to write up shorter notes but otherwise the pressure was constant.

As it was for Susan in her new job in York.

As it was for Nick in his old one at St Thomas's.

And in the second week in February news broke that was to affect them all. FRESH REPORT ON WANDSWORTH CRASH DELAYED the headlines said. RAILWAYS SOUTH TO SUE. The *Chronicle* dug out their old picture of Gemma being carried away from the crash on a stretcher and featured that on the front page too. It gave her quite a shock to see it on the news stands and it provoked a lot of interest and sympathy among her new colleagues in the staffroom.

'It was all a long time ago,' she said. 'I've moved on a bit since then.'

'Does it upset you, seeing it all again like this?' Mrs Muldoony asked.

'No,' Gemma told her, more or less truthfully, and she remembered what Andrew had said about being under fire in Cyprus.

'Actually I feel as though it wasn't me, as though it had happened to someone else. Memory softens things.'

Chapter 26

Tim Ledgerwood was riding a donkey and feeling extremely foolish. If any of his acquaintances in Cape Town had predicted that he would soon be living this sort of life on a batty little island in the Mediterranean, he'd have laughed them to scorn. And yet here he was, with a straw hat on his head and his legs dangling awkwardly on either side of the creature's rounded belly, plodding up the side of the Troödos mountains like a peasant.

It was more than seven weeks since he'd flown out to Nicosia and despite hideous economies his money was virtually gone. He'd had to take a job in a bar to eke it out. And he'd never imagined he would be reduced to doing that either. It was pleasant to be back under a Mediterranean sky again, even if it was a cold one, and he was glad to be out of the way of Mr Gresham's pressure, which according to Billie's letters was getting pretty insistent, but he still hadn't found the Papagathangelou family, although he'd courted every journalist he could persuade to meet him and followed every lead that offered.

But the more disappointments he had to endure, the greater his determination to succeed. By the end of that first month his self-imposed task was no longer a necessity. It had become an obsession. He *couldn't* let that gross man get away with it. He *had* to root out the truth, no matter how long it took or how much it cost. Which is why he'd set out on this ridiculous expedition into the mountains.

If it had been anyone other than Fat Nico who'd suggested it, it wouldn't have been so bad. But this man had led him on so many wild-goose chases and spoke such incomprehensible English that he really didn't have any hope of a useful outcome. Yet he was here, on the road yet again. What else could he do?

'You come!' Fat Nico had ordered. 'I find.' He'd arrived just after breakfast, wearing a smile like a slice of melon and leading two donkeys. 'Is mountain.'

Which was true enough. They'd been climbing for hours. Or what seemed like hours.

'How much further?' Tim called.

'Is here,' Fat Nico called back. 'Is village.'

Yes, Tim thought. I'll bet. It had been

'is here' for the last quarter of an hour at least.

But this time they really had arrived. Hardly a village. Just a cluster of low houses and an old lady sitting in the doorway of the nearest, hump-backed and dressed entirely in black.

They dismounted, stiffly. Fat Nico waddled across to the old lady. There was an exchange of murmured Greek and much nodding. Tim sat on the grass verge and lit a cigarette. This could be protracted as well as useless.

But no. Nico was back, sweating with excitement. 'Is woman,' he announced. 'Andreas Papagathangelou. Is cousin. You come. I trans-a-late you.'

She couldn't possibly be, Tim thought. The kid was sixteen and she's an old crone. But he got up and walked across to the old lady to be trans-a-lated.

'Ask her how Andreas was killed,' he suggested.

The answer was given in mime. An imaginary pistol held at arm's length. 'Boom!'

So there'd been a death. But that didn't really mean much. There'd been hundreds of deaths. 'Ask her when. Was it on Greek Independence Day?'

Long conversation. More nodding. Apparently it was.

This was beginning to get exciting after all. 'Can you ask her who shot him? Does she know? Who boom boom?'

There was no need to ask that. 'Soldier,' Nico said at once. 'British soldier.' And he picked up a twig and drew a cross in the dust.

'Medical orderly?' Tim hoped. 'Red Cross?'

'Soldier,' Fat Nico agreed.

Why can't the stupid man speak English? Tim thought. This incessant pidgin was frustrating. 'Has she got any evidence?' he asked slowly, looking at the old lady. But the word meant nothing to Nico. 'Something written?' miming writing. That simply provoked the watermelon smile. 'Papers?'

'Ah, paper!' Nico said. And returned to yet another flowing conversation in Greek.

I'm not getting anywhere with this, Tim thought, watching them with irritation. Trying to converse without a common language was like walking uphill on a sheet of ice.

The old lady got out of her chair and disappeared into the darkness of the house. That's the end of that, Tim thought.

But she came back, holding out an ancient newspaper, much creased and as brown as tea. And this time she addressed him directly, spitting the words at him, her face contorted with hatred.

'Paper,' Nico explained happily. 'You look.'

It was all in Greek of course but there was a page full of pictures — a funeral procession, a group of women standing round an open coffin, a snapshot of a young boy with a rifle slung over his shoulder and right in the middle, a wonderful familiar, helpful picture of a wrecked lorry, the young Dr Quennell kneeling beside it, a dead body crumpled on the ground. Almost exactly the same as the picture that had started him off on the search in the first place. Bingo! Nobody could argue with that.

The only trouble was that he couldn't find the words to persuade the old lady to part with the paper. No matter what he said, neither she nor Nico understood that he only wanted to take a photocopy. He tried charming her, telling her she was wonderful, promising extreme care, but the longer the conversation went on the tighter she clutched it to her black bosom. Stupid old fool! In the end he had to leave the damned thing in her possession. But he'd got the lever he wanted. He couldn't wait to get back to London and use it. Next flight, he thought, here I come.

It wasn't exactly a hero's welcome. Billie met him at the door of the flat with her face full of trouble, words spilling from her before he had a chance to say a thing.

'Oh Tim!' she cried. 'You can't *believe* how pleased I am to see you. I was just writing you a letter.'

'Well that's nice,' he said. 'Listen . . .' But she was still talking.

'I've been at my wits' end to know what to do. Mr Gresham's been on and on at me. It's been really awful these last few weeks. And now he's made us an appointment. I was just writing to you. We're to go and see him tomorrow.'

His triumph was wrecked. 'What do you mean, we're to go and see him?'

'Like I said. He's made us an appointment. He says it won't wait. There's the letter, look.'

'Don't you want to know how I got on?'

'Yes, of course,' she said untruthfully. 'What are we going to do about it? He sounds so cross. I mean, look at all these letters.'

A bit of sweet talk seemed in order at that point. His story would have to wait. 'Don't

473

worry about it, Poppet,' he said. 'If he wants to see us, he'll see us. I'll manage him. I manage most things, don't I?'

But when they arrived in his office, it was plain that Mr Gresham was in no mood to be managed by anybody. He was standing by the window looking out in a rather brooding sort of way and the first thing he said when they were ushered in was, 'Is your daughter not with you?'

'No I'm afraid not,' Tim said. Damn man. There's no need to come straight out with it like that. We haven't even sat down. 'She couldn't make it, I'm afraid. She's not very well. You know how it is.'

'This isn't at all satisfactory,' Mr Gresham complained, indicating that they should sit down and seating himself behind his desk. 'As I told you in my letter, I cannot proceed any further with this matter until I have your daughter's signature on the application.'

'She'll be here within the week,' Tim promised, assuming his earnest expression. 'I mean she can't help being ill, can she, poor girl, after all she's been through. But she'll be here.'

'So you say,' the solicitor sighed. 'But can we depend upon it? I have to tell you I am beginning to have very serious reservations about this case.'

'She'll be here,' Tim repeated. 'You have my word.'

'With respect, Mr Ledgerwood,' Mr Gresham said, 'I have had your word before, on several occasions, and nothing has ever come of it. There is also the little matter of my invoice, which is still outstanding I believe.'

'I'll take care of it,' Tim said, grandly. 'If you'll just give it to me.'

His bluff didn't work. 'You have received a copy of it twice,' the solicitor said, 'as I understand it.'

'Oh have I?' Tim feigned surprise. 'I didn't know. I've been abroad. I'll attend to it. Of course. Naturally. First opportunity.'

Mr Gresham took out his handkerchief and polished his face: nose, chin, forehead, neck. When he'd finished, there was still a slight film of sweat on his brow and his neck was decidedly pink. 'With respect,' he said, 'I've heard that before too.'

'With *respect*, Mr Gresham,' Tim said in his grandest manner, 'I am not accustomed to having my word doubted. A gentleman's word is his bond.'

The solicitor was momentarily wrong-footed but before he could think of a suitable retort, Billie joined in.

'The thing is,' she said, leaning forward to confide in him, before Tim could warn her not to, 'the thing is, Mr Gresham, we've got a bit of a problem. Our daughter's been enticed away.'

The solicitor's eyebrows rose in amazement. 'Dear me,' he said. 'What do you mean, Mrs Ledgerwood?'

'Enticed away,' Billie explained. 'By a doctor. She's been living with him ever since she came out the hospital. It's my belief he's enticed her away from us.'

'And why would he do that?'

'Because of the compensation.'

Mr Gresham's doubts about this couple had been growing for some time. Now they knotted into a certainty. 'Mrs Ledgerwood,' he said solemnly. 'That is a very serious accusation to make. I must warn you against saying any such thing unless you are entirely certain of your facts. You could be leaving yourself open to a charge of slander and if that were the case, I'm sorry to say I should have to ask you to find another firm of solicitors to act for you.'

Tim was kicking her ankle underneath the desk to warn her, but having been challenged, Billie defended herself vigorously. 'She's been enticed,' she insisted, her voice rising. 'Don't take my word for it. Ask him.'

476

Mr Gresham's neck deepened to turkeycock red. 'I'm afraid I have another appointment in two minutes,' he said, rising to his feet. 'I shall expect to be hearing from you *within two days,* Mr Ledgerwood. Now we really must say good morning.'

'Good morning!' Tim said his voice rising. 'You can't just say good morning, Mr Gresham. That's not good enough. There's still the matter of the compensation.'

'I have made that matter abundantly clear,' Mr Gresham said, ushering them both towards the door. 'Without a signature there can be no application. Ah, Miss Smith, Mr and Mrs Ledgerwood are leaving. Be so good as to show them out, will you.'

'This,' Tim said angrily as he and Billie walked to the car, 'is ridiculous. He can't refuse to work for us. We're his clients. We pay the piper, for Christ's sake.' Being put down so publicly had reduced him to aggression. And he was furious with Billie for being indiscreet, especially as he had to keep her sweet and couldn't rebuke her the way she deserved.

'It's all that doctor's fault,' Billie said. She knew he was blaming her, even if he didn't say so. 'That's who it is. If he hadn't taken her away she'd have signed weeks ago.'

'He needs dealing with,' Tim agreed darkly.

'What are we going to do now?'

'*You're* not going to do anything, my poppet,' Tim said, resuming his masterful expression. 'I'm going to take you back to the boutique and then *I'll* take action. You leave it to me.'

In the restaurant of St Thomas's hospital, Nick and his friends were recovering from too much action. They'd been on duty all night and now they were eating a much-needed breakfast.

'Roll on next Thursday!' Abdul said.

'So what's with next Thursday?' Nick asked, blinking. He'd been in A and E and could hardly keep his eyes open.

'It's Mother's Day and he's growing daffodils as a sideline,' Rick suggested. 'He's going to make a killing.'

'You're such cretins,' Abdul said cheerfully. 'We shall be on leave. Don't say you've forgotten. We've all got a long weekend. Thursday to Monday. Remember?'

For the past ten weeks, their lives had been so dominated by work that they'd almost forgotten about leave. The flu epidemic had run its course by the end of February but their elderly patients were prone to bronchitis and pneumonia and took a long time to recover. Now remembered plans came rushing back to encourage them. Abdul and Sacha were going to France early on Thursday morning 'if someone'll introduce us first!' and they were taking Rick and Bridget with them, 'if you're still an item'.

'Can't wait,' Rick said and joked, 'Bridget who?'

'Why don't *you* come with us Nick,' Abdul offered. 'It's going to be a great trip.'

'Oh I don't know,' Nick said, trying to sound casual. And failing.

'He's got a woman in his life,' Rick teased. 'This isn't hospital fatigue we're seeing. He's shagged out.'

That provoked a wry grimace. 'I should be so lucky!'

Having started, they went on teasing. 'So who's the girl?' Rick asked.

'There isn't one.'

'It's the crash girl,' Abdul said. 'That's who it is. The one you brought into A and E that night. Gemma Something-or-other.'

'Was,' Nick told him, 'is the operative word.'

'She's given you the elbow?' Rick guessed.

'No,' Nick said, his pride stung. 'Nothing

like that. We've just sort of drifted apart.'

'Oh dearie dearie me!' Rick mocked. 'What a wally! They've just sort of drifted apart, Ab.'

'Two young leaves caught up in the waters of life!' Ab was enjoying the joke. 'Maybe they'll just sort of drift together again.'

'Don't mock,' Nick said as lightly as he could. 'That's easier said than done.'

Ab was suddenly serious. 'Have you tried?'

'No.'

'Why not?'

'It's been going on too long. I haven't seen her since Christmas. I can't just ring up after all this time.'

'Why not?' Ab said again.

'Oh come on! What would she say?' Even the thought of it was making him flinch.

'Only one way to find out,' Rick said. 'Phone her and see. I presume you've got her number.'

'Yes,' Nick admitted. He'd taken it from his mother's address book when she was out of the room. Very underhand. It still made him feel ashamed to remember it. 'But . . .'

'No buts,' Ab said, talking to him like a Dutch uncle. 'Just do it and don't be such a coward. If you're serious about a girl you have to run a few risks, you know. Compromise and that sort of thing. You can't expect to have everything your own way all the time.'

'I don't.'

Ab smiled at him. 'Don't you?' he asked. And when Nick frowned: 'All right. I'll take your word for it. So there's no problem, is there?'

'We'll dial for you if you like,' Rick grinned. 'Only go and do it now. I can't take all this testosterone first thing in the morning. You're spoiling my cornflakes.'

'No thanks,' Nick said. 'I can dial.' Was it possible? Could it be done? There wasn't really time, was there? Was there? Maybe he *was* being cowardly. Maybe he ought to phone. He certainly wanted to. He'd wanted to for weeks. Dammit. He would. She could only say no. 'I won't be a minute,' he said to his friends. 'But don't wait for me.' If she was going to turn him down he'd rather not be in their company when she did it.

He found the most distant phone. Dialled, heart shaking. Struggled to think of something noncommittal to say . . .

And she was answering — 'Hello' — her voice so warm and close it made him feel weak to hear it.

'Hello,' he said, breathlessly. 'It's me. I'm in a rush. Got to be back on the wards two minutes ago. You know how it is. The thing is I've got a few days' leave and I was wondering if you'd like to have a meal with me or something.'

There was a pause. That's it, he thought, I've blown it. And he tensed himself for her refusal.

'That would be nice,' her voice said. 'When?'

Acceptance was so sweet and so unexpected he chose the first date that came into his head. 'Next Wednesday?'

'Yes.'

'Where would you like to go? I don't know much about the restaurants in Putney. Maybe you've got a favourite.'

'I tell you what,' she said. 'Why don't you come here and *I'll* feed *you*.'

'That would be great,' he said, weak with relief. 'Why don't I?'

Gemma was still feeling surprised when she put the phone down. But very pleased. There was no denying that. It would be good to see him again and to hear what he had to say for himself. Now that they'd fixed their date she remembered that next Friday would be the last day of her first half-term, so she had a reason to celebrate, even if he hadn't rung. I'll buy something special, she decided. Salmon *en croûte,* perhaps. It would mean a trip to the supermarket but she could cope with that now. It was high time she put her walking ability to the test even if it meant competing with a store full of two-legged women.

So that Wednesday, while Nick was working his last shift, she made her first expedition to a supermarket since her accident and was really quite pleased with herself. The trolley was difficult to manoeuvre but she handled it well enough, even when she was being jostled, and it gave her something to lean on when she needed a rest. She pushed it back to the car in some style, feeling competent, and packed all her plastic bags in the boot just like everybody else.

It wasn't until she got back to the flat that she hit trouble. Transferring bags from trolley to boot in a car park had been relatively easy, but now it was getting dark and it was cold and she had to carry them some distance, out of her poorly lit garage and across the cobbled compound to the flat. It didn't take her long to discover that she could only manage two bags at a time, so it was going to be quite a business.

I should have left my wheelchair here and

used that, she thought, as she struggled off with a heavy bag in each hand.

And somebody called her name. 'Gemma! Gemma!'

A man's voice. Not Nick, but someone who knew her. What good timing! Perhaps he'd give her a hand. She looked round to see who it was.

A dark figure was moving towards her from the visitors' parking area. It wasn't anyone she recognised but he obviously knew her, for he was calling to her again. 'Gemma! It *is* you!' his voice throbbing with some sort of emotion. As he got closer she could see that he was tanned and quite handsome in an old-fashioned sort of way.

What if he's a drunk? she thought, sniffing the air. And she decided to be cautious. 'Do I know you?' she asked.

He wasn't a bit abashed by the chill in her voice. 'Know me?' he echoed. 'I should just think you do, Poppet. I'm your father.'

She was shocked and, although it seemed churlish, annoyed. This wasn't the way she'd planned to meet him again. She'd always had it in mind that, when it did happen, it would be well organised and intimate, like a well-staged play, not out here in a cold courtyard on a chill afternoon, when she wasn't expecting it.

He was standing right in front of her now and of course, she recognised him. 'As far as I know,' she told him, 'I never had a "father". My father ran out on me when I was a baby.'

'I know,' he said, grimacing an apology, 'and I shouldn't have done it. You don't need to tell me. But there you are, these things happen. Anyway here I am, come back to make amends. Do you want a hand with those bags?'

'Well yes,' she had to admit. 'Thank you. It would be a help.'

'Can't have my little girl carrying great heavy bags about,' he said, taking the last four out of the boot. 'Lead the way, Poppet.'

They walked across the courtyard to the flat together, father and daughter carrying the shopping home. And although she was glad of his help, it felt surreal.

'How did you know where I was?' she asked as they walked into the kitchen.

'Polly told me,' he said. 'The cleaning lady at Amersham Road. Nice woman. Went and got the address for me at once, the minute I asked her. It's only your mother you never told, you bad girl. You've been a bit naughty to your poor mother. She's been very concerned about you, you know. You ought to have told her where you were.'

Being reproved made Gemma feel uncomfortable and being called a bad girl in that condescending way was irritating. 'I needed time,' she said, rather tetchily. 'I don't like being rushed.'

'Well it's all water under the bridge now,' Tim said smoothly. 'How about a cup of tea?'

She had to be hospitable whether she would or no. She hung up her coat, filled the kettle, began to unpack, covering her confusion with domestic routine. 'I've got someone coming in half an hour,' she warned, tipping the prepared vegetables into saucepans and putting the salmon *en croûte* in the oven.

'That's all right,' he told her. 'That's all it'll take. I shan't keep you. I only came to see how you were and bring you a little present. You'd like a little present, wouldn't you? All girls like presents.'

Not particularly, she thought, lighting the oven. But he was already taking it out of his pocket.

I suppose I'll have to thank him for it, Gemma thought, whatever it is. But her heart sank at the sight of the wrapping paper, let alone the present. It was pink with orange and blue powder puffs all over it.

'Go on, Poppet, open it,' he urged. 'It's lovely. You'll love it.'

There didn't seem to be any way of avoiding it, so she opened her present. It was a teenager's make-up kit, in garish colours and with a pink plastic mirror at the centre of it all.

'Neat, eh?' her father said proudly. 'You girls always like make-up, don't you?'

It was all beginning to be a bit too much for Gemma. She wanted to cry because he was such a disappointment but she knew she couldn't. She wanted to laugh because his present was so absurd but she couldn't do that either. She knew she ought to thank him but it was simply beyond her. Fortunately the kettle was boiling, so she made him a mug of tea and suggested that it might be more comfortable to drink it in the living room.

He took possession of the armchair and accepted the tea as though it were well-earned thanks. And Gemma sat on the sofa and drank her tea without saying anything.

Her silence didn't seem to worry him. 'I must say you look better than I thought you would,' he said. 'When I saw you on the news you looked dreadful. I thought you were a goner, as a matter of a fact. And now here you are, an absolute stunner, as good as new.'

'Well not quite,' she corrected, annoyed that he was making so light of her injuries. 'I'm scarred for life and I've got a false leg.'

'Nobody would know it,' he said, fingering his moustache. 'So tell me, how are you getting on?'

'I'm fine,' she said. 'As you see.'

He gave her a rather calculating look. 'I dare say you could do with a bit more cash, though.'

That's none of your business, Gemma thought, but she answered politely. 'I manage.'

He insisted. 'But you could do with a bit more, now couldn't you? For wheelchairs and things like that. Things you need. Cripple's things. I mean, take this flat for a start. It's very nice but it must've cost you a pretty penny. You can't deny it. And you've got a car, haven't you. I'll bet that didn't come cheap. Everything costs.'

That was true enough but she wasn't going to admit it to him, especially when he'd just called her a cripple. 'I work,' she told him. 'I manage.'

'It's a good job I came here, if you ask me,' he said, and leant towards her conspiratorially. 'I could help you manage a bit better. Well a lot better, actually. In point of fact, that's why I came to see you. I thought you might need some advice.'

She felt that he was putting some kind of pressure on her and didn't like it. 'No,' she told him firmly. 'I don't.'

'This is a nasty world,' he explained. 'There are some terrible sharks out there. You take it from one who knows. Terrible sharks. As soon as I knew you were in trouble I thought to myself, you ought to get over there, Tim Ledgerwood. You ought to get over there and protect your little girl before the sharks move in. Because they'll move in sure as God made little apples. They only have to get the slightest whiff of a bit of money and they're round.'

Gemma stared at him. I'm not in any trouble, she thought. What is he talking about? 'As far as I know there's no reason why sharks should move in on me,' she said. 'I haven't got any money for them to get a whiff of. Just my wheelchair. And they'd hardly be after *that*.'

'But you could have,' he said. 'That's the point. You could have. If you sue the railway for compensation you could be a millionaire. Think of it. Well, half a millionaire anyway. And that's where I come in. I could show you how to invest that money. Right out of the way where the sharks can't get their greasy paws on it. I could be really useful to you.'

Money, Gemma thought. I might have guessed. After all these years dreaming and wondering and building you up into a hero who was going to come and rescue me and love me, you turn out to be a money-grabber. And she turned to him with the sweetest smile she could conjure and began to play him along.

'You must tell me all about it,' she said, charmingly. Oh, she was a good actress! 'I'm intrigued.'

It was all the encouragement he needed. 'Well first,' he confided, 'you ought to come with me and see a solicitor. I know a very good one. Very good. In point of fact, I've got him to draw up a sort of document in case you were interested. We've done the ground work, so to speak. The thing is, time's getting on, and you ought to make a claim pretty soon or it could all go wrong. You wouldn't want that, would you?'

Smile.

'There's a lot of money at stake here,' he explained, his face avid. 'Half a million. And why not? You take them for every penny you can get out of them. That's my advice. They've asked for it.'

'Which you'd invest for me. Is that it?'

'Got it in one. Actually I've got some brochures, if you'd like to see them. Cast-iron investments.'

'And all I'd have to do is sign on the dotted line. Is that it?'

This time her smile was just a little too sweet.

'I could get you a good deal,' he told her defensively. 'All you've got to do is file the application. You want some compensation, don't you?'

'No,' she said. 'Not particularly. I've got enough to live on.'

He could feel his blood pressure rising. What was the matter with the girl? 'We're talking half a million here,' he told her. 'You're not going to tell me you'd turn down half a million.'

'Yes,' she said. 'I think that's exactly what I am saying.'

She's going out of her way to annoy me, he thought. 'Now look here, Poppet,' he said, assuming his stern face. 'All this play-acting's all very well. I mean I appreciate a joke. In the proper place. But you ought to be serious about this. If you play your cards right you could be a millionaire.'

Time to call a halt, Gemma thought. 'Let's get things straight, shall we,' she said.

'I'm *not* a millionaire. I'm not going to be a millionaire. I don't want to be a millionaire. And even if I were I wouldn't give my money to you.'

She was making him so cross it was all he could do to contain himself. 'Oh I see how it is,' he said, heavily. 'Somebody's been putting pressure on you, haven't they?'

The unpleasantness of his tone alarmed her. 'No,' she said.

'You don't fool me,' he said. 'It's that damned Dr Quennell. Well let me tell you something about your Dr Quennell. He's not the great hero everybody imagines.'

'Dr Quennell is a very good man,' she said springing to his defence. 'If it hadn't been for him I wouldn't be here now. He saved my life.'

'He's a phoney,' Tim said. 'And it's high time you knew it. He's no more a hero than that table. When he was out in Cyprus . . .'

'You don't know anything about him,' she said, before he could tell her something she didn't want to hear.

'And you do?'

'Yes, I do. I've lived in his house.'

'And that's another thing,' he sneered.

The implication was too obvious to be borne. 'I'm sorry,' she interrupted. 'I can't have you maligning my friend. If you go on with this, I shall have to ask you to leave.'

What happened next was so unexpected that it took her completely off balance. He jumped to his feet, took two strides across the carpet, seized the arms of her chair and leant over her, pushing his angry face so close to hers that they were locked in a stare. She could see the veins standing up on his forehead.

'Now you listen here!' he threatened. 'And you listen good! You want to stop being a bloody fool. That's what you want to do. I came here to help you. *Which no one else will.* D'you understand. No one. And do you know why? I'll tell you why. Because you're a cripple and no one wants a cripple. You ought to be down on your knees fasting for the help I'm giving you. Down on your knees fasting. Not coming over all hoity-toity and butter-won't-melt and Lady Muck and I don't want to be a millionaire. That's not going to get you anywhere and don't you think it. I've set everything up for you. I've gone out of my way. All you've got to do is come down to the solicitor's and sign the forms. So you just make up your mind to it and stop all this bloody silly nonsense.'

She was so shocked that for a few seconds she couldn't move or speak and she could feel her heart swelling with fear of him. Her instincts urged her to spring to her feet and run away from him but her prosthesis seemed to be locked. Something had to be said, even if she couldn't move. She stiffened her spine, took a deep breath and anger came suddenly and powerfully to her rescue. 'Go away!' she spat at him. 'Get out of my house! How dare you behave like this!'

He went on glaring at her for a long, long second but then he stood up, let go of the chair and took a step away from her. 'You're my daughter,' he said. 'I can speak to you how I like.'

Now that he'd moved out of her space, she was more in command of herself, although her heart was still throbbing painfully. 'I suggest you leave,' she said. 'Or I shall phone the police and have you thrown out.'

'All right then,' he said, struggling with his fury. 'I'll go for now. If that's the way you want it. But I'll be back, let me tell you. Don't think I won't. You've got papers to sign and I'm going to make sure you sign them.'

'You know where the door is,' she said. And looked away from him, willing him to go.

She heard the door open and close but it

was several seconds before she turned her head to check that he'd gone.

It was peaceful in the flat without him. And safe. Blessedly, blessedly safe. She got to her feet at last and walked out into the hall where she leant on the arm of her wheelchair for support, feeling limp with relief. Now she could cry.

Chapter 27

Nick drove to Putney that Wednesday evening fuming with impatience. Just when he needed a nice clear road, the traffic was worse than he'd ever known it, slow-moving, bad-tempered and bottlenecked at every turn, at Vauxhall, in York Road and virtually all the way through Wandsworth, where the one-way system hadn't eased the traffic flow at all. Consequently, he swung in through the archway to St Mary's Court much too fast and at exactly the same moment as a large BMW was driving out.

For a second he thought they were going to hit one another. 'Fool!' he shouted as he stood on his brakes. 'Look where you're bloody going!'

The driver took no notice, but drove arrogantly past, and much too close. If he'd been an inch nearer he would have scuffed the paintwork.

'Bloody roadhog!' Nick roared and screeched to a halt in the visitors' parking space. Then he belted across the compound to Gemma's flat, still in a temper.

'I've damn nearly had an accident,' he said when she opened the door. 'Some bloody old fool in a BMW. Driving out of here like a bat out of hell. Nearly had me off the road.' Then he realised that she had tears in her eyes and was turning away from him. And he knew he'd made a mistake. 'What's up?' he said, changing his tone. And when she didn't answer. 'Gemma?'

His concern was too late. She'd needed sympathy too, not some stupid masculine complaint about somebody else's driving. It hurt her that he hadn't noticed what a state she was in. 'Nothing,' she said and walked into the living room without looking at him.

Christ, what a bad start! He was instantly and totally reasonable again, trying to put things right. 'It can't be nothing,' he argued, following her. 'You're crying.'

She protected herself by being independent and stubborn. 'I can cry if I like.'

Now that he'd calmed down, he realised that she looked delectable, in a new red jersey and tight black jeans. He wanted to put his arms round her and comfort her with kisses. But it was too soon for that. Or too late. Oh, not too late. Don't let it be too late. 'What is it?' he said, as tenderly as he dared. 'Can't you tell me?'

'The man in the BMW was my bloody father, if you must know,' she said, her voice angry.

'Did you invite him?' She must have done or how else would he have known where she was?

'No I didn't. He just turned up out of the blue. Oh Nick, I thought it would be wonderful to see him again. I've been dreaming about it for years.'

'And it wasn't,' he understood following her into the living room.

She walked to the window, drummed her fingers against the glass, walked back towards him, tense with misery and disappointment. 'No,' she said. 'It was horrible. He hasn't come back to look after me. He's come back because he thinks I'm rich. He's after the compensation money.'

Nick felt awkward standing in the middle of the room but he didn't like to sit down for fear of doing the wrong thing. 'That's vile!' he said.

She was too near tears to be comforted. 'Don't sympathise,' she said angrily. 'It's my business. I can handle it.'

'Don't let it get to you,' he advised, deciding to sit in the armchair. 'They're never worth it. Parents.'

The fury she'd held in check while she was dealing with her father broke through her control and came pouring out of her mouth. She knew, in the more distant and reasonable part of her mind, that she was being angry with the wrong person but she couldn't help it. 'What's that supposed to mean? Are you getting at my mother?'

He hadn't thought about her mother until that moment. 'No, I'm not,' he said, looking up at her. 'But she's not exactly perfect either. Look how she went on when you were in St Thomas's.'

'Once.' She glared at him.

'Twice to my certain knowledge. And again at the Ps' house that time.'

'Oh yes,' she mocked, turning and pacing. 'I knew we'd get round to that.'

'I was there,' he pointed out. 'I heard her.'

'You don't know anything about her.'

Battle was joined. It was ridiculous but that's how it was. She meant to fight him even though he didn't want to fight her. He cast about for something simple and factual to say and remembered his studies. 'I know quite a bit about her, actually.' And he quoted from one of his textbooks. ' "You can tell a lot about the parent by studying the child." '

She rejected that as nonsense, snorting at him. 'Oh come *on!*'

'No,' he said. 'Seriously. This is a classic case of parental repression.' If he could get her to talk generally they might cool down.

But she roared at him, sparks flying between them so powerfully it was a wonder they weren't visible. 'So I'm repressed now, am I? That's nice to know.'

'That wasn't what I said,' he protested. But then he stopped and sniffed the air, lifting his head and turning away from her. 'Something's burning,' he said, jumping to his feet. 'Look!' There was smoke billowing out through the archway to the kitchen.

'Shit!' she said. 'Oh shit!' She went limping into the kitchen to open the oven. 'It's the bloody salmon.'

It was burnt black and the bottom of the oven was covered with bubbling lumps of black tar.

She removed the wreckage, fanning it with an oven glove, her face pink with heat and fury. 'Bloody rotten stinking thing!' she said.

He stood beside her in the kitchen and laughed, the tension of the last few awful minutes released in a roar of amusement. 'Oh Gemma, you're so funny!'

She wasn't amused. 'It's nothing to laugh at,' she scowled. 'That was our supper.'

'Never mind,' he said. Now they could be

normal and he could tease her and kiss her. 'We'll have a take-away.'

The kitchen was so full of smoke it was making her cough. She opened the little top window to clear it a bit. 'Oh God! Look at the mess.'

'Leave it,' he advised.

But she wasn't listening to him. She was still coughing and complaining. 'How could I have done such a thing?'

'I wouldn't worry if I were you,' he said, trying to cheer her up. 'It's part of your charm, burning food.'

She was too tense to be teased. 'I don't burn food!'

He gestured at the remains of the salmon, grinning at her.

'Once!' she said.

'What about the Ps' retirement cake?' he reminded her.

She was wafting the smoke towards the window with a rolled newspaper. 'That sank,' she corrected, between coughs. 'I didn't burn it.'

'Same difference. We had to cut a hole out of the middle.'

'And now I suppose I'm never going to hear the end of it. Is that it?' She looked wild, beleaguered, vulnerable, with her brown eyes watering and the rolled newspaper falling to tatters in her hand. He loved her so much it was making him ache.

'I think you should marry me,' he said. 'You need someone to look after you.'

He'd spoken instinctively, without thinking what effect such a proposal would have, offering his love simply like the great gift it was. And to his horror, she turned on him as if he was insulting her.

'That,' she told him furiously, 'is the one thing I *don't* need. I'm not a cripple . . .'

He was completely thrown and terribly hurt. 'I never said you were . . .'

'Yes you did. You implied it. I'm not a cripple. I'm not an invalid. I don't need looking after. Not by you or my father or my mother or anybody. I can look after myself. I've got a job, and I've got a home, and there's nothing I can't do if I set my mind to it. Nothing! I won't be looked after and I won't be pitied.'

'But I want to look after you,' he protested. 'I love you.'

She snorted. '*Now* he tells me!'

'Where's the harm in wanting to look after you? It's what husbands do.'

'I'll tell you the harm in it,' she said wildly. 'It's belittling. It puts me down. I don't want to be some stupid Barbie doll being pampered and petted and looked after all the time. If you want that, you'd better get a poodle. If I ever marry anyone I shall be his equal. An equal partner. Not some feeble thing that has to be cared for.' Some lines from *Pygmalion* sang into her head and she quoted them, feeling they were better than any words she could find for herself. ' *"Not a millstone round your neck. A tower of strength. A consort battleship."* '

'I never said you were a millstone.'

'It's Shaw,' she said in exasperation. '*Pygmalion.* I was quoting.'

Literary quotations were beyond him in a moment as fraught as this one. 'Well don't.'

'I was telling you how I felt.'

'And what about me?' he cried, too distressed to hold on to his control any longer. 'Or don't my feelings come into it? No I suppose they don't. I suppose it doesn't matter what I want. That I might mean what I say?'

'Isn't that just men all over?' she yelled. 'You take me out and then ignore me for weeks afterwards. We go to dinner and I end up in hospital.'

'That wasn't my fault . . .'

'You leave me without a word for months and months and then you come bouncing back and you think you can propose and I'll fall into your arms.'

If only she would. 'I don't. That's not . . . Anyway I didn't leave you without a word. I saw you at Christmas.'

'From the other side of the room. You never came near me.'

'But you said . . .'

'This is all wrong,' she said, suddenly overcome by an intolerable fatigue. 'We can't go into all this now. It's the wrong time. I think you should go.'

'Well I don't. Now we've started we should have it out.'

Her face was mutinous. 'Well I do and it's my flat.'

'All right then! I was a fool to come here. I might have known it would go wrong.'

'And you were supposed to love me,' she said bitterly.

'I do. I do, you stupid woman.'

'Don't call me a stupid woman.'

There was nothing for it. He would have to go before he made matters worse. 'This is bloody ridiculous,' he said and strode out of the flat, slamming the door behind him, in a storm of frustration and anger and incomprehension. How could she say such things? When he loved her so much. When he'd asked her to marry him. There was no sense in it. He fell into the driving seat, hitting his knees on the steering wheel, switched on the ignition as though he was wringing its neck, drove angrily and with no sense of purpose, unaware of where he was going. It wasn't until he turned into Amersham Road that he came to himself again and then he felt foolish, as though he was running home to Mummy. But, as he now realised, he was also extremely hungry so perhaps he'd just go in and see them and cadge a sandwich. He didn't have anywhere else to go.

He found his key and let himself in, calling as he walked down the hall, glad that his voice sounded normal. 'Hello! Anyone at home?'

'Is that you?' his father answered from the study. And when Nick put his head round the door: 'We weren't expecting you this evening, were we? Your mother's out. Gone to see the cousins in Peckham.'

'No, no,' Nick said. 'I only called on the off-chance.'

'You chose the right time,' Andrew said. 'We're off to Birmingham tomorrow after-noon.'

'How so?'

'I've been asked to appear on *Friday Fo-rum*. We're going to stay overnight and make a little holiday of it. It's the Wands-worth crash. It's back in the news.'

'Is it?'

'It was in the papers this morning. Or don't you read the papers these days?'

'I've been on A and E.'

'Ah!' Andrew understood. 'Have you had dinner? Or are you on the way there?'

'No and no,' Nick admitted. 'I suppose I couldn't rustle up a sandwich or something, could I? I'm starving.'

'See what's in the fridge,' Andrew suggested. 'Would you like a malt?'

Nick declined the whisky. 'I'm driving.' But there were two tins of Carlsberg in the fridge, which were a good substitute, and the remains of a cold chicken and some coleslaw.

'So how's life?' Andrew asked, coming into the kitchen, whisky glass in hand as his son set about his impromptu meal.

'Gruesome,' Nick said, and told him how hard pressed they'd been at St Thomas's all week. Talking shop was a comfort and something they both enjoyed.

But at the end of it Andrew asked a deliberately casual question. There was something so brittle about this son of his this evening that he felt it needed asking, despite his advice to Catherine to leave well alone. 'Seen anything of Gemma recently?'

Nick paused, thought hard and decided

to tell the truth. 'I saw her this evening,' he admitted. 'First time for weeks.'

'Is she all right?'

'No,' Nick said. 'Not really.' And when his father looked another question at him: 'As a matter of fact I've just asked her to marry me and she's turned me down flat.'

Andrew's next question was asked as though it was part of a consultation. 'Why was that?'

'She says she wants to be independent. She doesn't want to be looked after. I thought that was part of the deal, looking after your wife and making a fuss of her, that sort of thing, but apparently not. You'd have thought I was insulting her the way she went on. She doesn't want to be a wife, so she says. She wants to be a consort battleship.'

'Pity!' Andrew said.

'Yes. It is. But there you are.'

'No,' Andrew corrected. 'Not pity, what a shame. Pity the emotion. It's a poor substitute for love.'

The word made Nick remember. 'That's what she said. "I don't want to be pitied." But I don't pity her. I love her.'

'Are you sure?'

'Yes. Of course I'm sure.' His answer was vehement because he wasn't sure at all.

Could he have been pitying her all these weeks? That *was* the emotion he'd felt when he first saw her — and when she was coming round from the op — and when he examined her stump for the first time.

'It's a very dangerous emotion,' his father was saying. 'Leads to all sorts of trouble. Demeans the one who's pitied and makes the pitier feel superior.'

'All I want to do is to look after her and help her. Is that so bad?'

'Laudable but risky.'

'You help Mum.'

His father gave a wry smile. 'Only when she's not looking.'

Nick sighed. 'Why is life so complicated?'

'Because it would be dull if it wasn't.'

'Just when you think you've got everything sussed something comes along and knocks you back to square one.'

That required no answer, beyond a smile. Both men returned to their drinks.

'So what am I going to do?' Nick asked.

'Leave her alone for a day or two. Let her get over it.'

But where would he go for the next four days? He could hardly crawl back to St Thomas's. That would be a dreadful comedown. And he couldn't stay here either. 'I've got a long weekend,' he said. 'We all

have. Rick and Abdul are going to France.'
And *there* was the answer. Of course. 'Could
I use your phone?'

He tried Abdul's number first. Without
success, so he wasn't back yet. Then he rang
Rick and got through straight away.

'Hi!' Rick said, sounding surprised.
'What's this? God speed?'

'No,' Nick said, feeling suddenly awkward. 'Actually I was wondering. I think I
might like to come with you after all. Have
you got room for a little'un?'

Rick was wise enough to ask no questions.
'Yeah! I reckon we could squeeze you in,' he
said, as if it were no big deal. 'Where are
you? Do you want us to pick you up?'

'Well actually . . .' Nick said again. 'I was
wondering if you could put me up for the
night. My holiday's not going to work
out.'

'No problem,' Rick said understanding
what a large problem his friend was facing.
'You'll have to sleep on the sofa though. So
we'll have to amputate your feet.'

'Feel free!' Nick said gratefully. Thank
God for friendship. 'I'm going to France,'
he told his father as he put the receiver
down.

Andrew had worked that out for himself.
'Very wise,' he said. 'Just what you need.

Breathing space.'

Back in the wreckage of her kitchen, Gemma was finding it hard to breathe at all, what with the lingering smell of the smoke and a throat full of tears. She'd scrubbed the baking tin and now she was sitting on the floor trying to clean the bottom of the oven, working out her distress with wire wool and a bucket full of Flash — there being nothing like housework to bring you down to earth. How could he have been so crass? she thought as she peered into the oven. She simply didn't understand it. He'd always seemed so gentle and compassionate. She remembered his face, distorted by anger, yelling at her. How could he have yelled at her like that? But she'd yelled back, hadn't she. She'd given as good as she'd got. Or as bad.

She emptied the dirty water down the sink, and then had to pick all the sharp bits of debris out of the plughole. She was hungry and miserable, she'd burnt her supper and although the fridge and freezer were full of food she didn't have the energy or the inclination to cook anything else. In any case, after such a disastrous evening, it seemed appropriate to go to bed hungry.

To bed and straight into nightmare.

Trains screamed in upon her, slicing her in half, filling her throat with dust and pressing down on her chest as she struggled and twisted and fought for breath. She was on her knees trying to wash away the dirt and grease and the axle was inches away from her face and the grease turned to a stream of blood that ran and ran and couldn't be stanched. And Nick looked down at her through the jagged hole in the carriage with his hair untidy and an ink stain on his white coat. 'Oh Nick!' she cried. 'I'm so glad to see you.' And he turned his head away from her. 'I'm going,' he said, 'and I shan't come back.'

She cried and screamed, 'Oh please don't go!' trying to catch at his coat. 'What shall I do without you?' But he was beyond her grasp, walking away along the ward, his coat tails flapping. And her father had her by the throat and was choking her. 'Sign, damn you. Sign. Do as you're told.'

She woke screaming, 'I won't! I won't! I won't!' with sweat on her forehead, her heart pounding, confused by terror, still caught up in the nightmare. She was convinced that half her body had been cut away and put down her hands gingerly to feel what was left. I'll face it, she thought, however bad it is. I must. There's nothing else I can do. It took several seconds before she came to her full senses and knew where she was. Then she sat up and turned on the light and looked at the clock.

It was ten past five and she was all alone. And very hungry.

There was no possibility of any more sleep that night so she got up, found her crutches and went to the bathroom where she washed and put on her prosthesis, carefully, and dressed as though she was starting an ordinary day. Then she walked to the kitchen and switched on the radio for a bit of company, cooked herself bacon and eggs, made toast and a pot of tea, and ate a leisurely breakfast.

After that she felt better. What had happened had happened. Now she just had to get on with the day, which was dawning beyond the kitchen window. She could see the pale green of the lightening sky through the gap in the curtains. She pulled the curtains back and stood by the window looking out.

It didn't seem right that the day should be beginning in such an ordinary way. After such an awful row and a night devastated by nightmare, she should have woken to a biblical darkness covering the sun for twenty-four hours, or a hurricane with black and purple skies and winds of a hundred miles an hour screaming and howling and tossing trees aside like straws. But dawn was coming in like a peaceful tide, trailing rose pink ribbons across a pale sky, and outside the flat, the daffodils were in yellow bud and the Thames shone blue as the sky. It made her remember York and their trip along the river and how close they'd been that day.

Perhaps I could phone him, she thought, as she washed her solitary cup and saucer. But she didn't know where he was. He wouldn't have gone to Amersham Road. He was too proud to do that. So he'd probably gone back to the hospital, and if that was the case, there was no way she could contact him, short of phoning the switchboard and asking them to page him. Which would be much too public. She would have to wait for him to phone her — if he wanted to. And after all the dreadful things they'd said to one another, she had to face the fact that he probably wouldn't want to. How could we have behaved like that? she thought. It was too stupid.

The post arrived as she was cleaning her teeth but it was only bills, so she put them on the mantelpiece and went off to work without giving them another thought. Paying bills was the least of her worries that morning. For the moment she simply wanted to drive to Fairmead School and get on with her work.

As she turned out of the compound, she noticed that she'd left the kitchen window ajar and wondered whether she ought to go back and secure it. But what was the use of fussing over little details when she might never see him again? If the kitchen got cold, it would have to get cold. She'd think about it when she got home that afternoon. For the moment there were other things pummelling her mind.

She anguished all the way to the school, feeling more and more miserable. I didn't mean half the things I said to him, she grieved, and now I can't take them back. And, as she inched through the school gate, she knew she loved him.

Chapter 28

Tim Ledgerwood was in such a temper when he got back to the High that Wednesday evening, that he needed two stiff whiskies before he could manage to tell Billie what had happened.

'Well that's it!' he said, topping up his glass for the third time. 'She's left me no option. I shall *have* to go to the papers. It's not nice but she's asked for it.'

Billie made a commiserating noise. 'If you'd told me where she was,' she reproved, 'I could have gone with you and talked her round. I warned you she was tricky.'

'Tricky!' he complained. 'She was diabolical. She threw me out. All this time I've been working on her behalf, setting this up, looking after her interests, and she threw me out. *And* I bought her a present. Full make-up kit. Gorgeous, it was. You should've seen it. Cost me an arm and a leg. But does she thank me? Does she hell? No, she turns round and says she won't sign the application and she won't go to the solicitor, and then she gives me a mouthful and

515

slings me out. Me! Her father! It's bloody disgraceful.'

'She was always tricky,' Billie admitted, patting her hair for comfort. 'Even as a kid. It doesn't surprise me. You should've seen the way she carried on when we had the portfolio done. You'd have thought I was killing her instead of making her look beautiful.'

'Wouldn't have a word said about that damned doctor. I was right about him. He's got her well under his thumb. Well that's it. I shall go to the papers.'

'Yes,' Billie encouraged him. 'I think you should. Go to that Nicky girl. I've got her card somewhere or other.'

'What Nicky girl?'

'The reporter. The one that interviewed me. You remember. No, maybe you don't. It was before you came back. Anyway she interviewed me. I thought she was nice. And she gave me her card and said to ring her if I had any other news. Well we've got some news for her now, haven't we?'

'Maybe,' he said grudgingly. If he was going to the papers he would rather choose the reporter himself. 'It depends what paper she works for.'

'The *Chronicle*.'

'Ah,' Tim said. That was different. 'Then

she'll know Garry McKendrick. Yes, I think I *would* like to talk to her. You find the card, Poppet, and we'll ring her. First thing in the morning.'

Nicky Stretton had only just come in when the phone rang. She was standing by her desk, still in her driving coat, coffee mug in hand and more than half asleep, but when she heard who was calling she took up her notebook at once and struggled out of the coat as she talked, the receiver tucked under her chin. Yes, she did remember Billie Goodeve. And yes, if there was a story, she was interested. 'So tell me. Did she get her half-million?'

'Well that's just it,' Billie said. 'We don't know. She's being kept away from us. I'll hand you over to her father. He'll tell you.'

Which he did at considerable length. 'She didn't come home to her mother . . . I mean, that's unnatural for a start. I think she's been lured away. They let her out the hospital and he lured her away to live with *him*. Great house like that, it's a temptation.'

Nicky Stretton wrote 'family squabble' on her pad and prepared to give him the brush off.

'Someone in the family, you mean.'

'Oh no. Nothing like that. We're a very close family. Extremely close. No, it's that doctor.'

That sounded marginally more interesting. Doctors made good copy. 'What doctor was that?'

'The one that's on TV all the time, sounding off about the Health Service. Dr Quennell.'

Nicky signalled to her colleagues and wrote 'Quack-quack Quennell! Gotcha!' on her pad. The excitement the message generated was intense and gathered a crowd.

'Are you telling me she went to live with Dr Quennell?' Nicky asked and keyed in her headline. TV GURU AND CRASH HEROINE IN TUG-OF-LOVE TANGLE.

'Got it in one,' Tim said. 'He's enticed her away. I don't think it's right, do you?'

'Tell me about his house,' she suggested as she typed up the story. 'Where is it?'

'That,' she said to her audience, as she put the phone down, 'is tomorrow's lead, unless I'm very much mistaken. Garry'll go bananas. Quack-quack Quennell caught with his trousers down. Is he in?'

'Not yet.'

'Right. You can break the good news,

Jack. Give him this number, suggest he rings it and tell him I'm in Putney checking it out.'

Amersham Road was very quiet after the bustle of the office, and the Quennell house was the quietest in the road. Nicky knocked and rang and, as there was no answer, peered through the stained glass into the empty hall.

'Can I help you?' a voice asked.

Elderly man, tweedy, nice smile, neighbourhood-watch person with a Dobermann pinscher on a lead.

She gave him her sweetest smile and told him she'd come to see Dr Quennell.

'They've gone to Birmingham,' the neighbour volunteered. 'I'm keeping an eye on things. You've only just missed them, as a matter of fact.'

'Oh dear! Will they be away long?'

'No, no. Not long. He's gone there to appear on television, *Friday Forum*. Rather exciting, don't you think?'

Great! Nicky thought. Couldn't be better. What timing! 'Actually,' she said, 'the one I really came to see is Gemma Goodeve. She used to live here, I believe.'

'A lovely girl,' the neighbour said. 'Yes. She did. We saw quite a lot of her.'

'So she has moved. Isn't that just my luck!'

Now, and a bit late, her informant remembered his lookout duties and thought he ought to ask a few questions of his own. 'Are you a relation, by any chance?'

'No,' Nicky told him. 'I wish I were. She's just the sort of relation I'd *love*. Wouldn't we all! No, I'm a reporter. I'm the one who wrote up her story after the crash. We all think she's *wonderful*. Such *courage*.'

'Yes,' he agreed, relieved by her information. 'So do we. Like I said, a lovely girl.'

'And of course, she's in the news again, with this second report coming out, so we wondered how she was. I don't suppose you see so much of her now she's moved.'

'Oh she comes back,' he told her, 'regularly. She was here at Christmas in fact. We often see her.'

'They must be very fond of her,' she fished.

'Oh yes,' he agreed. 'Very fond.'

'She's lucky to have them to look after her.'

He agreed with that too. 'They're a lovely family,' he said. 'We all think very highly of them round here. Pillars of the establishment, you might say. Well we often do. It doesn't make it any less true for being a truism. He's such a good doctor. Nothing's too much trouble for him. And of course Mrs Quennell was a sister at the clinic. She used to run the mother and baby clinic before she retired. She looked after my Christabel when she had the pleurisy. So kind.'

'Very nice,' Nicky said, wondering how she could steer him back on target.

'And then of course there's the two boys,' the old man rambled on. 'They're both doctors, you know. The older one's out in Canada. Such a nice boy, although I dare say he's a bit more than a boy now. Time goes by so quickly. I remember him as a little lad playing in the garden with his brother. That's the younger son, the one at St Thomas's. He was at the crash too. Quite a family affair that crash. We all remarked on it. Especially with the daughter being involved. Such a nice girl and so clever. She wrote the report, you know.'

Nicky hadn't been paying much attention to him but at the word 'report' she was instantly alerted.

'What report was that?'

'Why, the report into the crash. The one that was in all the papers. She wrote it, the daughter.'

'How *wonderful!*' Nicky said and this time she wasn't gushing. 'I don't suppose you remember her name, do you?'

'Susan,' he said. 'Susan Pengilly. She used to work for British Rail but she's got a job in York now with one of the new companies. Such a nice girl.'

Nicky phoned Garry McKendrick as soon as she was back in her car.

'Listen to this,' she said and told him what she'd just heard. 'Front page or what?'

'I think I ought to talk to this feller of yours,' McKendrick decided. 'You check out the daughter and I'll get him to come in.'

Tim Ledgerwood was chuffed to be summoned to Wapping and went there at once. Strike while the iron's hot, he thought. And if he was any judge, this one was blazing.

It was an impressive place. Computers everywhere, like blue lights on every desk, smell of cigars, perfume, aftershave, men in shirt sleeves and braces, power-dressed women, just what he'd imagined. And Garry McKendrick was exactly what he expected too, heavily built, with a determined face that could be brutal, and a beer belly to rival Ken Clarke's. And he was flatteringly interested in what Tim had come to say.

'Bit a dirt on Quack-quack, that's the size of it. Right?'

'Rather more than a bit, I'd say,' Tim told him, casually. 'We're talking enticement here. He's after my daughter's money. Half a million.'

Garry McKendrick lit another cigarette from the stub of the one he'd just finished. 'And your daughter's Gemma Goodeve. Right? So what's the angle?'

Tim told his story coolly, provided dates, times and addresses, revealed Gemma's postcards with their vague messages — 'she didn't want her mother to know where she was and that's most unlike her' — and finally, with the air of a man who is clinching his argument, laid Mr Gresham's first letter on the worktop to prove that the claim for compensation was genuine.

'Right!' Garry McKendrick said. 'I'll tell you what I'll do. Can't promise anything, mind. It's up to the editor what we print, but I'll check it out and get back to you.' He grinned at his visitor. 'Be great to nail the bugger. I can't be doing with heroes.'

Tim seized his opening. 'Maybe he's not such a hero.'

'Won a fucking medal, didn't he?' the reporter said. 'I've got the cutting here somewhere. Fucking Cyprus.' He flicked through a bulging folder and pulled out a sheet of paper. 'There y'are. Military

Medal. Bravery under fire. Makes you sick.'

Tim drew on his cigarette, his eyes narrowed. 'What if I were to tell you he shot an unarmed man while he was out there winning his medal.'

'Did he?'

'A teenager,' Tim said. 'Sixteen. Shot on the road to the Troödos mountains. I've just come back from the place. I interviewed his cousin.'

'So tell me about it,' Garry McKendrick said. It would need checking out, but it would make a great follow-up to Nicky's story. And if it was really good it could run for days.

The copy for her own story had been composed in Nicky's sharp young brain, headline and all, before she got back to the office.

TV GURU AND CRASH HEROINE
Gemma Goodeve, courageous heroine of the Wandsworth rail crash at centre of tug-of-love tussle. 'My girl has been enticed away from us,' says Tim Ledgerwood, 46-year-old father of Gemma. 'I was forced to play detective to find out where she was. What does this man think he's doing?' Dark secret of TV guru.

Parents distraught. Grieving mother. Hidden heroine. Where is she now?

At that moment the hidden heroine was sitting in front of the window in her totally silent bedroom, looking out at the river and thinking hard. She'd been so busy at school that morning that she hadn't had time to think about anything except the job in hand — which in one way had been a very good thing because it had taken her away from her nightmares — but now the muddle of her emotions pressed in upon her.

In the calm of the afternoon it was hard to remember half the hurtful things they'd said to one another but the feelings that had been roused still lay dark and disturbing just under the surface of her mind. She'd been so angry to be offered help. She was angry about it now. Which was ridiculous when so many people had helped her and she'd been glad of it. She thought of the flowers that all those strangers had sent, of the way the nurses had treated her, of how kind they'd been at the rehab centre, of Catherine arriving in the restaurant to offer her the flat, of the couple from St Mary's driving her home. And here she was actually working as a helper. It was stupid to be so touchy. Ridiculous to feel such rage. But she couldn't be pitied. That was the bottom line. Couldn't and wouldn't. Especially by him.

And here you are, she told herself with a grin, pitying yourself. But the flat was spotlessly clean and she certainly wasn't going to sit and watch television, so what could she do to keep herself occupied and away from foolish thoughts?

I shall put on my coat, she decided, and go across to the couple who've just moved into the flat opposite and introduce myself and see if they'd like to join me for supper. She'd got more than enough food since her trip to the supermarket and it would be a pity to cook it just for one. Even if they didn't want to join her, they'd be company for a minute or two.

Chapter 29

Tim Ledgerwood was the first person in the newsagent's the next morning and one look at the headlines had him running back to the flat to show Billie.

'There you are!' he said, triumphantly. 'Look at that! What a revenge, eh?'

Billie was making the tea but she stopped to examine the paper. 'It's on the front page!' she said.

'Of course it is,' he said. 'It's important. Wait till *they* see it, eh. Oh I'd like to be a fly on the wall when *they* see it.'

But in fact, *had* he been turned into such an insect, he would have been a sorely disappointed one. For none of his intended targets saw the paper that morning.

Gemma was up too late to bother with news of any kind. She'd spent a cheerful evening with her new neighbours who'd invited her in 'to see how they were settling' and had accepted her invitation to supper providing they could supply the sweet. He was a paraplegic and she had chronic

527

asthma, but their motto, as Gemma discovered to her delight, was 'There's nothing wrong with *us!*'

'That's what I say too,' she told them. 'We ought to have it carved in stone above the entrance.'

'I'll do it tomorrow,' he joked.

'It wouldn't surprise me!' she replied.

She had gone to bed very late, feeling that she'd picked herself up again. And had then been sucked down into the horror of another terrible nightmare from which she woke at five o'clock, weeping and afraid. She recovered quickly, rebuking herself for being stupid, but once she'd had breakfast, all she wanted was to drive to school and get on with the day. She didn't even bother to listen to the news on the radio.

Nick was all on his own in the Tuileries Gardens and in no mood to read newspapers either. Paris is not the right place to be when you are young and in love and on your own. He'd enjoyed the journey because his friends had been such good company, he'd relished the food, and the first day had passed pleasantly enough, but in the evening the five of them had gone to a club and everything had changed. There had been plenty to drink and lots of kidding and laughing, but he'd been horribly aware that he was a gooseberry and he missed Gemma so much that her absence was like a physical pain. Now, mooching about the gardens in the early morning while his friends slept off their excesses, he was facing the fact that wonderful though this city was he really shouldn't have come here.

It was nearly spring, that was the trouble. He hadn't noticed it in London but here the air was stirring, chestnut trees in bud, flowerbeds sprouting long green spears, blackbirds fighting, jumping at one another, shrill with challenge, wings outspread, and there were lovers everywhere, strolling with their arms about each other, gazing into each other's eyes or stopping to kiss under the budding trees.

Even when he crept away into the Louvre it was no better. There were lovers depicted on every canvas, plump limbs erotically entwined, eye to eye, breast to breast. It was impossible. Oh Gemma, he grieved, my dear, darling gorgeous Gemma, why did you say such awful things to me? And worse, why did I say such awful things to you? How could I have got everything so wrong?

In Poppleton, the Pengilly morning had started in its usual way, the girls dawdling over their Sugar Puffs, Susan drinking black coffee as she checked her files, Rob eating bacon and eggs. But nobody in that household had seen the papers either because the paper boy hadn't delivered them.

'I'll pick them up on my way to work,' Rob offered as he stood at the kitchen door putting on his leather jacket.

'That's the third time this week,' Susan complained. She didn't look up from her work but Rob could tell she was scowling from the sound of her voice.

'Have you told Sheryl she's to pick up the girls?'

It was all taken care of. 'Yes, yes,' she said, still concentrating on the file.

'I shall be in York this afternoon. I'm going to make a start on the hotel gardens. I told you that, didn't I?'

She answered that vaguely too. 'Yes, I know. Don't take any more, Helen. There isn't time.'

'I'm off then,' Rob said. 'Be good kids.'

The girls waved to him, their mouths too full to answer. But Susan still didn't look up. Notice me, he willed her, lingering at the door. Leave those wretched files for two seconds and acknowledge that I'm alive. Don't let the job eat you. It isn't worth it. Just look up. Once. You need me as much as

I need you. But she went on working, biting her underlip.

'How about us going out tonight?' he tried. 'For a meal or something. We haven't been out for ages.'

No answer.

'There might be something on at the Theatre Royal. I could get tickets this afternoon if you like. Or we could go to the pictures. What d'you think?'

'Can't be done,' she said, not looking up. 'I've got this report to finish. You know how it is. There'll be all hell to pay if it's late.'

'Right,' he said, accepting defeat as he'd done so often since the New Year. There didn't seem to be any way he could get through to her. 'See you tonight then.'

'Um,' she said.

Catherine and Andrew were the only ones who were starting their day in a happy mood but although they'd read the *Guardian* over their hotel breakfast, they hadn't seen the *Chronicle*. Now they were back in their room, debating the important matter of which tie he was going to wear for his appearance on *Friday Forum*.

'The blue,' Catherine said. 'That always looks good with your grey. Not the other one. It's got zigzag stripes and they look awful on television.'

'It's grey,' he corrected, dangling it for inspection.

'The pattern's blue.'

'If I wear it, what d'you bet I drop gravy down it at lunch,' Andrew said.

'We won't order gravy.'

'Well, sauce then. Whatever.'

'Take the other one as a spare, just in case.'

'Now,' he said, 'where are my notes? I shall need to be on top of things on a show like this.'

The notes were found and checked. 'Ready for the off!' he said, happily.

The television centre at Pebble Mill in Birmingham is a handsome, prestigious building and fronts a wide, prestigious road. No one approaching it by taxi, as Andrew and Catherine did that morning, could fail to be aware of its importance, for it looks what it is, one of the major centres of the television industry. Taxis arrive and depart one after the other, as though it were an airport or a railway terminus, and the famous carry their recognisable faces in and out of the building with the insouciance of princes.

It made Andrew think of an ocean liner, although he couldn't have explained why.

The length, probably, and the dazzle of all those huge windows, or the ocean-green gardens that swelled below and around it, or the ramp that led from the pavement to the entrance like a long concrete gangplank.

He and Catherine climbed the steps to the front entrance, recognising the view they'd seen through the studio windows when they'd been watching the place on their TV screens and feeling, as Catherine put it, like visiting royalty. The feeling increased when they were greeted by a uniformed doorman and led to a desk in a foyer full of sofas and screens and pictures of the stars. There, a receptionist gave them name-tags and told them that someone would be down to collect them directly. And someone was, a brightly dressed, brightly smiling, cheerful girl who led them off through a maze of corridors talking all the way. She said her name was Sandra, and hoped they'd had a good journey and confided that she'd seen all Andrew's broadcasts and thought they were terrific.

'You ought to be in politics,' she said, as they reached yet another labelled door. 'Here we are, if you'll just follow me.'

More greetings, a visit to make-up, the usual briefing from a girl with a clip-board, then back to 'hospitality' where they were to wait until they were called. By this time all the guests for the morning's show had arrived and were standing about making small talk in the guarded way of men who would soon be adversaries.

There was a tall, untidy man from Railtrack and a short neat one from Railways South, a porcine young man with rimless glasses who said he was a politician 'for my sins. But a very minor one. You wouldn't have heard of me.' A thickset man with a beer belly was sitting at one end of a line of easy chairs smoking a cigar, and a sharply dressed, sharp-featured woman was pointedly displaying the longest pair of legs that Andrew had ever seen and, equally pointedly, not saying who she was or why she was there.

'A journalist,' Andrew guessed, *sotto voce* to Catherine.

Catherine thought it likely.

The politician began to hold forth about the value of privatization. 'Of course this inquiry is all very sad,' he said, 'but that in no way detracts from the success of our privatization process. Competition is the key to success, believe me. It's the making of any organization, large or small. It cuts out waste, it gives you an edge, it keeps you efficient. Lean and mean and efficient, that's the name of the game. That's what we need in this country if we are to succeed against our European competitors. It's tough but we have to cut out the flab. It's the only way.'

There wasn't time for anyone to argue with him because the cheerful girl had arrived to escort them to the studio. Drinks were finished, glasses set down and off they all went, the politician continuing his peroration all the way.

'That's going to be his opening statement,' Andrew said to Catherine. And so it was, word for word.

Sitting on the platform among his fellow speakers, Andrew listened to it all for the second time, thinking what a pillock the man was and how easy he would be to demolish. The journalist, who was sitting to his right with her long legs arranged for the camera, looked like a cat with a mouse in her sights. But the presenter had his opening sequence prepared too and moved smoothly on to the next speaker, the representative from Railways South, who folded his neat hands in his lap and spoke with face-creasing sincerity.

'We are disappointed that Railtrack is putting up a bureaucratic wall of silence at this time,' he said. 'The public have a right to know whom to blame for this tragedy. It is in the public interest for the truth to be told.' He laboured the point for several seconds, concluding that, 'if necessary', Railways South would take action against Railtrack to force it to make its findings public. 'If we have to go to court,' he ended, his voice ringing valiantly, 'if we have to go to court to get the answers we want, then we will.'

Andrew was irritated by the speciousness of these two men, making their set speeches without reference to one another, but he didn't intervene. Some of the studios he'd appeared in had been so young and brash that he'd had to fight for an opening, but this one was relaxed and established, so he knew his turn would come. He looked across to where Catherine was sitting in the front row of the audience and smiled at her confidently. It was going to be a very good show.

The representative from Railtrack was given his moment next. Their report was 'virtually complete', he said, but it wouldn't be made public, 'so as not to prejudice the separate findings of inquiries by the Health and Safety Executive and British Transport Police'.

Railways South snorted. 'There's an exercise in blame-avoidance if I ever saw it.'

Railtrack stood his ground. 'We are following the correct procedure,' he said, 'so as not to prejudice the inquiry of the Health and Safety Executive.'

'Is there to be a third inquiry?' the presenter asked. 'This is a new development.'

'As we understand it,' Railtrack stammered. 'We have been advised . . .'

The journalist leant forward slightly to signify her desire to intervene. 'Ms Cooper,' the presenter introduced her.

She spoke languidly but fluently. 'This,' she said, 'is exactly the sort of situation we have got to expect now that British Rail has been broken up into competing companies. It's a direct result of fragmentation and a very deplorable one. Had our railway system still been run by one national company, there would have been one inquiry and it would have been published and acted upon months ago. As it is, we have two smaller companies — or three, if there is to be a third inquiry — publicly bickering over whose fault it is. Or to put it another way, over who will be financially liable to pay out compensation. This is all to do with avoiding huge bills for compensation.'

'There's nothing wrong with that,' Railways South told her. 'Ask any businessman.

That's good business practice.'

The politician applauded him. 'Quite right!'

The presenter held out a warning hand. 'Dr Quennell,' he said and gave Andrew his turn at last.

Andrew smiled at him. 'Ms Cooper is right,' he said. 'What we should be concerned about is saving lives, not money. That accident could have been avoided in the first place if the new companies had paid proper attention to safety, if they'd kept the rolling stock in good order and maintained the track. That's what's important. Avoiding accidents and avoiding loss of life. I think I can claim to be the only person on this panel who was present at the crash and I can tell you it was a shocking event. Twenty-seven people died, don't forget, and there were some dreadful injuries. It isn't something to score cheap political points about.'

'I'm sure nobody here wants to score cheap political points,' the politician objected, plump hackles visibly risen, 'as you put it.'

'I hope you won't,' Andrew said, 'because *I'm* sure there are accident victims out there who are watching this programme very closely and they want to know what you are going to do to prevent anything similar happening in future.'

'One of whom was Miss Gemma Goodeve,' the man with the beer belly suddenly put in. He'd been so quiet since the broadcast began that Andrew had almost forgotten he was there.

The presenter turned, smiled and introduced him. 'Garry McKendrick.'

Oh for crying out loud! Andrew thought, struggling to control his surprise. That awful man! But he answered at once and boldly. Yes, Gemma had been one of the casualties.

'Right,' Garry McKendrick said. 'And you know her rather well, don't you, Doctor?'

'I was the anaesthetist when her leg was amputated,' Andrew agreed, his heart beating uncomfortably.

'Oh rather more than that,' Garry McKendrick insisted. 'You've been her — what shall I say? — her *landlord* ever since the accident, haven't you?'

The implication was so scurrilous that Andrew could feel himself colouring as his temper rose. The atmosphere in the studio changed perceptibly. Heads turned in unison towards him, breath was indrawn and held. Landlord! For Christ's sake!

'She stayed in your house,' Garry McKendrick said.

'For a few weeks . . . as a halfway house. Good God, man, she was in plaster. She couldn't walk. She needed care.'

'Which you gave her.'

'Now look here,' Andrew protested. 'This has no relevance to the matter we are supposed to be discussing.' He was making a mistake to react so angrily and he knew it even as he heard his voice.

'OK,' the journalist said smoothly. 'So try this for size. Isn't it true that your daughter is Ms Susan Pengilly?'

'Yes. It is.' Now what?

'That would be the Ms Susan Pengilly who headed the inquiry into the Wandsworth crash. The Ms Susan Pengilly who is now, if my information is correct, a senior executive with Rail North East?'

First Gemma and now Susan, Andrew thought, his heart pinched with distress. It was as if he was walking on quicksands. 'Yes,' he admitted, 'but that has no relevance either.'

Both officials joined in the attack, snorting with delighted derision. 'No relevance? A family connection? An inside source of information? Of course it's relevant.'

Andrew looked from one to the other,

knowing that the cameras had zoomed in on him and feeling exposed. Under such close scrutiny, it was imperative to keep his emotions under control and not let his eyes wander or he would look shifty and guilty. He tried to catch the presenter's attention but couldn't do it without making it obvious. He tried to glance at Ms Cooper, hoping she would help, but she was avoiding his eye. She's making mental notes, he thought. It'll be in *her* bloody paper next.

'You can't say it isn't relevant,' Railways South insisted. 'You gave your opinion about the cause of the accident at the scene of the crash, minutes after it had taken place. Long before anyone knew what it was. So how did you know? You knew because your daughter is a railway official.'

Andrew made a supreme effort to keep calm. 'I was called to the crash because that's part of my job,' he explained. 'I'm trained for emergency work. My daughter was appointed to head the inquiry after the crash and after my involvement in it. It was pure coincidence.'

That provoked an uproar and the presenter intervened at last. A row was good television but the audience had to be able to hear what was being said. 'Gentlemen!' he rebuked. 'Gentlemen! One at a time if you please.'

'May a lady speak?' Ms Cooper intervened, 'or would that be sexist?' And at that the tension was released in laughter. 'What I've been wondering is when Railtrack's report is likely to be published. And should it transpire that Railtrack share responsibility for the crash, what will happen to all the claims that are still in the pipeline?'

Her questions defused the situation because they couldn't be answered and that allowed her to pursue them until the presenter took questions from the floor, which were hot and pointed and all concerned the results of the crash and the sort of measures that ought to be taken to prevent another.

But Andrew was still feeling shaken when the credits began to roll and couldn't wait to get out of the building.

'I expected to come under fire sooner or later,' he said as he and Catherine walked down the ramp, 'but that was bloody awful. If Susan saw it, it'll have upset her terribly. And Gemma! What a thing to imply, for Christ's sake! They've got minds like sewers. *More than her landlord!* It's a wonder I didn't thump him. We'd better get hold of a copy of the *Chronicle* and see exactly what they said.'

'You handled it well,' she tried to reassure him.

'I did *not*,' he said. 'I lost my rag.'

Someone was running after them down the ramp. 'Dr Quennell. Just a minute.'

'Oh God!' he said. 'Now what?' And winced when he saw that it was Ms Cooper.

'I'm glad I caught you,' she said. 'I've got something to tell you. Something you ought to know.'

He assumed his disapproving face. 'Oh yes.'

She smiled at him. 'Oh yes,' she echoed. 'Look, I admire the stand you're taking. I'm on your side.'

He relaxed a little.

'The thing is,' she went on, 'McKendrick's got something else on you and I think you ought to know about it. He was bragging about it in the bar. Something about a kid getting killed out in Cyprus. Sixteen-year-old? Andreas Papa-something?'

He closed his face against her and the information. 'Well thank you for telling me but it was all a long time ago.'

'McKendrick's a nasty piece of work,' she warned, 'and he means business. If you'll take my advice, you'll step out of the lime-light for a week or two and let the dust settle.'

'I should say that was all the more reason for fighting him,' Andrew said.

She shrugged her elegant shoulders. 'It's your decision. Personally I'd keep my head down. Still, best of luck, whatever you do.' And she swept off to a waiting taxi.

'What was all that about?' Catherine asked.

'Nothing,' he said, regaining his balance with an effort. And he changed the subject a bit too obviously. 'Do you want to go straight home or what?'

This is trouble, Catherine thought, and if we go straight home he'll brood all the way. He needs a break to recover from it, whatever it is. 'If it's all the same to you,' she said, 'I'd like to have lunch and see St Anne's, the way we planned.'

'Lunch and St Anne's it is, then,' he agreed.

But although he didn't say anything about the boy in Cyprus, he read the *Chronicle* all through the meal, studying it intently. 'It's very clever,' he said, when he'd finished it. 'It's all wrapped up in reported speech. *"According to Mr Ledgerwood . . . Mr Ledgerwood tells us . . ."* and hypothetical questions.

"What does this man think he's playing at?" I don't think it's actionable. Have a look and see what you think.'

Catherine knew what she thought even without looking. 'Don't do anything in a hurry,' she advised. 'See what Gemma thinks about it. It affects her too. It's her father who's causing the trouble.'

'Money,' Andrew said. 'That's what this is about. They've dug up the old story about half a million compensation. Did she ever apply for compensation?'

'Not that I know of,' Catherine said, 'but I didn't ask.'

Andrew sighed. 'And now we're in the middle of all this nonsense. Just as well the boys are both abroad. At least they won't have seen it.'

'I hope poor Susan hasn't seen it either,' Catherine said. 'It could be very difficult for her, in her position.'

'I hope to God *nobody* in the family saw it.'

But, as they both knew only too well, it was a vain hope.

Chapter 30

Susan's managing director and chairman was one of the new breed of nineties entrepreneurs, a tough, determined man, self-educated, self-made and entirely self-centred. He'd made a fortune in the 1980s when the buses were deregulated, lost another as a financial adviser when he decided to diversify, and was now determined to become a megamillionaire as head of one of the newly privatised railways. His suite of offices dominated the top floor of a concrete office block called Yorvik Posterity House, and, because of his state of wealth and his paranoia, were fully equipped with every high-tech device any empire builder could desire — including a TV set and video recorder. For as he proclaimed to his secretary every time he switched on, 'Keeping abreast of the news is my number one priority, Miss Green, my number one priority.'

Nobody was surprised when he rescheduled his morning so that he could keep abreast of *Friday Forum*. For even though Rail North East had no connection with the firm that was running Railways South, it was good business sense to keep an eye on the opposition. And they all had to stay on the right side of Railtrack.

He was annoyed to see that that damned doctor fellow was being given air time again. Quack-quack bloody Quennell. There'd been far too much of him over the last few weeks, bloody commie. Garry McKendrick was bang to rights about him, as he was about most things. Still, the opening skirmish was amusing and he enjoyed the way the fellow from Railtrack managed to stonewall; and when the tables were turned and the commie doctor came under attack, he got up at once to check what the *Chronicle* had said and was hugely satisfied by their front page. That's the style! he thought. Root the buggers out. That'll show 'em. Bloody lefties! He poured himself a Scotch and put his feet up on the desk ready to savour the rest of the programme.

And at that point the broadcast went pear-shaped.

He swore so loudly that Miss Green could hear him in the outer office. Then he sent for Ms Pengilly.

Susan had spent the first part of her morning in Accounts checking the figures in her report. Now it was nearly complete and although she took the lift to the top floor with the usual trepidation that any employee of Rail North East was bound to feel when approaching their MD, she thought she could make a good case for herself. The deadline for the report was six o'clock that evening and the deadline would be met.

But the moment she stepped inside the door of his office she knew she was in a different and difficult situation. The chairman was sitting behind his desk and his entire body was belligerent. Sirens echoed in the air between them, a war map grew across the tinted glass of his wide window, guns bristled from every corner of his desk.

'Ah — um — Ms Pengilly,' he frowned at her. 'Come in. Sit down.'

She sat in the chair he indicated, feeling like a criminal in a court of law. What have I done? she worried. Or not done? Or more dreadful, what has he found out?

He pushed his copy of the *Chronicle* across the desk at her. 'What have you got to say about this?'

She saw her father's face, and Gemma's, and read the headline, her heart contracting with alarm, but before she could even think how to answer him, he attacked again, 'Your — um — ah — father, I believe.'

She had to admit it, but tried to tell him that it was just newspaper talk. 'There's no truth in it,' she explained. 'He's been on the television rather a lot recently and he writes a medical column for the *Independent*. This sort of thing is one of the hazards of being in the news.'

She felt she'd stood up for her beleaguered father rather well. But the thought was no sooner in her head than the guns began to blaze.

'Your father,' he said. 'The man who's been giving inflammatory speeches about rail safety. That *is* the one, isn't it, Ms — ah — um — Pengilly. Your father, the one you've been feeding inside information.'

She opened her mouth to protest but he wouldn't let her speak.

'Don't try to deny it,' he said. 'It's all come out. It's just been on *Friday Forum*. The proverbial cat is out of the proverbial bag. The connection is known.'

She fought back as well as she could but she was already defeated and she knew it. 'I see I'm to be judged before I have a chance to defend myself,' she said, her control as tight as her lips.

'There is no defence against disloyalty,' he told her. 'A company stands or falls by the loyalty of its employees, as you well know.'

'You have always had my total loyalty,' she answered angrily. 'I have never done less than my best for this company. I have never been indiscreet.'

'When you came for your — ah — um — interview, you may recall that I asked you whether there was anything that would prevent you from serving this company in the manner we required, did I not?'

She had to admit it.

'And yet you told me nothing about this relationship.'

'I couldn't see that it was relevant. I keep my business life quite apart from my private life.'

'You expect me to believe *that,* when your father knows everything that is going on in the industry and sounds off about it on every occasion, on every television screen. There's never any end to the man.'

'With respect,' she said, 'he is only saying what everybody says.'

'What he's saying is that the privatised railway companies are badly run, that we cut corners to save money, that we put lives at risk. If that's what everybody is saying perhaps you are saying it too.'

She'd been stung too much not to sting

back. 'I may not say it,' she told him, giving up hope and speaking boldly, 'but yes, I do think it. Thought is free and this is still a free country.'

He was furious at such insubordination. The woman was a commie like her father. 'Then feel free to consider your position, Ms Pengilly. Feel free to do that.'

She stood up and tried to look at him coolly but her stomach was shaking and she couldn't control it. 'My resignation will be on your desk within the hour,' she said. And made her escape.

Afterwards she couldn't remember going down in the lift or walking to her office. Events and emotions were blurred into one long slippery second and slid away from her as she tried to grasp them. This was what she'd dreaded ever since she took the job, what she'd known would happen if they ever found out, what she'd been refusing to face since the New Year. And now it had happened and she couldn't bear it. She felt as if her legs had been cut from under her and her thought processes were so fouled and furred up that when she came to write her resignation, it was almost impossible to get the words into grammatical order.

But at last it was done and seemed literate and dignified. She put the letter in one envelope and the report in another, cleared her desk, told her secretary to take both envelopes to the chairman, touched up her make-up, combed her hair and left the building. If she hurried, she could catch the one o'clock train to Poppleton. There was nothing in her mind except the urgent need to get home, to be inside her own house, inside her own room with the door locked against the world. Hidden away. Safe.

The house was completely empty, for the cleaner only worked mornings and it was much too early for the girls to be home from school. But emptiness was what she needed. The order and stillness of it was like balm.

It took an effort to climb the stairs, an effort to walk across the landing and, once inside her bedroom, she locked the door and collapsed across the duvet as though she was fainting. But she didn't cry. She lay quite still with her hands at her sides and thought and thought, dully and without hope. She'd come so far and worked so hard and now it was all dust and ashes in her mouth. She'd lost her job, just like everybody else. Her job, her status, her salary, her reason for existence. She was finished. All her patience and tact, all her hard-won education, all those hours and hours of work and effort had been a total waste of time. It couldn't be true. Oh dear God, it couldn't, couldn't be true. If it was true, how could she ever face anyone again?

For a brief moment, she thought of Rob and wondered where he was and what he would say when he came home. My poor Rob! Then grief overwhelmed her again.

Her poor Rob had been hard at work all day in the gardens of the Alhambra Hotel, taking up the challenge of grounds that had been neglected for nearly a decade and were now little more than a wilderness.

The gardens lay so far below the road that, unless they had been guests at the hotel, very few people knew they were there. Once there had been paved terraces before the drawing-room windows, and wide herbaceous borders, and stretching to the furthest bounds, a grassy path that led between rose beds and ornamental herbs to a central sunken garden, bordered by low hedges and containing a round pond full of carp where a fountain played perpetually.

Now the borders were full of weeds, the roses overgrown and straggly, the soil sour, the hedges dead, the fountain chipped and dry and the pond full of dog-ends and empty cigarette packets. But this was just the sort of work Rob thoroughly enjoyed, out in the open, in air that had a breath of spring about it, resuscitating and restoring.

He and his team had walked and measured all morning. Now they were making a start, turning over the earth and digging in compost to feed it. Two of them were dismantling the fountain so that they could take it back to the garden centre and work on it under cover. The centrepiece was a winged cherub holding a conch shell and, under Rob's orders, they were wrapping it in sacking to protect it on the journey.

'Pack the wings with newspaper,' he instructed. 'We don't want them to chip. Use plenty.'

But when they'd used all the paper they'd brought with them there was still a wing that wasn't protected.

'There's a couple of papers in my coat pocket,' Rob remembered. 'Use them.' This was an emergency. He could always buy another on the way home.

So the day's news was put to good use and his father-in-law's picture was folded round the cherub's right wing.

'Now what?' the two boys wanted to know.

The tower of the Minster was a pale shape against the darkening sky and blackbirds were shouting at one another in the hawthorn hedges. Pip, pip, pip. But the light still held and there was no need for him to be home early. Sheryl was going to collect the girls.

'We'll go on,' he decided. 'Get as much done as we can. We'll drain the pond and then it'll be dry by Monday and we shall be able to see what sort of state it's in.'

'It'll be cracked,' one of his men predicted.

'I don't doubt it,' he grinned. 'Fortunately cracks can be mended. That's what we're here for.'

Chapter 31

'She's late!' Helen Pengilly said disparagingly. 'Look at her!'

The two girls had been waiting at the school gate for a whole minute and their new nanny had only just appeared, hurtling towards them on her battered old bike, pedalling frantically, her ginger hair streaming behind her.

She was in a dreadful hurry. 'Come on,' she said, breathlessly. 'We've got five minutes.'

'What for?' Naomi asked.

'To get home. I've got a date. Come on!'

Helen couldn't see why they had to hurry because *she* had a date, but she was wasting her breath saying so. They had to run all the way home while she pushed her silly bicycle at a hundred miles an hour. By the time they turned into the drive Naomi was out of breath and tearful because her shoelaces had come undone and she hadn't been allowed to stop and do them up again and Helen was scowling with fury. But their mother's car was standing in the drive, so that was all right. Ever so badly parked, though.

Sheryl whisked them both into the kitchen where she skinned off their coats and ordered them to sit up at the table. Mummy wasn't there and she didn't come in to see them, which was odd. But Sheryl ran out into the hall and called up the stairs to tell her they were home.

'Now your mother's home so I'll give you your tea and then I'll be off,' she said. She took two miserable-looking digestive biscuits out of the tin and gave them one each — one biscuit for tea! Then she made two mugs of cocoa before Helen could remind her that they didn't like it.

'There you are,' she said. 'You sit there and drink your cocoa and eat up your biscuits like good little girls. Mummy'll be down presently. You'll be all right, won't you. I'm off then.'

After she'd gone, Helen and Naomi ate their biscuits 'like good little girls' and sipped at their 'nice cocoa', even though they didn't like it, but Mummy didn't come downstairs and the odd feeling got worse.

Presently Naomi began to worry. 'It's ever so quiet,' she whispered. It didn't seem right to talk out loud when it was so quiet. 'Do you think she's all right?'

'Yes. Course,' Helen said. She spoke in her normal voice and firmly because whispering is babyish. But the house *was* quiet. Usually there was music playing when they got in or a washing machine whirring or a hoover or something. Now there wasn't a sound. 'I expect she's in the shower.'

'Let's go and see, shall we,' Naomi urged. So they tiptoed through the silent hall, hand in hand for comfort, and crept upstairs. The quiet made their skin prickle and there was worse to come. Their parents' bedroom door was locked. They'd never known a door to be locked before. Ever. They both tried it twice, but it simply wouldn't open and nobody came to open it for them. The silence lapped around them like ice-cold water and now they were both afraid.

'Mummy!' Helen called, but not too loud just in case it was the wrong thing to do. 'Are you there?'

There was no answer, so she tried again, this time a little louder. 'Mummy, are you all right?'

And at that, their mother's voice answered in an echoing hollow way, as though she were at the end of a tunnel. 'Go away.'

The girls looked at one another, their eyes rounded.

'Is something the matter?' Helen ventured.

The answer was really alarming. 'Yes,' their mother's voice said. 'There is. Go away, I don't want anyone near me. Just go, do you hear me. Go away.'

'Are you hurt?' Helen asked.

'No.'

'Are you ill?'

That brought a tetchy answer. 'No. No.'

'Are you coming down to tea?' Naomi asked.

'No,' their mother's hollow voice called back. 'I'm not coming down to tea, or dinner, or breakfast. I don't think I shall ever go anywhere again. Oh please go away!'

There was no mistaking the anguish in her voice. The girls looked at one another, now thoroughly alarmed.

'Do you think she means it?' Naomi asked. 'What are we going to do?'

Helen knew the answer to that. 'Phone Daddy,' she said.

'Do you know the number?'

'It's in my address book,' Helen said, striding off to their bedroom to find it.

But dialling the number was one thing, talking to their father quite another. A strange voice answered them, in a laconic drawling sort of way. 'Sorry,' it said, 'he's not here. Not been here all day.'

'Where is he?' Helen asked, heart sinking.

'Out on a job,' the voice said. 'Do you want him to phone you back?'

'No,' Helen said miserably, and she put the phone down and explained the situation to her sister. 'He's out on a job. They don't know where he is.'

Out on a job was bad news. It meant that Daddy wouldn't be home until very late.

'Something awful's going on, isn't it, Helly?' Naomi said. She was very near tears, her bottom lip trembling. 'What are we going to *do*?'

Something awful *was* going on, but there was no point in speculating about it. Helen took command. 'We'll go to London,' she said. 'And tell Grandpa Quennell. He'll know what to do.'

'Why can't we go and tell Grandma Pengilly?' Naomi asked. Grandma Pengilly lived in York and that was much nearer than London.

'Because she's batty,' Helen said. She was very fond of Grandma Pengilly but she wouldn't be any good in a crisis, and this was a crisis.

'But we haven't got any money,' Naomi wailed, tears beginning to fall. 'How will we buy the tickets? And it's miles to London.

How will we know the way?'

'We'll use Mummy's ticket, silly,' Helen said. They always travelled on their mother's ticket and she knew where it was. 'Come on.'

Three minutes later they were on their way to Poppleton Station, wearing their padded jackets, their woolly hats and scarfs and carrying a bag full of necessities — a packet of chocolate biscuits, two cans of Coke, a Mars Bar and some chewing gum, two pairs of clean knickers, Naomi's teddy bear, her colouring crayons and her birthday book, Helen's silver bracelet, her purse with £4.54 in it, in case they needed something more to eat on the way, her new hairbrush that had never been used, an assortment of ribbons, their mother's concessionary ticket and, as a last-minute afterthought because Naomi was taking her birthday book, Helen's address book.

It was better when they were walking through the village. Naomi began to recover. They passed the school and waved to a group of their friends who were still hanging about by the gate, skirted the Lord Nelson pub and the White Horse pub and the church with the belfry, crossed the Green where they waved to Mrs O'Henry and set off on the walk down

Station Road, which was miles and miles long and took them ages.

Just as they reached the level crossing, the barriers came down and the York train buzzed past, its yellow face gleaming in the half-light, its three maroon and cream coaches clearly labelled REGIONAL RAIL-WAYS and lots of passengers sitting like black silhouettes beside the windows. They had to run to catch it, and only just scrambled aboard before the double doors closed behind them. There was no time for doubt or hesitation. They were on their way.

It was an easy journey into York because it took only ten minutes and they'd done it plenty of times before. But York Station seemed huge and very noisy by contrast, especially to Naomi who grew weepy at the sight of it. Not that weeping did her any good. Helen said not to fuss and hauled her off to platform 1 where an absolutely enormous train was curved alongside the platform like a great dirty-white snake.

'This is it,' Helen said and pushed her sister into a first-class compartment, where there were maroon curtains at the windows and grey carpet all the way up the walls and little Formica tables set between seats, which Helen said would be very useful for eating things and writing.

'We'll have something to eat in a minute,' she said. But rush and worry had given Naomi stomach ache.

'That's because you're hungry,' Helen said, quoting their father. 'We'll have half a Mars Bar when it gets started.'

But when the train finally *did* get started, it frightened them both so much that it put all thought of food right out of their heads. It went so fast that it leant over sideways like a rollercoaster ride and gave out an odd sort of smell like something burning, which seemed very peculiar to Naomi because she couldn't remember the trains doing things like that when they'd been travelling with Mummy.

'It's not going to crash, is it?' she asked.

'Course not,' Helen said. She spoke scathingly so as to quell her own fears. 'These trains don't crash.'

'Gemma's did.'

'This one won't.'

'Will we be there soon?'

'No. It takes two hours.'

'Two *hours!*'

'Look out of the window,' Helen advised.

They were swishing through the great wide plains of the Ouse Valley, past fields lying dark and mysterious in the half-light and a Tesco's lit up like a red-brick cathedral with rows and rows and rows of cars lined up in the car parks alongside it.

'What if a ticket inspector comes?' Naomi worried.

'He will come,' Helen said. 'That's all right. Leave him to me.'

But he didn't turn up until they were pulling out of Doncaster and it was getting really dark and then he was suddenly beside them when they least expected him.

'Travelling with your mother?' he asked, as he glanced at their ticket.

Helen looked him straight in the eye. It's always best to look people straight in the eye when you're going to tell them lies. 'That's right,' she said.

He'll ask us where she is, Naomi thought, and what will we say then? We shall be found out and he'll make us get off the train and how will we get back home?

But he didn't. He simply returned the ticket and said 'Have a nice day!' And that was that.

It was such a relief that they had a Mars Bar and a can of Coke to celebrate. After that the journey was easy. They ate their chocolate biscuits and had another can of Coke and did some colouring in while the darkening countryside passed beyond the windows. Now and then they rushed through a town where orange lights glowed in long symmetrical rows and they could see cars and people in the streets. And once Naomi fell asleep and woke with a start as they pulled up at another station.

Then they were driving between rows of houses and there were lots of streets and ever such a lot of traffic and they passed a station called Haringay where there was an odd blue bridge and masses of trains going in both directions in a very bewildering way, not cream trains like the InterCity ones or cream and maroon like the Poppleton ones, but blue, white and red like the French flag. Helen said she thought they were in London but Naomi wasn't sure because they'd just passed a long yellow notice on one of the buildings which said 'York the largest lofts in London' in big black letters. So perhaps they'd gone round in a circle and York would be the next stop.

But no, the next stop was King's Cross. The guard said so and reminded them to take all their luggage with them.

'There you are!' Helen said, cramming the colouring book back in the bag. 'We're here!'

York station had been daunting but this was much, much worse. It was an absolutely enormous place and full of echoes that reverberated round and round inside your head like gongs playing. It had great tall columns everywhere made of yellow bricks and a glass roof curved like a huge glass frame and hundreds and hundreds of trains, pulling in and huffing out and making dreadful hissing noises. There were people pushing terrible trolleys, and people running, all in a hurry, jostling past them on enormous feet and swinging bags and briefcases in every direction. They walked off the platform, hand in hand and too overawed to speak, and dared themselves along a huge ramp on to a concourse full of people all striding about as if they knew where they were going.

'What are we going to do now?' Naomi said, clinging to her sister.

'We're going to take a taxi,' Helen said, speaking with splendid confidence, as if she'd been taking taxis all her life. 'There's a sign up there. See? With an arrow. If we follow that we shall find them. Look! There's another one. Come on.'

So they followed the signs, clinging on to one another and both feeling very nervous. And they found the taxis. 'There they are! I can see them through the door.'

There was a circular space just outside the door where the taxis followed one another round like horses in a circus ring while their passengers stood in a queue and shuffled forward to be taken on board. The two girls joined the line, small and quiet among the tall suits, blue jeans and bulky luggage of their fellow travellers. There were four young men in front of them and after a while two fat Americans joined the queue behind them, talking to one another in loud fat voices, and behind *them* there was an Arab lady in a sort of black tent with a black headscarf over her head and forehead and a mask made of leather covering every bit of her face except her eyes. If being in the middle of it all hadn't been so terrifying, it would have been exciting.

The queue moved forward quickly. Before Naomi could worry about what they were going to say to the taxi driver when they got there, they *were* there and Helen was climbing in as though she was one of the grown-ups, saying 'Putney' to the driver, the way the young men had said 'Tower Bridge'. She'd watched them very closely.

The driver was a friendly man with a very wide face and a very wide smile. 'What part a Putney, darlin'?' he asked.

When Helen told him, reading the address from her book, he said 'Right!' and drove them out into the main road.

Now that they were away from that awful station, Naomi could relax again. It was quite fun being in a taxi, bowling along between so many cars with rows and rows of red lights ahead of them and all the buildings bright with lights. 'Is this all London?' she asked her sister.

'It's all London,' Helen said. She hadn't been at all sure that a taxi would accept two children as a fare so she was bold with relief. 'It goes on for miles and miles. Daddy told me.'

It certainly went on for a very long time and the red figures on the driver's little oblong clock were ticking up alarmingly. £4.80 — £6.20 — £7.60. It's an awful lot of money, Helen thought, wincing at it. I hope Grandpa won't mind.

'Amersham Road,' the driver said, speaking over his shoulder. 'Which one is it, darlin'?'

'That one!' Naomi said happily. 'The white one.' It was such a relief to have arrived that she didn't notice how dark the house was.

'If you wouldn't mind waiting a minute,' Helen said, rather grandly. 'We'll go and get our grandfather. He'll pay you.'

So he waited while they picked up their shopping bag, scrambled out of the cab and ran to the front door. But although they rang and rang nobody came, and after the third ring Helen was chilled by a fearful thought. She peered in through the stained glass hoping for reassurance. There was no movement in the hall and it all looked horribly neat and empty. 'They're out,' she said. 'Oh Nao, they're not here.'

'What are we going to do?' Naomi asked.

'We'll have to tell him.' Even though the mere thought of the bill they'd run up was freezing her blood, there was nothing else they could do. She knew that. Daddy said you have to face up to your mistakes no matter what. She left Naomi cowering in the porch and walked back to the cab, biting her lip in agitation.

'I'm ever so sorry,' she said, 'but they're out.'

'Then you'll have to pay, won't you darlin'. That's £8.80 you owe me.'

Helen put the bag down on the pavement and searched through it for her purse. 'I've got £4,' she said, offering him the coins, adding, 'and 54p.'

'That's not much good,' he said and his voice was suddenly growly. 'You owe me twice that.'

'Yes, I know,' she said miserably. 'But I haven't got it.'

He leant towards her and took the four coins into his huge hand, his nice wide face creased into a new shape by fury. 'Oh that's lovely!' he said. 'That's just dandy! And how am I supposed to make a living, eh? Ripped off by a pair a bleedin' kids. Tell me that.'

She hung her head and mumbled that she didn't know. She was so frightened she felt numb.

'I shoulda known this was a scam,' he said. 'You're a wicked little monster. That's what you are. Dragging me out all this way for nothing. A downright wicked little monster. I've a bloody good mind to call the bloody police to you. It's against the law what you're doing. You know? Against the bloody law. Fat lot you care. It'ud serve you bloody well right if I put you back in the cab and took you straight back to where you've bloody come from. How'd you like that, eh?'

Helen stood her ground. 'We didn't mean it,' she said. 'We thought Grandpa would be here. Please don't take us back. You can have my silver bracelet if you like.' She took it out of the bag and held it out to him.

He took the bracelet and was mollified but only partly. 'You've no business hiring a cab when you can't pay for it,' he grumbled on. 'I'll let you off this time but woe betide you if you ever do it again, that's all. I'll have the police down on you so fast your feet won't touch the ground.'

'Oh we won't,' Helen promised earnestly. But he'd put the cab into gear, turned it and was gone, leaving a snort of grey smoke and the heat of his temper behind him.

Naomi was crying out loud and this time Helen didn't scold her. They'd come so far and been so frightened and it was all for nothing. They'd been shouted at and humiliated and called names and there was no one there to help them. They stood huddled together in the porch and put their arms round one another and cried until there were no more tears to cry. But the house was still dark and there was no sign of their grandparents.

'What if they've gone out for the night?' Naomi said. 'We can't get in, can we? Not without a key.'

They searched all round the house to see if there was a window open anywhere but there wasn't.

'We'll have to go somewhere else,' Helen decided, putting her bag down on the drive.

But where? Neither of them could think. Uncle Nick was in the hospital and they couldn't go there. Uncle Chris was in Canada which was even worse. There *was* Grandma Pengilly but she was in York and they were in London now so it had to be someone here. Who else was there? They stood forlornly on the asphalt and looked down at their untidy belongings. And Helen suddenly had a brilliant idea.

'We'll go and find a phone box,' she said, 'and we'll ring Gemma. I've got her phone number in my book. *She*'ll know what to do.'

Chapter 32

The playground of Fairmead School was swirling with kids. They jumped and yelled and screamed and fought, plump in their padded jackets and shrill as a flock of starlings. Even after a second night torn by bad dreams, Gemma was cheered by the sound of them. She got out of her car and walked through the happy racket to the school entrance. And there was Francine, sitting up perkily in her wheelchair, waiting for her and beaming with good news.

She'd spent the previous afternoon in hospital. 'And guess what, Miss. I walked six steps. All on my own.'

'That's brilliant,' Gemma approved as she pushed her excited pupil to the classroom. 'I'll bet they were pleased with you.'

'An' guess what,' Francine went on. 'I done all my homework too, all on my own.' Her independence was the best thing that had happened to her since she'd been taken ill.

'You're a good girl,' Gemma told her.

It was a pleasure to them both to be able

to start their school day with praise. And the first half of the morning was equally rewarding. They tackled a difficult assignment together, with Gemma doing the fetching and carrying and Francine working happily with her group, thinking everything out for herself and writing up her conclusions in more detail than she'd attempted for a very long time.

'It just shows what a bit of confidence can do,' the teacher said as Gemma drank a well-earned cup of coffee in the staffroom at playtime.

'I wish I could bottle a bit of it and take it through to Matt,' Gemma said. 'We could uncork it and sprinkle it all over him before he could stop us. Can't you see it.' She mimed the action, uncorking an imaginary bottle and sprinkling the contents over an imaginary boy. 'He might even smile.'

The real boy was sitting in his usual place beside the window, gazing out at the playground with a withdrawn expression dull on his face. The hyacinths were in sculptured bloom in their neat pots on the windowsill, their summer blue bright among the dull buffs and browns of chairs and tables, but he didn't seem to be aware of them.

'It's a lovely day, Matt,' Gemma told him. 'Look at the hyacinths. It's nearly spring.'

He didn't look at the hyacinths or her. 'So?'

'So it won't be long before you can get out.'

'What for?' he asked, his face sullen. 'What's the point?'

'It's nice out of doors.'

'When you can run,' he scowled.

She decided to talk tough. 'It's nice whether you can run or not,' she told him. 'It's nice no matter what you're doing. Even sitting in a chair it's nice.'

'You don't know anything about it,' he said. His face was dark with distress.

'Yes, I do. You'd be surprised.'

'You don't,' he said. And suddenly he wasn't sulky and monosyllabic but had found a furious tongue. 'You don't know *anything* about it. It's all very well for you. You can walk about. You've got legs. I haven't. I shall never walk again. Never do anything — run, kick a ball, play cricket. Don't you understand? I'm stuck here in this chair for the rest of my life. I don't care if it's spring. It can stay winter for ever as far as I'm concerned. I might as well be dead.'

His onslaught was so unexpected and so passionate that for a second she didn't know what to say. Then she decided that having started tough, she would have to continue,

575

even if it made him worse. 'That's a stupid thing to say,' she told him briskly. 'You're not dead. You've got a lot of life ahead of you. It's about time you started to enjoy it.'

'You don't know what you're talking about,' he repeated, 'so you can just shut up.' And when she opened her mouth to rebuke him for rudeness — for distressed or not he couldn't be allowed to get away with that — he suddenly started to yell and twist about in his chair, both fists clenched and very near to violence. 'I hate you! I hate everybody! I hate this fucking chair! I can't fucking stand it! Go away! Go on, go away, or I'll punch you.'

Now she knew instinctively what had to be done. She raised her false leg until the foot was on the nearest chair and the shin within striking distance of his angry fist. 'Go on then!' she said. 'Punch me! Punch my leg. I dare you. I don't care either.'

'I will,' he warned, his face wild.

She looked at him steadily, accepting his rage, daring him. 'Go on, then.'

She felt the punch in her stump and straight up her thigh, but the pain of it was nothing compared to the look of shock on his face.

'Yes,' she answered him, 'I've got a false leg too. I know exactly where you are, and exactly how you feel. You're not the only one. Nothing is ever quite what it seems. Right?' And as he seemed to be calming, 'I'll show you if you like.' She realised that she would probably have to reveal her prosthesis to the entire class, but it could be the making of him, and she had no qualms about it. She looked at Colin Rainer for permission, which was given with a rapid smile. Then she rolled up the leg of her jeans until he could see the socket.

Children gathered round them at once, full of the dispassionate interest of the young. 'What's it made of, Miss!' 'Does it hurt yer?' 'Have you got a knee or does it go right up?' It was an inspired lesson and surprisingly painless.

'There you are,' she said to Matt when all the questions had been answered. 'I lost my leg but it hasn't stopped me. I can walk about and drive a car and do everything I want. You could too. And don't tell me they haven't fitted your prosthesis yet because I know they have. I've read your notes.'

'Yes. Well,' he said. 'I suppose . . .'

'Never mind suppose. You could.'

He was looking at her leg, thinking hard. 'Did you fall over a lot?' he asked.

They were on the same level, two amputees comparing experiences, friends. Now she thought, I can really help him. 'We all fall over a lot,' she told him. 'That's how you learn not to. Have you fallen in the shower yet? I've had some awesome bruises falling in the shower.'

'I slid out the seat the first time,' he confessed. 'Right on the floor. That was awesome.'

'I'll bet!' she said. 'Now what about this work we're supposed to be doing? Can we make a start on it, do you think?'

'Probably,' he said and gave her a smile of such ineffable sweetness she could have picked him up and hugged him.

By the end of the morning they were both exhausted but they'd made so much progress she could hardly believe it.

'You look all in,' Colin sympathised, as they walked back to the staffroom.

'Very gallant of you to say so, sir,' she teased him. 'I expect I do though. I've been up since dawn two days running.'

'Then you'd better stay and have lunch with us.'

Until then, she'd always rushed home when her stint was over. But why not stay? There was nothing to go home for, not now she and Nick had decided to finish with one another. But she wouldn't think about that, not yet anyway, not when she was on a high.

So she joined them at their crowded dinner table and had a school dinner which was more appetising than she'd expected. And afterwards she stayed on in the staffroom and talked to Mrs Muldoony about her two pupils.

'You must be feeling very pleased with yourself,' the headmistress said, when she'd skimmed through the lesson reports. 'You've done a good morning's work.'

To be praised so fulsomely was very pleasant and Gemma could have taken any amount of it. But the bell was sounding to start the afternoon session and Mrs Muldoony had a parent to see.

The afternoon had a springtime balm about it. Much too nice to spend cooped up in a flat that still reverberated with that awful row. I shall go shopping, she decided as she walked along the corridor to the entrance. I shall treat myself to something luxurious. I've earned it.

She was so cheerfully engrossed in her plans that she didn't see the reporters until she'd turned the corner and almost reached her car. Suddenly they were round her, a great pack of them, eager-faced with microphones or squinting behind the huge owl-eyes of their cameras.

'Gemma!' they called. 'This way,

Gemma!' Cameras flashed in her eyes and for a second she felt so buffeted by the pressure of their bodies that she was afraid she was going to lose her balance. 'Gemma! One more! This way!'

A young man thrust his microphone under her nose. 'Were you enticed away from your family?'

She was bewildered. 'I don't know what you're talking about.'

Other voices joined in. 'When did you last see your parents?' 'Your father?' 'Is it true . . . ?' 'Can you tell us . . . ?' The babble of their voices was worse than the pressure of their bodies.

She held up her hand, the way she would have done in the classroom. 'One at a time, please!'

But it was a waste of breath. 'Can you tell us . . . ?' '. . . this tug-of-love case . . . ?' 'He says you're going to sue for half a million. Is that true?' 'Can you give us a statement?'

'OK, OK,' she said. 'I'll give you a statement.' She waited until the noise had subsided and they were ready, microphones thrust forward. Then, speaking slowly and clearly, she said, 'I am not an exhibit. I have a life to lead and I want to be left alone to get on with it. Now will you please go away.'

They didn't move. Instead, the uproar began again. 'Can you tell us . . . ?' 'Gemma!' 'Gemma!'

'I've nothing else to say,' she shouted into the din. But they weren't listening because she hadn't told them what they wanted to hear. There was nothing for it but to fight her way out. She gathered her strength and struggled through the pack, pushing away microphones, cameras and bodies as she went. This, she thought, as she hauled the car door open, must be what it's like to be attacked by a swarm of locusts.

They pressed against the windows even as she drove away, cameras clicking and flashing. But at last she was able to inch through the gate and elude them. What was all that about? she thought. Then she remembered the second report. Of course. It's the crash being back in the news. They've dug out my picture and found all that millionaire nonsense again. I might have guessed there'd be trouble. And I stood in the staffroom and said it was all in the past — *as if it had happened to someone else.* I should have known better.

She was in the High Street by this time, heading south, and still feeling annoyed. No, she thought, I won't go shopping here. I'll go to Croydon, right out of the way, where they can't find me. I'll go to Croydon and buy myself a hat with a huge brim and a pair of dark glasses and if they come after me again I shall pretend to be someone else.

So she spent a happy afternoon in the Whitgift Centre and bought herself a dress from Monsoon, which was long and straight and beautifully cut and made her feel marvellous because it looked so good on her and because she couldn't really afford it. Then she treated herself to a cream tea and went to have a look at the furniture in Marks and Spencer's, as if she were a woman of means.

It was very late by the time she got home, and there was a chill wind blowing. As she walked across the compound towards her flat, she noticed that the kitchen window was still wide open. The sight of it gave her a shock because she was sure she'd closed it yesterday as soon as she got in. Obviously she hadn't. How careless! The central heating would have come on at one o'clock so she'd been heating the compound for five and a half hours. The thought of all the money she'd wasted made her feel really cross with herself. But as she approached the porch, a new and rather more alarming suspicion entered her mind, for now she could see that the window was open to its widest extent and she was quite sure she hadn't left it in *that* state, especially for two whole days. She would have noticed the draught. As the hair rose on the nape of her neck, she realised that somebody must have broken in.

She stood in the porch for a second, listening as she drew her keys from her pocket and wondered what she ought to do. It could be her imagination but she was sure there was something different about the flat. She couldn't identify what it was, but there was something. She put the key into the lock as gently as she could and turned it very nearly silently. The air that wafted towards her as she eased the door ajar smelt of stale sweat, leather and motor oil. Dear God, whoever it was, he was still inside!

Afterwards it occurred to her that she'd taken a risk just walking into the flat like that. But at the time she didn't think about it. She was so angry that someone was invading her home that she simply put down her shopping, seized a crutch as a weapon and pounded across the hall and through the bedroom door, switching on lights as she went.

Her neat square room was strewn with clothes. They had been tossed across the bed and the chair and hurled on to the floor, with empty drawers flung down on top of them. And sure enough, the burglar was still in the room, a thickset bulky man in dark jeans and a leather jacket with a black bala-clava covering his face, one foot inside the fitted wardrobe, both white-gloved hands rifling through the pockets of the clothes hanging there, hooded head turned towards her. For a fraught second they stared at one another, then he stepped back from the wardrobe and turned to run. But she was too quick for him.

'You sod!' she yelled. 'How dare you!' And bounded forwards at him, holding her crutch before her like a shield.

It was as if she'd frozen him to the spot. They were standing face to face, so close that she could smell his sweat and see that his eyes were pale blue and fringed by short gingery lashes, but he didn't step back and although he seemed to be trying to pull away from her, he didn't run.

'Geroff!' he yelled. 'Geroff! You're fuck-ing hurting.'

For a second she couldn't think what was the matter with him. Then she realised that she was standing on his foot with her pros-thesis. It was the thing she'd been warned about at the rehab centre, to take care where she was putting her new foot because she wouldn't know when she was standing on somebody. And now she hadn't taken care and she'd pinned a burglar to the floor. How perfectly bloody marvellous. 'Gotcha,' she said, and reached up to pull off his balaclava.

He fought her off violently, punching at her and twisting his body to get away from her. She had to struggle to keep the crutch under his chin and it took all her strength to hold him, even though she pressed down on her false foot as heavily as she could. She had no idea how long they fought. It could have been seconds or hours. At one point, she lost her grip on the crutch, and grabbed him by his collar, his T-shirt, scrabbling and pushing to beat off his punching hands. But seconds later she made an enormous effort and managed to pull that awful balaclava off his head.

With his face revealed he was far less frightening. Now he was just an uncouth boy, with a shaven head dyed blond, a line of earrings in one ear and a dragon tattooed on his neck, and young — fifteen or sixteen at a guess — and far less bulky than he'd appeared at first glance. But he went on fighting. By now she knew he'd certainly stolen something and that whatever it was it was stashed away in one of the pockets of that leather jacket. She pulled at it furiously as they struggled, throwing out various odd things to right and left, an oily rag, keys, a newspaper folded in half, a collection of credit cards that tumbled on to the duvet cover one after another like falling leaves. And at last she scrabbled her right hand inside his jacket, found an inner pocket and, panting with the effort she was making, pulled out a jeweller's velvet pouch and emptied the contents on the bed, all her little precious pieces — the signet ring, the diamond cluster Jerry had bought her in a rare moment of drunken affection, her gold chain with its two medallions, even the little gilt bracelet she'd brought back from a school holiday in Spain.

'You bloody little toe-rag!' she screamed at him. 'How dare you steal my things!'

But turning to tip out her belongings had given him the chance he needed and he was out of her grasp and halfway to the door.

He paused. She couldn't catch him now. Not on crutches. 'So I nicked 'em,' he said, sneering at her. 'So what? You got 'em back. Right? They're nothing special. Only worth a few quid. You can spare it. What's a few rings an' things to you. I know who you are.

I been watchin' you. Right? You got millions. Right? Millions. I seen it in the paper. That's well out of order. You wiv millions an' me with nothink. So you can spare me a bit, can'tcher. I got a right to it.' Then he was out of the room, hurtling though the hall, banging through the front door. Escaped.

She stared after him, open-mouthed and panting. What was he talking about? What paper? Then she got her breath and her senses back and remembered the reporters.

The newspaper she'd thrown out of his pocket was still lying on the carpet. She picked it up, put it on the bed and unfolded it. There on the front page was her own uninjured face staring up at her and below it a picture of Andrew Quennell with his mouth open and his hair bristling like a white mane. And in enormous headlines: TV GURU AND CRASH HEROINE. It was such a shock and made her so angry that the words of the text swam out of focus as she read them. But she saw enough to know what was going on. 'Dr Quennell, speaking on . . .' 'Gemma Goodeve . . . suing for half a million . . .' 'Tug-of-love tussle . . .' He's been talking about me on TV, she thought.

There was a sharp sound ringing behind

her. A sharp familiar sound. Oh shit! The phone! Well whoever it is can get off the line. I've got to phone the police.

'Yes,' she said crossly. 'Who is it?'

'It's Nick,' his voice said. 'Are you all right?'

She was suddenly weary and sat on the edge of the bed, glad to be off her stump. But she was too caught up in her anger to feel anything beyond a mild surprise. 'Where are you?'

'Paris. Look, are you all right?'

'I'm fantastic!' she said, cynically. 'Couldn't be better. I've just been burgled.'

He drew in his breath with alarm. 'What?'

'Rotten little toe-rag with a crew cut. Said he'd come for his share of my ill-gotten gains. Didn't get them though. I saw to that.'

'You mean he was there? You caught him? Oh Christ, Gemma. Are you all right?'

'Yes. I caught him.' There was pride in the answer. 'I can stick up for myself.'

'How did he know it was your flat?'

'Your bloody father's been opening his mouth on TV, that's how. Telling everyone I'm a millionaire. We're both all over the front page.'

'Oh Christ!' he said again. 'I *knew* it was a

mistake, all this media business. Are you sure you're all right?'

She was short with him. 'Yes, yes, I'm fine.'

'What did the police say?'

'I haven't called them yet. It's only just happened.'

The warning pips were sounding. 'Oh Christ, Gemma,' he said again. 'This is awful. Look, wait a minute and I'll find some more coins.' The line went dead. 'I'll come back,' he said, as the disengaged tone began to purr. 'I'll catch the first train. You're not to worry about a thing.'

It upset Gemma to be cut off in mid-sentence. There was so much more she wanted to say, so much more she ought to have said, and now that they were disconnected she was aware of all the distances between them that they hadn't begun to bridge. But there was no time for regret. There wasn't even time to think about it. She had to phone the police. She looked down at her hand as it replaced the receiver and was shocked to see that the knuckles were torn and bloodstained. It had been more of a fight than she'd realised. I'd better get cleaned up first, she thought, and have a look at my stump. It felt all right but it had taken a lot of pressure.

But the phone rang again before she could stand up.

'Hello,' she said, thinking Nick had rung back. 'You found your coins, then.'

There was a pause, then a small, uncertain voice asked, 'Is that you, Aunty Gemma?'

One of Susan's girls, Gemma recognised, and she softened her tone. 'Yes,' she said. 'Is that Helen?'

'Yes. Could you come and get us, please.'

It was such an odd request that she was alerted to trouble at once. 'Where are you?'

'In a station near Grandpa's. Putney South.'

'What are you doing there?'

The explanation was breathless with tears and very muddled. 'Grandpa Quennell's gone out and Mummy's locked in her room and she said to go away and Daddy's not in the garden centre and there aren't any lights on and the taxi driver was horrid. He said he had a good mind to take us back to King's Cross because we couldn't pay him and we ought to be smacked and it wasn't our fault because we couldn't help it if Grandpa was out. I did give him my silver bracelet . . .'

It *was* trouble. And pretty serious. The police would have to wait and so would cleaning up. 'Stay where you are,' Gemma said. 'I'm coming to get you.' Her response was so quick it didn't enter her head that she would be driving to a railway station.

Chapter 33

The two girls were standing just inside the station next to the flower stall, small, still, solemn and hand in hand. They looked like a pair of statues in their identical black padded jackets, identical blue jeans, identical bobbed blonde hair. There was trouble in every line of them.

Gemma pulled up as close to the station entrance as she could get and let down the passenger window, delighted to realise that there was no fear in her at all, only anxiety for their safety. She'd parked on double yellow lines, so she'd have to be quick.

'Come on you two,' she yelled. 'Hop in.'

It concerned her that they didn't run. They walked hand in hand with frozen deliberation, hardly like kids at all. And even when they were safe inside her car they sat bolt upright and pale-faced and didn't speak. But she wasn't worried about them. She was in a state of such extraordinary euphoria she felt she could cope with anything.

'Home,' she said. 'You can put me in the

picture as we go.'

But they couldn't tell her very much more than they'd told her already and it upset them to be questioned. They'd left Poppleton because they'd been alone in the house and their mother was locked in the bedroom and wouldn't come out. They didn't know what was going on, nor where their father was, nor where Grandpa and Grandma Quennell were, and they were cold and hungry and wished they'd stayed at home. No, they said, their eyes strained, they didn't know why their mother was locked in. She hadn't told them.

'Never mind,' Gemma reassured them. 'Your daddy'll know. He'll look after her, won't he.' But she was thinking hard. It was so unlike the power-dressing, high-flying, businesswoman she thought she knew that she couldn't make any sense of it. Why lock herself in? It hadn't been by accident or she'd have asked them to let her out. She'd said she wasn't ill or hurt. But then why did she say she was never going to come downstairs again? That sounded hysterical. It must have been something pretty traumatic to cause such an extreme reaction.

They'd arrived at St Mary's Court. 'Let's get you in the warm,' she said, as she pulled up at her garage. She took hold of their chilled hands and led them to the flat.

The air in the hall was so cold that Naomi shivered when she took her coat off. That damned kitchen window, Gemma thought. She'd forgotten all about it.

'There's a window open,' she explained, leading them into the living room and through the arch into the kitchen. 'That's why it's cold. Hang on a tick and I'll shut it.'

But it wasn't just open, it had been wrenched off its hinges.

'Crikey!' Helen said, roused out of her misery by the sight of it. 'How did you break that?'

There was no point in trying to hide what had happened. She'd have to call the police once she'd found their father and they were bound to see the mess in the bedroom. In any case she felt so confident in this odd euphoric state of hers that lying was out of the question. So she told them.

She expected them to be alarmed but they were thrilled, their faces animated for the first time since she'd picked them up. 'A real burglar?' Naomi wanted to know. 'In a mask?'

And Helen asked what he'd stolen.

'Nothing,' Gemma told them with great satisfaction, as she searched for a hammer and a box of nails. 'I caught him and made him give it all back.'

They were full of admiration. 'Really?'

'Really!'

'Crikey! Did you hit him? Is that why you've got blood on your hands?'

Gemma had forgotten her torn knuckles. 'I'll tell you all about it,' she promised, as she nailed the window shut, 'when we've phoned your father and let him know you're all right. First things first. We don't want him to worry, do we? What's your number?'

But although she let the phone ring for a very long time, nobody answered it and the girls began to sink back into anxiety again. 'Never mind,' she said. 'We'll try the garden centre. I expect he's there.'

'We rang there,' Helen said, miserably. 'They said he was out.'

'On a 'signment,' Naomi added.

'We'll try again,' Gemma said. 'He could be back by now.'

But he wasn't. All they got was his voice on an answerphone telling them that the garden centre was closed at the moment but would be open 'tomorrow morning at nine o'clock'. At which Helen looked more miserable than ever and Naomi bit her lip with anxiety.

'If we can't find your father for the moment,' Gemma said, 'let's see where your grandfather is. They might be home by now.' And she dialled Andrew's number.

They all felt quite hopeful when it clicked and his voice answered. But it was only another answerphone message saying they couldn't come to the phone at the moment.

Gemma left a message, feeling irritated. 'Just in case you've had a call from York, Helen and Naomi are with me and quite safe.' He's caused me enough trouble today, she thought. He's got no business being out at this time of night.

'I think we ought to try your home again,' she said to the two pale faces waiting beside her. 'Your dad might be back by now.'

'He won't be,' Helen sighed, 'and she won't answer.'

'We'll try,' Gemma said.

They tried three times, but the phone just rang and rang and rang.

'What are we going to do?' Helen asked.

It was pointless phoning any more. 'I'm going to put some Elastoplast on my fingers,' Gemma told her cheerfully, 'and then I'm going to cook supper. Do you like chicken?'

The thought of food cheered Naomi up a little. 'If it's nuggets,' she said.

It wasn't so they had to compromise with beefburgers and chips. But cooking cheered them and in the middle of the meal Helen suddenly remembered that Grandpa had put two phone numbers in her address book and that the second one was his mobile.

'Brilliant!' Gemma said. 'If they're out on one of their jaunts, there's just a chance he'll have taken it with him. You go on eating and I'll try it. Where's the book?'

Success at last. Andrew's voice, answering from a great and tinny distance on a very noisy line: 'Dr Quennell speaking.'

'Andrew. It's Gemma. Look, I've got Helen and Naomi here. There's a bit of a problem at home and they've come to London.'

'Is Susan with them?'

'No,' she said calmly. 'Susan is the problem. She's locked herself in her bedroom and won't come out. They travelled down on their own. But they're quite all right. I'm looking after them.'

The background noise was increasing. 'This is a God-awful line,' he shouted. 'What's the matter with her? Is she ill? No, never mind. I can't hear you. We're just pulling into Euston. We'll get a cab and come straight there. Gemma? Did you get that?'

'Just about.'

The line was crackling and fizzing as if it was in the middle of a bonfire. 'We'll be there as soon as we can.'

'There you are,' she said to the girls. 'Your grandfather's on his way.'

They were both relieved to hear it. 'But what about Daddy?' Helen worried, pausing with a chip halfway to her mouth. 'What will he say when he gets home and finds we're not there?'

Rob had spent a happy afternoon in the Alhambra grounds. The rose gardens had been dug over, the pond drained, the fountain removed to the garden centre, and they'd only stopped work because the light was so poor that they couldn't see what they were doing. He'd praised his team and sent them home and had then spent an hour and a half in the hotel discussing plans with the new manager. They parted after several drinks feeling well pleased with themselves. Now it was back to Poppleton and a well-earned dinner. He was hungry for it all the way home.

It was a surprise to turn in at the drive and find the house in darkness and the phone ringing dementedly in an empty hall. The damn thing stopped as soon as he picked it up. Typical. But it puzzled him that nobody had been there to answer it. Where were they all?

He walked into the kitchen, and turned on the lights. There was nothing cooking, which was a disappointment, but there were two used mugs left on the table and two plates with crumbs on them, so the kids must have come home and gone out again. Probably at a party somewhere. They were always going to parties. Sue must have ferried them there and hadn't got back yet. Having solved the problem, he switched on the radio to provide a bit of cheerful background noise and bounded upstairs to wash and change ready for her return.

At first, like his daughters before him, he thought the bedroom door was jammed. But one push showed him otherwise and at that point he began to worry. It shouldn't be locked. Nobody ever locked the doors in this house. So what was going on?

'Susan!' he called. 'Are you there?'

She didn't answer him until he'd called three times and then her voice was slow and slurred as though she was drugged. 'Go 'way.'

That sounded so alarming it made his heart jump. 'Open the door, sweetheart,' he urged. 'We can't talk through a closed door.'

'Can't talk to anyone,' she slurred. 'Go 'way, Rob. Please.'

He insisted. 'Open the door.'

'I can't,' she said and now her voice was anguished. 'I can't. *Please* go away.'

He tried another tack, asking her specific questions, as calmly and patiently as he could — if she was ill, or injured, if she'd had too much to drink, if there'd been a road accident, offering to call the doctor, urging her to open the door and let him *see* how she was. But she answered no to everything. Finally, he asked about the girls, because that was something she *would* know about. Were they at a party? Or out with Sheryl? But, to his horror, she didn't know where they were and didn't seem to care. Now he had two reasons to be alarmed, and alarm made him angry.

'You must know where they are,' he said. 'They can't have left the house without you knowing. Come on, Susan. This nonsense has gone on long enough. Get up and open this door and stop playing the fool. Did Sheryl take them somewhere?'

But she only groaned and told him to go away.

He was too worried and too angry to talk to her any longer. The girls were out somewhere and he would have to find them. 'I'll phone round,' he decided.

He lit a cigarette for comfort, and went downstairs to start his search. Sheryl's mother said, no, the girls weren't with Sheryl. She'd gone to a disco in Leeds. Helen's best friend hadn't seen her since playtime and wanted to know if she'd still got her Peter André record. Her next-best friend couldn't remember when she'd seen her last. But the third-best, who was called Alice, said she'd seen her after school, going off somewhere.

'Who was with her?' he asked.

'Naomi.'

'Who else? Weren't they with a grown-up?'

'No. They were on their own.'

The shock of *that* made him feel nauseous. They never went anywhere on their own. That was why they had a nanny, to ensure that they were always accompanied. 'Do you know where they were going?'

Alice was unconcerned. 'Down the road, I expect.'

'Which road?'

'The school road,' Alice said. And then her mother took the phone back again, wondering what was the matter. So he made an excuse that he'd come home, found the children out, didn't know where they were and was ringing round. Then he hung up before he could be asked any questions about Susan. He was sick with fear. They were out on their own in the dark with no one to look after them. Anything could happen to them. For all he knew it might have happened already. But that was too awful to think about and raised him to such a passion of terrified anger that he couldn't contain it. Damn you Sue, he thought. This is all your fault. He took the stairs two at a time, to let her know what she'd done.

'Thanks to you, our kids are out there wandering about in the dark with no one to look after them,' he said, his voice harsh with distress. 'I hope you feel bloody ashamed of yourself!'

There wasn't a sound from the bedroom. She didn't even answer *that*. He beat on the door with both fists, shouting at her.

'For Christ's sake, Susan, what are you playing at? Don't you care? I've rung everywhere, do you hear me? Everywhere. And I can't find them. Nobody knows where they are.' He remembered the phone ringing and ringing as he arrived home. 'Damn you, Susan. You couldn't even be bothered to answer the bloody phone. They could have been trying to get through to us and you just . . .' And then common sense began to reassert itself. He could dial 1471 and return the call. Without saying another word, he went straight back to the phone.

A London number. Not Andrew's but in the same area. Surely they're not . . . 'Hello! This is Rob Pengilly. You rang me.'

'Yes,' Gemma's voice answered. 'It's about Helen and Naomi.'

'Do you know where they are?'

'They're safe. I've got them here with me.'

He was weak with relief. 'Thank God. Thank God. I'll be there on the next train, tell them.'

'Do you want to talk to them?'

He was in too bad a state to face it, caught between fear and anger and afraid of what he might say to them. 'No,' he said. 'Just tell them I'll be straight there.' He was already working out what train he could catch, his mind leaping forward to the journey, to the need for a hired car — he'd order that on the Express — checking that he had keys, cash cards, cheque book. Thank God for the speed of InterCity!

It wasn't until he was pulling into the car park at Poppleton station that he remembered Susan and realised that he hadn't told her the news. After a second's guilt, he decided it served her right. She'd brought it all on herself by turning away from him. And turning away from the kids, which was much, much worse. How could any woman do a thing like that? Leave alone Susan. They could have been murdered wandering off on their own and, if they had been, it would have been all her fault. Let her stew in her own juice.

So many trains, so many stations, so much anxiety. Catherine and Andrew at Euston, standing in the queue for taxis, she taut with concern, he stamping with impatience. 'Come on! Come on! Get a move on! What's the matter with you?' Rob in York, prowling the long curve of the platform, willing the London train to arrive, wondering how on earth the kids had managed the same journey all on their own. Nick in the Gare du Nord, frantically trying to get a stolid information clerk to understand that he had to get to London that night.

'Mais oui, but le Shuttle is depart, monsieur.'

'It's ridiculous,' he fretted. 'I can't stay here all night. What about the ferries? Dover. Calais.'

'Is depart.'

'Newhaven?'

'Is depart.'

He asked his next question with exasperation. 'So when is the next train to London?'

'Tomorrow morning, monsieur.'

In the disapproving calm of her empty house, Susan was weeping at last. When Rob had shouted at her, she'd been so dulled by shock that it had simply been an irritating noise, a series of sounds somewhere in the background and with no meaning, but now the impact of what he'd said was seeping through the cotton wool in her brain to add the sting of remorse to her wounded pride and to rouse the most terrible fear. The girls were missing and he didn't know where they were. They must have walked out because she wouldn't speak to them. She must have driven them out of the house. Oh dear God, how could she have done such a thing? And now he'd gone out to look for them, and she didn't know where he was either or when he'd be coming back, and she was sick with fear.

She got up from the bed, moving slowly like an old lady, wiped her eyes, cleaned her glasses, put them back on, struggled to think what to do. Should she phone the police? No. Not yet. Not when Rob had gone off to look for them. And certainly not while she was in a state. They'd think she'd murdered them. They always suspected the parents. No, no, I can't think about murder. They're not murdered. They've just wandered off and got lost and Rob will find them. Please God let him find them and don't let them be murdered. No, no, I can't think about that. I'll wait until he gets back and we'll phone the police if there isn't any news. They can't have got far. Poppleton's only a small place. But he'd phoned round. He'd said so, hadn't he. He'd phoned round and nobody knew where they were. Oh dear God, what am I going to do?

The telephone book was lying on the bedside table where she'd left it that morning before she went to work. Was it only that morning? It felt like a week. She looked at it idly, wondering if there was anyone she could phone for help. Not her parents. They were the last people she wanted to tell. Nick? But he was always unavailable in that hospital. Chris. Of course. She would ring Chris. They were hours behind in Quebec so it would be early evening there and she might be able to catch him at home.

The same warm voice, the same affection, 'Hi there, Sis. Nice to hear you.'

'Oh Chris,' she said. 'I'm so glad I've caught you.'

His tone changed at once. 'What's up?'

She told him everything in an outpouring of guilt and fear, as though they were in the same room instead of thousands of miles apart.

'OK,' he said. 'Leave it to me for the moment. I'll do what I can. Phone me when Rob gets back or if anything else happens. I'll get back to you.'

She thanked him profusely, tears welling into her eyes again. It was the first time for years that she'd felt the need to depend on someone else for help. She and Rob had always been self-sufficient until this awful business. Shame was clogging her mind again and now she had another reason for it. How could she have sent him away like that? Why hadn't she explained to him the way she'd just explained to Chris? But how could she tell him she'd been thrown out of her job? That she was finished. How *could* she explain anything as dreadful as that?

'Are you there?' Chris's voice was saying. 'Sue?'

'I'm here,' she said. 'I'll wait to hear from you. Give me three rings first and redial. Then I shall know it's you. I can't face talking to anyone else.'

In St Mary's Court, her daughters didn't want to wait another minute. Once they knew their grandparents were on their way, they found their appetites and made a good supper but now they were fidgety with impatience. Naomi found a perch on the kitchen windowsill and peered into the courtyard. '*When* are they coming?'

'Give them time,' Gemma said. 'It's a long way from Euston. Come and have a look at my bedroom.' That was dramatic enough to keep them occupied for a few minutes.

It certainly surprised them.

'What a mess!' Helen said.

Naomi wondered if Gemma was going to clear it all up.

'No,' her sister told her. 'You mustn't. You're supposed to leave it for the police to see. That's what they do on *The Bill*.'

'I think that's for fingerprints,' Gemma said. 'He was wearing gloves so he didn't leave any.'

'Are you going to ring them now?' Naomi wanted to know. Seeing the mess had reminded her. 'You said you'd ring them when we'd found Grandpa. If you ring them, will they come while we're still here?'

'I doubt it,' Gemma said. 'You'd like to hear me report the dastardly deed, is that it?'

They were all ears as she rang, taking in

every gory detail and deeply impressed by how calm she was.

'Did he really have a dragon tattooed on his neck?' Helen asked. 'Crikey! That's well gruesome. Will you be on *Crimewatch*?'

'Are they coming to see you?' Naomi wanted to know. 'Will they be in a squad car like *The Bill*? I'll watch out the kitchen window for them, shall I?'

'You'll have a long wait,' Gemma said, laughing at her eagerness. 'They're not coming until tomorrow morning.'

'There's someone coming now,' Naomi reported from the window. 'He's parking his car right outside. It's a detective, I bet.'

'I shouldn't get excited,' Gemma said. 'It'll be someone for next door.'

But he was ringing her doorbell. Now what?

It was Tim Ledgerwood, squinting on the doorstep.

He didn't say 'Hello' or 'Good evening' but plunged straight into the attack, his face scowling. 'We've got to talk.'

After all the events of her extraordinary day, Gemma couldn't be bothered to be polite to him. 'Not now we haven't,' she said. 'I've got other things to attend to.'

'This can't wait,' he insisted. 'We've got to talk. There's a lot of money at stake. I'm

running up bills on your behalf. Right? Solicitors don't come cheap.'

'If you've run up bills, that's your business,' she told him coldly.

Her annoyance was getting through to
him. So he made an effort and tried a bit of
charm. 'Aren't you going to ask me in?'

'No. I'm not.'

'But we've got to talk. This is getting out
of hand.'

She made a decision, her mind needle
sharp with anger. 'OK,' she said to him.
'We'll talk. I've got plenty to say to you, believe me. But not now. Come back tomorrow afternoon. Teatime. And bring Mother
with you.'

'What if she won't come?'

'That'll be your tough luck, No Mother,
no talk. D'you understand that?' And she
shut the door, her eyes blazing.

'*Who* was that?' Helen asked.

'That,' Gemma told her, 'believe it or
not, was my father.'

'Crikey!' Helen said. 'He doesn't look like
a father.'

'There's the taxi!' Naomi yelled from her
perch on the windowsill. 'They're here!'

Chapter 34

As soon as Andrew and Catherine had finally climbed into their taxi at Euston, he erupted into furious and useless questioning. While they'd been waiting in the queue, he'd managed to keep his anxiety more or less under control but now he let rip.

'All that way, all on their own,' he raged. 'I've never heard anything to equal it. Anything could have happened. They could have got on the wrong train and ended up at the back of beyond and how would we have found them then? They could have been run over, crossing some God-awful road somewhere. Why didn't someone stop them? They've got a nanny, for God's sake. Where was *she?* I hope they sling her out on her stupid ear, damned stupid girl. I never did hold with nannies. And Susan ill.'

'We don't know she's ill,' Catherine pointed out.

'Of course she's ill. Why else would the children have run off like that? It was because she was too ill to notice. It's obvious.'

'It could be something else.'

'Like what?'

Catherine was remembering. 'Work, perhaps.'

He wouldn't consider it. 'You don't get into a state about work.'

'She got in a state when she failed her exams,' Catherine reminded him. 'She locked herself in the bedroom and wouldn't come out.'

He dismissed that as youthful dramatics. 'She was a child. This is different. She's ill. She must be. Or she's had an accident. She should have called a doctor. Got things organised.'

'Perhaps she has.'

'Then why hasn't somebody phoned to tell us? And where's Rob, for Christ's sake? The whole thing's bloody ridiculous.'

'Well at least Gemma was there to take them in.'

'And what if she hadn't been?' he said, his face a storm of anxiety. 'Tell me that.'

'But she was.'

'And what if she saw the broadcast or read that bloody awful paper? What am I going to say to her, Kate?'

'Nothing,' Catherine advised. 'It's late. We'll just pick up the girls and go home.

We can deal with everything else in the morning.'

The taxi edged towards Putney through the impatient traffic of the evening. They seemed to be moving through a blizzard of harsh lights and very very slowly. 'Can't he go any bloody faster?'

'When we get there,' Catherine said, 'no scolding the girls.' It was midway between an instruction and a suggestion. 'I know they deserve it but they've probably given themselves fright enough and we'd only be rubbing it in.'

'No scolding,' he agreed. It would be more appropriate coming from their parents. And she was right. It must have frightened them terribly.

'No questioning either.'

'We must find out what's the matter with Susan.'

'Let *them* tell *us*, eh?'

'They'd better. We need to know. It's all perfectly bloody ridiculous.'

But once they were in St Mary's Court and the girls were standing in Gemma's hall, waiting to greet him, he took one look at their poor little faces and the dark shadows under their poor little eyes and was filled with such pity that he simply scooped them up into his arms and gave them a bear hug. And Gemma didn't say anything.

'You should be tucked up in bed, the pair of you,' he said, leading them off at once to the waiting taxi, before anything could be said. 'I prescribe a warm bath, a hot drink and plenty of sleep. Come on!'

Catherine stayed behind to thank Gemma for looking after them. 'We do appreciate it,' she said. 'What a good job you were here.'

'Yes,' Gemma agreed, wryly, watching as Andrew led the girls away. The sight of him looking so handsome and self-assured made her feel angry. You open your mouth, she was thinking, and I get bloody burgled and you just walk away as if nothing had happened. 'Wasn't it.'

'I don't know what we should have done if you hadn't been. What news of Susan? You said she was locked in her room.'

Gemma told her what little she knew, warned her that it upset the girls to be questioned and added that Rob was on his way.

Then it *is* work, Catherine thought. I knew it.

'Come on, Kate!' Andrew called from the taxi. 'You can talk tomorrow.'

The two women kissed before Catherine ran to the taxi, where Andrew was waiting at the door.

'Quite right, Dr Quennell!' Gemma called to him bitterly. 'There's been far too much talking in the last few days, if you ask me.' And she went back inside the flat before she was tempted to say anything else.

'She saw the broadcast,' Andrew said, as the taxi edged out of the compound. 'I knew there'd be trouble.'

But Catherine hadn't got time to think about the broadcast now. She was concerned for her granddaughters, asking whether they'd had anything to eat and whether they'd brought their pyjamas.

'We'll find some for you,' she said, when they shook their heads. 'I've got some old ones of your mother's hidden away somewhere. And then we'll ring your mummy and daddy to tell them where you are.'

'She won't answer,' Helen said, bleakly. 'She hasn't been answering all evening. And Daddy won't either because he's on the train. He said he was coming straight here.'

Catherine could see that talk of phoning distressed them. 'Well we'll see,' she temporised. 'The first thing is to get you bathed and to bed. There'll be time enough for phoning in the morning.'

But when they got in, the answerphone was flashing and had to be dealt with.

'I'll see to it,' Andrew said. 'You take

them up to bed. They've had enough for one day, haven't you girls? I'll come up and tell you if there's any news.' He waited until they were out of earshot before he switched on the machine.

There were five messages from reporters, which was predictable, all saying much the same thing. Would he care to comment on the allegations made on *Friday Forum*? No he would not. At least not now and not to them. That could wait for his column and would have to be thought about very carefully, when he had the time and energy for it. The sixth message was Gemma's, now out of date. The seventh and last was from Chris: 'I've just had a call from Susan. Please call me back as soon as you can.'

Heart thudding with alarm, he dialled the number.

When Catherine came downstairs more than half an hour later, she found him slumped in his armchair staring at the blank television screen. It was such an uncharacteristic position that she was very alarmed.

'Oh Drew!' she said. 'What is it?'

'You were right,' he sighed. 'It *is* work and it's all my fault, according to Chris.' And he told her what he'd heard. 'I didn't realise this job was so important to her.'

'She knew there was a price to pay for it,'

Catherine told him. 'Right from the beginning. She said she had a choice. To tell them you were her father and be turned down there and then, or to keep quiet about it and risk losing the job when they found out.'

'Which is what's happened, according to Chris. She couldn't phone *me* and tell me herself. She had to phone Chris, all the way across the Atlantic. It's very hurtful.'

'Ring her now,' Catherine suggested.

'I have,' he sighed. 'Twice. She doesn't answer.'

I knew this would happen, Catherine thought. I ought to have warned you. But you wouldn't have listened to me if I had. You'd have told me not to imagine things. There was no point in saying anything about it now. Fortunately they had a better language for comfort. She knelt between his knees, put her arms round his neck and kissed him.

'I've hurt her, Kate,' he said. 'I've cost her her job. It's the one thing in the world I should never have done to her — and I've done it.'

'Not intentionally,' she said. But he wasn't comforted.

'Intentions are irrelevant,' he said. 'It's the end result that counts.' He took her hands and held them. 'That broadcast was a nightmare, Kate. I knew it would make trouble. I'm not complaining. I went into this with my eyes open. I always knew I'd have to face the opposition, and I knew I'd have mud slung at me, sooner or later. That's the way the system works. But not like that, not through Gemma and Susan. Not through my daughter. That was below the belt.'

She kissed his hand and held it against her cheek. 'Yes,' she said. 'It was. But that's the way the system works too. If you go around telling people the emperor's got no clothes on, they'll nobble you in any way they can, through the people you care about, or your job or your pension. You can't expect to tell the truth about politics and not get punished for it. Not in the 1990s.'

'When I started all this,' he said, 'I thought I could. That was the object of the exercise. Tell the truth and shame the politicians. Stand up for the NHS. Shed light on murky places. I can remember saying I was the only one around who could tell the truth and get away with it. The arrogance of it. Well, I was wrong.'

'I don't think you were arrogant. Or wrong. You're too hard on yourself.'

'What am I going to do?' he asked. 'I've had six reporters on the phone since the broadcast. What do I say to them?'

She gave him a wry smile. 'Tell them the truth?'

'You're saying, fight on.'

'I'm not sure what I'm saying,' she told him, 'except that I love you and I can't bear to see you hurt.'

'And then there's Cyprus,' he said.

She waited.

'I thought it was over and done with,' he said. 'I'd almost forgotten it. And now they're going to dig it all up again. Dear God!'

He was gazing into the middle distance, reliving it, feeling it, the sun warm on his shoulders, the mountain rising before him, covered with trees where gunmen could watch without being seen, the prickling sense that they *were* being watched, dust swirling back at them from the lorry ahead, the smell of sweat, his mouth dry with fear.

'They'd shot one of our doctors the day before,' he said. 'He was driving through Nicosia and they shot him. In broad daylight. The one that took our lorry out was a "toffee tin bomb". Blew it to bits.'

A spurt of bright red flame. A roar that filled his ears with pain and reverberated through his body, making his guts shake. Bits of an arm flung into the air. A hand, its

fingers spread, frozen in the instant of surprise. Chunks of metal. And such fear and
anger flooding his system. He was leaping
from his own car, running to the debris
even before it had finished falling. Something pinged against his tin hat as he ran. It
was nothing. He didn't stop to see what it
was. His anger was so extreme even a bullet
wouldn't have stopped him. Fucking evil
monsters! How dare they do this! A body
sprawled on the road, another trying to
crawl away. Still alive. Must get to him.

Then that dark figure dodging between
the trees, running away. Bloody running
away. His own voice screaming. 'There he
is! Shoot him! Oh for Christ's sake, don't let
the bugger get away. Kill him! Kill him!'

'Oh Kate!' he said. 'I've never hated anyone in the whole of my life the way I hated
that boy. I could have killed him with my
bare hands.'

'Did you shoot him?' she asked. She was
very calm, her face creased with sympathy.

'I honestly can't remember. I'm not even
sure I had a gun. I was running to the lorry,
you see. To pick up the injured. But I
wanted him shot. *I* gave the order to fire.'

He heard the fusillade, the roar of triumph. Down on his knees trying to reassure
the crawling soldier, trying to stem the

bleeding, wishing he had more skill, afraid the poor kid would die, willing him to live . . .

'It was crazy,' he said to Kate. 'There I was doing everything I could to save the life of one young man and screaming obscenities to kill the other one.'

'War,' she said.

Then there was a gentle silence between them. A soothing silence. She held his hand lovingly in both her own, caressing it with her thumb. 'Why didn't you tell me all this before?' she asked. There was no criticism in her voice, just curiosity.

'Because I'm a coward,' he confessed, looking at her. 'I thought I'd lose you if you knew how foul I could be. I couldn't risk *that*.'

'It wouldn't have been a risk.'

'It was to me,' he said ruefully. 'Well, there you are. You know now.'

It was the first time she'd seen a vulnerable expression on his face. 'Yes,' she said. 'I know now.' And she smiled at him. 'I'm very glad I know. It's a weight off my shoulders too.'

That puzzled him.

'It's hard work being married to a good man,' she said, the teasing note returning to her voice. 'It's a relief to know you've got clay feet. It levels us out.'

'Oh come on!' he said. 'I'm not a good man.'

'You are. You're a very good man. An honest man. Ask your children. Or your patients.'

'You're the good one,' he said. 'I wouldn't be anything without you.'

'I had an illegitimate child,' she pointed out.

'That was love.'

'That was stupidity.'

The terror of the memory was receding. They were in their own world again, at ease in their healing house, closer to one another than they had ever been. There were decisions to be made, difficulties to face. But weren't there always?

Chapter 35

Alone in her nice quiet flat, Gemma was working off her annoyance by clearing up her bedroom — the police having given her permission. It was a quarter to eleven but it felt more like two in the morning. She was tired and hungry and her stump was aching but once she'd started she worked on doggedly, partly because she was cross and partly because being in a mess annoyed her. The nerve of that damned Tim Ledgerwood, turning up on her doorstep like that. The nerve of that damned Andrew Quennell, to talk such nonsense to the press.

She limped about, gathering her scattered clothes, then she sat on the edge of the bed with her stump supported by a pillow, and folded them into neat piles, item by item, ready to put away. It took a very long time but restoring order restored her temper. Now, she thought, as she gathered up a tangle of bras and stockings that had been slung under the dressing table, I'll sort these out and then I'll find a meat pie or something and leave it in the oven to cook while I take a shower. She would have liked to indulge in the luxury of a nice long bath — just the thought made her stump ache for the ease of it — but although getting into a bath would be easy enough, she wasn't sure she could manage to get out again without slipping. Maybe, she thought . . .

And at that moment somebody rang at the door.

I really can't deal with anything else this evening, she thought, as she went to answer it. I've had more than enough to cope with already. But when she peered through the peephole and saw that her visitor was Rob Pengilly she changed her mind.

'They've gone,' she said, as she opened the door.

'I know,' he answered. 'I've been there.'

She stood back to let him in, noticing how weary and travel worn he looked. Poor man. 'Are they all right?'

'They're in bed and asleep,' he told her. 'None the worse apparently, thanks to you. I can't get over them running off like that.'

There was such distress on his face that she knew she had to help him. Whatever it was that was upsetting Susan it was plainly serious. 'Have you had anything to eat?' she asked.

He shook his head. 'No. I meant to get

something on the train but I couldn't face it. It's all right. I didn't come on the cadge. I just wanted to thank you.'

'It's been a long day,' she told him, 'and I haven't had anything since lunch myself. I was just going to put a pie in the oven. We could share it if you like. It's all prepared.'

His face lifted. 'Are you sure?'

The change of expression pleased her. 'Quite sure. I'd be glad of your company. It's been a very odd day.'

'Well if that's the case,' he said, smiling for the first time since she opened the door, 'I'll take you up on it. Is there anything I can do to help you?'

They cooked and set the table and talked as they ate their homely meal. He told her how he'd come home to find Susan locked away and the girls gone. She told him how they'd been waiting at the station and how sensible they'd been to phone her — and, as he smoked his after-dinner cigarette and didn't seem to want to tell her anything else, she added the story of the burglary to entertain him.

He was shocked and full of admiration. 'Weren't you scared?'

'Not at the time,' she said. 'I was too angry.'

'And then my two idiots come barging in to add to your problems.'

'They're not idiots,' she said. 'They're sensible kids. I told you. Anyway I was glad to be able to help. It made me feel like a fully paid-up member of the community again.'

He exhaled, taking care to blow the smoke away from her. 'I can't imagine you as anything less.'

There was something about this conversation that made honesty not just possible but necessary. Something about their situation: two people who'd been coping with unexpected and frightening events suddenly at peace at the end of an extraordinary day. 'I've felt less sometimes,' she confessed.

'Because of your leg?'

'And my scar,' she said, touching it with her fingertips. 'It *does* change things, being injured, even though I try not to let it.'

He leant back in his chair, inhaling thoughtfully. 'That's something I can relate to,' he said.

That didn't surprise her but she wondered how. 'Have you been injured?'

'It was a long time ago,' he said. 'Not a major injury. Not like yours. Though I thought it was when it happened.'

'When what happened?' she said encouragingly.

'I was working in a nursery,' he explained. 'I must have been about nineteen or twenty. Sue and I had just moved in together. Anyroad, it was my turn to run the potting machine and it jammed. We'd all been shown how to work it and warned how dangerous it was, but I was cocky. I used to run risks to show I could get away with it. I ran one too many that day. Put my hand in the thing to get it started up again and it went off with a rush and caught my fingers. They switched it off at once, of course, but it took a long time to get my hand out. I can remember looking at all the blood and thinking, that's it, I've lost my fingers, that's me finished. But as you see, they weren't gone. Just mangled up a bit. I've never forgotten it, though.'

She took a medical interest. 'Did you get the use back straight away?'

'No,' he said, making a grimace that pulled his beard sideways. 'They were in splints for weeks. I didn't know how they'd be until the splints came off. Nobody did.'

'Then you're scarred too.'

He held his right hand across the table for her to see the long white scars ridging all four fingers. Such a strong, capable hand.

'Aren't we all in one way or another?' he said. 'I know my Susan is.'

She examined the scars with her forefinger, thoughtfully and gently, sensing that what he was about to tell her was personal and difficult. 'Is that why she locked herself in?' she asked, not looking at him. If it was too tender a subject, he could turn from it more easily if there was no eye contact.

'Work's always been much too important to Susan,' he said slowly, withdrawing his hand. 'Success. Getting to the top. Being the best. You don't have to be a psychologist to see why — with two younger brothers like Chris and Nick she was bound to be competitive.'

'I can't imagine Nick competing with anyone,' she said. 'He's too laid back. *Were* they competitive?'

'Not consciously, no. Nothing like that. They were great kids. Full of fun. I used to call them the sunshine boys. You couldn't help liking them. But they were clever. That was the trouble. Hideously clever. They could pass exams without trying. Sue was the one who had to compete. I don't think she was ever jealous of them. They were always very close. Look how she's just phoned Chris. Couldn't tell me, you notice. Couldn't even let me into the room. But she phones her brother in Canada.'

Now Gemma looked straight at him. 'Tonight, you mean? She phoned him tonight?'

'She phoned him, he phoned Andrew, Andrew told me. How's that for a way to get information from the woman you love?'

He sounded so bitter that she wasn't sure she could ask him her next question, but curiosity got the better of her. 'So what did she say?'

He told her, speaking slowly and carefully as though he was trying to make sense of it himself. 'They gave her the sack because Andrew was her father and they thought she'd been feeding him inside information. Or rather, they threatened her with the sack and she jumped before she was pushed.'

'That's monstrous,' Gemma said. 'They can't do a thing like that.'

'They can. They've done it.'

'But she hadn't fed him information, had she?'

'No, of course not. Not that it matters now. The damage is done anyroad.'

'And she's locked herself away.'

'She can't face the shame of it, she says. So she's gone into purdah. She told Chris it made her feel like a nobody. She won't speak to anyone — except Chris — and she won't answer the phone. Andrew tried twice, so he says. We've been married fifteen years and this is the first crisis we've ever had to ride we've not talked through. It makes me feel useless.'

She could see that and was torn with pity for him. 'Do the girls know all this?'

'Not yet. I'll tell them tomorrow. I'm taking them home first thing in the morning.'

'She'll talk to you about it in the end,' she tried to reassure him. 'She can't stay locked away for ever.'

'Never mind the end,' he said. 'She should have talked to me from the beginning. There's no two ways about it. She's rejecting me. That's how it is.'

She looked at him steadily. It was such an intimate confession and there was such bitterness in his voice that, although she felt it couldn't be true, she wasn't sure how she ought to respond to it.

'It's been work, work, work, all the time since she started this job,' he went on, staring at the table. 'I've not had a look in. It's no surprise she won't talk to me now. We've been growing further and further apart for weeks.' He sighed. 'I'm beginning to think I've lost my touch. I shouldn't be telling you all this, should I. It's not fair on you.'

'It's all right,' she promised. 'It won't go any further. Did you try to talk to her?'

'Yes. I did. To tell the truth, I was that angry when I knew the girls had run off, I ended up shouting at her. But I did try. Didn't make a scrap of difference though. How can you talk to someone when they've locked the door and won't answer?'

'It's a problem,' she admitted, 'but not insuperable.'

'Feels insuperable to me,' he said. 'I can't see a way round it. I mean, what would you do?'

Ideas tumbled into her head. 'Go into the room next to hers and tap on the wall in Morse code,' she suggested. 'Stage a fainting fit just outside the door with lots of groaning and rolling about. Find a ladder and climb up to the window and make faces at her through the glass. Hold up a placard with a message on it: *"Guess what? I still love you"*, or *"Come out, come out wherever you are"*.'

That made him smile again. 'You would an' all,' he said.

She smiled back at him. 'It's my stage training. Dramatic situations, dramatic solutions.'

'It might be worth a try,' he admitted. Then he thought for a second or two. 'Look,' he said, 'this is probably out of order. Say if it is. But you wouldn't put me up for the night, would you? If I do the dishes or something?'

'I've only got one bedroom,' she said, 'but you can sleep on the sofa if you like.' The request surprised her. 'I'd have thought you'd want to stay at Amersham Road with the girls.'

'I'd rather not. There's too much disapproval in that quarter at the moment.'

'Which is why you came here.'

He nodded.

'It's because of Susan, isn't it? You think they're blaming you for what's happened to Susan.'

He thought about it for quite a long time and then gave an honest answer. 'Not altogether, no,' he said. 'He's taken quite a bit of blame to himself being it was their relationship that did the damage. But I think he blames me for other things, for not seeing it coming, not preventing it, not being there to stop the girls running away. I could be wrong. But it's what I feel. I'd be more comfortable here if you'd put up with me.'

'I'll put up with you *and* put you up,' she joked. '*And* I'll let you do the washing up. How's that?'

'Handsome. You've not to let me keep you up, though. I tend to talk all hours when I get the chance. As you see.'

'No problem. When I'm tired I go to sleep.'

'Now what?' he asked. 'Shall I make some coffee?'

She took him up on that offer too, but followed him into the kitchen to talk on. They had progressed to such an extraordinary state of intimacy that she felt she could ask him virtually anything.

'When we were all together at Christmas,' she began, 'you said something rather odd.'

'Sounds likely,' he said, measuring instant coffee into her two mugs. "All the world's queer save thee an' me, an' I can be reet odd when I like."'

'It was something you said about the Quennells. You said, "They include you in." What did you mean?'

He explained easily, standing before her, teaspoon in hand. 'They never make you feel an outsider. They extend the circle and include you. But . . .'

'But you feel an outsider just the same,' she said as the kettle boiled. 'Welcomed but not part of the family. I felt that too. It's because they're so close.'

'That's part of it,' he admitted, as they carried their mugs into the living room. 'But there's more to it than that. The truth is, I've never felt welcome. Tolerated would be nearer the mark. Not welcome.'

It seemed ridiculous that anyone could feel unwelcome in the Quennells' friendly house. Welcoming was what they were good at. And yet Andrew had made all this trouble for her by speaking out of turn. 'Why not?' she asked, sitting at the table.

He drank his coffee, debating whether to confide in her. 'I was a jobbing gardener when I met Susan,' he said at last. 'Very lowly sort of job, is that. Especially to a doctor. I never felt approved of. I always had the feeling they thought I was below her. Not the sort of husband they wanted for their daughter. And they were right, seemingly. I've failed her altogether now.'

She dismissed his pessimism and sprang to their defence. 'You couldn't be more wrong,' she said. 'They're very fond of you. I've heard the way they talk about you.'

'Oh, they're fair,' he admitted.

'Not fair,' she told him, irritated that he was misjudging them; 'fond. They're fond of you.' But the smile he gave her showed he didn't believe her. 'Look,' she said, 'I've got an axe to grind now — I'll tell you about it later — but I *know* you're wrong about this. Andrew may have all sorts of faults.' Hadn't Nick told her he wasn't perfect? 'We all have. But he's not prejudiced and he's not a hypocrite. If he says he likes you, then he does. He tells the truth. It's one of his strengths.'

'An axe to grind?' he said. That was as hard to believe as everything else she was telling him. 'You? About Andrew?'

'Yes,' she said. 'Me. About Andrew. It was his fault I was burgled. The burglar as good as told me so.'

'What?'

'He'd brought a newspaper with him. Said it was all over the front page that I was a millionaire so I deserved to be burgled. It was too. I saw it. There was a picture of me and a picture of Andrew. He'd been talking about me on some television show.'

'Are you sure?'

'It was in the paper. I saw it. It's in the bin now but I'll show it to you if you like.'

He finished his coffee, thoughtfully. 'I think you're making a mistake,' he said. 'He wouldn't talk about your private affairs in public. Not Andrew. It's not his style.'

She shrugged.

'What does Nick say about it?'

'Nick's in Paris,' she said shortly, and when he raised his eyebrows: 'We had a row and he went off with his friends.'

'Ah! When was that?'

'Wednesday evening. We were going to

spend the evening together but then he proposed to me and I said no and he went off in a huff.'

That made him laugh. 'And you're surprised?'

She felt she had to justify herself. 'He said I needed looking after and I ought to marry him.'

'And you said, no thanks. I don't want your pity.'

There was a hint of mockery in his voice and hearing it, she didn't know whether to be pleased or annoyed that he'd understood her so well. 'Very perceptive,' she said.

'It's one of the first things I noticed about you,' he told her, speaking seriously. 'Your independence. You were independent at the party, wheeling yourself about, determined not to be a nuisance to anyone. You made your own bed. You washed the carpet when you spilt your coffee. We were impressed.'

'Actually,' she remembered, 'Nick washed the carpet.'

He gave her his wry smile. 'So you *do* let him help you sometimes.'

'I was in a wheelchair,' she pointed out, with some asperity.

He smiled at that too. 'Point taken. So. Nick's gone to Paris and missed all the excitement. Does he know what's been going on in his absence?'

'No, he doesn't,' she said. 'He phoned earlier this evening and I told him about the burglar but then the time ran out and he didn't ring back.' It still upset her that he hadn't tried to contact her again. This time she had hoped it would be different. But it hadn't been. He didn't care. 'He made sympathetic noises but he didn't ring back.'

'We're a pair,' he said. 'Rejected lovers the both of us. You've been on your own since Wednesday and I'm on my own to-night. Our stars must be crossed.'

'Something's crossed certainly,' she said. 'I've never known a day like today. Nothing's been what it seemed.'

'Nothing?'

'Not much. I feel as if I've been at sea all day and in a force nine gale. I've got a pupil who usually sits in a heap and won't talk, and this morning he suddenly finds his tongue and turns out to be a really nice kid. I come home for a bit of peace and quiet and catch a burglar. Your girls turn up.'

He joined in the litany. 'My sensible Susan locks herself in her bedroom.'

'Right,' she said. 'It must be the stars. And then there's you. I thought you were the most laid-back, contented guy I'd ever met and you turn out to have a chip on your shoulder.'

He was stung to hear her say such a thing but swallowed and took it. 'Is that how it looks?'

She returned his gaze, afraid that she might have gone too far but standing her ground. 'That's how it looks.'

He considered for quite a long time. Then smiled. 'OK,' he said, 'you might have a point. But . . .' returning fire with fire, 'what about you? I thought you and Nick were in love.' And when she made a face: 'OK. OK. That's what it looked like at the party. And yet you bawl him out when he proposes.'

She winced at that and decided to close the subject. 'You're right about one thing,' she told him. 'You talk too much. I'll get your blanket.'

He took the hint. 'Right. I'll do the dishes. As promised.'

As she walked through the hall towards the bedroom, she remembered her original plans. 'I *was* going to have a bath,' she said. 'My stump's a bit sore. I've been on my feet since five o'clock this morning.' And as she pulled the spare blanket out of the wardrobe, an idea occurred to her. 'I suppose you wouldn't lift me out when I've finished, would you? I can get into a bath, but getting out's tricky.'

'I'd be honoured,' he said, 'if you'll trust me.'

'After all the things we've been saying to one another this evening, I think I could trust you with anything,' she said. And limped into the bathroom.

It was bliss to be lying in hot scented water at last, letting the warmth ease the ache in her stump and listening to him clattering about in the kitchen, knowing that the chores were being done. Domestic bliss, she thought, and the idea pleased her. It was quite a disappointment when the water chilled and she had to get out.

She hung on to the handrail and struggled to her remaining foot, got her balance, pulled the bath towel round her as well as she could and called.

He appeared at once, in his shirt-sleeves, his hands speckled with traces of soapsuds, his hair untidy. The change in his appearance made her suddenly aware of how attractive he was, of how he must look at work, Rob the gardener, with his strong shoulders and those competent hands and that thick springy beard. He seemed to have brought his outdoor life into her little steamed-up room. She half expected trees to branch out of the walls, or fruit and flowers to blossom among the tiles.

'OK,' he said.

She waited for him to stand still so that she could lean on him while she hopped over the edge of the bath but instead he scooped her up in his arms and lifted her out like a child. It was done so quickly and so easily that she was being held before she could protest. And very pleasant it was, this sense of being held close and protected.

He stood for a while, with the steam swirling behind him and looked down at her as she lay against his chest, one rosy arm flung about his neck, her dark hair damp, brown eyes lustrous in the muted light of the little room. And as she looked up at him, the moment held and extended and became unreal. It was as if they were under a spell. Then he recovered his common sense and lowered her gently into the chair, sat on his heels before her, so that they were eye to eye, and tried to joke.

'Aren't you taking risks,' he said, 'allowing a strange man to see you like this?'

The Elastoplast had come unstuck. She peeled it all off and threw the tatty pieces in the bin. 'You're not a strange man,' she said and was alarmed to realise that she was breathless.

'I'm a man.'

She struggled to control her breathing. 'That's no problem,' she said, speaking as lightly as she could. 'I've got one leg.'

'Ah!' he said and there was a depth of meaning in that one little sound. 'And you think that makes you unattractive. Is that it?'

'Well it does, doesn't it,' she said, looking round at the discarded clothes littering the floor and the prosthesis standing against the bath in the full glare of its surgical ugliness. And she tried joking too. 'I haven't got a leg to stand on.'

'Is this what it is between you and Nick?' he asked. 'You think he's pitying you. That he only loves you because you've been injured. Is that it?'

She hadn't faced it quite so squarely and his question confused her; she knew there was more to Nick's love than mere pity. But she tried to answer. 'Well possibly. Yes. I think it might be. I mean . . .'

'No man alive could pity you,' he told her. 'You're gorgeous.'

She looked a question at him.

'Yes,' he told her honestly. 'You're turning me on.'

She should have been shocked to be in such a compromising position, shocked to hear him say such a thing. But she wasn't. She was delighted. Suddenly she felt superb, normal, worth loving. 'Really?'

'You're beautiful,' he said. 'There isn't a man in his senses who wouldn't be turned on by you. You. As you are now. Gorgeous.'

It was a wonderful moment. *You. As you are.* But a very unfair one. 'If that's the case, you'd better clear off and let me get respectable,' she said.

When she hopped out of the bathroom, swathed in her bathrobe and very respectable indeed, he was sitting on the edge of the bed, smoking.

'I hope you don't mind,' he said. 'I needed . . .'

She nodded to show that it was all right and then continued with their conversation as if there'd been no intermission. 'I was rotten to Nick,' she said. 'I should have explained. Not bitten his head off.'

Rob had been thinking much the same thing. 'I was rotten to Susan,' he confessed, 'shouting at her like that.'

'I shall explain next time.'

'I shall try your placards.'

'Very sensible,' she approved.

He put the cigarette in his mouth and picked up his bedding. 'Time to sleep,' he said. 'It's been a long day.'

'And we've come a long way.'

He gave her his wry smile as he left the room. 'True,' he said.

Chapter 36

When Gemma woke the next morning, the first person she thought of was Nick. It was nearly half-past nine, the birds were singing in the garden, the room was warm with sunshine and Rob was gone. If it hadn't been for the pile of bedding left neatly on the sofa, the events of the previous evening could well have been a dream.

Then she remembered that the police were coming and got up at once to wash and dress. I should have set the alarm, she thought, as she pulled her last clean Ottobock sock over her stump.

That wasn't all she should have done. As she walked through the hall to the living room, she saw her shoulder bag and the bag she took to school flung in a heap in the corner, and with them the carrier bag from Monsoon. She'd left her lovely, new, expensive dress lying on the floor all night and forgotten all about it. What a way to go on! She took it into the bedroom and hung it up at once to make amends. Then she got her breakfast.

She was touched to find that the table was laid, complete with a blue vase containing six newly picked daffodils, a newspaper propped against the milk jug and a leaf from a notebook lying across her plate.

Thanks for everything. Have phoned Amersham Road. The girls and I are going back to York on the first train to write our placards. Saw the daffs in the garden and thought you would like them. Found this newspaper in the bin and have read it. Suggest you do too. Very interesting. Will ring when I have any news. R.

It was the *Daily Chronicle* that the burglar had taken out of his pocket and flung on the bed. There was her picture on the front page, and Andrew's, and the headline: TV GURU AND CRASH HEROINE. What a lot had happened since then. It was as if she'd seen it first in another lifetime.

She read it as she ate, as if it were an ordinary day and an ordinary newspaper. And discovered, to her horror, that it hadn't been Andrew who had talked to the press, after all, but her wretched father. What a load of rubbish, she thought. Tug of love! What does he think he's talking about?

The more she read, the more upset she

became. How unfair I've been, she thought. Rob was right. It's not Andrew's style to give trashy interviews to the press. I condemned him without looking at the evidence. It shamed her to remember how readily she'd jumped to conclusions. As soon as these damned policemen have come, I'll go round and put things right, she decided. And at that moment, with perfect timing, the police car arrived.

Her visitor was a stolid, middle-aged sergeant who took his time over everything and kept checking his facts. He wrote down every word she said, and when she handed over the stolen cash cards, not only did he produce a plastic envelope and seal them away, but he composed an elaborate description of each and every one and where and how they'd been found.

'Well ma'am, you've given me an excellent description,' he told her, when he finally put away his notebook. 'We should be able to find our chappie with all this information, especially the tattoo, and the cash cards. There'll be a few people happy to see them again. I assume you'd be prepared to attend an identity parade.'

She would.

'Splendid!' he said. 'Now I'm sure you won't mind if I give you a little warning before I leave you. It's sometimes necessary to point this out, you understand. Having a go is often admirable — it was in your case — but usually I have to say it's foolhardy. You don't mind me pointing this out, do you?'

'But I caught him.'

'Yes, ma'am, you did. But you might have been hurt.'

'I lost a leg in a rail crash,' she told him with pride. 'My burglar was nothing compared to that.' She was delighted to see that she'd thrown him.

'I'm sure he wasn't,' he agreed, recovering quickly. 'It's not wise for all that.'

But I'm not wise, Gemma thought. I've never pretended to be. I've always made mistakes. I shall probably make a lot more today, and the day after and the day after that.

He stood up to take his leave. 'Your daffs are pretty,' he said. 'First I've seen this season.'

In York the daffodils were still in bud. Their straight leaves massed like spears on the grass embankments below the city walls but the blaze of their flowering was still to come.

'It'll soon be spring,' Rob said to his daughters. 'Let's buy some daffodils for your mother.' There was just time to pick up a bunch from the stall before the train to Poppleton was due. 'Two dozen,' he said to the assistant. A single bunch was nowhere near enough. Massed, they might cheer her.

The house was full of sounds, music playing and people talking. They could hear it all quite clearly as they stood on the doorstep.

'There you are,' Rob said, 'she's up and about.'

But to his disappointment, it was only the radio playing. He must have left it on when he went rushing out. And as it was still playing, Susan must still be locked away. So they went upstairs to see, and called her, one after the other, and all together. But it was a waste of time.

'Never mind,' Rob said. 'I know what we'll do if you'll help me.'

They were ready for anything. So he led them to the garage and between them they carried the ladder round the side of the house and propped it against the bedroom window. Then they got a basket and a length of rope and the daffodils and several sheets of card on which they wrote messages. And when everything was ready, he climbed up to the window.

Susan was lying on the bed with her eyes

shut. She'd taken off her shoes but apart from that she was fully dressed and she lay stiffly, like a corpse laid out for burial, her arms straight at her sides and her heels set neatly together.

'Sue!' he called. 'Sweetheart!' And tapped at the window.

She turned her head wearily but although her eyes were open and she seemed to be looking at him, there was no expression on her face at all.

He signalled to the girls to put the daffodils in the basket, hauled it aloft and held them up for her to see.

'For you,' he mouthed through the window. But there was no response.

He gave another signal and the basket was let down and hauled up again. When he looked back at her, she'd turned her head towards the window.

He held up the first placard, hopefully. *Dinner is served.* No reaction.

He tried the second. *Your carriage awaits.* No reaction, not even a smile. So jokes wouldn't work.

Now there was only the last placard to offer. It was bigger than the first two because it had been decorated with blood-red hearts and sheaves of psychedelic flowers and signed by all three of them. But the message was bold and direct. *'We love you very much.'*

For a long anxious second he held the placard to the window and hoped. She didn't even smile. It's no good, he thought, we can't reach her. He pushed the cardboard at the window as though he would propel it through the glass if he had the power, his face taut with entreaty. And she got up, swinging her long legs over the edge of the bed, stood up, very, very carefully, as though she was an invalid, and staggered across the room towards him.

He let the placard fall, mimed that she should open the window, begged her with his eyes, his face, his entire being.

She seemed to be thinking, standing with her hands on the sill and her face withdrawn, a few impossible inches away from him.

He mimed again. 'Open it up. Please, sweetheart.'

She stretched out a hand towards him as if she was going to touch his face and was puzzled by the glass.

'Open it!' he begged. 'Just an inch.'

But she still stood before him baffled and withdrawn. If he could only touch her. 'Please!' he said. 'Lift the window.'

And at last she did as he asked, lifting the window, jerkily and with difficulty until there was a gap large enough to admit his hands. After that it was easy. He raised the frame, opened the window to its fullest extent, held out his arms to her, and, with a little moan, she burst into tears and fell against his chest.

He held her as she cried, balanced precariously on the ladder and looking down to show the girls that everything was all right. After a while she was recovered enough to stand back and let him climb in through the window.

'I didn't mean to hurt the girls,' she sobbed as he put his arms round her again. 'Are they all right? I didn't mean to hurt them.'

He was leading her to the door, rubbing her back as they went. 'I know.'

'I've lost my job.'

'I know.'

Her face was creased with distress. 'I'm finished.'

'You've got me and the girls,' he said. 'We still love you.' And he unlocked the door and let them in to prove it.

It was an emotional reunion, as they clung to her waist and hung round her neck and told her how much they loved her. 'I've lost my job,' she told them.

That didn't worry them in the least. 'Does that mean you won't be going to work?' Helen asked. And, when her mother nodded, 'You'll be at home for half-term.'

'For a lot longer than that.'

'Yippee!' Helen said. 'We can all go to the Yorvik Centre.'

'Do you want to go to the Yorvik Centre?'

'Oh yes,' Helen said. 'If it's with you and Daddy.'

Have they missed out? Susan thought, looking at their faces. Have I cheated them by working such long hours? They've never said anything about it. And for the first time since she'd handed in her notice she saw the faint possibility of some good coming out of it. Maybe it would be better not to work quite so hard. To try for a job that didn't take all her time.

'We'll go there on Monday,' she told them. 'How will that be?'

Rapturous.

'But be warned,' Rob said, pleased to see her making decisions again. 'Your mother won't be on holiday for long. She'll get another job in no time.' And when Susan looked at him: 'Yes you will. This is the result of one man's prejudice. You're too good to be out of work for ever, even in this day and age.'

Naomi was clamouring for attention. 'I'm starving,' she announced. 'Is there anything to eat?'

'We've got a meal ordered at the Fox,' Rob told them.

'Now?' Susan asked.

'Ready when you are.'

'What is it?'

He gave her his slow, loving smile. 'Fatted calf.'

'Oh!' she said, crying again. 'I do love you.'

There were daffodils budding in the gardens of Amersham Road. But Nick didn't notice them. He'd come home on the first shuttle and in a turmoil of rage and impatience, angry with the railway for making him wait in Paris all night, at himself for not being there when Gemma was burgled, at his father for putting her at risk in the first place. He was unwashed and he was hungry because he'd had no lunch and it was now mid-afternoon. But none of that mattered. There were more important things to attend to.

In the whole of his easy life, he'd never had an out-and-out row with his father.

They'd agreed about most things or agreed to differ in a fairly amiable way. He'd stood up to him that day in York but that was nothing compared to what he was going to do now. Now he was going to tell him he was wrong. He couldn't avoid it. It had to be done even though the thought of it was tying him in an anguished knot, making his palms sweat and his heart judder.

He let himself into the house and stormed into the attack while his courage was reckless. His parents were in the living room, sitting in their favourite armchairs, deep in conversation and his arrival was so precipitate it made them jump.

'Now look what you've done!' he shouted, glaring at his father.

Catherine half rose, ready to rebuke him, but Andrew put out a hand to check her. He was alarmed but he knew he had to be reasonable. There were bound to be repercussions and he'd accepted that he would have to face them.

'Sit down,' he said. If he could get Nick into a chair it might calm him a little.

But it was wasted effort. 'I'd rather stand.'

Andrew sighed. There was nothing for it but to get up himself, which he did, taking up a stance on the hearthrug with his back to the grate. 'I had no way of knowing this would happen, Nick,' he said.

Nick was too agitated to stand still. He prowled about the room, stopping briefly to let his hand rest on a chairback, or the bookcase, or his father's desk. 'I warned you. I said it would happen. I told you not to mess with the media. Right at the beginning. But you wouldn't listen. You never listen to anyone.'

There was truth in that and Andrew couldn't argue with it. 'I wasn't to know it would hurt your sister,' he protested.

That caught Nick off balance. 'Sister? Who's talking about her?'

'I thought you were. That's what all this is about, isn't it? Susan losing her job.'

'No it is not. This is about Gemma. What you've done to Gemma. She was burgled yesterday. And it's all because of something you said on television. The burglar told her so.'

Catherine's face wrinkled into instant concern but Andrew lifted both hands and tore at his hair in exasperation. 'This,' he said, 'is beyond a bloody joke. I can't be held responsible for burglars.'

'Yes. You can,' his son insisted, prowling again. 'Directly responsible. You were on TV. You made a public statement in front of millions of people and the burglar must have heard it. She could have been injured.'

Could have been was comforting. 'But she wasn't.'

'That's not the point.'

'No,' Andrew said angrily, 'the point is political. I *am* making statements. They're political statements and they need making. Or have things come to such a pass that no one is allowed to stand up and tell the truth? Is that it? We've all got to kow-tow to our masters and accept their lies and say nothing. Yes sir, no sir, Mr Health Minister sir, the NHS has never been better. There are no problems. We don't have closed wards and patients dying in corridors and operations postponed over and over again. Everything is for the best in the best of all possible worlds. Is that what you want?' Rage made his hair bush about his temples so that he looked like a lion in full roar.

Nick had grown pale during his father's tirade, but he stopped prowling and stood his ground, now that they were really fighting. 'No,' he said. 'You know it's not.'

'Well then. I've got to go on. No matter what it costs.'

'If you pay the cost yourself, but not if Sue and Gemma have to pay.'

It was the crux of the problem: they both recognised it and could find no answer to it. Now that they'd stopped shouting Nick realised that he was panting and that, bad though all this was, he was feeling proud of himself. He'd stood up to his father. He'd actually stood up to his father and told him he was wrong.

Catherine was on her feet, walking towards them, standing between them, putting a conciliatory hand on each taut chest. 'We know,' she said to Nick. 'We've been up all night talking about it.'

Nick was still bristling. 'And?'

'We don't know the answer.'

'We do,' Andrew said heavily, turning away from them both. He walked across the room to the drinks cabinet and poured himself a whisky. 'I just don't like accepting it, that's all. I shall have to give it up. You're quite right, of course Nick, when it comes down to it, you can't hurt your children. That's how they keep us quiet. Through our children.'

It was a victory but it felt like a defeat. 'I'm so sorry,' Nick said. 'I know what this has meant to you.'

'Drink?' his father offered, holding up the whisky bottle. 'Or are you driving?'

There was someone ringing the doorbell.

The sound made Andrew tetchy. 'Oh not now!'

'I'll get it,' Catherine said and left the two men to their whisky.

She was disturbed to open the door and find Gemma on the step, although she might have expected it. She was bound to come sooner or later if she'd seen that article.

'Are you all right?' she said. 'Nick says you've been burgled.'

'He's here?'

'Just arrived.' There was no point in trying to hide what was going on. They could both hear the voices in the living room. 'They've been having a bit of an altercation.'

'I know what it's about, don't I?' Gemma said. 'It's that rubbish in the *Chronicle*.' And she walked straight into the room to put it right, hauling the newspaper out of her shoulder bag as she went.

It gave her a jolt to see Nick again, especially as he looked so fierce. But when he turned and saw her, his face smoothed with such open affection that she felt as if all the pieces of her life had suddenly fallen into position.

'Hello,' she said, keeping her voice casual — but only just. 'You're back, then.'

'And giving me a bollocking,' Andrew said. 'I hear you've been burgled and it's all my fault.'

'Yes, I have been burgled,' she said, 'but it's no big deal. He didn't take anything and it's all over and done with now. And it wasn't your fault. That's what I've come to explain.' Which she did quickly, spreading the newspaper on the coffee table. 'I saw the headlines and our photographs but I didn't read the text. I jumped to conclusions and they were the wrong ones. I was in a state. The burglar was still in the room.'

'Ah!' Andrew understood. 'You were in shock.'

'I didn't read the damned thing until this morning. And I've come straight over. I told you it was your father's fault, Nick, and I was wrong. It was *my* father, opening his rotten mouth and telling lies. "Tug of love! Enticed away from her loving parents." I never saw such rubbish.'

Andrew motioned them all towards chairs and this time even Nick took a seat. This was a practical problem that he could deal with rationally. 'We can't let them get away with it,' he said to Gemma. 'But it isn't libellous.'

'We must write to the editor,' Gemma said, 'and tell him to publish a correction. If

659

I can use your word processor I'll do it now. I know exactly what to say.'

Action carried them away from trouble. Nick made helpful suggestions. Catherine made sandwiches and tea to sustain them while they worked. And when the letter was done they were all pleased with their work.

'Two copies,' Gemma said. 'One to send to the paper and the other for my so-called father.'

'Sounds like trouble,' Nick said cheerfully, thinking how richly it was deserved.

They were laughing when the phone rang. 'That'll be Rob,' Andrew said, anxiety returning.

But it was Susan to say that she was fine and to thank him for looking after the girls. 'Chris told me where they were,' she said. 'I never thought they'd leave the house. I only meant for them to go downstairs. I'm *so* sorry about all this.'

'I'm the one who should be apologising to you,' he told her. 'I wouldn't have had this happen for worlds.'

Her voice was warm with affection for him. 'I know that.'

'You should have told them I was nothing to do with you. You'd have been within your rights.'

She was appalled at such a suggestion. 'I

couldn't do that. You're my father.'

'Only technically.'

'Oh what nonsense!' she rebuked him. 'You're my father. You've always been my father. Not technically but in everything that matters. I couldn't have wanted a better one. How could you possibly imagine I'd deny that?'

He had to blink because tears were pricking behind his eyes. 'I won't hurt you again,' he promised. 'I've decided not to do any more broadcasts.'

'I hope this isn't on my account.'

'Well yes, of course it is. I can't put you at risk. Once was enough.' He smiled at Nick and Catherine. 'It's not fair to make you pay the price for what I'm doing.'

The old strong Susan spoke to him along the wire. 'Now look here,' she said. 'I can't have this. You're locking the stable door. The price has already been paid.'

'One price,' he agreed. 'There mustn't be any others. TV appearances are too risky.'

'Well I hope you're not going to give up your column too,' she said.

'I don't know about the column,' he told her truthfully. 'I haven't thought about it.' And he remembered Garry McKendrick. *If I continue with it, it'll be me he'll attack. His animosity is personal.* But as he and Kate looked at one another across the room, he knew he could cope with it.

'Well,' his daughter said, 'take my advice and don't give it up.'

'I think your mother would probably say that too,' he told her.

'What?' Catherine asked.

He explained briefly. 'Not to give up my column.' Then he turned back to the phone. 'She's hovering. Do you want to talk to her?'

So Catherine took the phone and Andrew returned to the word processor.

'She's right,' Gemma said, as he switched off the machine. 'You mustn't give up your column. Think of all your fans.'

'Someone else will write for them,' he said.

'Personally,' she told him, very earnestly, 'I would much rather you did. Don't you agree, Nick?'

Nick tried to joke his way out of it. 'Oh that's right,' he said. 'Put me on the spot.'

'He agrees,' Gemma said. 'You can see by his face.'

'I can see the point of the column,' Nick admitted. It was safer than TV because the written word was considered and edited.

Gemma had finished addressing the envelope and, looking round at him, caught sight of the clock. 'Oh God!' she said. 'Look at the time! I must go.'

'Why?' Nick asked.

'I've told my parents to be at the flat at four o'clock.'

'Am I to come with you?' he asked hopefully.

It was a moment of decision for them both. 'Yes,' she said.

Chapter 37

There was so much to say, so many apologies and explanations, so very much to declare, but they didn't say a word. Because suddenly and wonderfully, words were unnecessary. They left the house hand in hand and as soon as they were in the garden and hidden by the hedge, they fell into one another's arms and kissed until they were dizzy, while the daffodils nodded their bright heads beside the blue of their jeans and a pair of blackbirds leapt from grass verge to pyracantha bush, piping shrill as they renewed their springtime battle.

'Beautiful — wonderful — gorgeous — consort battleship,' he said between kisses. 'I love you so much. You *are* all right, aren't you?'

The sun was dazzling patterns into her eyes. There was so much electricity between them that she was supercharged, her skin tingling. 'Six feet off the ground,' she laughed. 'Kiss me again.'

As if he needed bidding! 'Let's go home,'

he said. 'I can't kiss you properly out here.'

She turned in his arms to open the car door. 'I thought this place was your home,' she teased.

'Not any more,' he told her. 'Home is wherever you are.' So naturally he had to be kissed again. And again. It was so simple. So easy.

They settled into the car side by side still yearning for kisses. 'One more,' she said, 'and then we must behave or I shan't be able to drive.'

'You could do anything,' he said, with his arm round her shoulder. 'I'll never offer to look after you again.'

They could even tease one another about *that.* 'Never?' she laughed. Oh such laughter, bubbling in her throat like champagne, lifting her.

He was laughing too, blue eyes blazing with love, sunshine patterning his face. 'You don't look after a consort battleship,' he said. 'Not when its guns are blazing. You damn nearly blew me out of the water last time.'

'Yes,' she said with delight. 'I did, didn't I? Well you can't say you don't know what you're letting yourself in for.'

'Yes please!' he demanded and kissed her

with such passion that he took her breath away.

'We must stop,' she said, kissing, kissing.

'I've stopped.'

'It looks like it.'

He began to clown. '*Please* take me home!'

So she controlled herself and put the car into gear.

'Where's your car?' she asked as she drove out into Amersham Road.

'I left it at Abdul's.'

'So how was Paris?'

'Gruesome.'

'Good.'

He feigned surprise. 'I never knew you were a Francophobe.'

She grinned at him. 'It means you missed me.'

This time he pretended to be nonchalant. 'Well yes, I suppose I did. Now and then. In a small way.'

'I love you,' she said, champagne laughter bubbling again.

They drove down Putney Hill aching with desire, and she negotiated the High Street with his arm around her shoulders. From time to time, he stroked her cheek, as if he was about to turn her head and kiss her again. 'I warn you,' she giggled. 'If you keep on doing that while I'm driving we shall end up on the pavement.'

That provoked more laughter and more provocative caresses. 'I'd rather we ended up in bed.'

'You're one-track-minded.'

'Um, but what a track!'

She turned the car into St Mary's Court at last. 'You're out of luck,' she teased him. 'My parents have arrived. We shall have to deal with them first.'

They were sitting in the BMW, staring through the windscreen, Billie in her best suit, looking anxious, Tim instantly flashing his most charming smile at them.

Nick struck his forehead with his fist, happily play-acting. 'Thwarted!' he cried. 'Dead! Dead! And never call me mother!'

'How did I ever get involved with such a ham?' she giggled as she parked the car. 'Be sensible.'

But he couldn't be sensible. Neither of them could. Their happiness was so entire and so obvious that Billie and Tim were quite heartened by it and followed them into the flat as though they really had been invited to tea.

Gemma arranged a circle of chairs around the table, unconsciously imitating the circle she'd just left in Amersham Road but this time with Nick sitting close beside her. Very close beside her. Sparks leaping and dancing.

It was time to be serious. 'You know Dr Quennell, don't you,' she said to her mother and was pleased when Billie winced. Then she turned to sting her father too. 'Dr Quennell,' she told him, 'was the doctor who saved my life in the crash.'

Tim tried charm. 'Pleased to meet you.'

'Right!' his daughter said briskly. 'Now you've been introduced, I've got a bone to pick with you.' She produced her copy of the *Chronicle* and for the second time that afternoon spread it out for inspection. 'What's the meaning of this?'

'They got me wrong, Poppet,' Tim said, giving her the full beam. 'You know what the tabloids are like.'

'Oh no,' Gemma corrected. 'They didn't get you wrong. You told them lies. This is lies from start to finish. I've never been enticed away by anyone and you know it. And you can hardly call yourself a loving father, now can you?'

'Now that's where you're wrong,' Tim said. 'You couldn't be more wrong. I know I got a bit cross with you the other evening — I'm sorry about that — but I did it all for you. I always had your interests at heart. After all I *am* your father.'

Gemma gave him her sternest look. 'You share half my genes,' she told him. 'That's all. By an accident of birth. But you're no more my father than that table leg. I've learned a lot about fathers in the last few months. I've seen two very good ones in action. Men who put their wives and children first. Men who are prepared to sacrifice anything to protect their children. Even their principles. And that takes some doing — although you wouldn't know that because you haven't got any principles. Oh, I can tell you a lot about fathers. Fathers are men who look after you while you're growing up, pay for your keep, buy your clothes, help you with your homework, teach you moral values, dear God! Like telling the truth.'

'You can't tell the truth in this world,' Tim told her. 'People don't expect it. Good God, you'd be eaten alive if you went around telling the truth all the time. I mean, look at the way the politicians go on. You don't think they tell us the truth, do you? Once in a blue moon, if ever. And certainly not when there's an election in the offing.' He was on one of his hobby-horses now and felt much more comfortable. All that talk about other men being better fathers had been very unnecessary.

But she cut him off short. 'We're not talking about politicians,' she said sternly. 'We're talking about you and the lies you told to the press. What are you going to do about *them*?'

'It'll blow over,' he said, dismissively. 'If you'll take my advice you'll just ignore it. Nobody takes anything seriously when it's in the tabloids, now do they?'

'It might interest you to know that a burglar took that absolutely seriously. He came here yesterday evening to relieve me of some of my half-million. I had to fight him off with my crutch.'

Their faces were a study of disbelief and horror.

'Oh Gemma,' Billie cried. 'He didn't!'

Tim tried to bluff. 'You don't know it was because of the paper.'

'Yes I do. He told me so. That's his copy on the table. I wouldn't have seen it if it hadn't been for him.'

'That's awful!' Billie said.

Gemma pressed home her point. 'And if he's read it and believed it, all sorts of other people will have read it and believed it too. So something will have to be done about it. Right?'

'I don't see what,' Tim said. 'It's over and

done with now. In print. You can't unprint it.'

'No,' Gemma told him, 'but they can publish a correction. I've got one written. It's in the post now, signed by me and Dr Quennell. I've brought you a copy. I'll read it to you if you like.'

He didn't like it at all but how could he refuse to hear it?

She took the letter out of her bag and read it slowly.

Sir,

Contrary to the false impression given by your front page on Thursday, I would like the following facts to be brought to the attention of your readers:

I have not been enticed away from my parents.

My father, Mr Tim Ledgerwood, who was named in the article, deserted me when I was six weeks old. I have only seen him on three occasions since then.

I live on my own in my own flat and earn my own living.

I have never sued the railway for half a million pounds and do not intend to sue them.

Railways South offered me £10,000 compensation soon after the accident, which I

671

accepted. I signed a disclaimer agreeing that I would not sue for any further compensation.

There was a long silence. Nick was grinning with delight at the way she was handling this, Billie had her mouth open, Tim was obviously shocked.

'D'you mean to say you've taken it?' he asked at last. 'You've given up half a million for a paltry £10,000?'

'A paltry £10,000 was all I needed,' Gemma told him. 'It bought my car and furnished this flat. It pays the rent. I don't need half a million. Millions are trouble.'

'I don't believe I'm hearing this,' her stunned parent said. 'I ran up debts on your account. Thousands. You never stopped to think about that, did you?'

'Tough,' she said. 'That's your problem.'

'Yours too. I did it on your account.'

'No,' she corrected. 'You did it because you thought you were going to take a share of the pickings. It was the thought of getting your hands on half a million. Well there aren't any pickings. The dream's over.'

'But I've got bills to pay. Solicitors' fees. How am I going to pay them?'

'I don't know,' she said. 'Like I said, that's your problem.'

'Billie!' he begged, turning to her for support. 'Speak to her. Tell her.'

But Billie was no help to him. She could see him much too clearly now. 'I suppose you'll have to sell the car,' she said. 'You don't own anything else, do you?' All these years dreaming about him, seeing him as her dreamboat, hoping he'd come back to her, wanting to live happily ever after, and he was just a con man after Gemma's money.

His answer was sullen. 'I can't do that.'

'No,' she said, very sadly. 'You can't, can you. Because it's on hire. All this talk about the high life and how good you are at business and you haven't got two ha'pennies to rub together. I'm sorry to have to say this, Tim, but you're a fraud.'

'Oh lovely!' he said. 'That's really lovely. After all I've done for you.'

'Like what?' she asked, her face creased with sadness. 'The last thing you did was to borrow £3,000, as I remember. When am I going to see that back?'

'I don't have to take this,' he said, standing up. 'I'm going.'

She was quite calm. 'In that case,' she said, 'I'll have my door key.'

He took it from his pocket and flung it at her. 'There's your key. And much good may it do you.' Then he turned for a Parthian shot at his daughter. 'And as for you young lady, don't think you'll ever make a model now. You might've done with a bit of money behind you but you've blown that.'

Nick decided he'd been a spectator for long enough and stood up to take over. 'Ready, are you?' he said and began to edge their unwanted visitor towards the hall, following him to make sure he left the premises.

'I'm so sorry about all this,' Billie said, when she and Gemma were on their own together. 'I never thought he'd tell lies to the papers. I mean, I thought you really had been enticed. I suppose the truth of it is I wanted to believe him. I thought he was such a good man. He said all the right things. He was going to look after you. He was going to look after us both, come to that. But there you are. No fool like an old fool! I'm so sorry.'

She looked so woebegone that Gemma put out a hand and patted her arm. 'I know,' she said.

'I only wanted the best for you.'

'I know.'

Billie began to cry. 'I wanted to give you a good start,' she wept. 'That's all it was. I thought if you were a model you could have a really nice life.'

Gemma passed her a tissue. 'I've got a really nice life,' she said. 'I've got a job and a home and a man who loves me. What more could I want?'

Billie blinked back her tears and glanced at the door. She didn't want the young man to come back into the room and find them talking about him. 'This doctor?' she whispered.

'This doctor,' Gemma said, as he walked in. 'I've just been telling Mother how lovely you are,' she told him.

'That's me,' he agreed. Then he saw that Billie was crying and embarrassed. 'We got off to a bad start, Mrs Goodeve,' he said. 'Could we start again, do you think?'

She gave him a smile, watery but full of hopeful affection. 'It would be nice, wouldn't it,' she said. 'I never meant half the things I said to you. It's no excuse but I was so worried about Gemma I said the first thing that came into my head.'

'Me too,' he said. 'I thought I ought to be looking after her.' And he grinned at Gemma. 'Big mistake!'

'You're right there,' Billie agreed, smiling at Gemma. 'She won't let anyone look after her. I've been trying to for years.'

'Well I'm glad you've both seen sense at last,' Gemma teased them. 'Now I can get on with living my life. There won't be any more nonsense about me being a model, will there?'

Billie shook her head. 'I've made a lot of mistakes in my life,' she said. 'But that's one I won't repeat.' And she sighed. 'All those years getting it wrong, thinking he'd come back to me and marry me and everything in the garden would be lovely. What a fool!'

'You wouldn't want to marry him again now though, would you?' Gemma asked.

Billie gave her a wry smile. 'I never married him in the first place,' she confessed.

'But I thought you were divorced. I thought you went back to your maiden name.'

'I never changed it,' Billie admitted. 'He said he didn't believe in marriage. I added the Mrs bit as a sort of courtesy title. To be respectable. Stand on my own feet, sort of thing.'

'Well good for you,' Nick applauded. 'So that's where she gets all this independence from.' And he put his arm round Gemma and gave her a hug.

The gesture was so affectionate that Billie knew they wanted to be alone. 'I must be off,' she said. 'Come and see me some time, both of you.'

Gemma put her arms round her and gave *her* a hug. 'I'll phone you,' she said. 'Now you know where we are, you can come and see us again. It'll be better without him and I'll feed you next time. You'd be surprised what a good cook I am.'

'She is,' Nick said. 'I can vouch for that. You should see her baked salmon.' And got punched for his presumption.

So mother and daughter parted with affection and kissed goodbye on the doorstep as lovingly as they'd ever done.

'You make a very pretty pair,' Billie said as she looked back at them. It was almost as though she was giving them her blessing.

'Amazing!' Gemma said as she and Nick walked back into the living room.

'You were,' Nick agreed. 'I'd fire a six-gun salute to you, if I had any guns.'

'I thought that was a gun in your pocket,' she said, enjoying the old joke.

'No,' he said happily, 'that's because I'm glad to see you.'

'I do love you,' she said. 'I know I said all sorts of stupid things to you when you proposed, but I *do* love you.'

'I said all sorts of stupid things too,' he

admitted. 'It doesn't matter whether we get married or not, really. The great thing is being together.'

'Equal partners?'

'Equal partners.'

'We'll marry when we're both ready for it,' she said. 'What are you doing on Monday?'

'More to the point,' he said, pulling her into his arms, 'what are we doing now?'

We hope you have enjoyed this Large Print book. Other Thorndike Press or Chivers Press Large Print books are available at your library or directly from the publishers.

For more information about current and upcoming titles, please call or write, without obligation, to:

Thorndike Press
P.O. Box 159
Thorndike, Maine 04986 USA
Tel. (800) 257-5157

OR

Chivers Press Limited
Windsor Bridge Road
Bath BA2 3AX
England
Tel. (0225) 335336

All our Large Print titles are designed for easy reading, and all our books are made to last.